White City

Chance Delgado

First published in Great Britain on Amazon.

TABLE OF CONTENTS

PART ONE

1 THE VALLEY

Blindfolds itch. They make you sweat. I'd been wearing mine for almost an hour: a swathe of red cloth secured in a knot at the back of my head. My driver was disinclined to talk, and when I'd attempted to adjust the band he'd cursed at me and warned me of his terms: keep it on or be thrown out, abandoned on this mountain road. I considered the option, and was about to take him up on it when the car pulled up abruptly and threw me, hands forward, towards the dashboard. On his instruction, I freed my eyes and got out of the vehicle, squinting in new surroundings.

He auto-locked the doors, covered the car with vegetation and broken branches and strode off into the undergrowth, gesturing me to follow with his small spade. His name was Maica, a native South American Indian, and out here, I was utterly reliant on his knowledge and protection. I tucked my empty bag into my jacket and clambered downwards in the mist on a weaving pathway, now completely hidden from the road. It was hard to balance on the incline, boots slipping on cold rock, but feverish expectation kept me stumbling, breathless, towards our goal. There was no sound but our footfall. No jet traffic in the sky – not even a bird. Just a cool quiet, and the slit yellow eye of the coming dawn.

I'd flown from Arequipa to Cusco to meet him, and Maica had driven his minibus like a demon out of the airport car park and out of town, stopping briefly for petrol, water, and supplies. It had taken us seven hours to drive here. Ten miles back, he'd stopped and blindfolded me.

In this region of Peru, near the border with Bolivia, the Andean soil is iron-rich and turns to thick, orange mud in the rainy season. The sun is merciless in the thin air, and far more dangerous for the skin than it feels. Up near the snow line, the cold is dry and penetrating, but as we descended into the vegetation, the dank humidity was just as unpleasant.

I was suffering from *soroche*, altitude sickness: blocked nose, raging thirst and a dull headache at the base of my skull. Sore lips cracked as I tried to moisten them with saliva. It was hard to breathe, but despite my discomfort, I acknowledged the beauty of the place, which was clearly visible once we'd descended through the cloud forest

Maica, only twelve yards in front of me, was becoming increasingly nervous: body tense, eyes darting around him. He gripped the spade like a weapon. I, too, was jittery and alert. I parted the leaves in broad sweeps, my excitement hand-in-hand with anticipated dismay. Maica's tall truths about my expected prize could have been warped by the depth of my pockets. This entire caper may be just a hollow Peruvian promise. But, having paid in advance for exclusivity, I expected nothing less. I was quietly gearing myself up for volcanic anger if he tried to deviate from the script and fob me off with anything other than promised. We'd been walking for almost forty minutes. I was impatient.

"Are we near now?" I asked.

"*No se preocupes. Sígueme*!"

He answered without turning, but his reassurance to keep following didn't ease my nerves. It can't be a secret. How long has it been here? Wouldn't someone have found it by now? Surely, I won't be the first. I'm not that lucky. Not me. I've never so much as won a bottle of ketchup at a raffle. Nothing I have ever owned or achieved has come to me by chance or good fortune, only by graft, wit, and animal cunning. Can I really be that close to such a discovery? Can't be! Can't be! *Can't be!* And so on, whilst underneath my breath I was praying to a god I don't believe in:

"Please, please, *please* let it be true."

Needless to say, my brother Anthony, Golden Boy, wasn't here to help or protect me, though to feel his presence, I was wearing his bracelet of *pashaquilla* seeds, the common Peruvian talisman for good luck, health and protection.

"Wait till I get back," he'd instructed, but Maica, my guide, wanted our visit to be now, so now it was. And here I was: big shopping bag, masking tape, empty bottle of water, wad of cash – and no brother.

Though I'd slept a little on the journey, I hadn't urinated. My bladder was full but inhibited by *soroche,* which constricts the urethra and gut. Trapped wind was trying to make its way to the Peruvian air. This could be embarrassing. Nevertheless, I didn't see the point of tying my intestines in knots for the sake of social convention.

Meanwhile, to combat the worst excesses of *soroche*, Maica had provided me with a ball of coca leaf to chew. With it, I was given a piece of *llucta*: mineral lime and wood ash. Wrapped in the leaves against the gum, it breaks down the alkaloids and releases the cocaine. But I sucked with care. Lime touching flesh burns like hell. I hated the taste, but respecting Nature's cure, slowly medicated my headache.

My dry mouth was not just due to the altitude. I was very disturbed knowing I was so close to the *cocaleros*: cocaine growers and their barons. They must have look-outs. They could be watching us, though we were not here for cocaine.

Finally, after an hour, we reached an open clearing. Maica hesitated as his mobile phone beeped, answering in a whisper. With a sharp turn of his head, he squinted his dark eyes sun-ward, the phone still pressed to his ear. I followed his gaze to the dawn horizon, shading the brightness with my hand, but couldn't see what he was looking at. He squatted down abruptly, snapping the phone shut, then leapt up and sprinted forwards. I spat out the coca.

"Hey! *Qué pasa*?" I yelled, but he didn't look back. I started running after him, and, as we turned away from the rising sun, I could see two figures clearly silhouetted on the other side of the valley. They carried something heavy on their shoulders.

"*Rápido! Rápido!*" Maica hissed. "*Apúrate!*"

The urgent tone of his voice kicked at my adrenaline. He was far ahead and widening the gap. A sudden surge of energy crackled down my spine and into my legs. I felt the full agility of muscles and tendons. I was fleet, like an athlete, and within my fear I remembered my delight at my own speed and grace, feeling coca's effect as a natural vasodilator, widening blood vessels to my heart and lungs.

I almost glided across the turf, and was within arm's reach of him as he headed over an embankment to a small building with a smoking chimney, only yards from us. At its side, I could see the open door of a tiny *pozo* shed, a pit for stomping and mashing coca leaves. An acrid smell enveloped us. Caution made me pause.

I looked at the hut. A little black dog ran out, yapping and snarling. Maica flung down his spade and ran fast to the left of me as a whistling sound rushed forward in cascades of orange soil. Man and dog rolled past me in a flame. A vacuum engulfed me as the light dimmed to black, buzzing velvet.

I heard a thick, foggy *crunch* as my head hit the earth.

2 THE BLACKNESS

Fear raised me fast from oblivion. I sat bolt upright and drew in my breath, choking on dust. Two things were immediately evident. First, I had survived an explosion. Second, my bladder was now empty, the trapped wind expelled. As the dust cleared, I could see the hut was gone; Maica's spade smashed and burning. My face was scuffed and a sharp pain stabbed my right wrist. The bracelet had broken, shattering its promised powers of protection. My head lolled as I mouthed Anthony's name.

To my left was a smouldering leather boot with a foot and ankle still inside it. Ten yards to my right was a lump of smoking flesh, covered in black hair. I looked slowly around. Nothing was moving. The only sound was a low buzzing. My hand was bleeding, and I could see it was wreathed in thorns. They tore my flesh and spiked my soupy consciousness as fear dictated: '*Run*!' '*Run*!' ...the instinct not met by the ability. I was in stasis, shocked and still. Time glooped like cold treacle.

In the cool of the Andean dawn, all that Maica had promised was there before me, inches from my face. The native man, who had guarded this piece of land and had known of its secret, died delivering it up to me. My eyes focused. One nanosecond was long enough to absorb and remember for my lifetime the first sight of such ebony beauty: the black rose.

Still swaying from the force of the explosion, her dark, petal vulva was unbowed. She pulsed and flexed in micro-moments as the sun rose slowly behind the hill, arching her head back from the silver-green collar, upright and proud on a red-brown stem. Beyond blood maroon, beyond midnight blue, she was the deepest and purest of blacks, collapsing all light's frequencies to liquid darkness. Delicious. Noble. *Intense.*

I was in love with her an instant. Nauseated and enthralled with the want of her. Intoxicated and afraid. She was that most rare beauty all men desire and want to possess. Alive and vibrant and sexy. I *had* to have her, and would risk all I had to take her. From the first moment Maica told us of the black rose, I had identified with her isolation and uniqueness. She was the reason I was kneeling in this valley. To come so far and not to take her would be unthinkable.

My hands were shaking. Time shifted back from eternal to instant. In large black letters: 'NOW!' wrote its command across my milky vision. 'NOW! NOW! NOW!' The word flashed and thumped and impelled me to action.

Frightened of more explosions, I dug at the earth with bleeding fingers, tearing deep into mud, terrified of breaking her, terrified of losing her, cursing the fact that I had not brought my trowel. I could not find the courage to retrieve the buckled spade from the smouldering heap I knew to be a body, so I ripped at the soil until my nails splintered and split.

Slowly, slowly, the taproot revealed itself: thick, curled, yellow against the orange soil. Two more moments and I knew I would have it all, yet something made me look up from my frenzy. I turned my head to where I had seen the figures. Instead, there seemed to be a mist at the base of the hill. Then, slowly coming through it on the far right of me, I saw them. Planes. Small, buzzing planes.

I eased the rose root free and picked up what I thought was a fallen petal. It was torn, with a sticky, red edge. For a second, I thought I'd been duped, that my new paramour was not a black rose but a painted, scarlet whore in dark drag. Another rip-off. Another con. My lip curled with momentary disdain when an emotion far more sickening took over. I realised in horror, it was no petal; it was the little dog's ear. I stuffed my fist into my mouth. I could hear screams; they seemed a long way from me and then suddenly, so very close.

Covered in mud and blood, I flung down the doggie ear and crammed the rose into my half-melted bag, clasping her to me as I ran, breathless and aching in the thin air, looking back across the misting valley.

Crop sprayers! Crop sprayers! And a military helicopter! Looking for *cocaleros,* probably. They must have bombed us. A bazooka, maybe? Here, on the stark beauty of Incan soil, two governments had colluded to commit legal murder. The valley dissolved in a deadly miasma. Not only the coca crop, but all organic life would die within hours. Then would follow living death: water pollution, birth defects. I could never go back, no one could. Not for years. My rose was safe inside her cradle and, if Maica were to be believed, the only one of her kind.

It was early. I had money. If I could find the road I could catch a bus or flag down a car. No, mustn't cause attention. White skin and blue eyes are too memorable here. Thank God I had my *chullo* hat and sunglasses.

I tied my jacket around my waist to hide the urine-soaked jeans; then I ran, clutching my prize, shivering and disorientated, back up the covered pathway. Scared by the possibility of police, I decided to wait a few hours before I walked out into the open. Maica was dead, that was real. Black volcanic ankles now deep in scarlet. Were we seen? Were we filmed?

"You've done nothing wrong," someone said, far above me. "You only wanted the rose." I gasped between the words, not recognising my own voice, then sat down on the grass, embracing her, and passed out.

Shock, Nature's way of helping us detach from the unbearable, is followed, like earthquakes, with aftershocks, often more deadly. As I sunk down on the Andean turf, beneath the line of consciousness, my mind flipped a thousand images, threading cold terror through sensuous beauty. Synapses stormed and crackled their impulses inside my skull.

Why were some images sexual? And why, wreathed into the scramble, was there a progressive smell of burning? Where was I? In what place? And with what sense of knowing?

Here comes the genie in fields of corn. A scarecrow warns –

The death of the Monarch in grand theatre.

Answer the burning telephone, for life is seeping down to black

volcanic ankles and I am running – anywhere, everywhere,

away from death's combustion.

Gentle fingers I invest, to pry into her velvet dress

and peel her to her openness.

But, watching us – the silent, toxic snowdrop, white-faced with shock. It

tore my flesh; it ripped my sleep as folded sevens stain the paper.

Little muse lights mighty fuse.

Now the birds circle – and I am rising, I am rising, I am rising.

3 THE BIRDS, THE BUSES

I woke with a start, lying on my back. The sun had moved higher; birds wheeled and glided in the bright sky, soaring on the cool air currents, hundreds of feet above me. They were condors, the eagles of the Andes. A tearing sound filtered through the soup of my hearing. It was llamas, grazing close, ripping at the grass.

I reached for my phone to ring my brother, my best and only true friend, but his line was dead. Texting anyone was out of the question. I could hardly hold on to the handset as I shook and pitched on nausea's wave, so I concentrated on the animals, grateful for the company of other living things. The closest was a baby alpaca with a collar, but the big llamas had ear decorations made from wool.

Immediately, my artist's eye engaged, sharpened by the dulling of my other senses. Their coloured ear tags were lollipop gaudy: lipstick pink and vibrant orange. Discordant. Demanding. I reached out my hand, hoping for the warm communion of flesh with fur, but I was spurned and spat at as the animals fled down the terrace, hooves thumping.

Then I was sick, gagging up the bitter taste of coca. The memory of recent events revisited in full effect as I remembered something else. This is Peru. Even if I had committed a crime, which I had *not*, the authorities would surely take a bribe to leave me alone. I could no longer see planes, nor could I smell any herbicide spray. But the rose in my bag told me it was no dream.

Bruised and concussed, I staggered back up the path we had come until I reached the road. There was no sign of Maica's *combi* minibus. Had it been stolen? Or impounded? Had the authorities known about his coca field? About me?

I walked down the mountain road into the afternoon. Coca's effects had worn off. Back came *soroche* and the killer headache. I was hungry, sore and breathing hard. The 'copter was droning on the periphery. Could I be monitored by satellite – relayed back to a distant screen? I steadied myself as I remembered paranoia is the ghost of coca. Though my ears were still ringing, my jeans were drying as I weaved, unsteady, hour upon hour, desperate for water.

The tomato sun was all but ripe by the time I saw people in the distance. I tugged my *chullo* hat down and hugged the rose close to me inside the bag as I walked up to the strangers. Seven people were standing together, chatting. Mostly *cholo* women with wide, coloured skirts and shawls. Bowler hats and pigtails. They were carrying bundles of *arroba*, compacted coca leaf.

My brother had told me that the mountain women are often financial dealers for the *cocaleros*, given authority because they're considered less corrupt than the men. These women were from the Aymaran tribe: dark brown skin like chestnut horses; genetically unchanged by the Spanish conquistadors, who had corralled and impregnated thousands of them under the command of their generals.

Such were the spoils of war for conquering soldiers. But the sins of these Catholic fathers, perhaps confessed and forgiven, were surely paid for by the rape children. What kind of mindless injustice and racism did the first-born half-breeds have to put up with – from both sides?

Ah-ha! Hello anger! My fuel and survival juice. The shock of the explosion was wearing off. Anger is my barometer. When I can't feel the passion of my ranting, I know I'm in deep trouble.

The locals were standing by a one-storey building, where a man sold tickets. A few enquiries in Spanish told me they were going by bus to Puno, a two-hour ride, so I joined them. Three other people arrived separately after me, knowing the bus to be due.

Most spoke in their native language, marking my difference, but I did not suffer the exclusion long, and within minutes was climbing into the bus to hear Spanish voices I could understand.

Ill-at-ease in my company, the rural people had little or no contact with *gringos* and held them in a mixture of fear, awe and contempt. Judging by the way they acted, they didn't know what had happened a few miles over the hill: crops poisoned, livelihoods gone. No one but the driver seemed to have a mobile phone. Once we reached Puno they were likely to find out exactly who had been messing with their coca. These country people, the *paysanos,* had every right to be murderously mad. I just hoped it wasn't with me.

On my flight to Peru, the politics of cocaine were explained to me by my fellow passenger, Per Linstrom, a Swedish ecologist. He'd told me, in strongly-accented English:

"America gives millions to the Peruvian Government to burn and spray the coca crops and arrest the peasants for growing and refining it. Meanwhile, corrupt officials pocket the dollars and stick a few poor devils on TV in handcuffs, so that the DEA can show the public what a good job they're making of the war on drugs. It's the US Government marketing itself to get votes, and the price is no more expensive than paying a big PR company."

Apparently, Peruvian officials benefit in good relations and greased palms, while a few more peasants are shat on in the name of justice.

Once in Puno bus station, I bought a ticket to Arequipa, water, crackers, a quart bottle of rum and a stronger plastic bag for the rose in the only colour available: bright yellow. I spent a few minutes in the *Servicios Higénicos Públicos,* the public lavatory, having paid the attendant four soles for access to a cubicle with a pan rather than just a hole in the ground.

I was afraid to show my face in the waiting room as my cheek was swollen, my wrist still bleeding, and I'd hesitated to look at the rose in case it drew attention. Nonetheless, I was thrilled and titillated that she was mine; that now, at last, we could be alone together in safety.

I washed my hands, smoothed my hair and examined the bruises, then slugged at the rum. Who had bombed the hut? The DEA? Did they know I'd escaped? Am I being watched?

A young Peruvian woman entered. She began combing her hair and eyed my reflection in the mirror. Her front two teeth were encased in gold. Smiling, to reassure myself rather than her that I was somehow still in control of my faculties, I re-entered the closet. She walked into the cubicle next to me and sat on the pan, but did not, by the sound of it, appear to be doing anything. I bent down and stared under the gap. Small feet. Thick socks. I coughed and fidgeted. My ears strained to hear her excretions. The silence was palpable and embarrassing, thankfully broken when a mother with two noisy children entered the place.

Relieved, I leant down to pick up my rose, to blot out the events that had led to it being here, with me, in this place. From all that I'd been told, I was now the only person to own such a prize; but more than this, I was feeling again. The rose had engaged my emotion. For the first time in two years, I felt something other than angry or numb. I touched her beautiful petals.

Children were laughing in the far stalls. The announcer called us to board for Arequipa, blotting out all sensuous fantasy. Rising, I grabbed the rose and zipped the yellow bag. I flung open the door and walked quickly outside. Tiny feet left the adjacent cubicle moments behind me and followed me out to the bus.

Two uniformed policemen stood either side of the coach steps. As we boarded, they eyed every passenger carefully, yet smiled and chatted with the women who had the bundles of *arroba*. The driver was then cleared to shut his doors. Thus we embarked on our journey via the dangerous mountain road out of Puno, which winds and twists at angles of more than one hundred and eighty degrees. Drivers go hell-for-leather, Anthony told me, regardless of fog and oncoming trucks. The sheer drop on one side is inches from the wheels at times.

Fortunately, today's driver was not drinking. Thank Christ, I was. I hoped he'd snorted a nose-full of cocaine to keep awake.

This road was well repaired, but still a white-knuckle ride for at least nine dark hours. None of the passengers seemed vaguely perturbed and most nodded off despite the blaring movie on the big monitor. I hung on to my tattered nerves, whilst in the film, Jean-Claude blam-blammed his way through endless assaults at ear-shattering volume. Peru is not a culture where silence is valued. Peruvians have incredible vocal projection and loud, loud voices, perhaps because from nappyhood their yells have to compete with the blasting TVs and radios in every shop and home. Padding my *chullo* with earplug wads of toilet paper, I slumped down, bludgeoned into a fitful sleep full of misty planes, bloodied boots, and exploding soil.

I was harshly woken by another whistling BANG, as the door of the bus opened at the Arequipa terminus. Still concussed and shaking, I re-emerged in the White City and staggered out into another Andean dawn.

4 AREQUIPA: THE WHITE CITY

I walked unsteadily through the bus station clutching my bag and hailed the nearest taxi, which slewed out of the car park, instantly making me nauseous. The driver wanted to strike up a conversation, but I was in no mood to talk; so, pretending this was my first time in his city, I let him burble the tourist tour. He was articulate and polite and started a standard intro: that next to Lima, the capital, Arequipa is the richest city; the second capital of Peru.

"Peruvians call Arequipa the '*Ciudad Blanca*', White City, because many of the forts, monasteries and grand buildings are made from *sillar*, the white volcanic stone."

I gawped out of the window at everything he pointed to, letting him think his *información turística* would gain him a big fat tip. It would. I could stay silent and concentrate on not being sick.

"We are embraced by the fastest growing mountains in the world, and the altitude is more than five thousand metres; no humidity and no *insectos*. The sky is blue, every day." I found that one hard to believe, but there was no stopping him.

"Blue sky, every day. And the temperature is always between twenty-one and twenty-seven degrees Celsius." He trilled like a travel brochure as the day began to warm. I looked out at the sky. The light in Arequipa is perfect for painting – clear, truthful light; an honest dialogue with its source is possible here. No wonder the Inca worshipped the sun.

I was in Peru at the invitation of one of its most famous artists, Marina Del Prado, whom I'd met at my own retrospective exhibition in London. It was a desperate attempt by my agent to make some sales, as the year had been slow and no new work had materialised. Marina had engaged me in animated conversation, showing me a photograph of one of her paintings. She was mainly a portrait artist and she burbled on about those who'd influenced her: Soutine, Otto Dix and Arcimboldo, of whom I knew only a little. She was a confident gay woman, and I think she was trying to pick me up. No, I'm sure she was.

There were no portraits at all in my exhibition, just some abstracts, some installations, conceptual stuff, and five pieces of simple sculpture.

"Your work is good. Simple but strong!" she noted. "But why do you never use blue?"

She was a little drunk and waffled on about chroma-variables: tint, hue, nuance, shade, relishing her role as the more experienced painter. It was difficult to be moved by her enthusiasms when my own were so jaded, so I changed the subject to my brother, Anthony, who had been nine months in her country, in Arequipa, on a prolonged holiday.

"*Arequipa*? That is where I live, Sybil! Come to Peru! Change your life!" she ordered. "They want nothin' but dollars in Lima, but in Arequipa we have the painters, the intellectuals. We have the *volcano*. You will paint differently when you see *El Misti*."

It was this last remark that had got me on the plane, as I was out of love with both my own painting and the London art scene. Anything that could make me pick up a brush these days needed serious investigation. So, there I was, shaking her hand again within six weeks of our first encounter.

Marina told me to refer to her only as 'Mavis' when in Peru. Why she chose this sobriquet above her own name was a mystery. Luz Marina, her full Christian name, meant 'light of the sea', which I thought quite beautiful, but henceforth, 'Mavis' it was. I subsequently found out that many of her social class preferred a less Spanish-sounding name.

But though I was now injured and in need of a friend, I did not trust Mavis with news of Maica's death, and could not tell her why I was so bruised and shaken. I had sworn to keep his secret; but what really stopped me calling her was the intolerable thought of another artist poring over my new muse: the black rose.

The driver's voice drifted back to me: "Yes, blue sky, every day; and never too hot, because of our light winds, señora." I was a señorita, but no point telling him or he would have seen it as an invitation. What he hadn't included in his blurb was that the afternoon breeze dances arm-in-arm with a billion discarded polythene bags.

"The big volcano, '*El Misti,*' is named after one of the Qqechua words for God. Can you see? On the left. It last erupted four hundred years ago." That would have been when the conquistadors were busy burning and raping and turning the rivers red. Misti must have witnessed it all, as it witnesses all now, dominating the landscape – watching us – watching it. I had seen Misti all right. I had seen its grey cloak rise up as the plane prepared to land, many days ago now. The conical mass was burned into my consciousness. The White City seemed like a church, Misti its altar. Misti stirred something in me that I didn't know I could feel. But I still wasn't painting… yet.

"Misti, Chachani and Pichu-Pichu surround the White City, señora. This is the Atacama, señora, the driest desert in the world. Without the melted snows of the volcanoes, we would have no life here in Arequipa."

He made no mention of their implied threat: the fact that they smoke and steam in tiny puffs, sleeping, but fitful, their awakening an ever-present hint. Thus, instability and the transience of life becomes an obvious contemplation in the White City. And the price the citizens pay for living in such a beautiful region is the constant reminder that theirs is a paradise built on sand. Grey, volcanic, ever-shifting sand. Running close to a major fault line, Arequipa can have as many as twenty small tremors a day, and in much the same way that the citizens sleep through a blasting movie on a bus, they just ignore them.

Beside the white stones that built it, Arequipa could have been called the White City for racial reasons, my driver explained. The *pitucos:* upper-class, white-skinned citizens from pure Spanish descent, like Mavis, and my brother's friend Charlie, live privileged lives. Next to Lima, Arequipa has the highest percentage of them. I'd noted their imperious presence, day one. Servants' quarters are mostly sheds on the roofs of the houses, and the native peoples serve their masters for up to eighteen hours a day. Such social demarcations seem incongruous to visitors, but it pays to be careful when voicing judgments. In this parochial environment, nearly everyone and everything is connected by very short strings.

The cabbie weaved through the backstreets of Cayma, his voice fading and blurring as my stomach churned. He pointed out the grand houses of local dignitaries. The mayor; a judge; a famous cabaret singer. I looked around at the swept streets and noted the amount of construction the townsfolk had undertaken. Such industry makes ants look lazy. On every corner were new apartments or extensions to the houses, thrown up from ground-break to light bulb inside six months. Linstrom, the Swede on the plane, had explained:

"Dirty money is washed through legal businesses, mostly smart hotels, discothèques and restaurants, all consistently empty. My ex-wife's family had one. They just fill in the accounts as if they were busy every night and *bang*, legal income! Pay a little tax, everyone's happy. No one checks. A huge proportion of businesses are built on coca money."

He was right. Maica had bought a fleet of minibus *combis* to cover up his coca dealings. Anthony explained that this was how the *cholo* justified to everyone how he'd paid for his children's private education: a coach business. Without subterranean coca in this economy *no pasa nada* – nothing happens.

"The *Arequipeños* are spirited people, proud of their place in the country's history. They call it the *Estado Independiente de Arequipa.*" The driver banged his chest and checked his mirror to ensure my backseat attention.

“We are known for our revolutionary trade unions; our stance against central government. Our history of *insurección* comes from very intelligent peoples and brave native *paysanos,* who will be slaves to no one.”.

All remain curiously silent, however, when asked about the hidden cocaine dollars upon which their economy is based. Spend one week at Diego the dealer’s house, my brother had said, and count how many judges, doctors, and civil servants rely on the coca bush for their daily enthusiasm. Not to mention the ‘brave, native *paysanos*’ who grow it, and happily chomp the leaves.

Drug tourists who consume the white powder that Arequipa offers certainly know it as the ‘White’ City. Apart from the countless Mormon missionaries, most visitors who choose to stay here for any length of time fall into two distinct categories: full-on addicts or emotional refugees.

My brother Anthony and I were no exception.

5 BRUISE, MUSE AND BOOZE

The following day, I awoke early after endless nightmares, still nauseous and confused. Inside the yellow bag on the kitchen table was my rose, snug in a plastic bucket full of soil I'd bought from a plant shop, two blocks away. I'd firmed the root in, and cut back the foliage, first making a hole in the bucket for drainage; but I couldn't bring myself to cut the bloom. Ripped from her bed, the rose should have been clipped short and given a chance to recuperate.

Folklore says that to a give a newly-planted rose the best of chances place a rusty nail, a pound of lard and a bag of horseshit next to the root and water it all with rainwater. Mine had a scrap of orange soil and a bag of sterile soil, all doused with the horseshit of hypocritical praying.

A plant under these conditions is in conflict. It either invests energy in the flower and progresses it to fruit and seed, or jettisons this chance and makes a stronger root with its existing life force. My love of the bloom was jeopardising her existence and I knew it. She was as stressed as I was. Though her dark crinoline was creased and dull, it had not fallen. I watered her, willing her to survive, and spoke softly, promising her immortality, reminding her again of her duty to represent her unique species. I used to talk that way to my reflection in the bathroom mirror, willing myself to prevail and triumph over sorrow, depression and lethargy. "*Better paintings coming*," I would promise. "*Don't give in*."

I needed to talk to Anthony, but having seen his phone charger on the hall table, I realised why his line was dead. Unless he'd bought a new one, difficult to source in the Valley of Volcanoes, there would be no contact until he returned. Even if he'd borrowed a phone, he would not have remembered my new number. I was feeling his absence like an aching.

Apart from the *taxista* and the girl in the plant shop, I had not spoken to anyone since I'd returned from the valley. There were three texts from Marina Del Prado, signed 'Mavis', of course, but I was in no state to have one of her fractured conversations. Other than Mavis and Maica, I'd met only a few people in the time I had been here: Mavis' friend Armando; the redneck Todd and his girlfriend Laura; Joseph, a Mormon missionary; Charlie the idiot; and Diego,
Ant's drug dealer. I couldn't seek comfort from them and didn't trust any of them with knowledge of the black rose.

It was time to try Diego's phone again, just to see if he knew anything without me giving much away. I'd tried twice already since my return. Now I was convinced his dead line meant he'd been detained by the police. Maica was his main supplier and friend; Diego had introduced us. If Maica had been earmarked for extinction, maybe all his associates were, including me. I was staring at my wilted rose as I dialled. The line was still dead. Of course, there was no point ringing Maica. He and his mobile had been blasted to oblivion. Atomised in the Andes. Face, voice and boot still uppermost in my imagination.

Maica Cauac Lloque Yupanqui had been a perfect genetic representation of his people. Dark-skinned and squat, they called him a *cholo* – an indigenous native. His stature, race and lack of education had automatically debarred him from many of the opportunities here. Consequently, he'd learned to refine coca from his own valley crop. And, like regional wine makers in France, or private olive grove owners in Greece, he'd perfected a personal formula. Pure and smooth, with no edginess, it was a powder you could eat, sleep and work on. Simply, the best coke in town, my brother had said.

Anthony, who loved Diego and Maica with that special *amor* reserved for all his candy men and dealers, had explained to me the meaning of the word *cholo,* pronounced as if with a double L in English.

"The descendants of the Spanish rulers use it to describe the indigenous people, while the *cholos* call the white Spanish upper classes *los pitucos*."

Ant's dealer, Diego, with his European features, felt superior to the dark natives, and used the word negatively, although with affection. Unable to afford a *cholo* servant, Diego delighted in referring to Maica as 'his' *cholo,* even though the native man had obviously been the more successful partner, since he was higher up the chain. They'd met whilst in jail, and the bisexual Diego had a filial loyalty to him. In prison, Maica was the shoe-mender and fellow cook. Or fellow crook. Or fellow cock? Who knows the secrets of *that* relationship?

Maica first mentioned he had a black rose growing in his valley the first weekend I was in Arequipa, while giving me and my brother a lift back from Diego's house. I was commenting on the flowers we passed outside the houses, and how surprised I was to see so many common to Britain. Snapdragons, pinks, hollyhocks, and of course, roses. I told him that I always grew unusual flowers in my garden at home, blabbing on about how I would love to buy some roses for my balcony if only I could find where to look, and that I wanted to buy large, mature plants and was willing to pay well for the best specimens.

I can't live anywhere without a garden. If I were going to make this place my home for a while, I needed my own green space. I remember I gave a sanctimonious little speech about how, to me, a godless artist, the garden was my church. "*Pachamama* is the only thing worth worshipping," I'd added, invoking the Incan earth goddess Ant had told me about. Maica seemed impressed.

Realising there were dollars to be made, he then told us of the rare black rose, insisting, almost hysterically, that we should not mention it to *anyone*, including Diego, lest he wanted a cut, I supposed, for having introduced us. Ecstatic at the prospect of owning such an utter rarity, I was resolute, particularly when he explained that there was only one rose bush of such a colour.

An imaginary pair of shears was thus wielded by the high priestess of horticulture, ready to cut off the head of any rival. No bastard is getting that black rose before I do, I vowed.

Maica could speak a little English, but Ant insisted on helping me negotiate. At first, Maica said he would bring the rose to me.

"No way, *amigo*," I'd said. "If you want to see the colour of my money, *I'm* the one who's digging it up. Have you ever transplanted a rose?" I'd asked. "No? Well, you don't know how careful you have to be. Unlike other plants, the soil does not cling to a network of roots. They're fine and easily damaged. You can't just lift it on a spade and replant it. The taproot can go two feet down or more, and if you dig it up and damage the big root, you'll lose the rose."

He was very attentive to my knowledge, and immediately mentioned money. He wanted $3,000 to show me, two more if the rose were brought back successfully, with roots intact and still growing.

"*Huevon*! *Por favor. Es demasiado*! *No seas pajero*!"

My brother chided and swore at him, trying to lower the fee, but there was no beating him down. Half believing it to be a scam and that I would never really have to pay, I agreed his price. Yet he'd still not been keen to take me to the valley. I offered an extra $1,000 sweetener. He agreed, but said I'd have to submit to being blindfolded part of the way to preserve the secret.

So excited were my passions then, it was all I could do not to put my hands around his scrawny throat and demand he take me to the rose immediately. It would be risky, because when he'd referred to 'his valley' I knew that meant his coca crop. Anthony wanted his cut of the money as translator and protector, at least a couple of *falsos*, the paper folds containing coke.

"Why is it called a *falso*?" I'd asked.

"It's just over half a gram, but the *gringos* are so naïve that they think it's a full gram." I expect he had too, until enlightened.

As Maica drove off, I explained to Ant how much a genuine black rose could be worth, but he was more curious about a trip to the growing areas. My sweet, addicted sibling, a junkie to his own adrenaline as well as cocaine.

A visit to a secret valley! We could hardly wait.

6 *EMBRACING THE VELVET*

Now that my head was clearing, I began to realise the full implications and cost of getting the rose. I walked over to her and picked up the bag, taking her into the tiny bathroom, the only room in the house with a lock. Her petals contrasted sharply with the garish plastic, black with yellow, like a wasp. Like a hazchem warning. I wondered perhaps, if the petals were steeped in boiling water, would they liberate some delicious narcotic… a luscious opiate that takes away all pain? Could the thorns be poisonous? Or medicinal? A precious herbal remedy, maybe, hence the careful guarding by Maica.

I lifted her from the bag. The ache of my wrist, the shock of the explosion and the death I'd so recently witnessed all dissolved as I touched the rose. Her head was bowed, her petals opening in the warmth of the morning. I brought her closer to my face. She brushed velvet against my lips and I raised her to me, cradling the bulk of her in my palms to support her.

The weight of a beloved in one's arms is intimate and special. Yet, in the delight of the embrace lies an exquisite insecurity: fear that the object of desire will someday no longer be yours: that death, or rival, will have triumphed; that disease, or age, will have overcome. Worse, that you yourself will have discarded that which you now hold so close.

With my left hand, I raised her slender neck and breathed deeply of her. She did not disappoint. A rose without perfume is like a beautiful but unintelligent woman: stunningly decorative, but lacking character. But like its colour, the perfume of this rose, had no rival. Roses have a bewildering range of scents, and though, in essence, rose perfume is always 'rose', it is differentiated in tiny molecules. The wild dog rose has peppery top notes; bourbons and quartered roses are laced with anise. Damasks and gallicas are the sweetest… but the full spectrum is in the Chinas and the old-fashioned breeds, though modern hybrids are fast matching them.

But *my* rose… how to describe her? Liquorice, cinnamon and blackberry, a deep base note of spicy *rugosa* but with an almost citrus overtone. If the perfume of this rose could be extracted, she would be worth millions. But, so too would her colour. Her debut in horticulture would be a licence to print money.

Since I'd first heard of the rose, the idea of exclusively owning her, then cloning her for a percentage of every sale, had been part of my motivation for turning rumour into tangible fact.

Of course, I'd have to get into bed with commercial growers to achieve it, but every gardener in the world would want to buy her sister clones. Fêted and famous, she would bear my name and join with me forever throughout time. She was better than any child; not that breeding had ever remotely interested me, but I still couldn't pass up a sure shot at immortality. How easy my choices would be if I still only wanted the rose for gain.

But here, in this little cubicle, where first we fully engaged with each other, I found myself overwhelmed with a jealous need to protect her from the ravages of commerce. Like a possessive lover, I was heady with the idea that only *I* should know her perfume and touch her form, only *my* eyes gaze upon that dark, exotic vulva of petals. The idea that any exposure of her might soil her, or diminish her, enraged me.

I thought through the furore of her disclosure. I imagined they might advertise her in Sunday supplement magazines next to kitsch figurines of royalty, exploiting her beauty for mindless consumers anxious for new icons. Petty horticulturists would leer and preen, congratulating themselves on their connoisseurship.

Suburbia would swarm over. Spending. Stroking. Salivating. And her uniqueness would burn out in flames of prurient curiosity.

My grandiose fantasy was that at the reading of my will I would have gifted her to a charitable foundation, and all profits in perpetuity to them, revealing only then that she had been mine and should bear my name.

But unlike me, the black rose was not grandiose. She was Nature's art, unfiltered through ego and narcissism. Only a form such as hers gave a yardstick by which to measure the worth of my own efforts as a creator. I was overwhelmed by her. Humbled that I might now be the guardian of a lone species. Guilty that her beauty had been tainted by blood; that her life with me was wreathed in death.

From the first rip of her briars on my wrist, why didn't I see this was a dangerous, deluding passion? Because, it was I, not the rose, who was culpable. I became responsible for all that unfolded because of her. But regardless of warnings from the brokenhearted, from the world's greatest poems, songs and stories, I was totally blinded by love.

Neurotic, needy and lost, I stepped into the darkness. And, like many an obsessive lover before me, I handed over power to something irresistible and uncontrollable… to another life-force, wilful in its own agenda; despite me and without me.

And I knew that by doing so, I had conjured love's cliché: empowering the thorn by embracing the velvet.

7 WAYNE'S COCAINE WORLD

Before I came to Arequipa, all I knew about Peru was that it was the world's largest source of cocaine. No literature or website mentioned the legend of the black rose. Nothing. The only plant ever mentioned in relation to this country was coca. My travel book confirmed twenty thousand hectares of land were registered for licit coca cultivation near the Bolivian border in the north-west in the country. Many thousand more hectares were growing illegal coca.

"The legal crop is exported, mostly to the US, previously for soft drink flavouring, now for numbing agents and pain-relievers. Farmers registered with the National Coca Monopoly (ENACO) can legally sell to local markets for coca tea and leaf chewing. Possession of the leaves in any amount is not illegal in Peru or Bolivia," the book said. You could bathe in them nightly and wear them in your hair with no fear of reprisal.

Yet, considering it's a home-grown high, only a small percentage of wealthier Peruvians take refined coke. Ant told me that the natives prefer to chew the leaf, and even rub it on babies' gums for teething problems. *'Matte de coca'*, coca tea, is a legal cure-all; everything from period pain to arthritis soothed by coca leaves immersed in boiling water.

I took the rose back into the kitchen, grabbing a pen to write a shopping list, then flipped on the TV to the Miami cable channel. I watch the screen, hunched forward, slurping my own coca tea. What it cures for me is the ringing in my ears and continuing nausea.

"Welcome to *America Today*."

An ultra-white set of capped teeth are smiling to camera: "Continuing our series of discussions on America's anti-drug policies, we have as our studio guest Mr. Wayne Sheridan, the new head of the Drug Enforcement Administration." Camera cuts to red-haired man.

Flashy ring glints on his left hand. Camera pans the suited 'experts', host introducing:

"Dick Havens MD, director of the Bon Haven Addiction Centre; Wallace Newsam, crime correspondent from the Miami Herald; Señor Rodrigo Balén, Vice President of Miami law firm Balén Valdivia; and lastly, Dominic Meisenberger, Professor of Economics at U.C.L.A."

The presenter is slick. I've seen him before. He seeks sensational statements and likes to provoke them.

"In his recent documentary on the rise of cocaine use, Marv Benton of CBS described it as 'the white caterpillar in the cabbage of our cultural heart, eating away at the moral fabric of society'. Mr. Sheridan, what is your agency doing about the frightening increase in our young people using cocaine and crack?"

The drug tsar shifts in his seat.

"Well, Barney, we have to address that at source and target both the manufacture and the refinin' of cocaine, which, as you know, is mainly grown in Peru."

Sheridan looks like a genuine good guy, neat, smiley, and fighting on the side of the Almighty. Nature has not been kind to him; he is pear-shaped, overweight, with a red, bulbous nose. He seems too benign to match the formidable drug traders he seeks to oppose. A seeming Father Christmas to their evil elves.

"Part of the reason it's so easy for our kids to get hold of cocaine is because of the efficient drug distribution network," says the journalist.

"So, the drug cartels are winning the free market game?" poses Barney. "Dynamic distribution without interference!"

Sheridan winces. He knows it's true. No longer a private vice: cocaine, the crystal concubine, now offers her charms to all.

"We've doubled the amount of officers; doubled the amount of cocaine seized; and we're targetin' the growing fields. But we gotta educate our children, too. Cocaine is dangerous for minds and bodies. It will destroy their health and finances and their families' lives."

"But in most of South America it costs a couple of dollars a gram," says the economist. "Affordable for most people."

The others raise their eyebrows, knowing he's right. If you like cocaine, living in Peru has its advantages. Ask my brother, Anthony Sands, Golden Boy. The white knight on the white diet, currently enjoying an Andean sleigh ride in a snowstorm of purest cocaine.

"Isn't it true they also use dangerous pesticides on the coca crops?" asks the presenter, raising his game to faux eco-warrior.

"Yes, it's used against coca fly," he's informed. "Traces of it stay in the finished product, no matter how well refined."

"Coca is considered to be a sacred plant," says the journalist.

"Sacred? A dangerous drug – *sacred?*" asks Mr. Teeth.

"In its unrefined state it is. The leaf is still used in rituals of mourning; at weddings; for herbal medicine; to praise the gods and to appease angry spirits. You can't stop that," the journalist says.

"More to the point," says the doctor, "coca is necessary for those living and working at high altitudes. It helps them breathe in the thin air by dilating the blood vessels to the lungs. It's a part of their daily lives. They won't work without it." The journalist nods:

"They think it's been given to them by God."

"Perhaps it has been," interrupts the only Peruvian in the studio, Señor Balén. "Why else would it grow in these high places and serve the people with exactly the chemical they need in order to negotiate mountain life? It is a miracle drug: a gift from *Pachamama*."

The presenter explains to the TV audience this pagan reference to the earth goddess. Sheridan's ring catches the lights. He can feel the initiative drifting. He must emphasise the case and strategy for curbing this menace, and fast. He hitches his trousers over his knees and leans forward. I lean forward, drifting in and out of concentration, spilling tea. The doctor speaks next.

"Cocaine is the most efficient dopamine transporter in the world, more than all its derivatives and analogues, both man-made and natural.

It's guaranteed to raise your feel-good factor; that's why it's popular, particularly among depressives."

"Perhaps you should explain the medical terms, doctor," says the patronising host, aware of the limitations of his viewing public. Havens expounds on brain chemistry and its effect on personality, the morale-boosting properties of the brain's dopamine, serotonin and adrenaline levels. Cocaine, he says, changes their proportions in the mental soup, elevates mood; gives focus. I focus on my shopping list. It only has one word one it: rum.

The lawyer makes a case for the peasants: unable to live without farming coca; few other ways to earn money. Sheridan unbuttons his jacket and grimaces.

"The American Government appreciates the role of coca in the lives of the indigenous mountain people but we have a duty to our own citizens to stop the production of refined cocaine. The Peruvian Government understands this well and is prepared to help with new measures."

Meisenberger plays his economist's card:

"Cocaine is the most successful cash crop on the planet. It's harvested three or four times a year from the same plants. In thin soil and at high altitudes it would be impossible to grow anything else with the same financial yield."

"So, the DEA seems set to destroy the livelihoods of some of the poorest Peruvian farmers?" say the Teeth. Sheridan clears his throat.

"New coffee varieties, developed in co-operation with our two governments and Gentrex International, will help improve their livin' standards by offering an alternative GM crop," he says. Up flashes the name 'Gentrex' as the presenter blah blahs and introduces cut-away footage. Chief Executive of Gentrex, Alec Abelman: designer suit, wire-rimmed glasses, explains their new contract with the US government to develop a genetically-modified coffee crop to rival and replace coca.

"This new technology has already introduced 'golden' rice, a GM rice variety enriched with iron and vitamin A, which is having a major impact improving nutrition for the world's poor. Coffee, as we know, has a proven market. Peruvian farmers deserve a chance to develop this new crop and make good profits."

The words 'good profits' make everyone smile. Focus returns to the studio. Focus returns to my list. Two items: 1) Rum. 2) Coca tea.

"That won't stop the farmers growing coca," says the lawyer.

"Coca gives them a sense of purpose and meaning, as well as a cash crop. Their ancestors have grown it for millennia. Even newly guaranteed coffee prices won't change that."

A sweating Sheridan addresses his colleagues:

"One thing that will kill off the cocaine trade for good... *Disease*. That's the other reason why we've brought a modern company like Gentrex on board." The group stiffens. He expounds:

"Somethin' genetically-engineered to terminate fertility within the coca plant, or to give it an incurable disease, but at the same time providing a high-yield coffee as a substitute crop." He sounds like a zealot, the pitch of his voice is rising as he warms to his theme: "A mould perhaps, somethin' to kill coca forever, and cocaine addiction along with it." He slows for dramatic delivery: "Biotechnology is the answer."

Sheridan looks round at the assembled company in florid sincerity, as if he's just played an ace. Christ! I'll be surprised if he makes it out of the studio alive.

Cue everyone talking at once. Cut to adverts for drain cleaner, *matte de coca* and Nike trainers: loud music; big feet. Bomp, bomp, bomp. Nike! Nike! Nike! The ad man's magic three repeats to seed your subconscious.

Alcohol is great at keeping nausea and nightmares at bay. I needed more. Food might not be a bad idea either. I dressed and walked down towards the liquor store on the main street. A red-faced man in cowboy boots was walking unsteadily up the road towards me with a bag full of beers, stinking of drink and laughing. He saw me and called out loudly:

"Hey there, missy. Y'all comin' up fer a swaller?"

I slowly focused my eyes. It was Todd.

8 TODD

Todd Whale and his girlfriend were in Peru for the usual reasons, though this time it was Laura Snow who was the addict and Todd the emotional refugee. He knew nothing of roses, of Maica, or Diego, and was emphatically anti-cocaine. Todd was a cowboy: a redneck, rodeo-ridin', truck-drivin' cowboy from Colorado. OK. Rewind that. He *had been* a cowboy, back in the day, before the accident. Todd had also been a helicopter mechanic, could fly them at a push, though he had no licence; but he'd earned his living as a truck driver, the biggest rigs America could make.

"Hell, there ain't nothin' with wheels I kin't handle," he liked to boast, and, at one time, you knew it had been true.

Todd's problem was that from an active life of going to truck fairs and waving his monkey wrench, he'd had a terrible accident on a jet-ski at a Colorado lake resort. One fine day, a fellow skier had crashed into him and ripped his face off. When they pulled Todd from the water, his nose was sitting on top of his head and his eyeballs were hanging out.

No oil painting before, he now resembled a mid-period Picasso, even though a fine surgeon had managed to stitch it all together in a not too scary arrangement. He had a squint in his right eye, a scarred nose and no sense of taste or smell. Self-conscious about his looks, what pissed Todd off more was that he'd lost all interest in food. A 'rump-steak with all the trimmings' man, he now found it difficult to trust the freshness of meat because he couldn't tell if it were spoiled. He hated Peruvian fish stalls and butchers and their lack of hygiene. I'd once pointed out that local fish was fresh daily from Lake Titicaca. He'd retorted:

"Well, they sell a lot of bottom-feeders, and I ain't eatin' them scum-suckin' bast'ids! They eat shit all day and turn to mush in yer mouth when ya' eat 'em. 'Sides, I only drink beer cuz it's 'bin cooked. Only drink water if I hav'ta."

Everything was: "Hell, no!" and "You bet yer sweet ass!" And it greatly amused Ant and me when he said: "The biggest goddam assholes I ever met in mah life were the Briddish!" At least we were the best at something, I'd joked. He didn't notice. Todd still believed that the fires of hell and the Second Coming of Christ were realities. Darwin, he said, couldn't possibly be right because: "If that wuz true, why's them apes still around? That jis don' mek sense t' me."

Like Laura, his girlfriend, he was naturally intelligent, but completely uneducated, never having read anything more challenging than adventure fiction. But, try as I may, I couldn't dislike him. I was both fascinated and angry as to how his culture had led him to such primitive conclusions. White trash Todd was the real deal. Pictures come to life. He could never resume work as a driver as his eyesight had been badly affected, but he was far too proud to take my pity. Sadly, his relationship with Laura was floundering, and his dislike of us 'Briddish' kept her from seeing us, even though she was a good friend of Anthony's. Maybe Laura used Todd as the excuse. She could have slipped away for a drink with us had she wanted to. Hell, you can't make someone like you, but Ant was incensed on my behalf:

"Rednecks! Don't they know *anything* about art?"

"Bro', right now, I don't know anything about art either," I'd said at the time.

I was surprised, therefore, when Todd invited me to his apartment for a celebration. I needed human company, and as alcohol was on offer it seemed like a good idea.

"What are we celebrating?" I asked, as we climbed his steps.

"I 'jis got me a jawb as a security guard," he said, struggling to retrieve the key. He opened the door and reeled into the kitchen. Laura was out. Todd was coy about telling me more. He tapped the side of his re-stitched hooter and winked.

"All y'need to know, missy, is they're payin' me $600 a week."

Well, that was a bloody good wage for Peru. I could see that the status conferred by this position had elevated Todd's self-esteem, and thus his magnanimity to me.

"Hell, you took a punch, lady?" He noticed my bruised cheek as he staggered around the kitchen.

"Yeah that's right, Todd… for being too Briddish."

He didn't hear my quip. Too busy struggling to find a bottle opener. He must have been used to seeing beaten-up women because he didn't mention it again. He lit a cigarette with a shaking hand and opened the window.

"Don't tell Laura. Hates smokin'."

Though he could no longer taste the beer, it was obvious he hadn't lost his liking for the effect, which kicked like a mule just as before. I waited till he'd downed his lotion, then I asked more about the job and how he came by it.

"Steve Colby rang me," he shouted over his shoulder, "one of my best buddies from the 'copter days."

Steve was now working for a private company flying small planes for officials and business moguls, he explained. Steve, apparently, had a contact in Arequipa.

"Told 'em he knows a guy down in Peru you could trust if yer life depended on it, an' the next thing I know, I got me a jawb."

Well, the detail wasn't easy to wheedle out of him. Seemed it was a laboratory complex called Gentrex, the company I had just heard about on the TV. Controversial biotech, very modern for Peru. Must be the cheap rent and labour, I thought. They'd had two break-ins at the lab and had been forced by insurers to redesign all their security systems and hire new guards. I asked why they'd hired a foreigner, Todd replied:

"Didn't trust them sneaky Peruvian bast'ids!"

I registered his racism and poured myself another drink. Wondered how well he'd fit in with the Peruvian workforce.

“But hey! It’s pretty hush-hush, so don’t go shootin’ yer mouth awf,” he said, shooting his mouth off.

Two large beers later and he’d glazed over, slumping down onto the sofa, almost drooling. Todd’s nasal impairment inured him to his armpit aroma, which reeked of rancid goat. And the chemical reactions in his trainers had long since gone critical. This noxious funk wafted to the street as I left; the ripe supply within ready to greet girlfriend Laura, whose nose, I supposed, would be too numb to notice.

9 GENE GENIE

Despite Todd's liquid hospitality, my nerves were still shaky. Maica's boot was kicking my subconscious. More alcohol was needed to dull the angst. The internet café was on my way to the liquor store, so I decided to check my e-mails on a bigger screen than my phone. It was still hard to focus after my concussion and we didn't have a Wi-Fi connection at the house yet.

The café was full of kids playing online games. Music blasted out from Lima's retro-pop station, mostly in English. I swung into a booth to 80's synth pop. Depeche Mode's: *Everything counts (in large amounts)*. I opened my mail, having waded through the endless pop-ups and click bait, one for an online dating site called *The Love Club* fronted by a spectacularly bosomy blonde, and one flashing advert exhorting me to buy the very latest drone-mounted camera at an *u n b e l i e v a b l y* low price. I ignored all the mail from my UK contacts: the Cook Street Gallery; De Montfort's; my framer; and instead, opened the one from Ant.

"Home in couple of days, sis. Tour bus awful, food worse! Gigs great though. Hope u love the White City as much as I do. Hope u painting. Miss my favourite girl. A XX."

Anthony comforted me like no one else. I needed to embrace my brother. I didn't want to tell him about the rose or the valley in writing. I was still paranoid. He'd know soon enough. "Hurry back." I wrote.

The second message I opened was a newsletter from the 'Green Soldier' environmentalists, to whom I'd occasionally donated funds. I was a great admirer of their derring-do, stopping the Japanese whaling fleet; door-stepping the shareholders of animal labs. I followed a link entitled: 'New Dangers'. I clicked the title and out popped Jack and his toxic snowdrop.

"The proliferation of biotech companies based in South America continues unabated," the report began. *"In 2013, the US*

administration approved a $60 million grant to the government of Peru to fund a contract for Gentrex International, whose research will concentrate on attacking coca crops with bio-engineered fungi. Gentrex has persistently refused to answer our enquiries concerning the effects of its GM fungal organism on other crops. Their main research laboratory is to be found in Arequipa, Peru."

It gave the address. I wrote it down. The report continued:

"GM crops are often touted as a solution to famine, but they are unsafe and motivated only by profit. In 1999, Armand Putztai, an immunologist, proved conclusively that genetically modified potatoes that were transgenic with snowdrop lectin were toxic to rats and compromised their immune systems." Jack Colby, Green Soldier correspondent.

Genetically modified spuds? Compromised immune systems? Hmm. Bet it didn't compromise anyone's bank balance. Next heading: 'Wings of Death' in gothic red letters.

"Maize modified with an insect-resistant gene has been proven to poison the Monarch butterfly, which feeds on corn pollen."

I read the next part with glee. Apparently, in cahoots with British activists, Green Soldier re-enacted the death of the poor insects. An ear of corn was marked with a giant X and all the greenies dressed up as dying butterflies and mock-fainted in the field.

The death of the Monarch in grand theatre.

The photos were hilarious. The press lapped it up. Sadly, such camp antics could only invite mockery from the media. But at least it was an honourable thing to do with your time: enlighten people through humour. These pranks affected banks. Shares went down. Yeah. Down. A direct hit! Through imagination and wit. Linstrom, my fellow plane passenger, knew all about biotech, he'd started to lecture me when the unctuous hostess had tried to serve sweetcorn to his dinner tray and he sneered her away.

"Stupid American farmers adopted GM crops without question," he told me, refusing to eat the delicious yellow beads. "Trans-genesis is routine for maize and tobacco. It's been used for almost thirty years. More than a trillion modified crops are grown throughout the world. Now you know why the bees die, eh?"

Yup, he was the life and soul of the party was Linstrom, for twelve bloody hours, though he did cheer up once he'd had a drink.

Back to Jack… I read a couple more items of rant and was about to exit the site when I noticed the words: 'Bio Business Latest'. Out-clicked concise information on Gentrex and another company, Lifex Laboratories. The item was in bold letters:

"Lifex Laboratories has put in a friendly bid for Gentrex International, the American biotech company, now with an extensive research base in southern Peru. Gentrex issued a profit forecast of $300m last week. Share prices have moved fourteen points on the news."

Green Soldier went on to enlighten me with some startling financial facts. In the last twenty years, the US Government has deregulated over two thousand transgenic crop varieties for commercial field release, many developed by Lifex Laboratories, generating $14 billion worth of business under the stewardship of their CEO, Bill Lerner.

I leant back in the seat and squinted at the screen. Fourteen billion balloons, eh? That generates *huge* power. The Mode were right: everything does count in large amounts. Biotechnology is the new gold rush. Multinationals and millionaires are investing now and investing *big*. Since Bill Lerner became vast earner, they're on it like bluebottles, patenting the genes of every living organism.

"This technology will change everything we have come to understand as normal," Linstrom had pronounced.

"Science invented a new wheel," I'd replied, and continued munching the airline's GM sweetcorn. Linstrom put it more strongly than that.

"God is redundant. Pensioned off. Put out to pasture."

"Yeah, probably grazing on GM crops."

He became very animated, not in the least amused.

"They'll soon have the maps of life itself! Don't you understand? Once they know *how* to get there, it's only a matter of *when*. People become *Nazis* when they have such power! They will start their Eugenics programmes again. My grandfather was murdered by Nazis because he was an epileptic. Genetically inferior. They took him to the camps!"

Sobered by his story, I asked the Swede if he thought some biotechnology was good, that it could defeat Nature in some ways. He was horrified.

"The patenting of genetic codes?" he spat. "They'll want to be the owners of your DNA next and grant you a licence to use it. You'll need a permit to *breed*."

I suggested that at least Mother Nature alone won't have the blueprints. Whatever happens from now on, I reminded him, *she* never played to the rules of cricket. All those creative little flaws: cleft palate; cystic fibrosis; autism. That shut him up… for a full ten seconds.

Linstrom had passion, I'll give him that. A passion I had left behind in London, nailed to the last of my canvasses. Swedes are often thought to have none: to be cold and pragmatic and not given to the warm-blooded, demonstrative frothings of south Europeans. But his light blue eyes were full of warnings: gene terrorism and the strangest of creatures; unheard-of life-forms in Petri dishes – *abominations*. A shuffle of the genetic pack makes a pig with six legs, to better feed the world.

Some smart artist would likely make an installation of it. …Probably me, if I ever got my mojo back. Now, what would I do?

Ah, yes. A large magnifying glass set over a tiny, six-legged pig foetus sculpted in pork fat, set in a womb made from torn dollar bills. Title? '*What pigs are we*?'

I refocused on the screen. A picture of Bill Lerner, dark-haired and smiling in a smart, pin-striped suit. I read the quote:

"GM crops are safely grown all over the world. My family regularly eat them." Bill Lerner, CEO Lifex International.

OK. I get it. Not only was the genie out of the bottle, it was busy with mischief in a field near us at this very moment.

Closing down the screen, I paid the pimply-faced *chico* at the desk and walked back home via the liquor shop. Usually, it was full of destitute drunks trying to swap stolen light bulbs for libation, but now it was shut. I banged on the door. A small brown hand exchanged rum for local currency, ten new soles in coins. Great! I walked home, sucking on the bottle and musing on the trans-gene genies.

Once I had watered my wilted rose, I drank myself to sleep. But my rest wasn't peaceful. I fell back into cryptic nightmares…

Glinting wings, up and to the right, and far below
a bird is diving to the sea.

When secret science drips with handsome karma
Silhouettes wait to chew my lies
I am a kneeling cliché, so hard to breathe.

The dog in haunches humps behind –
a gripping, slavering, one-track mind.

A cracking, tight head easily silenced.
And a time to run, anywhere, everywhere,
away from flame

As the cool driver tasted dirt.
I bend, to weep dark dreaming wrapped in orange, while feathers fall
in palls of smoke.

Thunder. Heartbeat. Thunder.
I am rising I am rising I am rising.

10 PROJECT PHOENIX

Wayne Sheridan, the DEA's new drug tsar, wheezes up the last of the steep stairs to Meeting Room 3 in the Gentrex building with his heartbeat like thunder. "What is it with these South Americans?" he wonders: "Who builds a five-storey building with no goddam lift?"

Schwab, his somewhat slimmer aide, introduces him to the senior project manager, Ramon Suarez Montez. They shake hands. More scientific personnel arrive and are greeted. The party seat themselves, concentrating on the papers before them.

"Well, gentlemen," says Suarez, without bothering to acknowledge Ursula Velesquez, the only woman present, "we can tell señor Sheridan that Project Phoenix is viable from the end of this month, no?"

The leader dog peers at the assembled faces around a table punctuated by coffee cups. The pack is almost cringing, except for a confident American, Stannard Fischer, the chief scientist, staring at the folder in front of him with autistic intensity. Ignoring the snub of her sexist boss, Velesquez answers Suarez's question, casting her gaze at the important new drug tsar:

"Yes sir, as you know, Project Phoenix has three parts. First, we are genetically modifying fungi that will attack the coca crop. Second, we are genetically modifying the insects that attack the coca to be more fertile; and third, we are genetically modifying two varieties of coffee plants, which we will offer to the coca farmers as a substitute crop. The coffee plants are ready. We have significantly altered the output traits of coffee A. This is explained on page one of my report."

She points to the document. Sheridan shifts in his seat and fiddles with his ring. Schwab smiles at everyone, handing papers to Sheridan and pointing at the English translation. Velesquez, a Hispanic-American, continues speaking:

"This is *Coffea arabica tanzanicus*, the indigenous coffee grown on Mount Kilimanjaro in Tanzania, Africa, but it's a far superior plant now."

"Coffee B, the other modified variety, has been more difficult, I understand. Is that right?" Sheridan asks.

"Yes, its modifications were more complex than just chimeraplasty, but we persevered. It would be unwise to only plant a monoculture of coffee A."

Sheridan tightens his jaw, aware that the science might prove too complex to absorb in one sitting. He is grateful to his aide, Larry Schwab, for his preliminary notes. Suarez, the project leader, barks an order at the oldest man present:

"Cortez, describe the process to señor Sheridan."

"Well, sir, we are able to take one section of DNA out of an organism and insert it into another. This is called chimeraplasty. The second hybrid coffee we have developed is *coffea fadenii mongensis,* Coffee B. We bombarded the meristems by gene gun, grew out the shoots, then took seed from the mature plants and introduced plasmid constructs into them. The yields are proving better than coffee A."

"How much greater yield than the indigenous cawfee?" Sheridan asks, aiming his question at the six faces, concerned only with the implied financial gain, not the brilliant manipulation of *Pachamama's* little secrets.

"Three times for coffee A. Four times for coffee B."

This is music to Sheridan's ears. He can see glory beckoning. Headlines. Handshakes. Honours. *'The man who conquered cocaine'* will be his sobriquet and epitaph, he is sure.

"Excellent," he says, eyes bulging. "And how far have you gotten with the diseases?"

"We have modified the genes of two fungi that affect coca leaves," says Cortez. "If we introduce the fungi during the rainy season, when the coca-eating insects are most active, it will have a devastating effect." He hands Sheridan a sealed test tube containing a living insect.

Sheridan clenches his jaw, peering at the ant, and hands the tube to Schwab, who puts it down on the table immediately, wincing. Hates bugs.

"The fungi gain entry to the coca plants by the activities of a leaf-cutting ant, and the *aegoidus pacificus* beetle, mostly during the rains." Cortez passes a close-up photograph of a mouldy leaf to Sheridan. Velesquez fingers her crucifix, adding:

"There are seventeen types of coca plant that produce cocaine alkaloids, but project Phoenix will concentrate on the five most commonly used for cocaine production. We can show some effect on all of these plants by the GM fungi, but there are two varieties that are most affected, as you will see on page three."

She smiles at the two men. They smile back and bond with their fellow countrywoman; she's smart and they admire her expertise. She maintains the smile, thinking Sheridan to be a pompous, red-necked idiot promoted above his competence.

Sheridan reads the Latin names of the plants. *Erythroxylum coca ipadu; Erythroxylum species novogranatense var. truxillense.* He never studied Latin, nor did he have any exposure to it, save for a few legal phrases. Some information makes the brain wave a white flag of surrender, he muses, pouring himself more black coffee from the steaming jug.

"Are the modified fungi ready in large quantities?"

"Yes, but we need more equipment and more space."

Cortez, anxious for acknowledgement of his own input, says:

"On page four, you will see I am continuing modification on the other insects that destroy coca."

Fat fingers lift the paper. More Latin names, this time of the larvae. *Aloria noyesi* moth; *eucleodora* coca fly. Data tables show infestation rates; amounts of leaf consumed by the insects and over what period.

“The insects have been engineered to breed earlier, so the damage will be more widespread,” continues Cortez. “We need a dual approach for maximum effect. These insects are a more reliable weapon, as the fungi depend more on temperature changes and weather.”

Discussion continues on finance and the time lines for delivery of the fungi and coffee plants.

“Excellent,” Suarez concludes. “It seems we are on time and on budget, gentlemen. I trust the figures I need to prepare my final report for señor Sheridan are here?”

“Yes, sir,” they answer in unison.

Suarez spits his final command at the troops:

“There will be extra work in the run up to our second meeting with the DEA. I expect you all to work the hours required to rehearse the final presentation. *Bueno*, that concludes our meeting, unless you have more questions, gentlemen?” he says, standing up. Sheridan shakes his head. He thanks everyone for their diligent pursuit of a GM solution to the problem of cocaine. More handshakes.

Chief scientist, Stannard Fischer, breaks his silence and leans purposefully over, offering a clammy hand:

“Project Phoenix will deliver all we’ve discussed, Mr. Sheridan,” he beams.

Cortez shows the Americans out as the technicians meekly file back to the lab. Suarez waits a moment till the door is closed, then addresses the bearded Fischer.

“Señor Abelman wants to arrange our payments. He will call you at your house tonight.”

“The house phone is off right now. Engineers are re-laying the line outside in the street. Tell him to call this number.”

Fischer picks up a tiny notepad with a lurid picture of Jesus on the cover, but seeing every page full of calculations and scribbled notes, tears the cover off the ring binding and writes on the reverse, handing it to Suarez. Suarez pockets the Saviour inside his jacket and turns to leave.

Fischer watches him close the door, drinking deeply from his dark coffee.

11 CHARLIE WIGS OUT

I woke from my dreams in the early afternoon and made a pot of dark coffee. The practicalities of getting my prize back to the UK were vexing me. Once the rose had recuperated and shown signs of new growth, it would be safe to keep it in the dark for twenty-four hours, in a suitcase. But I couldn't take it through America on the Miami-London flight because since 9/11, they search more, and are very strict about any food or plant brought in. Better to fly via Spain, I thought. No sniffer dogs, unlike the Dutch airline.

Supposing it were found and confiscated? It would surely show up on the X-ray. I needed another as insurance. But, according to Maica, there was no other, and nothing would be living now in the poisoned valley.

I was terrified of any knock at the door. Since I'd returned, nothing had been reported on the local news, though I'd watched all the channels. Diego did not use social media and his phone line was still dead. I didn't know his new address. I could visit the old one and ask, but I was afraid. Charlie, my brother's close friend, hadn't answered my texts. No one was answering and my drug-addled brother had obviously been too stupid or too forgetful to write down my new number and call me.

In case the authorities paid me a visit, I had thoroughly cleaned the apartment of any visible traces of Ant's cocaine. I knew he had a secret stash somewhere, but I couldn't find it. As I searched the pockets of his clothes, I found little scraps of paper with scribbled chords and words among the detritus. Some were so beautiful, just screwed up and forgotten: throwaway ideas other songwriters would have killed for.

I needed Ant's advice. I needed to talk through a plan for the rose because I wanted it with me, alive and growing, wherever I might next choose to live. I thought that a company like Gentrex would possibly have the same gel and growing medium that I expected to find at the commercial nurseries in England, and I already knew someone who worked at Gentrex. Todd. My plan began to form. Yes! I needed to start some cuttings and cell growths, professionally. No one need know the rose was black. I can pull off the petals. I could say it was a rose that grew in my garden in Peru and I wanted its clone as a permanent memory in my English garden.

Peruvians can't know that a black rose is so valuable or surely someone would have commercialised it by now. They wouldn't know that the Brits spend billions following the Holy Grail of horticulture. Not that I wanted a slice of these possible profits. Not anymore. Money was the least of my worries; bank account bulging from past success; studio paid for.

Maybe I could find a willing technician through Todd. This is a poor, developing country and many of its citizens will do anything for money. I could take the plant cells in Petri dishes in my suitcase maybe, disguised as make-up, or secreted under powder puffs. My head filled with airport scenarios. Endless ideas seeded themselves in hatchery of my devious mind. I spent the next hour working out possible excuses if I were caught. Again I called Charlie. I didn't expect Diego to answer.

"Charlie? *Holá*! It's Sybil."

"Er... it's Diego," the dealer stuttered, in English. Relief rushed over me. Diego was alive! Therefore, no imminent vendetta against Maica's other close contacts, I hoped.

"Diego! Where've you been? D'you know what's happened?"

"Don't worry! I'm with Charlie. I dropped my phone in a toilet."

"*What?* Well, I need to see you. Are you at Charlie's now?"

"Er... with Charlie, in the car, in the Plaza. But it's OK, it's OK. I am not at my house for a while, maybe."

"What Plaza? Are you in hiding? Have the police been round?"

"*Police?* Er... No... No. My phone is drying out. It will be OK next week." Charlie interrupted, slurring:

"Sybil, this phone will run out, I have to get some…"

Click. Dead. No more talk time. No longer able to pay for a contract, Charlie's pay-as-you-go timed out.

I decided I must speak to Diego and took a taxi up to Charlie's house to see if they'd returned. No luck. The driver took me on further to Plaza de Cayma, Plaza Yanahuara then the central Plaza de Armas. We drove around twice but couldn't see Charlie's car; that is – I saw a similar black one, but with a woman driver and female passenger.

Still paranoid, I was hungry and I needed a drink. I wanted to avoid the bars in the well-policed centre, so I took a cab to Avenida Dolores, the main street for Latin entertainment. Ant had told me that bars in the heart of town only cater for tourists. Locals, he said, are refused admission if they are too native-looking, even if they could pay the entrance money. The white *pituco* class are allowed in alongside the more affluent *mestizos*: those with mixed blood. Though he played in these bars, he preferred to hang out with the poorer kids in the street drinking Pisco. The national drink is passed round anti-clockwise in a tiny plastic cup, sharing inebriation and bacteria in equal measure.

I needed human company and chose a bar with live music. As the singer came off stage, I offered to buy her a drink. She had a good voice. To make conversation, I asked her if she'd heard of my brother.

"*Sí, sí, mucho talento*," she smiled. Perfect teeth. Very black hair. A *mestiza*. Her name was Rocio and she spoke some English. She was young and smelled of ambition. A perfume I no longer wore. She had a degree in biology from the Catholic University but her goal was to sing and be famous. Her mother was against it, since Rocio had a baby to support. A steady job would have been far more respected. She wrote her own songs, but the bars mostly wanted covers.

“You can always earn a crust as a copyist,” I told her, “but have an original idea and the doors slam straight in your face; you may as well be a leper. Once you break through though, everyone wants a piece of you.”

From London’s art scene I knew that game backwards. Having pressed my nose against the glass, looking longingly inward, I then found myself trapped behind it with all the bastards whose attention I thought I’d wanted clamouring for a slice of my soul.

“Are jou a musician, like Anthony? How many jears between jou?”

“No, I’m an artist. I’m his elder sister.”

“Jou looks much jounger.”

My brother, careless with his looks, had been prematurely aged by his addiction; but for me, improving on the boring base canvas Nature gave me was dictated by narcissism and the desire to create. Day one, I adopted the Surrealist’s manifesto: ‘For art and against nature’. In fact, I’m a temple to artifice: dyed hair, capped teeth, masterly make-up. Plastic surgery beckons. I’m all for grinding my high-heeled boot into Nature’s grinning savagery. It’s my job, deceiving her, denying her. Like I’d said to Linstrom, Nature doesn’t play fair. She doesn’t need perfection, only breed-ability, and in this I delight in denying her most of all.

“Jou will paints me, yes?” Rocio asked.

Faces weren’t my thing but I could make an exception for her. She was lovely. I should introduce her to Mavis. Her portraits look like scrambled egg, as bent out of shape as Bacon’s. But not as bent out of shape as I was when Rocio answered my next question. Her day job? Gentrex. Lab drone. Filling vials; recording the data; cleaning equipment.

I felt light-headed with the possibilities for my velvet rose. I had so many questions. Rocio wanted to improve her English and I readily agreed to teach her. We didn’t discuss a fee. She would be doing me a favour if I could persuade her to help me. I could avoid Todd’s monopoly of events and go straight to jailbait without passing go. I gave her my phone numbers and email and left the bar, smiling.

As my cab returned via the Plaza de Armas, it cruised past the four-by-four I'd seen earlier: the one that looked like Charlie's. I caught a close look at the occupants. Charlie and Diego in badly fitting wigs; Charlie in dark glasses. As I screwed my head round for a better look, they roared off.

What I'd just seen was so camp and ridiculous, secret transvestism came to mind. Ant had told me that Diego was bisexual and very kinky, according to his wife. Given that cocaine makes people take risks they wouldn't normally take, could Charlie have been bent in Diego's direction? For extra candy, maybe?

No! *Surely* not?

Not the snortingly heterosexual Charlie?

12 MONKEYS IN SUITS

In the bright morning sun, I made breakfast, slicing a dripping orange guava into a bowl of yoghurt. I stared at the rose as I ate. There was intensity in her demeanour, even in this cowed position, and I still felt acute agitation at the recent death that had delivered her to me. I lifted the dark, flopping flower and held it gently between my fingers.

Unusual beauty stirs unusual emotion. Such perfect symmetry can render a subject almost religious. Philosophical. You just can't stop staring. Contemplation of the atom, of creation itself, is demanded. I always found that talking to someone who is very good-looking is mesmerising. Elevating, yet sad. Because the innocence of a natural beauty makes a mockery of our own imperfections with its genetic good fortune. Yet *total* perfection can seem almost sanitized. Too far removed from corruption or blemish it becomes representational rather than real. Perfect people can look like puppets. It was this feeling of unreality that overwhelmed me every time I looked at the rose.

Her perfume was missing, and I took this to be a bad omen. Though the flower was still bowed, the petals had not fallen, and the existing leaves looked a little fresher. I talked to her, trying to encourage her to grow, knowing that I might never see her upright again – that the death and fear and expense may all have been for nothing. I started praying, hard and long. Not to Jesus, never that, but to *Pachamama*: mother earth, the most relevant ear to call upon in Peru.

"Let the rose live," I said. "*Please*, let her continue. Help me preserve her beauty." I caressed the stem and cradled her. "Come on," I whispered to the bloom. "Death is the easy option. Living is the tough one. You don't want the bastards and the Philistines to prevail, do you? Fight the good fight, just being as you are: distinctive, with integrity; it's enough. You don't have to ripen to fruit; you just have to be seen to exist; to be experienced by others; to interact with them by being you and no more. Don't give in, or crudity and ugliness will have no balancing force. Find your will. Find the strength. Sweet energy, come back. Come back to me." And of course, I knew, deep in my narcissistic soul, I was also talking to myself.

I still wasn't painting, and I remembered with frustration the patronising advice I always give and never take: 'baby steps', the modern trope of positive thinking. 'When there's a big mountain to climb, don't focus on the far away summit, it will demoralise you. Focus only on your next step, even if you're fearful and aching.'

But so far, I had taken no baby steps. Not one. Hadn't even put on the climbing shoes. And no amount of contemplating the rose or the volcano had so far helped. Misti should have been inspiration enough. It looked beautiful in the morning light: a velvet, folded mantle of lilac-grey rock, textured by sunlight and shadows. No photograph I've ever seen of Misti does it justice. At night, the city lights ring the mountain base in a skirt of winking jewels, but the summit is invisible without the moon, though its mass is acknowledged by some other sense, beyond optics.

My bruised wrist was now a rainbow, and the mark on my face easily covered with make-up. I'd transcribed the Gentrex address from the back of my hand to my notebook and decided to cruise the Yanahuara district to look for it on my way back from the market. Fifty minutes later, laden with peppers, strawberries and papayas, I found it.

Green Soldier's information had been correct. In front of me, at number 121, was a small, polished plate marked 'Gentrex International in thin, capital letters. No buzzer, bells or doorknocker, only an automated keypad dial and a swipe-card strip. No camera that I could see. These people didn't want, or expect, visitors. And whose distinctive car did I see parked in the lot at the rear of the building? Charlie Mendoza's!

As I drifted past, a large sedan car pulled up. My curiosity curdled with dread; the hair on my neck riffled. The same panic I'd felt in the valley came upon me. Predators in close proximity. I could feel the weight and presence of the two men who got out of the car as if I had eyes in the back of my head; I didn't need to turn round to catch the menace. It was by looking to my right, at their reflection in the shop window opposite, that I re-affirmed my instincts. The passengers were a red-haired man and a woman, but their two 'minders' were shaved apes. Monkeys in suits. Cheap beef in expensive pastry. What were men like this doing sidling through the smart door of the Gentrex building?

Time I paid Todd a visit. If Ant were back, I could borrow a *falso* and slip the cowboy a White City tickler, a little chaser to his six-pack of Coors. It would be a guaranteed jaw-loosener, if he didn't get too paranoid, that is. But then I remembered, Todd Whale was an abstainer, unlike the lovely Laura.

I needed more information. And more rum. As I turned the next corner and crossed over to the liquormart, I was confronted by Charlie himself, hailing a cab, despite his four-by-four being less than a block away in the Gentrex car park.

"Charlie! Are you well? I saw you last night, didn't I? In the Plaza de Armas, in the car? With Diego?" He kissed my cheeks.

"Er… no, no, I was in my house," he said, looking startled, eyes turning back to the *taxista*, trying to negotiate the price. Why is he lying? Maybe it *was* a tranny thing. Charlie looked agitated, unable to concentrate on anything.

"Charlie, how can I find Diego? What's his new address?"

"Er, I think his house is in the *Urbanización Romanzo,* J106 or 109. In Cayma. Are you OK?" he asked, not really caring to hear the answer. I noticed a white, crystalline film in his nose. I didn't tell him. Let him advertise his habit. Anyway, Charlie couldn't know about the rose, why should he? He was never in the loop. My brother and I swore an oath to keep the enterprise secret, and I was sure Maica had not told anyone. Diego, if indeed *he* knew, was too greedy to share the possible spoils with Charlie, even if they were now doing the weird frock thing together.

"I am going to see my lawyer," Charlie announced. "Can you lend me ten soles? I can pay you tomorrow."

All amused notions collapsing, I conjured lies:

"Sorry, Charlie. The bank screwed up my card and now I can't take any money out."

He found the change he was looking for in those oh-so-deep pockets, kissed me again and climbed clumsily into the cab.

"We must have dinner," he said. "Call me. You have my number, yes? Arequipa 612 612."

13 CHARLIE LOVES CHARLIE

I walked home, musing on Carlos 'Charlie' Mendoza. His manner disturbed me. I should have asked him about Gentrex but the timing was wrong. Like Mavis, he had a great command of English, marking him out, along with his pale skin and big car, as an upper-class *pituco*. Ant had first introduced us in an expensive bar in the city centre on my second night in Arequipa, then left us together while he nipped out to restock their coke supply. He'd warned me Charlie was a lush, a roué, and a flirt, his philandering well known in the city. But I found him friendly and amusing, that is, until I asked if he were married. Immediately, he began to speak of his impending divorce, traversing high emotion in self-pity, spite and an apoplectic rage.

"My wife was a virgin when we met, and, you know, useless at sex."

Charlie whispered this from the side of his mouth in a manner that passed the barrier of intimacy between near-strangers, checking furtively for a reaction. I had stayed impassive and unreadable as I acted as the unpaid therapist. He slurped wine, proceeding with the saga, admitting he'd tried, unsuccessfully, to sleep with his wife again. Furious she'd begun an affair with her personal trainer, he denounced her as a prostitute, invoking murder:

"*Puta!* I want to *kill* her."

I asked him if his attitude wasn't just a little hypocritical, given that he played the field.

"*But I never loved any of them!* I was *always* faithful to her," he said, looking shocked; denying love but not infidelity.

"Faithful to *what?*" I'd asked. To an idea of her as the Madonna? And his lovers as mere sexual spittoons, undeserving of emotion? Ah! The trilogy of Catholic constrictions for the womenfolk: Virgin. Mother. Whore. *Faithful* he'd said! Words alone can't rationalise that one. Biology is amoral. Mother Nature loves deceits, along with the widest possible spraying of sperm.

"He's *nothing*!" Charlie foamed on, oblivious. "He runs a hotel used as a brothel! And I'll tell you something else. He uses *drugs!*" He emphasised the point with no sense of irony whatsoever, having found out her lover was a client of Diego's, and, worst of all, darker-skinned than Charlie.

The urge to laugh had almost overwhelmed me. That his wife could fuck a commoner and have a better time than with him galled Charlie utterly. It undermined everything he offered her and made it worthless. He'd married her for her pure Spanish pedigree, like prime breeding stock. Respect for her class was the basis of his love. Now she was acting shamelessly, he felt that this lowered his status to that of common cuckold.

The whole family was putting pressure on the poor woman as to what was expected of someone in her position. But what was her position? Ex-wife of an ex-winner. My heart went out to her. I hoped that from the corset of Catholic virginity and unfulfilled lust she was at last sweating it out with muscle-boy in the hotel of sin.

The barman, who was obviously gay, swished a cloth over our table and asked if we would like more drinks. Attention suddenly drawn from his pet subject, Charlie had seemed confused; his hands patted his pockets and he looked at me. Since I was on a roll with it, I stuck with impassive and unreadable. Mona Lisa mute. Da Vinci himself would have painted me. Savouring the sight of the squirming Charlie, the barman shot me a tiny glance long enough to register my wink.

"Sybil, er… I'm sorry; would you like a drink?" Charlie asked.

"Orange juice please, Charlie. Thank you." Before being blown up in a coca field, I hardly ever drank alcohol.

After two minutes, the barman flitted up to the table with a folded napkin, on which he placed a glass of juice, asking: "My friend wants to know if you are Sybil Sands, the *artista Inglés*."

He inclined his head to an effete young man perched on the farthest stool who looked over and raised his glass. I smiled and nodded. Charlie, incensed by the servant class trying to muscle in on his conversation, waved the barman away with a dismissive backhand. But, taking his cue from the boy's question, asked about my art. He was unaware of my work.

"Anthony told me you were an artist. Are you a painter? Or do you make those, erm, erm... 'installation' things?"

"Painting and drawing, mostly. A little sculpting and a few installations."

"What style?"

"Well, some are very naïve and childlike in the designs. I use one simple moving line and don't take it off the paper till I've said all I need in the simplest way possible. It's called 'taking a line for a walk'. I like it to be whimsical sometimes; other times it's very dark. The wax figures are also very simple bent shapes to get the idea across. The collages are much more complex. The paintings are usually more textured but I'm also into 3D art now."

"Are you famous?" he asked.

Not, why are you an artist? Or, what motivates the work? Or, what influences do you draw from? No. Just the modern value system: notoriety over serious critique; attributes over accomplishment. I sensed his titillation if I answered 'yes'.

"Well, a few years ago, I was one of the new kids on the block on the London art scene that had good reviews. Me, Roddy Marks and Christine Mbegwe."

He didn't know them, even though Christine won the Turner and Roddy was currently showing at the Met in New York.

"I had major exposure, so you may have seen pictures. I was part of the London Eye exhibition at the Southbank."

"How much do your paintings sell for?"

If I told him the truth I'd never get him to pay for the drinks, and for me, it was a matter of manners and principle, not cash. People change when they know you have money, and it's rarely for the better.

"Has Anthony been exaggerating? He talks rubbish when he's high." I sipped the juice.

"You haven't come to take him away, have you? Please don't take him back. We love him so much here. Everyone loves him. He is our star."

Mona Lisa recomposed. Enigmatic. Non-committal. Everyone has always wanted a piece of my brother.

"If you are successful in Europe, why are you here?" Why are you in Peru?" Charlie demanded. "To see Anthony – or to paint?"

I forced a smile, showing all my expensive teeth. In my head came the action replay: the radio and press interviews; the invitations from New York and Venice; photographs of my work in the art magazines; better prices at the Cook Street Gallery, where I'd gained three big commissions and a bright, bright, future.

And I remembered the determined wrestle with my intellect that allowed me to produce the concordance of line, texture and colour that best represented my soul at that point. Undoubtedly, I was as fluent in the commanding of my energies as I had ever been, painting out my anger and misery to canvas; turning the deepest of hurt into an external thing of beauty by transmuting pain, first to positive, then to neutral, then finally, to negative. There, torpor overcame me and set me drifting, all the way to this wooden chair.

My fury had only sustained me until 'The Blackness', the last of my canvases that they cooed and dribbled over; the dark full stop to my colourful line of enquiry. It was an abstract, a block of seemingly solid black, which, when perceived at close quarters, revealed a threading of textures in minute quantities – black butterfly wings, cock feathers, human hair. How they raved! Even Ryan Sitwell, The Times' art critic, liked it.

He said that I'd added infinity to the absence of light, and produced a masterpiece. And I knew, the moment I stood back to examine the work, that I'd made my name. After the exhibition, Tate Britain wanted it. So did Saatchi and De Vontfort. But I couldn't let it go. As I recalled its place, muslin-wrapped in my London studio, I was becoming uncomfortable.

Reaching for my glass, I lifted the orange liquid with its clinking cubes, avoiding eye contact with Charlie. The gallery had several potential buyers and my agent had almost threatened, I recalled. Then he sent an arse-licking letter, begging me to reconsider on the grounds that the world should have the benefit of my genius. Really, he meant that he should see the benefit of his commission.

"Why am I in Peru?" I chirped, affecting gaiety. But my smile was set like quicklime, my face aching from an ace of faking.

"To paint, Charlie... to paint."

14 ROCIO

All thoughts of Charlie evaporated as I hauled the shopping bag up the stairs of my apartment to the ringing of the telephone. I hoped it was Ant. His initial holiday in Peru had stretched beyond the planned six weeks to nine long months, and, when Mavis invited me here, I was relieved to be reunited with my darling brother. I scooped up the receiver.

"Si-vil?" the voice said.

It was female, soft and light, and poured into my ear. I hardly remembered her words as I luxuriated in the texture of it. It wasn't until I had put the phone down that I noticed I'd scribbled: *Rocio, 2.30pm* on the phone pad, below Diego's number.

Ah! Diego. He'd said his phone would not work until next week but I tried nonetheless to rehearse a conversation with him. What could I say? "Did you know that your supplier, Maica, is dead?" Of course not! I couldn't tell him the truth of my visit to the valley. He'd blab about the rose, or want it for himself. How could I explain that Maica was dead if I didn't tell him why I was in the valley? I sat quietly ruminating, doodling on my pad until Rocio broke the silence by ringing the bell, a full forty minutes late.

Peruvians are *never* on time. My brother told me it was a racial trait. I couldn't help but remark on it the minute I opened the door, having first hidden the wilted rose in the kitchen cupboard.

"*Lo siento, Si-vil.*" she lilted, "*No tengo un reloj.*" OK, so she didn't have a watch. Someone should have bought her one by now, I thought, an obvious gift from an impatient lover. I ushered her past me on the marble steps, but when the sun from the atrium shone down on her, I forgave her in an instant.

She had the kind of complexion so often found in Latin maidens of mixed race: glowing, burnished skin that made even her ice-blue T-shirt look warm. As she passed me to walk up the stairs, oestrogen-bathed and at the apex of her beauty, a thousand white birds flew out of my heart.

It was the tone of her, the gentle weight of her female consciousness and breathy voice that sat so well in my senses. Her rounded bottom swayed level to my face as she rose up the steps, pressing the cream cotton of her trousers into a rapturous crease under each buttock, like a cat's smile.

Such nubile curves I knew were a signal to the males of her tribe. Clear and vivid as a crimson flag, they would call many a snorting bull to press upon her. But her physical grace provoked chivalry. She was worthy of loyalty, faithfulness and honour, and I found myself wishing, with tears in my eyes, that she should find those three things long before the weight of disappointment hunched her down.

After a few preliminary questions as to her standard in English, I made her a coffee. I was cynical enough to stick to my brief, and politely questioned her about her job while she sipped. Rocio described the lab and her work in her best English and I made her write down some corrections. I asked about her duties, her boss, the staff, the work. The head honcho was a Peruvian, Ramon Suarez Montez, but the chief scientist was an American, one Stannard Fischer. 'Stan' to his friends. "*Muy crudo,*" she said of him. I thought she meant crude, but found out later from Ant that it meant 'uncooked', raw, pink-skinned. It was popular slang for the white folk, more insulting than simply '*gringo*'.

Rocio described the staff as seventeen scientists, five office staff, fifty laboratory assistants, two women lab cleaners and six security men, including:

"A new Americano, Meester Todd. *Un vaquero.*"

"A cowboy," I translated. She'd recognised him as a redneck. We both laughed.

Sadly, judging by her more racist comments, mixed-race Rocio thought the dark-skinned cleaners to be beneath her. They were natives who spoke in the indigenous language, Qqechua, and washed the floors and windows every morning. She described them as short, ugly *cholitas*. I thought it even uglier that a woman so beautiful should have petty notions of self-worth piggy-backed on those she considered inferior. I later discovered that all the *cholo* Indians, no matter how dark-skinned, ill-educated or discriminated against, think themselves a cut above *morenos*: blacks, or those mixed with black racial features. In Peru, these poor people were always relegated to the bottom of the pile.

"*Por qué necesitas esta información*?" Rocio asked, watching me write. I explained that I would use the information as the basis of our lesson, that I would need her to describe everything to me in English and, because it was her daily job, she would not run out of things to say. Nice touch, eh? How easily I lie.

I didn't tell her I knew Todd; didn't want him poisoning her against the 'Briddish'. Her job was to record data from written sheets to computer. She also cleaned and set out equipment, mixed chemicals. The wage was low, but it fed her and her baby and paid for rehearsals. The experiments were rigid and precise, she said, with rows of glass vials and Petri dishes and a complex hydroponic growing system.

She moved her hands gracefully, looking into my face with those dark eyes. They were currently completing trials of a new genetic combination in the plants, she said, having already tried seven different genes, some from the plant itself, some transgenic from other orgasms... er... organisms. God, she was beautiful! OK. Great! They'd definitely have what I needed: all the right science to perpetuate my black rose.

Rocio mostly worked in the outer office, but there were two other rooms. In the cultivation room, lit by grow lights, sat the technicians. The only woman scientist was Ursula Velesquez, a middle-aged Spanish American from Florida.

"She is *muy religiosa*," said Rocio, touching her crucifix. "Jou believes too, Si-vil?"

"No, sweetheart. Only in the powers of my perception and the depth of my rage."

She looked away, not understanding or wanting to challenge me, so she effected a genteel evasion by asking again, as she had before in the bar:

"Jou will paints me, yes?"

Rather than a portrait, I promised to make a life mask of her, urging her to continue talking. I started by asking her to describe the boss, Ramon Suarez Montez.

"*Machista*," she said immediately, explaining that he wanted everyone to know what a stud he was. He was stern and given to rages. Stannard Fischer was warmer, funnier, and a collector of rare cacti.

"Suntines 'ee give me cactooz for my mudder," she laughed

"S o m e t i m e s," I enunciated.

"S u n t i m e s," she said, through soft lips.

Good, he sounded approachable. Fischer was often causing arguments over procedure, she revealed.

"Suarez want to get 'im to go, I thin'."

"How do you know all this, Rocio?"

"Stan tell to me when we are drinkin' togethers."

Ah! She'd been for a drink with him. Flirting. Flexing her power.

"I 'ears Suarez makin' bad words to Stan. 'Ee say bad thin', but Stan says señor Abelman never will to be removing 'im." Hmm, her tenses need some work.

"D'you want to go to bed with Stan?" I heard myself asking.

"No," she laughed. "Ee 'as too many jears."

"How many years has he? I mean, how old is he?"

"More than forty, I thin'."

Anxious to advance my plans for the rose, I asked her if she knew how to grow plants from a single cell. I explained that I wanted to clone some Peruvian plants to take back to England.

“I can ask Stan,” she said brightly. “’Ee does it for his cactooz many times. ’Ee make the new variety always with the biotechnology.”

I resolved to try and meet Stan Fischer as soon as possible. Scientists are rarely interested in art and I didn’t expect him to know who I was, so I asked Rocio to set up a dinner for us if she could, in an Italian restaurant in town. But, by meeting her for lunch and a couple of evenings after work at the Gentrex entrance, I bumped into Fischer within the week, and set it up myself.

He was younger than she’d said, about thirty-eight or forty, intelligent, nerdy. That he was a total coke fiend became obvious. Having watched my addicted brother, it was easy to tell.

For a start, despite the hot weather, his hand was cold and clammy when I shook it; he rubbed his nose continuously and spoke at machine-gun speed. His eyes looked wired and he didn’t smile easily; but finally, given that my sense of smell has the acuity of a bloodhound’s, I could detect cocaine through his sweat.

How could I say for certain that he was an addict and not an occasional user? Because it was 12.30pm on a Thursday the first time we met and 5.30pm Monday on the second occasion. Both times he was bouncing.

Nevertheless, tooter or no tooter, the twitchy cactus fancier was the best bet for the rose.

15 GUINEA PIGS

Stan Fischer was fiddling with the cactus in front of him as the telephone rang. He cradled the phone against his neck as he answered.

"Yup. Yup, fine," he said, distracted.

"What do you mean *fine*? Señor Abelman needs *figures*."

Silence simmered for five, maybe six seconds. Suarez spoke again:

"Look Fischer, you are here to get results. If you don't get results, we can find someone else. Señor Abelman can call Lifex and have someone here in the morning. We need to see the *results*. Señor Abelman must make a demonstration to his superiors with *all* the results, not just the coffee and the *insectos*."

"It's in the safe. The Cuca figures are in the blue folder next to it. It's only the latest stuff that I haven't written up yet."

Fischer put the phone down and resumed his work. He picked up a rare cactus, cutting a tiny piece from its flesh with a scalpel. His hand shook. Only when the scrape of life was cushioned on nourishing jelly in a Petri dish and put to bed under a sealed lid, did he reach for the cocaine. From a glass vial in the top drawer of his desk, he tapped a small amount onto a tiny pair of brass scales.

The weights were ranged from one gram down to a thin metal wafer equal to two micrograms. With as much precision as his shaking hands would allow, Fischer measured the powder. Turning to a chart on the wall behind him, he marked the time of day and the dose. He snorted the measured amount, rubbed his nose and sniffed loudly. There was a gentle tap at the door and a female voice called:

"Don Stan, *tienes ropas para lavar?*"

He quickly replaced the powder in the drawer.

"No, I'm fine; no clothes to wash today. And, er… don't call me Don Stan, Juliana. It's just Stan, OK?"

Fischer was embarrassed to be formally addressed by his native Peruvian cleaner. The only thing he hated more than subservience to him was someone looking down on him.

"OK, Don Stan," the maid said.

Fischer resumed his private obsession as the small feet shuffled off. Her class always referred to their male bosses as 'Don', the Spanish 'Sir'. Diffident though he often was, he found it difficult being an overlord; he had a conscience. He cared about justice.

Though his studies had taken up too much time for him to be actively political, he'd regularly funded the liberals of his college year. He was a maverick though, and never stuck to one party, seeing merits and demerits in all of them. But Fischer was no racist and never thought of the Peruvian natives as *cholos*. Nor did he court the association of the Peruvian ruling class; he'd never met a mind that could compete. His ego centred on his intellect. His sense of superiority came from that, not from his white skin.

As a schoolboy, Fischer had been bewildered as to why other children did not share the transcendent wonder he felt at the elegant patterns of nature; the fascinating matrix of math. Naturally, after the bullying, his parents had their little prodigy privately tutored, and he learned fast. Numbers yielded to him and unlocked their secrets; he was giddy with the journey they offered. Little Stan loved naming and collecting all the insects and plants in his garden. His knowledge was encyclopaedic, and all his life he'd been used to being the brightest and the best.

At Harvard, IQ groupies would run to impale themselves on his Ivy League lingam, and good fellows all would warm their hands on his genius, kudos gained by association. But despite his workload, he wasn't without humour, and his ready wit would have colleagues laughing wildly, which made him popular with everyone.

News of such genius percolates, behind whispered hands and in private phone calls. Soon, Stannard Fischer reached the attentions of the security services. Thus, at the age of twenty-one, he was approached to work in covert communications for the Federal Government.

Unused to moral dilemmas until that point, the patriotic Fischer almost had a breakdown making his decision. Morals weren't like math. They were messy and grey and flitted between worlds. Clarity was what engaged him. He began to understand why his fellows read philosophy. For the greater good? What was for the greater good? Government foreign policy always meant war and death; funded insurgency; dubious double-dealing. His decoding would be for the military. He couldn't be in any scenario that he didn't control. After a week of hand-wringing, his answer was a clear 'No'. The Feds, undeterred, entered his name on a 'try again in two years' list. He was too bright to be only asked the once.

Alone now, with just his cacti, Fischer was content. He rarely needed anyone, except to fund his research and, occasionally, warm his bed. Casually cruel, in the way that preoccupied men often are, he could be insensitive to the needs of others. He was a passionate lover though, but only for the duration of the act, after which he would resume his focus in other areas. It wasn't that he had no feelings, it was just that he could compartmentalise them so easily, and evoke them only when the moment demanded, spilling no excess onto the clean sheet of his proximate project. So, as he teased the sliver of flesh from the cactus in front of him, riding the rush of his crystal high, all thoughts of the last conversation were dispelled.

Ramon Suarez, meanwhile, had gone straight to the safe, and, just as Fischer had told him, the blue folder marked *Cuca* was lying next to a bag of cocaine and a large batch of other documents. He scanned the information. He was no scientist, but his administrative skills walked him through the basic facts within. Animal experiments, no matter how extreme, caused no flicker of conscience. In his world, everyone was a potential guinea pig, there to serve his needs and submit to his will and take whatever was given.

It's common in Peru to keep guinea pigs, but not as pets. Raised in cages behind the house, they're valued as a great delicacy, the tender meat tasting a little stronger than chicken. His grandmother would cut their throats and pull their skins right off in front of him when he was a child, and she taught him, aged seven, how to do it. Young Ramon enjoyed the control over their little lives, petting them all first before he decided which were to die. Sometimes he killed more than was needed and granny would admonish him and send him back to the house.

Though Suarez hated any situation where he had no control, he instinctively knew when to bow to a smarter, crueller master, but only until he could gain strength and move up. This he learned at his father's knee, a father who was eaten up with shame at having been the darkest-skinned boy in his private school among the *pituco* class; forever teased about his *cholo* complexion despite his European roots and family name that could be traced back to Spain.

Then, to compound the indignity, he had fathered a much lighter-skinned son, Ramon, who'd inherited his mother's pale complexion and whose spirit never seemed cowed, despite the regular beatings. But the beatings had only strengthened the boy's resolve.

Convinced he was born to be subordinate to no one, Suarez realised now just how he could take the reins from the clever American scientist. He didn't trust him. His instinct had registered caution from the minute they shook hands. Now, he had a plan. He picked up the phone and dialled the direct line of the local prison governor.

"Hernan? This is Ramon. Do you still have those ten young *cholos* you caught stealing bags at the airport? Yes, that's right, the gang. Two women? OK. OK. Have them all brought to the back entrance at Avenida Goyaneche, 146. About three in the morning. OK, of course, $3,000. Yes *amigo*, of course, as always. But use your best men. No one must know. No one. OK?" He rang off and dialled again.

"Chicau, Chicau, can you hear me? This is Suarez. I'll need ten mattresses tonight. Bring them to the basement at the Avenida Goyaneche building between twelve and one o'clock. Go to the warehouse and tell Ronaldo to give you ten sets of leg irons. And bring two more of the electric coshes. I will ring him and tell him you're coming. No-one should see you. No one. Do it yourself, no one else, understand? Oh, and we'll need ten buckets."

Suarez clicked the phone shut and opened the safe. He pulled a chart from the blue folder, studying the written experiments with the animals. He leant in to the still open safe and was about to pocket two small bags of the cocaine when his mobile phone trilled. A familiar voice spewed invective at him:

"You fuckin' bastard! You won't get away with this, I'll..."

"You'll *what* my friend? You'll phone the police? I *own* the police in Arequipa. I ow *you.* You're lucky you still have breath, you stupid, fat *pendejo.* Call again, Mendoza, and you and that fine young son of yours will be found face down in the river." He snapped the phone shut, continuing to read, optimistic and smiling.

The drunken, bumbling Charlie Mendoza had no power over anything anymore, having blown his wealth, health and potential away in a cloud of coke. But Suarez respected the powder. He never abused it. He was above addiction. Only when events demanded, when the body was tired and spent, or concentration had to be at maximum, did he indulge.

Control… that was his drug. And now he was high on the prospect of taking it back from Fischer.

16 STAN'S THE MAN

Stannard Fischer's beard was easy to spot at the restaurant's far table. I shook his hand anew and asked if Rocio had called. She hadn't, her phone was going straight to voicemail. Sitting in the corner seat was Stan's girlfriend, Neri. Morose and monosyllabic, she would not be drawn out. Perhaps they'd been rowing, but he gave nothing away. He was bespectacled and geeky, but not without charm, except for when his whisky arrived with an unsolicited lemon wedge. I thought he overreacted somewhat, calling for a completely fresh drink and remonstrating loudly with the waiter. Neri was drinking Chianti, so I opted for the same.

I'd understood from Rocio that Stan was a computer genius, a prince of the binary world; he'd also studied chemical engineering and biology.

"Rocio tells me your company deals with plants," I said, determined to get the commitment I had come for.

"Yeah. It's biotech. Cutting-edge hocus-pocus." He Mexican-waved his fingers and added in a demonic voice: "Ve vill take over ze vorld!"

"How's it done – plant cloning and genetic modification?"

He laughed, saying, "With a gun, baby!" and bit into a breadstick.

"A gun? You mean you point it at the plant and tell it to mate with a different species or you'll blow its head off?" I deadpanned the line, hoping my dark humour would finally relax the twitching scientist.

"Exactly!" he said, and made a gun-shaped hand pointing at me, then at Neri. Even that didn't make Madam smirk. I poured more wine into her glass. She took the smallest sip known to man, gazing past me to some invisible point over my shoulder. Stan continued:

"It's a gene gun. It bombards the plants with tiny particles of other genetic material. Not as accurate as the old method, problem with mutations, but less time-consuming."

"What was the old method?"

"Bacteria." He raised his eyebrows, bouncy and animated, waving the truncated breadstick like a wand.

"We used it as a carrier of genetic material to 'infect' the plant. The trans-gene integration was good, but slow. There was a vacuum method, which was better, but even that's old hat now."

The waiter hovered politely, asking for the orders.

"I'll have transgenically-modified chicken please," I said, grinning. Stan caught the ball immediately.

"And for me, the DNA recombinant steak with chimeric corn. Neri will have mutagenized soya and fish-gene tomatoes."

The waiter was lost and affected a sort of lopsided grin, holding his pad poised, inviting translation. I explained Rosy's absence and asked politely to come back later.

"I've eaten chimeric corn, on a plane," I said. "What is it, exactly?"

"You've probably been eating it for weeks here. It's corn, genetically changed by chimeraplasty."

"What's that?"

"Now that the genomes of plants are coded, we can insert a small amount of chimeric DNA and shift the expressions of the genes."

"What, from a 'smiley face' expression to a 'get your fingers out of my fucking genes' expression?"

I swear too much, but it's my only real vice so I indulge it. One of my early paintings was described by my agent as 'swearing in oils'. Stan looked shocked, then he got the joke and smiled.

"Well, my work halts the expression of allergens, to make toxic plants more benign," he said.

"And benign plants more toxic, presumably?" I countered.

He rolled his eyes, "Yeah, I know, *Frankenstein foods*."

"No moral ambivalence, then?"

He slurped his whisky. Stan Fischer and I had a great deal in common. Like the scientist, the artist wishes their enquiries to be separate from morals; to be excused responsibility and never called to account. Let the politicos and chattering classes cluck over the significance and implications of one's work.

How shocked would society be, I wonder, if they could inhabit *our* state of mind, a state that elevates enlightenment and curiosity and fixates upon it beyond all else. But they can't do that. Though they enjoy the steak, good citizens prefer that someone else slaughters the bull.

"Morality rests on intent," Stan said evenly. "Ask Oppenheimer. Or Salman Rushdie. Or Monica Lewinsky."

"Or Andres Serrano," I said.

"*Who*?"

"The artist who made *Piss Christ*: a picture of a crucifix surrounded by his own urine. Or what about the guy who grew a human ear on a mouse's back?" Yeah. Intent. Corrupt or innocent? I took his point.

"Working outside a moral framework can be just as valid as the constriction within, Sybil. It's always the opposing view that *defines* morality; shapes it; grows it to maturity."

Now that he'd engaged my intellect, I began to trust him. I felt disturbed, yet optimistic. I was also getting drunk. He continued:

"*Choice* means the ability to understand the argument. *Both* sides. If there are no moral adventurers mapping out new territory, how can we send back postcards? How can we move forward?" He opened his hands.

"I agree. I'm an information junkie, just like you, Stan. What I object to is corruption, falsifying trial results, withholding information through fear it may stop the funding."

"We're all prostitutes, Sybil. Pioneers need funding; we need momentum."

"Can't be weighed down with the lead boots of caution, right?" Yeah. Since when did bio-tech have caution? The glyphosate scandal had already been the subject of one of my collages: half woman / half plant, kneeling in a field fellating a scarecrow. Title?

'Her Beside Seduction'.

Neri suddenly looked up from the mobile phone she had been glued to, and leant forward, saying:

"Biotechnology eez a good thin'. It will feed the starvin'."

"I wish someone would feed me," I said, blood sugar at basement level, outer flippancy no indication of turmoil within. Stan looked at his watch and drained a second whisky. Still no Rosy. No reply from her phone or texts and still I had not mentioned the rose. Having eaten all the olives and most of the breadsticks, we perused the menu for our starter.

"Could chimeraplasty alter any plant then? Mix characteristics of one with another?" I asked.

"Sure. In less than twenty years, all non-wild plants will be GM. We can engineer algae to eat oil spills; develop new fuels from seaweed; enrich crops with extra vitamins. There's already five hundred million acres of GM crops worldwide, all with better yields and engineered to be resistant to the chemicals that kill the weeds between them."

"But supposing the GM crops mate with wild ones and the weeds get the anti-herbicide gene? That could be disastrous."

"Can't make an omelette without breakin' eggs!"

That was it, the trite little aphorism that summed up the depth of his concern. I was right, he was amoral. But then so was I, busy pursuing my own selfish agenda. I looked straight into his bearded face.

"Could you clone a Peruvian plant for me? Only they won't let me through customs with anything green and I'd love to take back a couple of cuttings from my plants and grow them in London."

"What kinda' plants we talkin' about?"

"Oh, just Peruvian garden plants."

"Couldn't you take the seed?"

“I could, but there’s no guarantee they’d germinate in our climate, and I don’t have a greenhouse.”

“I see,” he said, eyeing me. “Well, if you’re found with plant material at the airport it’s a $10,000 fine. I guess I could grow some cells in a Petri dish, but you would still have to explain it if they found it in your bag and I don’t want any problems for the lab. How ’ya gonna explain it?”

I’d already thought that through.

“It doesn’t have to be in a Petri dish does it? Couldn’t I transfer the stuff to a face-cream jar and if they opened it, I could make out a mould had grown or something.”

He burst out laughing. “Hey, that’s a great story, but you’d have to sterilise the jar. And you couldn’t keep it out of the light for more than forty-eight hours.”

“What would you need from the plant itself, to clone it? How much material, exactly?”

“Hardly anything. It isn’t cloning you need. If the plant is totipotent it will develop from one of its own cells anyway. But you’d better bring me the whole plant, so I can pick the healthy cells, the ones at the growing tip, with the most hormone.”

He described the cell matrix; the maths of the structure; the GM dream. I realised his knowledge was worth a fortune. I asked him if he’d rather be working in the States. “I was up in Denver for six years, but I like this particular line of research here. I was following it in my own time and I got head-hunted to run this project.”

“Denver, Colorado?” I said. “Did you know a guy called Todd Whale when you were there?”

“Todd Whale, you mean the new security guard?”

“Seems to be particularly against the British for some reason.”

“Doesn’t speak to me ‘cos I had a thing goin’ with Laura, his girlfriend, before he arrived. Hates Brits ‘cos it was a Brit that ripped his face off with a jet ski. You know about that?”

"Yes. Poor man. Didn't know it was a Brit though. I hardly see them; they don't like me much."

"Shouldn't lose any sleep over that one," he laughed.

Neri excused herself to the *baño*, squeezing past, clutching her phone and pursing her lips like she was chewing a wasp.

"Is Neri OK? She seems a little distant."

"Jealous," he said, crunching the last of the breadsticks. I thought he meant of me, but he qualified it: "Caught me phoning Laura last night."

Just then, I was aware of a ripple in the vibe as everyone in the restaurant fell silent. I saw Rosy enter before Stan did and took a huge gulp of wine. She was so late I wanted to tear her head off, but when she took off her coat, murder was the last thing on my mind. I wanted to embrace her, to show everyone in the restaurant that she was mine. All I did was to sit very still and not say anything. Me, the mouth-on-a-stick of London's avant-garde. Mona Lisa mute. Again.

She had pinned her hair up and was wearing a black velvet dress with a green and silver necklace, a collar of Peruvian jade, red-gold skin, polished and glowing. Nothing she could have done would have made her look more aesthetically perfect. Every head turned to see my dark rose, perfumed and breathing.

My hands burned with the urge to paint her. But I knew I couldn't, even if the power to do so had returned to me. Portraits reveal more about the artist than the sitter. Unlike a photograph, a portrait would capture what I felt about her with every brush stroke; show my hesitation and uncertainty. It would fail as a piece of art; and, over time, would act as a visual séance, recalling only the ghost of her beauty, and my ability. It might condemn us both to mourn. And one of us was already in mourning.

17 MURDER ON THE MOUNTAIN

The wine had delivered a powerful hangover and I vowed to keep the whole of the next day alcohol-free. As I sipped my fourth cup of coca tea, the mobile *wha-wha*-ed for attention. It was Mavis, inviting me to her studio, a call I had been waiting for since my arrival, many days ago now. I took a taxi and she came out to greet me, watching me pay the driver.

"How much did you give the *cholo*?"

She tutted when I told her, pulling her cashmere beret down and blowing out a cloud of French cigarette smoke. Mavis definitely had style: a great haircut and unusual clothes for a Peruvian woman. Even her champagne-coloured dog, Wishbone, cut a dash. An English cocker spaniel, in Peru of all places!

She invited me in and showed me her latest portraits and charcoal sketches, some really good work, likenesses of her ex-girlfriend. I was surprised by the number of staff she had and how subordinate they acted. Mavis constantly barked orders: snacks, drinks, ashtrays to be emptied, dog to be fed. Her maid brought us coffee on a tray. She offered me a choice of the cups. I chose the red over the blue.

"So, you have not solved the blue question!"

Mavis stated this with a condescension I found hilarious, reminding me my exhibition work did not favour the colour. I asked her what she meant.

"I forget, you are north European," she pronounced. "You know, of course, that the Egyptians had the first true pigment for blue and they used it with joy, without trouble. It is because of the light. Egyptian light is solid. The light is what makes blue easy to work with; that is why you have problems in England. In Peru, near the equator, the light is pure. You will understand."

“Blue is uncomfortable, for me,” I said. What I meant was, you can’t trust it. It moves, shifts its tone. At its edges I love it: Turquoise... Purple. But alone? In its centre bandwidth? No. Blue wavelengths are shorter than the other colours. They refract and disperse too easily and bend out of shape. It’s horribly mutable. That seems like infidelity to me.

“You should not seek comfort from it, Sybil; you should seek enquiry – *mysticism* – the *unknown thing*. It is beautiful in its mystery. It can be powerful, too.” She pulled close to my face and whispered:

“Only when you accept inconsistency as its most interesting quality will you begin to have a relationship with it.”

I laughed outright at her dramatic tone. She remained serious.

“The Greeks had no word for blue, you know, because it was such a natural relationship for them. The light, Sybil, the light, like Peru!”

We continued talking about art as I was looking around the studio. I picked up her brush holder, an ancient Peruvian pottery jar: two figures in a twisted sexual position.

“They only look about twelve years old!” I said. “Was that the age they were married off?”

“Aah! Have you seen Juanita?” she asked. “The *Capacocha* maiden?”

“*Who*?” I thought she may be referring to a child bride, or a lurid Lolita painting.

“Ah... I will take you.”

She instantly gave orders to the staff, clicking her fingers. Call a *tico*; fetch the dog; lock the studio.

“Museo d’Arequipa,” she told the *taxista*, turning to me, saying: “Juanita will help you to paint.”

Mavis spent most of the journey arguing with the driver as to what the final fare would be. When we pulled up to the curb, she debated with him for a further two minutes, accusing him, with no irony, of racism and greed. She ushered me to the museum entrance and encouraged me to take the guided tour of Juanita, The Ice Maiden. I still had no clue as to what this meant. She would wait in the outside foyer with Wishbone she said. It only takes half an hour. No dogs allowed. She lit a cigarette and stood by the door.

"Go in and look round. They usually close for siesta, but the guide, he knows me well, he will come when he is ready and you can pay him then. Ten minutes, maybe." That meant half an hour at least in Peruvian time.

I entered the first room, which was dimly lit but with spotlights on the various artefacts. No paintings. In the centre, in a glass case, was the mummified body of a child. Its dark, shrunken appearance made me think of burned flesh, of blackened boots and matted hair. I began to shake. So, this was Juanita, this little shriven child, *she* was to help me to paint? The guide seemed to appear from nowhere. He touched my arm with his left hand, a small triangle tattoo sited below the joint of his thumb.

"She is beautiful, no?" he said. Beautiful wasn't the word that sprang to mind. The child was hugging her knees, head down, lips shrunken back to reveal her teeth roots. She wasn't pretty. She was scary. He began the story of her, enchanting but horribly sad.

"For five hundred years, the body of this girl child was cradled in snow, in the arms of Ampato, the sleeping volcano. The mountain god protected her and kept her perfect. But across the valley, Sabancayo, the bigger volcano, was jealous. He erupted in anger, heating the air for miles around. On top of Ampato, Juanita slowly began to move as her cradle melted, and her body, solidified like rock, slid from Ampato's rim down into the womb of the dormant crater. There she lay, folded like a foetus, until she was found in 1995." He stood back, opening his brown palms.

"The Inca venerated her, señorita, but they could never have dreamt of her future. She was delivered into the arms of scientists and they are moved by the rituals of her death, just like the Inca."

I looked at him. He was very dark-skinned, an *indigeno,* yet educated. Unusual poetic phrasing in perfect English.

"The child had been paraded to the top of Ampato with great ceremony; her status was *Capacocha* – chosen for the gods." He put his fingers to his forehead, lips, then his heart, and touched the glass with them in some kind of respectful salutation.

"Her journey to the *waka*, the sacred mountain, was many days travel. She was from one of the ruling caste families, the *Atunrunas.*" He drew the word out dramatically and invited me to look closely into the case. I expected his camp performance and gestures were partly to elicit *una propina*, a tip, but I felt his awe and respect were genuine.

"Juanita's tomb contained a tiny doll dressed in exactly the same clothes as she was wearing, a miniature self, carved in *concha* shell, more valuable to the Incas than gold. So, Juanita was probably sacrificed to a Water God, because there was a drought, and discovered at the top of the world, where the earth met the sky. This holy place preserved her, and five hundred years later, they laid her here in our museum where we can keep her safe. Her body is kept at a constant temperature of minus twenty degrees Celsius. The temperature she experienced at the moment of her death. The temperature of immortality." He walked me across to a different glass case.

"Her hair was braided and among the twists, inside her head cloth, they found her umbilical cord. It was DNA-tested by our modern technologies. Dried umbilicus is used as medicine even now by the *indigenos*, señorita, if ever the child is sick. We make a powder from it, to drink in water."

He pointed to Juanita's headdress, decorated with a sunburst of red and yellow parrot feathers, and to tiny shoes, woven from *ichu* grass. There were necklaces and a bracelet of *pashaquilla* seeds, like the one I lost in the valley. No. It didn't protect her either.

"She's was tiny. How old was she?"

"Twelve or thirteen. Healthy. Perfect. Her virginity and unblemished skin were necessary to be *Capacocha*. She would have been selected when her first blood proved her worthy."

Thirteen. Same age I was at my first period. Pure, fertile earth, where no man had ploughed. Perfect for a sacrifice! Poor little kid. The guide sensed my disgust.

"The maiden would not have been afraid. She had eaten only vegetables and coca leaf, but the shaman had given her *mescalina* and *chicha*, which is forty per cent alcohol. They did not want her to feel pain. She did not know what would happen."

That was kind of them. I was tempted to point out that men who drug and murder teenage girls are not known as 'shaman' in my culture. But, he explained, those who crushed her perfect little body looked upon her with awe and gratitude, whilst howling and singing her towards her death. So that was all right then.

Juanita was expecting to commune with the gods on behalf of her people, he said. She'd have thought it meant a conversation, not a sacrifice. My guide moved closer in a weird intimacy. He raised an arm and opened his palm.

"Higher, higher they trod. It was hard to balance on the incline, *señorita*, you know, up near the snow line, but their expectation kept them stumbling onwards.

The holy men had risked all to get her there. She was their future, their salvation. A beautiful rose in the bud of her life," he beamed. "Can you feel her isolation? Her secrecy? Her uniqueness?"

I shrank back from him, full of my cryptic dreaming, breathless and alone again in the valley. The mist; the planes; the rose. Thunder. Heartbeat. Thunder. He turned to look full at me, then back at Juanita.

"At the point when they could climb no higher, Juanita was halted and asked to look to the sky, to speak with the gods."

I knew what happened next. She was looking upward, then came a whistling sound, and a vacuum engulfed her. The light dimmed to black buzzing velvet. There was a thick, foggy *crunch* as her head hit the earth, her tiny skull smashed at the temple in one fatal blow.

A rushing sound filled my ears. His voice was getting dimmer. Time was clogging and I was losing my peripheral vision. I could only focus on her corpse.

"As she rose, chosen for the Gods, heartbeat increasing with every step, did she believe she would live forever? Because such a belief was no fantasy. She is here still, with us. Will stay with us until we, too, fade. Was she afraid? What was she thinking?"

I am rising I am rising I am rising.

"Her *chchuspa* feather pouches have been unopened for five hundred years." He cupped his dark hands together in the shape of a vulva.

"X-rays show they are full of coca leaf. But I know that if they are ever opened, the curious will also find petals, and one single leaf, from a most beautiful and unique plant, different from all the others, señorita; darker than all that came before. *Capacocha* – like the maiden herself."

A little dog ran out yapping at my feet. It was Wishbone, breaking the enchantment. Mavis called after him. I dug for a fifty sole note with shaking hand and pressed it into the brown palm as I exited to the light. Mavis saw my ashen face.

"What is the matter?" she said.

"The guide," I said, pointing back into the room.

"The guide was extraordinary. He seemed to know..."

Mavis strode in to the exhibition room, returning quickly to say:

"What guide? There is no one in there, Sybil. The guide is over there, still having his lunch."

18 A QUESTION OF GENITALS

I took Charlie up on his dinner invitation and called him at 6.30pm the following day. I explained that Ant was on a twelve-day tour in the Valley of the Volcanoes as guest guitarist in a famous Peruvian band, so I would be alone. We made a date for eight. Here was my chance to find out if Diego knew anything about the rose and had told Charlie. I also wanted to question him about his involvement with Gentrex, and about Maica, to test what he knew about the *cholo*'s whereabouts, and if anyone were enquiring after me, or my rose.

I'd been very disturbed by the blackened corpse of little Juanita, who'd joined my nightmares. But I didn't believe in the occult. The guide was real. Who he was and where he disappeared to wasn't what disturbed me. It was his hinted knowledge of my dreams, my rose, and the petals in Juanita's purse.

At eight-fifteen the buzzer rang. Not bad time-keeping for a Peruvian. I descended to find a cologne-splashed Charlie pacing the steps and blowing his nose in front of a taxi. We chatted in the back seat on the way to what I thought may be one of the better restaurants in town. I told him I'd been to see Marina Del Prado, Arequipa's famous artist, at her studio. Out of the side of his mouth he said:

"She is a lesbian, but I will protect you."

I didn't know he was acquainted with Mavis. But then I remembered Arequipa's short-string connections. He confessed he was drinking again, which must be why he'd come by cab rather than bring his smart four-by-four. Apparently, we weren't headed for town as his housekeeper had prepared us a meal in his apartment. Disappointed, I presumed he was desperately trying to save money. I accepted the offer because I needed information, and because he told me his son was at home – a sensitive boy who was studying art, Ant had told me. I hoped it meant that Charlie would not be talking about the imminent divorce.

But the son was already in bed and I was stuck with the father. An alarm bell started quietly ringing in my head. I should have jumped ship there and then, but if hindsight were foresight, we could see out of our own backsides.

Charlie offered me a drink of cheap Peruvian wine and handed me a small plate of cold cuts, unwrapping a paper *falso.* With the corner of his defunct Amex card, he took a snuff-sized sniff in each nostril, blowing away his tales of abstinence.

"I won $200 playin' with Diego yesterday," he said, pointing to a cheap chess set.

"How is Diego? He said he wasn't at his house for a while."

"No, he stayed here. He was rowin' with Christina. We were drinkin'."

"And snorting?" I needed to know if Diego had taken delivery.

"No, he has run out. It's due soon. He's waitin' for Maica."

Waiting for a dead man. He can't know then. Charlie must have scored this coke from another supplier.

"Do you know Maica well?"

"No, I've only met him once. He's a fuckin' *cholo*; they are all the same. Would you like to play?"

He pointed to the chessmen. I've never liked chess; there's no element of luck in it, save for the mistakes of one's opponents, but it's popular in Peru. Ant played it in the parks on little tables painted with the board. He was shocked to find an intellectual pastime so embraced by all ages and classes: one of the few places where the Dons and *cholos* met as equals.

"You see what I mean about the Brits, Syb? They're jaded," my brother had said. "This country's full of young, questioning minds. Poverty means you can't take anything for granted. Education and knowledge are valued. Music and art are valued by everyone, not just the smart set. You'd think the powers that be in Britain would put some bloody chess tables in local parks at least, but no. They think the plebs would vandalise them. High culture has given up on the 'don't knows'."

My brother, who had a distaste of authority of any kind, was never more animated than when heaping opprobrium on British 'culture'.

"No thanks, Charlie, not chess," I said. "I prefer puzzles and codes. I *love* cards: trying to make the best of what you have. Skill *and* luck. Like real life. Cards here are dealt anti-clockwise, aren't they? Ant showed me. Like water going down the Peruvian plugholes. You know, the Coriolis effect." I circled my index finger. Charlie registered the remark and looked utterly perplexed. He stood up and reeled to the bathroom. I poured the sweet wine into his potted plant.

On the side table next to the cold meats and salad were share certificates weighted down with a Virgin Mary paperweight. I craned my neck in the dim light to make out the name: *Gentrex International*. Is that why his car was over at the lab the other day? Or is he more than just a shareholder?

I was preparing to ask him about Gentrex, when suddenly, my phone blipped with a message. I hoped it was Anthony. Only a handful of people knew my Peruvian number.

"*No se preocupes, todo es seguro,*" it read: "Don't worry, everything is OK." No name; and when I rang back, the number was blocked. Who the hell was texting me? Was it Ant? What were they anxious I shouldn't worry about? Charlie? Maica? *The rose*? Was it a wrong number? A mistake, maybe? Or did they text me then block me?

Returning to find me mesmerised by the tiny words, Charlie seemed jealous my attention was distracted from him. He leant over and snapped:

"Who is it?"

I wished I knew. I started to sweat as I lied.

"Er... Anthony's friend Laura, wanting to meet next week."

"Laura? The American girl? She has very big tits," he said, ominously, like it was a death sentence.

"And she uses very strong cocaine. I bought a large amount from her at a ridiculously cheap price. I only took a little *tuerto*, but I couldn't sleep for days."

"Really? Have you been giving it to Ant?" I was worried for my brother's nasal tissue.

"No, no! It is too good to share. I have it here, but I mix it with the suave one I usually get from Diego's *cholo*. It lasts longer and I can sleep better. His is very suave. Maica, the *cholo,* makes the best you know."

"Maybe hers is pharmaceutically pure, from a bent doctor, perhaps?"

"No, I think it was from an American guy who lives here."

"Joseph? The Mormon missionary?" I was joking. Joseph had tried to engage me in a conversation about Jesus when I was shopping. He had lovely teeth. I happily listened to his zealotry because of his teeth. Charlie's eyes goggled at this useful gossip.

"The *Mormon* guy deals *coke*?"

"Sure." I said, mischief-making. "It's a perfect cover." I checked the facts again:

"So, the stuff you just snorted wasn't from Laura or Diego?"

"No, this is from my son."

He made this admission so very casually and continued:

"Laura hardly sees Diego now. He would like to fuck her. His wife goes crazy!"

I had the information I wanted. Time to get the hell out. I was bored and uneasy. Waxing my bikini line would have been more fun, or preferably, waxing someone else's. Someone dark-eyed and perfumed.

"Anthony is one of my best friends," Charlie slurred.

His lips were stained by the wine and he smelt sulphurous. He was drooling and had an odd body posture. Without missing a beat, he leant forward and said: "I want to kiss you," while trying to cup my face in his hands. I backed away fast and picked up my jacket.

Warning bells rang as loud as Notre Dame's.

"Sybil, have you got a cunt?" Quasimodo blurted.

"I *beg* your pardon?"

"Have you got a cunt?" he repeated.

Realising he may have confused ideas on gender and sexuality I challenged him.

"Well, may I ask you a question, Charlie? Are you a transvestite?"

"Maybe *you* are. You're not like other women."

"Charlie, I'm not like any women *you* know; I'm not like any women *here*. I don't think you have ever met the kind of woman that doesn't want a family, have you? Even the career girls here seem to want to settle down. This is a Catholic country; motherhood reigns supreme."

"Yes, but do you have a cunt?"

"I'm biologically female, if that's what you mean."

"With a cunt?"

"Of course; don't be ridiculous!"

"Do you have tits?"

"*Charlie, for Christ's sake!*"

"Let me see your tits," he said, lunging forward again, trying to open my jacket. I grabbed both his hands and looked him straight in the face, incensed by his amorous effrontery.

"Charlie, this is not appropriate behaviour. You're supposed to be a friend to my brother; you're being disrespectful to both of us."

"Yes, I know, but do you have a cunt?"

I said a curt goodnight and left. Charlie followed me out but neither offered money for a taxi, nor waited with me to catch one, reeling back into his courtyard and slamming his front door.

The night was starry and quiet. It was a downhill walk to my apartment. Vigilantes were guarding the expensive houses from possible *ladrones*: opportunistic thieves. *Watchimen* they call these guards, and they do watch – everything and everyone. I could feel several pairs of dark eyes following my footsteps all the way from Cayma down to Yanahuara.

Watchimen often collude with a little thieving themselves, waiting for a building to be vacated, turning a blind eye for a greased palm. But some are brave and honest and risk being accosted by villains nightly. They use a whistle if they're in trouble. If blasted really loudly, it signals to other guards on the corners of all the blocks that mischief is afoot and they need help. But their normal signal is *beep, beep, be-eeep*: "Don't worry. Everything is OK." It was the same assurance I had received by text from an unknown hand:

"*No se preocupes, todo es seguro.*"

The nonsense with Charlie had temporarily emptied the question and the identity of its sender from my mind; but now, like the proverbial elephant in the room, I was confronted with its enormity. How can it be that twice in two days, unknown strangers appear to have such easy access to my disturbed mindset?

As I turned into my street, a little black dog ran out yapping and snarling in front of me.

The skeletal remains of my nervous system walked like a zombie over my stomach.

19 THUMBS UP

On our next meeting, Rocio came bubbling in with news that one of the largest record companies, Sony Latin, was interested in signing her band. She was full of it: demo tapes; record deals; executives impressed with photos. I was in our tiny bathroom rinsing out a T-shirt. She flung her arms around me, smiling, full of her news.

Here, in this little cubicle, where first we fully engaged with each other, I found myself overwhelmed with a jealous need to protect her from the ravages of commerce. Like a possessive lover, I was heady with the idea that only *I* should know her perfume and touch her form, only *my* eyes gaze upon that dark, exotic vulva of petals.

I disengaged myself, politely congratulating her on her good fortune, persuading myself not to feel sexual towards her, but she was definitely flirting with me. I wasn't sure if she even knew it. I didn't want to ask her if she'd ever had a lesbian affair, or even mention the word, and had told her nothing of my past. She spoke of an ex-boyfriend who had been married, but he wasn't the father of her child.

She'd asked about my former lovers but I was vague; I didn't want to complicate the relationship; I was on a mission. She would facilitate my dream, not be part of it. I told her that Stan had agreed to grow the plant cells, and thanked her for introducing us.

"Why you cannot to buy another plant the sames in London, Si-vil?" she asked. I had the story ready.

"We don't have plants like those in Peru. I want to take the plant back but the airlines won't allow it. *Es illegal, me entiendes*?"

Yes, she understood it was illegal but the remark skimmed the surface of what really caught her attention.

"Jou have someone you are loving in England?"

"Er, no. Not really." I sensed where this conversation was going and was keen to change the subject and coerce her to help. "You can come and see me in England. I'll send you a ticket, but I need to take a part of Peru for my garden, as a permanent memory."

That seemed to settle her. She put her hand in mine. Latin women are so tactile. Rosy was always touching my arm and leaning in to me. She was fascinated by blue eyes, but flattery never softened me. I know what I've got and I'm no natural beauty. I'm not a natural anything. I've had to work at all of it. Besides, she was far lovelier. Delicious. Noble. *Intense*.

I had enough to worry about... paranoia and nightmares; headless corpses; buzzing planes. All I wanted was for the rose to recover, so that I could give a stem to Stan when it was full of sap, healthy. Then I would have new cells growing as well as the original rose. I knew that if it were dying and beyond redemption, I would need to get a stem to Stan quickly, before all the sap had gone out of it. It was a waiting game. A couple more days and I could make the big decision. My whole focus was the black rose until Rocio crept under my skin. She was twenty-three. Fourteen years between us was a big gap.

After our lesson, I decided to make a life mask of her. The previous week, she'd brought a photograph of herself to help me paint the likeness, but the other half of the picture was missing. Who was it that deserved to be cut out? I didn't ask.

Once I'd covered her eyes and prepared the plaster, gauze and Vaseline, I made her lie down on the floor. I put a tube in her mouth so she could breathe and closed her nostrils with cotton wool. She yielded to my expertise so sensuously, and while we waited for the plaster to set, I played her some CDs of Anthony's compositions. When the mask was done, she washed, and I prepared something to eat.

The sun was going down, lighting the mountain sisters in rosy gold. On my balcony, vermilion hibiscus flowers were glowing in the sunset, the reddest of all possible reds, enlivening my senses. But I had lost the courage to use such a colour; my world was black and white. Anthony was due back anytime and I was hoping that he would have a chance to meet Rocio. Secretly, I wanted his approval to go ahead with an affair. Anthony alone knew why I had been celibate for so long.

Rosy wanted to go out for a walk, so, arm-in-arm, we stepped out, carrying wine in a carton and water in a plastic bottle.

"Oh! I forgets, Stan eez invitin' us to Nazca. Jour brother would maybe like to comes too?"

"Nazca?"

I was temporarily distracted from carnal thoughts. Next to the Lost City of the Incas at Machu Picchu, Nazca's geoglyphic lines were Peru's greatest tourist attraction.

"Yes, 'ee has a plane. 'Ee loves to fly when eez not workin'."

His own *plane?* They must be paying him a fortune!

"I 'ave never seen the Nazca lines," she said, squeezing my hand. "They were made before the *wiraqocha* came."

"*Wiraqocha?*" I figured it was a Qquechua word.

"It eez the word for the white men."

Our racial difference was freighted in that word. I knew what the white conquistadors would have done to girls like Rosy.

We sat on a bench and I kept my arm through hers. She was giggling; we were a little drunk, not enough to be blunted, just relaxed. We were looking at the mountains from the Mirador in Plaza Yanahuara. The moon was beautiful, lighting up Misti, snow on the summit. Rosy said:

"If jou smell sulphur, jou knows Misti will maybe explode."

"Ah! When the mountain farts we must all run!" I laughed. She giggled when I asked:

"Why are Peruvians so uptight about breaking wind?"

My brother had said the first time he accidentally broke wind in front of the band they all stopped speaking to him for a day. She said it was a cultural hangover from the Spanish. I said maybe it was because if the conquistadors farted in their metal armour they couldn't escape or walk away. She really laughed. Mocking her country's ruling class was part of her own culture. But she said that after the pain and blood and excrement during childbirth, nothing now made her feel ashamed about her body. The little stretch marks on her belly, she said, were scars in the battle for life, and she had won and brought forth her daughter, healthy and yelling, and loved beyond reason.

Such honesty and humanity excited my passions. I wanted to embrace her, to feel her outline. We were joking about the indignities of having female bodies. She said at least it was better than having a male one, but if she were a man, she would want to have a really big penis, which she said was rare in Peru.

"Have you seen them *all*?" I asked.

We screamed with laughter and she fell over backwards, banging her head on one of the white *sillar* columns, spilling the bottle of water.

"Rosy, Rosy are you OK?"

"*Sí, no se preocupes*," she laughed and hiccupped, reassuring me.

Relieved, I leant down and picked up my lovely. Her head was slightly bowed and her petals had opened in the warmth of the night. I brought her close to my face. She brushed velvet against my lips and I raised her to me, cradling the curve of her bulk in my palms to support her. With my left hand I raised her slender neck and breathed deeply of her. She did not disappoint.

I couldn't take her home, Ant was due back. He might be there, slumped on the sofa or in bed. We couldn't go to her house, she lived with her mother. But a hotel seemed to cheapen it all. I pressed my face against her breast. It should be now. I knew it… and so did she.

I turned her away from me, and leant her against the pillar. My hands felt for her breasts as I kissed the back of her neck and bit her shoulder. Upright and proud, she arched her spine and thrust her bottom back at me. I pressed my pubic bone into her behind and she moved in small circles against me, leaning her dark head down. She tried to turn, but I firmly placed her hands palm flat, either side against the stone, and felt up into her skirt, my hands on her sturdy hips. I could feel the energy in her body. Alive and vibrant and sexy.

She was moaning very softly and I eased her knickers down to just above her knees. Time was slowing down again, dripping in the gloops of our wetness as my dreaming instructed me.

Gentle fingers I invest, to pry into her velvet dress. And peel her to her openness.

She knew what was coming and spread her legs for me. I slid my two thumbs into her very gently, making sure not to catch her outer labia or push them into her vagina. She widened her legs further and let out a soft sighing sound as I moved my thumbs against each other and her, like pistons. I was pressing forward against her G spot, to the back of her clitoris from inside her. My middle fingers were outside her, either side of her clitoris, rubbing gently at the same time. Occasionally, I would pull one thumb out and circle her anus, then push into her pussy again.

I don't know how long I stimulated her, but she rode me, and I knew she didn't want it to stop. The force of her rebound told me how hard she wanted it. She was drooling. Her saliva wetted the pavement. We could not be seen by anyone here, only if they walked under the arches.

She started to breathe harder. I wanted to hold her when she came, but couldn't from this position, so I interrupted and held her breast with my damp right hand, roughly pinching at her nipple, whilst bringing my left middle finger round to circle her clitoris. Anti-clockwise. Peruvian style. She hesitated at first; then began to ride my circling rhythm, guiding me to buzzing velvet.

After about four minutes she was coming, bucking her hips backwards as I ground myself against her. She was noisy. Too noisy for public sex. I brought my right hand up and put it firmly over her mouth as she strained in pleasure. It was a good hard orgasm. I only let go of her when she'd fully come to rest, riding her downward curve very gently with my finger so she got the full length of her cum.

We hadn't said anything. She turned to me and readjusted her clothes, pulling up her knickers and smiling. I put my fingers in my mouth to taste her. Rosy opened her mouth to speak but was suddenly interrupted by a flashlight. We froze. We thought it was the police.

"*Discúlpeme señor, pero mi amiga está muy borracha. Necesitaba orinar,*" I explained in badly-accented Spanish. I thought that by saying she was drunk and needed to pee, I would cover any panty-pulling-up scenarios they may have seen, along with the water on the pavement and the groaning. It was a masterpiece of quick thinking, and I looked round at Rosy, probably for approval. She was open-mouthed. Then I realised – we were holding hands.

The flashlight crossed my face slowly. A husky voice called out: "Sybil, is that you?"

"*Who's that?*" I said, startled beyond belief. But I knew the answer before she told me, because just then, a little dog ran out yapping by my feet. It was Wishbone.

"*Mavis?*" I called her by her ridiculous nickname, shading my eyes in the headlights of a swerving Mitsubishi. It swished past the kerb and back-lit her silhouette.

She had a small gun in her hand.

20 BOTTOM AND TOP

Suarez swerved the big Mitsubishi round the curving streets of Yanahuara. Like steam under pressure, he hissed and shook with frustration. He needed release.

Elated at the prospect of his forthcoming $2 million pay cheque and the flesh and privacy it could buy, he drove fast, past the river to the edge of town, parking only sixty yards from the blinking yellow lights of *'El Paradiso'*. Behind black-tinted windows he eyed the revellers spilling from the club onto the pavement, sashaying back and forth like ocean fronds.

Now, towards him, came Luis José Muñez Pacheco. Hair dressed with glittering gel, the slender nineteen-year-old weaved and streamed like a beautiful, intoxicated fish through the dark water of the night, unaware of his proximity to the waiting shark.

"Here's one," thought Suarez, immediately aroused. He flipped a button. The darkened glass zipped smoothly downward as the boy rippled past. Handsome Suarez looked straight at him. Mesmerised, Luis sidled back to the car. His soft voice, with its inquiring inflection, drifted upwards like bubbles into the shadow of the interior. Leaning across to open the passenger door, Suarez squinted sideways, forwards, and up at his mirror, to ensure no one had seen the lad enter.

Lithe and pretty, with beads at his throat, Luis sank into the wide, comfortable seat. He appraised his potential client with an undulating flutter of his eyes and body, stating the price again. Suarez, swollen with anticipation, pressed a crisp, crackling note into the cupped palm, driving to a place of privacy for his reward.

Fee now exchanged, attention and affection were generously served up, albeit without tenderness of heart. Luis placed his hand on the serge trousers and began massaging gently, feeling up through the cotton shirt to stiffened nipples. He cooed and flattered, stroked and admired. Meanwhile, his eyes flicked around like a lizard's, slyly evaluating his new surroundings for any small trinket he might steal, or ask for as a gift. Men like Suarez would probably be married or, at least, feigning interest in women, while secretly desiring boys such as Luis.

As they pulled into an arched courtyard and parked under a large fig tree, the drunken boy was slowly exposing his inflamed client. Reckless and raised, Suarez flung his jacket onto the back seat, already perspiring. He licked his lips, fixating on the boy's hairless, smooth chest, pulling roughly at his clothing to feel his firm buttocks.

Like a good psychiatrist, with a patient needy to be heard, Luis wanted his client to feel empowered and well cared for, thus ensnaring him as a paying regular. Not with his professionally willing ear, but a willing anus. Pulling down his jeans, he readied his hired orifice. A client this handsome need not pay for pleasure; he *wanted* to pay, to make it clear this was solely a service agreement with no invested emotion. Both parties mirrored a sense of control:

'I want; I pay; I get.'

'I've got; you pay; I give.'

Doing his best to be accommodating in cramped circumstances, Luis thought the choice of front seat over back was due to the urgency of repressed need. But he was wrong. Suarez, knowing his only weakness in life was this secret, visceral flame, could not afford to ever be caught. How much harder it would be to explain why he was ensconced in the rear seat with an obvious gay boy. His caution was justified, for as the transaction was drawing to a climax, a sharp whistle came from no more than ten yards away.

At lightning speed, Suarez flung down the condom and zipped up, caging all bestial emotion and pushing Luis hard to the floor of the front passenger seat. With alpha-male confidence, he opened the driver door and stepped down, acknowledging the *watchiman* on his nightly security rounds with a curt cordiality. Suarez began chatting to the man, polite but imperious, slowly walking him away from the steamy interior of the car. Luis could smell petrol and was feeling queasy.

He noticed a loose flap in the carpet and was delighted to find a *falso* of cocaine underneath. His client had been brutal, declining lubricant and pulling his hair. Luis pinched a *tuerto* of the powder to both nostrils and was sobering up fast; he rubbed a little on his anus for the numbing effect.

Minutes passed. Sore, and bored with waiting, the boy's eyes drew level with Suarez's discarded jacket, now fallen to the floor behind the driver's seat. Dipping fingers into pockets, he could hear the *watchiman* distantly laughing as Suarez, offering a cigarette, revealed that he had been waiting for a woman, but had fallen asleep when she had not kept their assignation. They were sneering at feminine foibles and making sexist remarks.

Luis had to work fast, his pickings yet to find gold. Nothing but sweets and a small bunch of keys in the right-hand pocket, nothing at all in the left but two electronic pass keys. He tried the inner breast pocket. The groping fingers pulled upwards: $800 and 600 soles in a steel clip, a CD, a silver USB flash drive, and a picture of Jesus. He fumbled, dropping his swag in the passenger seat-well. Luis pocketed the money quickly, scrabbling to hide the unwanted extras under the carpet flap, and threw the jacket backwards onto the rear seat.

Suarez extinguished his cigarette and said goodnight to the *watchiman.* He turned back towards his pleasure just as Luis quietly stole out of the passenger door, slithering back into the liquid night, softly and swiftly away from the car. Suarez saw the interior car light flash as the pretty rent boy made his escape, but, knowing he must not draw attention to him, restrained the urge to run the last thirty yards.

Realising his mistake in leaving his jacket unattended, Suarez grimaced. His curled lip showed his eye teeth as a long, low hiss escaped in exhalation. Still to be satisfied, his previous sexual tension turned from lust to seething rage. With accelerating heartbeat, he leant over the reclined seat, snatching the jacket and feeling for the contents of the inner pocket, checking to see it had not fallen out behind his seat.

He did not know about the loosened carpet flap, presuming, incorrectly, that the boy had taken it all.

Vexed and utterly compromised, Suarez knew that his own life would be at risk if anyone found out about the experiments. It was unlikely the boy would, or could, decode the information, but why take the chance?

He pulled on the jacket and flexed his fingers into tight leather gloves, unlocking the glove compartment to reveal a pistol. He paused. A gunshot at this time of night would attract all the *watchimen* for sure. He felt for a silencer in the car's side pocket, and screwed it into the barrel. In cold calculation, he reached down to his ankle strap and army knife, checking he had a choice of weapon for a near or far encounter. Then he focused, inhaled deeply, and gunned the engine to life. He knew exactly what he had to do.

'All's well,' came the *watchiman*'s whistle. *Beep, beep, be-eeep.*

Suarez drove out of the courtyard, cursing the filthy little whore. In the moonlight, he caught a glimpse of the lemon T-shirt darting to the left on the far corner, about seventy yards in front of him. Suarez slit a smile, his tongue flicking over his thin lips. He knew this area well. Recently, he'd used the river path and the backstreets for his jogging regime, keen to be as fit now as he had been in his army days.

Luis could not have dreamt of the significance of the discarded memory stick and CD, oblivious to the panic that their supposed loss could engender. Ahead and widening the gap, he was full of cocaine confidence, excitedly planning to spend the money: clothes, shoes, and, of course, a present for his mother. He'd crossed into a street that had only one exit; an exit that led through another small group of houses, then to the river path.

Suarez knew how to intercept this route without taking the tell-tale car. He drove fifty yards, killed the engine and alighted with menacing agility, pupils dilating to black.

Glancing backward to check the *watchiman* was out of sight, the predator flexed and sniffed in the night air, then moved fluidly through the dark. Closing fast on the glistening boy.

21 A SNOB, HER DOG, A RACIST, A ROSE

Mavis pulling a gun on us had been a shock. Despite my worldliness, I couldn't just write it off as experience. I was very angry. I knew our rustling in the shadows had frightened her, but Mavis was *always* popping up unexpectedly.

Having invited me here, I now felt as if she were following me. Almost every other day I'd bumped into her and her dog: at the cash machine; in the cake shop; even when my taxi had stopped at traffic lights two days previously, up sidled Mavis in the cab beside me, Wishbone hanging out the window, ears flying. Yet, how could I justify the irritation? Without her I wouldn't be in Peru, and it was Mavis, or rather her best friend, Armando, who'd first told me the legend of the black rose.

Rosy patted Wishbone as we exchanged forced pleasantries under the archway, and Mavis duly holstered the gun and bid us goodnight. Rosy was very intimidated by the confident *pituco* and asked me how I came to know her.

"Mavis is a respected international artist," I explained, knowing Rosy had no knowledge of the art world. "Her real name is Luz Marina Alvarez Del Prado."

"Why she has a gun? She is police, no?"

"No. She's from an old Spanish family, very rich. She did join the police force at detective level, years ago, when she was young, and eventually became the private bodyguard of a politician's wife, but she left after eighteen months."

I didn't also say that it was an easy way for her high-born family to hide their butch lesbian daughter… in a uniform, away from friends and neighbours. Away from the shame. Nor did I remind her that gun-toting paranoia is a common companion to cocaine addiction.

"She pulled the gun on us because she thought we might rob her. It's dark, she thought we were *ladrones*. Thieves." *Cholo* thieves no doubt; because despite her Bohemian credentials, Mavis was a snob and a racist. She always referred to the natives as *cholos*, just as her ancestors would have done, thinking always that 'they' had no culture, education or manners. Though she would feign politeness if she were introduced to a dark-skinned person, she held a genetic repulsion to them. It was difficult to see how her generation could ever change. I had shown her my photo of Rosy at our last meeting in the bakery and asked her if she thought she was beautiful.

"She's OK, for a *cholita*," she said.

"She's *mestiza*," I corrected. Mixed race.

"Yes, but very dark," came the reply. "You havin' a thin' with her?"

"No, no. I'm going to make a life mask of her. Besides, she's not gay; she's got a small baby."

"She's a *brigera*. She only wants your money, Sybil. You don't know these *cholitas!*"

"What's a *brigera*?"

"*Jerga*: slang. It means she wants to build a bridge out of Peru by usin' a *gringo*."

Of course, I didn't repeat this to Rocio and risk hurting her feelings. But ironically, though *she* didn't need their money, Mavis too, liked to socialise with the *gringos*. Like her use of French cigarettes, she thought that it reflected well on her 'international' persona. Consequently, she wanted to show me off to her friends in the first week I arrived, and had invited me and my brother to a party at the house of Armando, an art lecturer at the university.

Armando was gracefully waving my exhibition catalogue at me as I entered the room. He immediately engaged me in a conversation about art, which developed into a reflection on inequality and racism in South America. Armando then gave a lucid, well-argued speech about

Humanism and diversity; about the brotherhood of man, universal suffrage and education.

His bookshelves were impressive: modern political thought, beautiful art books, as one would expect, but peppered with classics in different disciplines. The location was his apartment on the top floor of one of the hotels his family owned. There was plenty of cocaine and grass available, along with the wine, and the sound of snorting soon filled the room.

"OK, *hombre*, now the Bolivian style," Mavis instructed Ant. She nipped a pinch into her nostrils directly, laughing. "No one does lines, man. This coke is so pure it does not need to be wasted. Lines are for ignorant *gringos*. Very *huaychafo*."

"*Huaychafo*?" Ant looked to Diego to explain.

"Not so good, man. Unhip. Uncool."

Mavis was rolling joints and snorting with Ant. As the powder animated him, an audience gathered round his shining blondness. Someone produced a guitar and that was it – *bang!* They were all in love with him. Diego was pulling out wraps and pocketing money. A few snorts came free, of course, just to whet the appetite.

Mavis urged Armando to show me his roof garden. He loved roses, priding himself that he'd every colour possible, she said: "Except black. He would kill for a black one."

"There's no such thing, is there?" I'd asked.

"Well, yes and no," Armando said.

"It is a legend," Mavis slurred.

"What legend?"

"Well, five hundred years ago, near the city of Juliaca, there was a terrible massacre, you know, by the Spanish," Armando lisped.

"The natives used to grow roses in the *chakras*, for food," said Mavis, rubbing her nose.

"Really? They grew roses as a crop? To eat? *Roses*?"

"*Sí, por los vitaminas*."

Apparently, rosehips are a richer source of vitamin C than oranges. They made a paste that they dried into a resin, giving it to the babies to suck.

"*Jarabe de escaramujo*," she explained. Rosehip syrup.

"But how do you know the roses were black?"

"We don't, but in the field where roses grew, a great battle took place, just before they killed Tupac Amaru, the last Inca chief. The legend says that the blood of the Incas soaked into the soil and turned the roses black."

Armando sipped his blood-red wine and smirked.

"What? You mean the petals turned black because the bushes fed on blood?" Preposterous, I'd thought at the time.

"It's only a *cholo* legend," Mavis answered, waving her hand as if to waft a fart. I was silent. The strange romance of it was sad, like the blood-red poppies in the fields of the Somme, the leitmotif of WW1; the Christian metaphor: Transfiguration. A metamorphosis of death into beauty and goodness. It was a wonderful story, but I had not thought of it as anything other than a myth until a week later when Maica had mentioned that a black rose grew in his valley and sent my passions raging.

Armando continued showing me round, guiding me away from the roses to the rear of the apartment. We could hear the guests clapping as Ant cruised through his repertoire. As we entered the bedroom, I noticed a small door. There was a sound from within, a muffled whimpering and what seemed like scratching.

"What's in there? Have you got a dog?"

"It's a just a washroom and toilet," Armando said, fumbling for a key in a drawer. He unlocked the door, pulling it open in annoyance and speaking harshly to the interior in lisping Spanish. I craned my neck to see if I could encourage the animal to come out and join the party. What I then saw closed my mouth shut and made me hold my breath, delighted expectation crushed by the weight of disbelief.

Inside was a pretty, muscular, and almost certainly gay boy. He was wearing only shorts, showing his gorgeous body. He was, however, a timorous *cholo,* and possibly of low intelligence judging by his odd, camp body language and furtive, gawping expression. He blew a kiss to Armando and tried to grab his hand. Why was he ironing shirts in this windowless bathroom when we, the brotherhood of man, toked and smoked ourselves to oblivion on the other side of the door?

Uninvited due to his status and colour, the sex-slave/servant cringed back as Armando re-locked the door with a sharp shout, returning his gaze to me and beaming as if all this were perfectly acceptable and the norm. I turned away, thunderously angry. Unable to stay one moment longer in Armando's company, I made my excuses and left. If I never saw that contemptible little cocksucker again, it would be a day too soon.

I made a note to make a tissue paper collage of this memory… If my brain ever reconnected with my hands. Title?

'Shallow homme, hollow sham.'

22 BED OF ROSES

I stopped my internal rant. The shock was wearing off. To chill us both out, I decided to give Rosy a comedic explanation of all that was Mavis, explaining that I'd introduced her to Ant the first day I arrived. He'd agreed with my assessment: that Mavis was more than flaky, she was totally nuts. Watching her interact with Ant was how we'd drawn such a conclusion.

Mavis spoke in a stream of consciousness, dashing off in all directions, sprinkling platitudes and nonsenses like salt and pepper on the supper of logic. And she loved to sing. Ant started singing one of his songs and although she couldn't possibly have known it, Mavis pitched in with confidence 'la-la-ing', making up word shapes and slurring all over the melody, trying to second-guess the next note. She also scratched a lot and kept sticking her tongue out.

Undoubtedly, she was a good portrait artist in a splotty, Pointillist sort of way, but the problem with Mavis was cocaine. One sentence was enough. Her nasal pronunciation sounded like an advertising voice-over for cold remedies. Nostrils burned to hell. Septum melted. She liked to smoke grass as well. In fact, she'd been busted for it because of the dog. I explained to Rosy how Mavis had bewildered us by suddenly announcing, apropos of nothing previously mentioned:

"It was terrible! *Terrible*! They all shouted at Wishbone!"

She'd said this, almost in tears, patting his silky head. Then she'd barked. Actually *barked...* and rushed to the bathroom, so that we just had the dog. And it was strangely sad, the dog without Mavis, Mavis without the dog, even though she was only yards away, squatting over porcelain.

"I'm not that worried," she'd sniffed, returning from lavatory, not realising that we hadn't the faintest idea what she'd been talking about. By her demeanour it was quite obvious she'd just snorted a line.

We eventually discovered that whilst on a ferry, another hound had attacked Wishbone, and Mavis had sent it flying with a swift kick, only to discover it belonged to the captain of the customs officials. Oops! Not a judicious act when you're carrying drugs. So there it was, the humiliating search, the nosy passengers; and now she was waiting to see the local judge, having first delivered $1,500 into the sweaty hands of corrupt officialdom. A goodly amount in Peru.

"I have papers from the doctor saying I need it for medical purposes. It stimulates me to eat."

A faint light began to dawn. She was talking about marijuana. Ant laughed:

"That's the first time I've heard 'the munchies' used as a defence."

"What monkeys? There weren't any monkeys, darling, it was the dog! Anyway, I'm a US citizen, *entiendes? Tengo dos pasaportes*."

And so it went on in a mixture of Spanish and English as we bridged the cultures to laugh; commiserate; advise. She then pulled out a wig in a polythene bag from her jacket pocket and gave it to Ant saying:

"I don't need it anymore; I'm better now," with no further explanation. We felt disinclined to ask. Rosy really laughed when I told her that. She liked to hear stories and descriptions in my wobbly Spanish.

We walked farther up into Yanahuara to my house once more. The kitchen light was on, so I asked Rosy to wait while I checked if Ant had returned. I was relieved he hadn't. The anticipation of what was coming next fired all my pistons at once. Within minutes she was in my arms on the stairwell and in my bed moments later. I even forgot to check the rose until my passion subsided and I stole a look in its hiding place. Definitely surviving. Ready for the next phase.

I went back to the bedroom with a glass of cold mango juice for my other dark obsession. Her dress was discarded on the floor, along with her wet knickers and shoes. That sight alone was profoundly erotic.

Ebony hair splayed out on my pillow as the gorgeous rust red skin of her curvy thighs nestled on cream sheets, her feather purse an exquisite, dark quill.

Leaping on the bed, spilling the drink a little, I noticed her bag was open on the chair. I saw, quite clearly, a metal security key in the gaping interior. Her Gentrex pass key. I leant over for some of her tissues and pulled it out.

"Is that an electronic key?"

"It eez the key for work." She took it, replacing it in the bag, in the inner pocket, where I noticed she had a second.

"Why do you need two?"

"There is more than one security door," she explained.

"Must be top secret," I laughed, "*Muy secreto*," searching her face for a reaction.

"No. Eez because of bacterias. When jou goes in the second room, jou needs to put no dust an' germs in, so they keep it lock. Jou has to cover all your hairs and wear a mask for to breathes."

"Do you have to remember the number, like a pin number?"

"No, they takes it each week and puts a code on, then the door knows jou are OK to go in," she said, closing the bag.

We sipped together and began kissing. She lay by my side, my left-handedness better facilitating our reciprocal pleasure. We were sober now and made love for a further hour, whispering in Spanish and English, gasping and screaming then falling back, sticky and satisfied. I was the happiest I'd been for months.

She curled herself into me, like a child, her dark head resting softly on my shoulder.

"Si-vil, Is it true jour brother is a *cocero?*"

I owed it to Anthony to give her a broader view and to speak of his talent, so I explained that yes, he was a *cocero*: a cocaine addict, and it led to bad behaviour, but he was also an artist, a creator of original work. That to be an artist was no easy thing. That you had no choice but to give your life's focus to making the work, regardless of where it took you.

Music was imprinted on his soul and he was a genius at conjuring her mysteries. He couldn't do anything else. He could never be anything else. There was such a simple honesty in that. He had no guile; no ego; no ruthless ambition like his sister. Like his sister *used* to have. He was simply devoted to his guitar and their continuing dialogue.

"Jou really love jour brother, no?" said Rosy, holding my hand. I nodded. What was the point of trying to make her understand the way we grew up and the complexity of our love? The greatest antidote to my loneliness is not the embrace of a body. It's what Anthony gives me. It's the understanding of my art. This can't be said in some company without inviting mockery, yet I'd long since given up being self-conscious about pretension.

"*Pretentious* is the word they spit at you when faced with their own lack of daring and ideas," Anthony used to say.

Only Anthony knew my artistic compulsion, the power and depth of it, the force of its will, the journeys I had made to the point of insanity, trying to get it right. I didn't just love him, in part, I *was* him. Of all the critics that had passed comment on my work, there was only one whose opinion I respected and sought. Ant always gave me the truth, direct and pure, engaged only with the work.

I felt comfortable with Rosy; our intimacy allowed me to relax a little. I told her that I had heard about the legend of the black rose. Had she ever heard of it?

"We 'ave all 'eard it. Maybe it is true but I don' know anyone who has seen the rose. But, if she is real, jou can never to see her, Si-vil. Never."

"Why?"

"Because you are *wiraqocha,* the white peoples."

She looked down and shook her head slowly.

“It is a symbol of the end of the Inca; it carries only the sorrow. Sorrow eez because of the white peoples. The sorrow would return to jou. Maybe it could destroy jou.”

23 THE QUEEN

What superstitious nonsense! How wrong Rosy had been! After months and months of waiting, my rose is displaying two beautiful new blooms and all my ambitions are slowly being fulfilled. I had smuggled my dark beauty back to Britain in an ordinary suitcase, and here, the black rose is met with fanfare and acclaim. How strange a power it is that I have something so coveted. I feel a nervous sense of guardianship, the way a father may feel for his pubescent daughter.

On this sunny day at the Chelsea Flower Show in London, a fat official guides me by my elbow through the warmth of the grand pavilion. The throng is white, middle-aged and mostly middle-class, with a few genuine toffs in tweeds or linen. Eyes glittering, they're all around the tent with curiosity.

I stand close to the floral displays and wait, breathing deeply of the delicious, narcotic scent of silver morning glory, datura, leonotis and passiflora, while my guide mops his ginger brow. Queen Elizabeth, who visits every year and is said to love this event, is now approaching, silhouetted in the entrance of the tent with a clergyman on her right. I retain enough composure to meet her steely gaze and professional smile. She is here, with me, specifically to see my black rose.

At close quarters, the Queen is far more frightening than she appears in pictures. She manages to be charming yet diffident, self-conscious and impenetrable, whilst an air of cold, executive calm prevails around her. She also has very small feet.

I am flushing; hot and nailed to the floor with nerves. She is the opposite: cool and at altitude. I have to fight back tears even to speak. Me, never fazed by fame or out-quipped by the quick wits, I suddenly feel like a child. Though I keep my composure, how can she *not* know she affects everyone but her family this way?

She looks me in the eye as she greets me, immaculately dressed in a lemon suit, velvet petals of black in her hat; tight gloves; black handbag. The stiff, designed appearance shrieks ‘money’; ‘confidence’; ‘ignorance’. I wish I hadn’t worn my heels. I seem to tower over her. Yet this does not diminish her presence. The tiny Elizabeth Regina wears her fame like a robe, as is her right. Fame given to her by accident of birth, and by me and others like me by my expectations: my sense of her history; my excitement and projection of whom she might be.

The fat, red-haired man introduces me as the other lackeys simper on the periphery, standing back, so that the exchange is personal, direct, and blots everyone but Her Maj and me out of the frame. In the momentary press of her flesh, my wrist begins to ache. A thousand cut-and-paste images fill my mind: her coronation; the royal weddings; Christmas broadcasts; Diana’s funeral; the endless bouquets.

My mouth is dry. My lips are sore and cracked. I try to moisten them with saliva. It’s hard to breathe. Somehow, the formal dress and hats of the assembled crowd remind me of a funeral. There is a darkness here, shrouding my optimism.

Elizabeth has blue eyes, small and beady. The contrast with her lemon dress is startling. Her handbag seems huge. Surely, she must have a gun in it these days, and a mobile phone. And maybe... a small bottle of rum? Outside in the clear, bright day, the royal helicopter hovers above the misted tent, blades thumping like a heartbeat. She looks up at the canvas as if to acknowledge it, then smiles directly at me.

“The black rose!” She points at my gold medal certificate. “Of course, we shall want one for the Palace garden.”

The heady scent from the flowers is making me feel drowsy – distant – as if I’m in a vacuum. Her minders look like monkeys in suits. I stare at the tiny feet. Why is the soil orange? Why is she wearing Nike trainers? Bomp, bomp, bomp. Nike! Nike! Nike! The ad man's magic three repeats.

A little black dog runs out yapping and snarling from under the table, followed by a whistling *BANG* as the Queen pulls a gun from her bag and fires at the little mutt. I hear a thick, foggy *crunch* as its head hits the earth. The Queen puts the gun in her mouth and fires.

The death of the Monarch in grand theatre

"Jesus!" I shrieked, sitting up in the bed. Rosy stirred and opened her dark eyes. I was sweating. The little clock said 6.40am as the Queen dream burst like a bubble, leaving a sticky residue of angst and anger.

"*Maica wore trainers*. Nike trainers! They were striped! Maica's trainers: they were navy and white!" I said, in growing disbelief. He must have escaped! Whose black leather boot and ankle and had landed beside me then?

"Evie, he *isn't* dead!"

"Who is no dead? Who is Evie?"

I returned to my rationale long enough to remember that Rosy knew nothing. It was a bad dream I told her, nothing more. But *was* it a dream? Please let it all have been a dream. I sprang out of bed. My head was hot and my throat dry.

I headed for the kitchen as reality crystallised. Would he still have his phone? I hadn't thought to ring it. Atomised in the Andes, remember? I never looked at the disembodied head – at the face. I was too preoccupied with the rose. Maybe it was someone behind us who died. Or someone from the refining hut? Yeah. The little dog had to have an owner. It had a collar.

Once Maica had decided to take me to the rose we had used a code for our calls to each other. Three rings – stop. Count to ten and ring once. Stop. Count to ten and ring again. I thought he was paranoid, but rightly so if he were dealing in drugs. I grabbed the mobile and dialled as prescribed, holding my breath, temper smouldering.

Answer the burning telephone.

"The number you require cannot be reached at this time." I slammed it shut, shaking. Rocio was standing in the doorway.

"*Si-vil, estás triste*? Why jou has bad drims?"

She walked over and put her arms around me, resting her head on my shoulder. Yeah, that was it. The dog must have had an owner, and they caught it full on, as Maica nipped off to my left. *Bastard!* He never checked that I was OK. He left me to fucking die out there in the jungle. Must be why his *combi* had gone. He just bloody abandoned me, and the dead dog, and its owner, without as much as a second look!

The cool driver tasted dirt –
then buggered off.

"Yeah," I thought. "Fuck you!" What trauma I suffered! And it was business as bloody usual for him. He took my dollars, showed me the spot and thought *he* had the better part of the bargain. But I found the rose. And he didn't know I'd found it, so I wasn't obliged to pay the other part of the deal, was I? Besides, if I could track the little bastard down, I could insist on getting back my original four thousand bucks by threatening him with the police. Yeah. That would teach him to leave me for dead. Ah! Hello rant! Shock wearing off. Again.

I could stake out Diego's house for Maica's next visit. Charlie had said the little *cholo* was due to make his delivery soon. Verbal intercourse with señor Maica was surely imminent, but preferably not by phone. No! Eyeball to eyeball, that's how I wanted us to be when he explained his callous indifference to my predicament in his coca field. And to right the wrong, for the benefit of my own moral equilibrium, I was going to lie through my cosmetically-adjusted teeth about not finding the black rose.

"Si-vil, are jou OK, baby?"

I kissed her hair. "Sure, Rosy. I'm just fine. And I'm getting finer by the minute."

PART TWO

24 BURNING RESENTMENT

Chicau was sweating as he wrapped the small brown woman in a plastic sheet and dragged her body up the basement stairs to the van, the fabric of his jacket straining at the armpits and shoulders.

When he'd taken the call from Suarez, his boss, he hadn't expected *this*. The woman had died, so it wasn't murder. It wasn't *his* fault. But he, Chicau, had brought her here. Hernan knew it. Suarez knew it. The fact that anybody knew it greatly troubled him. Supposing the others died? All the others? What were they doing to them? And why did it have to be a woman? He *liked* women. He *loved* women. Women were his life. His motivation for corruption was to gain money to spend on them. With money you could have any almost any woman you wanted.

Brutality to other men was easy... but *women*? His conscience told him that harming women, of all sins, was deeply wrong. Though not strictly religious, Chicau was always anxious to appear so. He'd kept the patina of faith because, in Peru, the ladies liked a pious man. As a youth, he had de-flowered many a Catholic virgin by saying how close to God he felt and how spiritual was their sexual union. He crossed himself, nonetheless, as he closed the van doors, going back to check on the others. They would all be moved tomorrow. He made the call.

"Don Suarez? Yes, it is done. Yes, I'm leaving Avenida Goyaneche now. The *crematorio* building at the back of the Sanchez Farmacia? Yes, I know it. I have the keys, señor. Yes, señor. One hour. OK."

Driving four miles across town, Chicau found the Farmacia and pulled the van into the *crematorio* car park, backing it right up to the door. Unloading the body was easier than loading it.

Still sweating profusely, he fumbled with the key of the incineration room. A small polythene sack full of dead guinea pigs leant against the wall, faces squashed, paws clasped shut. Chicau opened the metal door. The smell of charred flesh stung his nostrils. He pushed the woman's body in, flipping the switches as instructed, hearing the burners spring to life as he slammed it shut. A sense of relief bathed his nerves.

Carefully removing his gloves, he let out a long, slow breath and waited the allotted time: time spent musing on his latest girlfriend. She was sexy but she was cold. Ruthless even. He admired her for it. If he were a woman, he would definitely use sex to advance himself: sleep with the tourists, like she did. Sleep with the *gringas*. Get to go to Miami, maybe, and fuck some of those rich, fat Americans.

He still had sex with his wife once a week, like a good husband, and she still liked it and wanted more children. But Chicau's chain was always jerked by any passing ripe egg. Regardless of the basket it came in. He gladly serviced depressed divorcees; sexy students; eager teenagers and frisky matrons on the brink of menopause. Then there was the *cholita* he'd met at the market. Petite. Perfect. He flicked his tongue over his lips. If it weren't for this damn business at Gentrex, he'd be a happy man.

He wasn't a romantic, but had fancied himself as a serenading lothario, and had learned to play guitar at school. He always wanted to be a musician. A star. Women loved them. If you could play guitar and stand on stage and sing, well, you could get any number of women. Young ones. Pretty ones. But he was self-conscious about his bulk and just didn't have the voice or the musical talent.

There was a blond *gringo* who'd made a big splash in Arequipa singing and playing his guitar. A cousin had talked of nothing else for weeks and persuaded Chicau to go and see for himself. The *gringo* had that special talent. Grace. Passion. Poetry. Chicau was as jealous as it was possible to be watching the adoring girl fans hysterically calling and cooing. But behind dark glasses he was overwhelmed by the performance, despite himself. He'd made his excuses and left the concert early. Yeah, if only he'd been a rock star. A blond rock star. Queues of willing women. Young, willing women. He sighed, switched out the light and closed the door.

Back in the basement, over at Avenida Goyaneche, nine brown faces strained to hear the voices outside their door. Their noses were bleeding as they twitched and rocked in their chains. Two of them could just stretch to reach each other and were holding hands.

The air was thick with the smell of excrement from the buckets and cocaine from their sweat. They were murmuring in Qqechua to each other. Then, in unison, and with rising intensity, they began to chant:

"Intiq quillaq
sutimpi orqo willka nunaqpas kunan Pachacamaq
kuna uyariwanman, key allpaq ñat` in rurunmanta, pa` qcha
yawarniymanta pacha, mana riqsisqa hanaq pacha wichaymanta,
Wirakuchakunaman kachayamuni ñakayniyta.
Chey allpaykunapi raphra tupa kunturpaq hamunqa ñakay.
Huaykunman yuraq chiri sunqonkunapi willkakuna
cheymanta rumikunaman kutirachinman. Wawankunata ima uynikuy
pasaqpaqpuni hamuchunqa huk nishu unquy, atinman key nuna q`ora.
Apanchis karan ñuqaykuna inkaman pachakamaqkunaman
achhuynanchispaq, kunanqa apanqa wirakuchakunata kushka
saqrakunaman.
Key ñakayqa Atawallpaq sutinpi, qhapaq Inkakunaq Mistin, llapan
llaqtaypaq sutinpi, nishallashaqpuni wañunaykama yawarniywanpis
mukisqa."

The intonation was unmistakable: the rising inflections; the contempt; the passion. Now, in their darkest hour, the only power they had as *prisonieros* from a conquered race and a beaten people lay in these ancient phrases.

This was a curse, not a prayer. Together, they knew for certain that its incantation would conjure the Devil himself – to rain down upon the *wiraqocha* and their children. Forever.

25 *ATAHUALPA'S CURSE*

Rosy had been shocked by my nightmare and could not get back to sleep, so we made an early breakfast. The Queen dallied, prodding my consciousness again and again with her little gloved hand, presenting me with the startling new fact: Maica was alive; going about his business as if nothing had happened. I was livid he had treated me so callously.

Even if I could understand his fear in running away, I couldn't forgive him for not even enquiring after me by phone. Perhaps I had underestimated his hatred of *gringos*: the hatred that all his people felt. And, having read their history, I now knew why.

Marina Del Prado had filled me with curiosity about her country the night we'd met at my exhibition, so, once I'd accepted her invitation to visit, I decided to buy a few books on Peru. The fresh-faced lad at the bookshop, who took my money, handed me the purchases with this portent:

"Peru will change your life. *And* it will change your dreams."

"Good," I'd replied, not caring to hear a space-cadet prophecy from one of the shiny, happy people. Days later, in the soft aircraft seat where I first opened the pages, characters from Peru's dark history began dancing before me in rivers of blood.

In 1522, Francisco Pizarro brought less than two hundred conquistadors to South America from Spain. Like me, they found a treasure that possessed them. But in contrast to the velvet darkness of my current obsession, theirs was shining gold.

"*Sanctioned by the Holy Catholic Church, Pizarro's quest was to claim the natives' souls for Christianity and plunder Peru's riches for the throne of Spain. The tithe was a fifth of all the treasure, to be sent back to his King by galleon*," the book informed.

Apparently, Atahualpa, the incumbent ruler of the Inca natives, had just presided over his brother's murder in a rivalrous civil war, so the timing of Pizarro's invasion could not have worked better.

"*The Inca nation, once united across a vast land mass, was deeply divided. Rival tribes betrayed them to the Spanish. Genocide followed.*"

What the text didn't say was that to justify their sadism, the Catholic conquistadors were given licence by the Holy Church of Rome to regard these 'heathen' tribes as having a status equal to animals. As in Nazi Germany, hundreds of years later, it was a racist ideology proposed by educated Europeans.

The book showed ancient ornaments and artefacts juxtaposed with a lurid impression of Atahualpa's slaughter: red feathers falling into blood as they downed him.

The death of the Monarch in grand theatre

"They were frightened of the horses… never seen them before," Linstrom was leaning over my book. "They thought man and horse were joined together as one creature, and that it was an omen: the fall of their empire the astronomer priests had predicted from the position of the stars."

Obviously more knowledgeable, he enlightened me as to what happened next:

"Pizarro captured Atahualpa, but then decided to ransom him back to his people. His price was a room full of gold and a room full of silver."

The Incas, who had mined precious metals for centuries, gave up their jewellery, altars and ornaments, brought by llama from every corner of their vast territories, he explained. But when Pizarro saw how easily the gold flowed, he demanded seven times more. Linstrom sneered:

"Makes our modern bankers' corruption seem reasonable now, eh?"

It wasn't just the easy conquest that would still rankle with the native community, it was the callous shaming and deliberate degradation that the white men imposed. Atahualpa was chained to a stake in the central square. His people, who would have looked just like Maica, begged for mercy as their king entreated the stone-faced governor for the safety of his family and the sanctity of his own corpse.

Desperate that his body should not be burned, Atahualpa made a bargain with Pizarro and agreed to be baptised as a Christian: to die as Don Francisco Atahualpa if his corpse were left entire. "*But justice was stolen from him by a swift garrotting*," the book explained.

So, in a story that makes the trial of Jesus seem like a fair deal, Pizarro executed him under false charges the minute the treasure was in his hands. A callous butchering. And, despite promises to the contrary, the king's body was partly burned.

The smell of roasted flesh drifted up from Linstrom's airline supper, served by our pristine hostess. I marked the page. Put the book aside. Even in business class, my vegetarian option tasted like damp cardboard. As night stole the sky, the plane began to buck and rear, spilling our wine. To distract from my fears, I re-engaged with my book, as we could no longer eat, and had to belt in again.

The mutilation of Atahualpa's corpse had prevented the Indians from mummifying him: their ritual for creating a martyr. Nothing was more defiling to the Inca. It was never forgiven, nor forgotten.

The conquistadors, meanwhile, were busy learning the secrets of the coca bush. Reserved for chiefs and shaman, coca had been a way of opening consciousness to the spirit realm, to be closer to the gods. To give it to peasants *ad hoc* was profoundly disrespectful to those gods, as peasants were only allowed it to stave off hunger, cold, or occasionally, for religious rites. But the conquistadors gave it to all the natives, to control and manipulate them and gain their loyalty.

Enraged and conquered, Atahualpa laid a curse on the coca bush just before he was slaughtered and cried out in Qqechua, moments before his death:

"*In the name of the sun, moon and the mountains, may the gods hear me now! From the fruitfulness of this earth, through the flowing of my blood, up to the unknowable sky, I send out this, my curse on the wiraqocha, across all my lands by the wings of the mighty condor. May the coca enter their cold white hearts and turn them to stone. May it poison their children and may a great sickness come among them for all time. May our sacred coca, which has brought the Inca closer to our gods, now bring the wiraqocha closer to their devil. This I have cursed in the name of Atahualpa, King of the Inca, on behalf of all my peoples, and will repeat as I drown in my death blood.*"

Unintelligible to the metal-clad Spanish, they thought the King was commending his own soul to his god rather than theirs to the Devil. Since there was no written Incan language, Atahualpa's priests and shaman spread the words of his curse across the land, and his people learned it well and taught it to their children.

"Guess what the locals think when they see the hordes of *wiraqocha* now?" my brother had asked me when I told him I'd read Atahualpa's curse.

"Hey! I'm in search of adventure, me! I can afford the airfare! Full belly, great clothes; all I need now is *meaning*!"

I'd burbled on about Europe's spiritual vacuum in our post-God age. The Valhalla of consumerism that attempted to fill it. Blah blah blah. He was far more succinct and poetic in his summary:

"Yeah." he said, "The Devil's in therapy. God's gone bald!"

'Great title for a painting' was all that registered at the time, coupled with the desperate unease that I would never paint it. But he was right about the tourists needing ritual, symbols and esoterica. They want to be reassured of a greater mystery. A greater intelligence than that of mere humans, with all its betrayals and weaknesses. Hope invests in Utopia.

According to my book, full capitulation of Incan culture took a further thirty years from the death of Atahualpa. Tupac Amaru was the last of the crowned Incan kings to defy the Spanish and thought he was safe and hidden in the Machu Picchu secret settlement. Linstrom pointed to the iconic picture on page 142 and told me:

"The kind Christian soldiers tied Tupac to four horses and pulled him into quarters, having first cut out his tongue and made him watch as they murdered his wife and son. Creative, eh? Truly, Renaissance men!"

I closed the book. My brother had explained that Peruvians think their own country is useless. Corruption and self-interest at the top, no opportunities for the lower orders but continuous poverty. They laugh, he'd told me, at the fat-arsed *gringos* and the prices they pay for a line of cocaine. Pink-faced Swedes; hearty Germans; Israeli conscripts in post-army shock; Aussies in outback chic. He'd pointed out all the tribes during my first week in Arequipa.

I glanced around the plane. I could feel the anticipation. I could smell the tourist dollars ready to be mined from the rich seam of curiosity and cynicism in the hearts of the affluent. Like the lad in the bookshop, many come to Peru it to be a more spiritual place. Thousands of eager, mostly white, faces look to the Peruvian ancients for meaning. Some are naïve; some jaded; but all as curious as a cartload of monkeys.

All are desperate to trek down the sacred valley to Machu Picchu, the Lost City of the Incas, ready to titillate themselves with a mouthful of legal coca leaf, just to say that they have. The more daring will seek a refined version: cocaine crystals laced with toxic chemicals.

Then, higher than the condors, the poisoned children of the *wiraqocha* will stand on old Incan land looking for spiritual meaning;

on the soil where loyal shaman first repeated Atahualpa's curse – and curse them still.

The fact that I would soon be face down in the same soil, and, some days later, tearing over it in a stolen car, never occurred to me at the time.

26 ANT RETURNS TO THE NEST

When Anthony returned from his final gig in Mochegua, he dumped his guitar in the hallway and held me close for a full three minutes, weeping, laughing and hugging. He gave me a brief description of the gigs in the Cotahuasi canyon; the audiences; the antics. He'd spent all wages in advance of receiving them and had run out of cocaine. Consequently, he was now suffering from the dreaded '*gripe andina*': the Andean flu. This is the name given to symptoms of coke withdrawal, or indeed excess, describing the red eyes and running nose.

The food, he said, had been awful. Roast guinea-pig, deep-fried cat and buttered cow teats. He then produced a sweaty Chuquibamba cheese as a gift, still angry that the tour had lasted so long, elastic timekeeping stretching the planned ten days to a generous fourteen.

Apparently, the coach travel took forever. Some roads were washed out by waterfalls that cascaded over them into the canyon. Still, the audiences seemed to enjoy the concerts, never having seen a *gringo* before, let alone an authentic rock 'n' roller. He leant all his weight on me, tearful and tired, just as he had when we were children.

The next words out of his mouth were to ask if the Wi-Fi were connected. It was – finally. He put his phone on charge before disappearing into the bedroom to snort the remainder of the home stash I hadn't been able to find. Then he asked for money, while shedding his clothes along the hallway to the bathroom. I said I could lend him $200. He jumped into the shower, anxious to get to the dealer's house with my cash.

Since I had come to Peru, I had been picking up the tab, paying the rent, buying the food. It was me who had given him the original airfare and spending money after my flush of success in London. When I arrived, he was living in a filthy *casita*, so, on day two, I rented us a good apartment, with a balcony facing the volcano.

I indulged my brother because he was clever, talented and he made me laugh. He was also my best friend. As I'd explained to Rosy, he understood art and its motivations and would happily talk technique and ideas with me for hours on end. He encouraged and supported my lines of enquiry and took equal interest in the end result. No one was a more sincere champion of my work and his delight in my success was genuine. But he had always suffered mood swings, and when his drugs wore off, so did his personality. Back came the hair-trigger temper.

In Peru, his addiction had progressed. He was just a stoner before, not even a big drinker, but unable to function without his spliff. Now, if his cocaine supply were temporarily interrupted, he would dope himself with sleeping pills and only surface to pee or eat and then return to his bed. When he spoke, he was tyrannical, kicking the furniture, verbally abusing me, demanding money or stealing it.

I forgave him his tantrums when he was younger, as both our parents had died before I was seventeen, Dad from a heart attack, Mum in a car crash. I had virtually raised him alone, and always felt protective. He was lost until he discovered music. It calmed him, gave him expression.

I stood the other side of the shower curtain and laid out the facts: the valley; the bloodied ankle; the disembodied head; the dog's ear; the Nike trainers; the black rose. He stuck his head round, dripping.

"*What*? Is Maica dead? Shit! What happened? Are you OK?"

He grabbed a towel, embracing me with real concern. I pulled the rose from her hiding place in the kitchen cupboard and proudly set her next to the stove in the sunshine. Despite recovery from near death she did not impress him, though he was genuinely pleased for me that I'd rescued her. But mostly, he wanted to know about the explosion, making me repeat the details again about the smouldering foot in the boot that was not Maica's.

Furious that I had been blown up without warning and left for dead, he promised he would find out what happened to Maica from Diego, without divulging the secrets of the rose.

"Any new paintings, sis?" he asked, as he dressed. "There's loads of amazing scenery here. Remind me to take you to the Carmen Alto. It's only two miles up the road."

"I told you, I don't want to paint right now."

He stood behind me and rested his hand on my neck.

"It'll come back, Syb. It will." Without missing a beat he said:

"I've got a new song. Wrote it on the bus. I'll play it for you later, princess."

For an artist who cannot work, to hear another's tale of creative flow evokes thoughts of suicide, or worse... *murder*. My rage still burning from Maica's betrayal, I turned to face him and told him about the incident with Charlie: how damned angry I was. Not that the man had made a drunken pass, but that it was his so-called friend: a man born with the silver spoon in his mouth; a man who had blown his chances in every aspect of his life. I wanted to see Ant acknowledge the worthlessness of his cocaine buddies, and I surprised myself at the venom that I heaped upon them.

"They want you to *fail* bro', just like they've failed. Can't you *see*? They want you to be a burned-out, wasted 'could-have-been', so you can keep them company."

He brushed aside my concerns: "Don't worry, sis, words will be said. No one's gonna treat you like that." He kissed my face and hugged me, allowing himself the theatricality of 'aggrieved brother' in a country where family honour still mattered. But he was play-acting. For him, this incident had no real meaning. I knew that. I wanted him to protect me. Not because I needed it, but because he should *want* to protect me. I wanted him to stand up for me and for himself as the male of my race against the tide of disrespect I felt as a *gringa* in this culture: endless passes made at me by cab drivers convinced all tourists were easy; men speaking to him across me in social gatherings without making eye-contact once with me, without ever acknowledging my presence or consulting my opinion.

"Don't worry about Charlie," he said. "I can legitimately go nuts. They kill people for things like that in this country."

He embraced me again and duly borrowed some money, taking a bottle of my rum to the dealer's.

Mavis was also with Diego for lunch. They were agog when Ant told them about Charlie and the 'cunt' story, commiserating and downing the alcohol my dollars had paid for.

"That's attempted rape," cried Mavis, convinced that most men were pigs. "He's a shit!" said Diego.

And while they debated the demerits of such behaviour, who walked in but Charlie himself, in his silk suit, all sweaty for his *falso*.

Ant used Charlie's Spanish name and courtesy title when admonishing him, having left him in no doubt of his anger:

"Don Carlos, if I spoke to your wife like that, you'd want to kill me. Apologise, or you will never see Sybil or me again."

Covered in confusion and backtracking wildly, the thoroughbred Charlie professed to memory lapse due to alcohol.

"Let me think, let me think," he stammered.

Diego looked on, giggling, as the *pituco* Don Carlos was caught on the back foot. Diego's upper-class clients were ashamed to be seen out with him because of his criminal record and thought themselves superior. This type of snub cut deep into the dealer's psyche. So, as the red-faced Charlie departed in a taxi with Mavis, now not so offended that she couldn't hitch a free ride, Diego suggested to Ant that they steal Charlie's car – 'for retribution'. And, of course, the obvious profits from the sale to be spent on cocaine. He hinted that he might involve his *cholo,* Maica, from whom he bought in bulk each week. Ant took the opportunity to ask:

"How *is* Maica?"

"He's OK. He's been in Trujillo, in the north, but he's coming over as soon as he gets back."

It seemed to Ant that the *cholo* had not mentioned to Diego a single word of the explosion, the black rose, or the bloodied *gringa* staggering back to safety.

When my telephone rang, Ant's voice quietly whispered to me from Diego's bathroom, firstly of the luncheon tableau; then the situation with Maica; then the plot for Charlie's wheels. I bristled at the first two pieces of information – and laughed at the third. Had I felt any inclination to involve Maica in fencing a stolen car, which I most certainly didn't, it would have been a perfect plan. No one in Arequipa knew him. He came by night on the bus and left with a fistful of dollars in the wee small hours, having laid his shiny white egg in Diego's lap.

Since the four-by-four and a few ageing, quality suits were Charlie's only visible assets, taking his car would certainly whack him straight in the ego. I didn't feel particularly vengeful for the 'cunt' incident. Nor did I want to make money from the stolen car, but when Ant told me of the idea, my mood was immediately elevated to one of high glee. I wanted to punish machismo, impertinence, insensitivity and sheer bad manners. It was a sense of justice that led to criminal thoughts; that, my love of pranks – and the demon boredom, which had flogged my backside for far too long. Hard core adrenaline might unblock me. Maybe I could start painting again.

Besides, we could always leave the car somewhere so he could get it back. But how to do it? Wait till he was drunk? Steal the keys and get them copied? Well, it couldn't be us. Too memorable. *Gringo* faces are easy to spot, easy to recall. We both had blue eyes and the natives resonate with that really quickly and stare and stare. After the melting pot of London's streets, I felt uneasy being the stranger in a strange land, marked out by my racial difference. But Ant explained that following an hour of discussion, Diego gradually began to renege on the idea, and started murmuring:

“Well, you know man, he’s a friend and he isn’t insured.”

Ant’s call, having elevated my mood, now brought me back to cold reality. As he described Diego’s degenerating appetite for the plot, I realised, once again, that an idea conceived under the influence of cocaine and fuelled by its false enthusiasm, rarely, if ever, bears fruit once the drug wears off.

Motivation, however, is the oil in the engine of execution. *My* will for justice was fertilised with mischief manure and unpolluted by cocaine. ‘Grand theft auto’ embedded itself, deep in my brain. I resolved there and then to use all my elegant cunning to bring it about. I had only just hung up on Ant when a second call beeped.

Well, well! If it isn’t dear Charlie and a spluttered apology in English! I accepted, of course, having first said how shocked I was that someone of his ‘breeding’ could act so crudely, feigning my surprise and hurt. Since his status mattered so utterly to him, I used it as a stick. It worked. Flustered and stuttering he asked:

“Er, perhaps we could have lunch? I shall be in town later. Can I make it up to you? Anthony is my friend and I do not want to lose either of you.”

I politely declined lunch. I had nothing to say to a man like Charlie that wasn’t going to act like paint-stripper on his ego. Better I keep my acid tongue to myself.

Besides, stealing his big car would be all the apology I needed.

27 MISTER MIRACLE

Twenty-four hours later, I walked into the kitchen to witness a miraculous recovery. Firm in the soil, but with a few leaves dying, the black rose had lifted. She was beginning to emit a positive energy. The root had definitely connected to the soil. I watered her and left her in the daylight, next to the stove. Now, I can cut a stem and give it to Stan, knowing I have the original as insurance.

I telephoned Rocio and asked her to set up a meeting with him. She said she would ask him at work the following day, and she invited me out to a local festival. As I left the house, I saw two men standing by my electricity meter at the side wall. "They must be reading it," I thought, as I hailed a taxi. But no. Though I did not know it, they were cutting us off. Why? Because, in the eternal spirit of Spanish '*mañana*', our landlady hadn't paid her bill. An omission that was soon to cost me all I had. At that moment though, I was filled with optimism and plans: a state I had not enjoyed for the longest time.

In Plaza San Francisco, the jacaranda trees were in full purple blossom, framing a throng of worshipers for *El Señor de Los Miragulos*. I thought I'd been invited to a festival of culture. I'm shocked to find myself at a religious knees-up.

The procession crushes its way down the side streets, with shoals of barefooted women walking backwards. The faithful are dressed in purple and white, to match the decorations. They pray; wave flowers; collect money. There is distorted choral music from big speakers on the church roof and local TV crews are filming God's PR man in his robes and pointy hat, swinging his incense handbag. Menopausal matrons file past fingering plastic crucifixes, their heads covered in lace.

The congregation is predominantly *mestizos* and *cholos*. Not once do I see a Spanish *pituco* face. This is too lowly for the upper class, thrust together with the plebs, close enough to smell their sweat.

Heaven forbid that one might be equalised with one's servant in the name of devotion!

Rosy is nestled up against me. Whispering behind her hand, she insists we drop money into the priest's collection box. "No," I say, wondering who divides the cash and how naïve she is to put her faith in them. Well then, she insists, we must buy a ticket for the church raffle, the proceeds of which go to repair damage to the steeple from constant small earthquakes. I look up at the huge cracks in the *sillar* wall and relent, handing over ten soles; she grabs a ticket, smiling, and holds it out to me.

Just then, the procession stops. Coming up the road, I can see a huge sedan carried by twelve burly men: six in front, six behind. On this silver throne sits a seven-foot, framed picture of Christ, arms outstretched, face beneficent. He is decked with streamers, flags and flowers, and is white-skinned and blue-eyed: the Aryan re-imagining of a charismatic Jew.

As 'Jesus' passes me by, I recognise one of the bearers. Hairy hands remind me why I thought of him as a monkey in a suit. He inclines his sweating head at Rosy.

"Who's that?" I demand.

"Eez Roberto Chicau, from where I works." She waves and smiles at him. I draw back against the wall and look around me. The incense is spicy, resinous. The good behaviour of the crowd impresses. This crew want to feel – not transported by chemicals like a posse of ravers – but transported by religion. They paid no entrance fee. No money up-front for happy pills. Yet they seem to be having just as intense an experience. Penitential sinners: barefoot before a blue-eyed image of the supposed son of the supposed Supreme Being.

Rosy was utterly mortified by my lack of spiritual fervour. As she held my hand, unseen in the squash, I had sacrilegious thoughts about copping a sly feel of her *mons veneris*. Instead, I took the opportunity to thank Mother Nature for reviving my beautiful black rose.

It's the Peruvian custom to offer the first of one's drink to the earth goddess, *Pachamama*. I spilled a little water from my bottle onto the pavement before I drank, and spoke her name. How reluctant even I am to relinquish Paganism, the only religion that Nature reveals to all, without the need of prophet or martyr.

I had been keeping my hands on my pockets in this thief's paradise, but I was beginning to feel less cynical; beginning to understand the celebratory atmosphere. Atop the buildings, spectators jostled, looking down and waving purple flags. The entire street entourage swayed to and fro behind the procession, following Jesus down the Calle San Francisco. Then it happened. I'd taken my hands off my pockets for a few seconds and I was robbed, $300 lighter. Just as I became mesmerised by the twining snake of bodies, it bit me.

"Why you bring money today? Eez very estupid, Si-vil."

"Well, *excuse me*," I spat in English, knowing she wouldn't fully understand, "but what better cover for the parasites than the canopy of religion? This parade is more likely to be infested with thieves than a rave. Chemical ecstasy means a lower crime rate than religious ecstasy it would seem."

The procession duly passed, and we turned into the church courtyard.

"Peruvian *fuckers*!" I was still frothing. "Man, they love to rip off the *gringos* here. The people with pure Spanish blood are no different from the natives. They're worse! They're educated for Christ's sake. Yet still perpetuate an immorality that they're so ready to lay at the feet of the *cholos*."

Rosy looked startled. She'd understood the sentiment, if not all my words.

"Always eez *ladrones* in crowds Si-vil. Eez sames in London, yes? Sames everywhere."

"Yes, but not in every bloody shop and staging post, slipping you counterfeit coins, overcharging just because you've got a white arse." I inhaled, and let the air out slowly as I steadied for the onslaught:

"Oh, and you need to pay your public servants properly. Why wouldn't a policeman take a bribe when he earns a pittance? Here, his commanding officers would steal the bribe from him if they could.

Welcome to bloody South America!" I was ranting again. The shock of being robbed had worn off.

It was nearly 6.30pm and both Rosy and I were hungry, physical needs gainsaying moral outrage. Whom should we see in the pizzeria but Charlie and a new girlfriend openly holding hands. He introduced the perfumed lovely as 'Lupe', a common shortening of the prettier 'Guadalupe'. She glanced at both of us and flashed a painted smile, instantly dismissing Rosy as inferior because of her dark looks.

Lupe was a cabaret singer, swift to mention her forthcoming chat show appearance in Lima. She seemed familiar to me. Perhaps I'd seen a poster, or maybe a TV appearance. Lupe only spoke Spanish. So began a conversation, advising Rosy about singing and show business, whilst Charlie whispered to me,

"Please, don't say anything!" Meaning of course, his disgusting behaviour when trying to knock me into a blanket and grapple with my 'dubious' genitals.

"She's accompanying me to Lima at six tonight. I will be away on business for a week," he said.

Lupe, her antennae fine-tuned to rich, old men, was at least forty, but Charlie assured me she was thirty-two. Immaculate in the way that only brittle, brutal women can be, Lupe had raised personal grooming to an art form. Every lacquered nail and separated lash glinted with applied perfection. She was flawless: a doll woman, almost air-brushed. Jules and Gilles, Vargas, and Jeff Coons would all have been impressed by her inspirational kitsch.

Lupe was a natural courtesan with the gift of making useless men feel important. If she had any feelings at all, they had long since crystallised into tactics for getting what she wanted. Jealous of any perceived rival, she spoke to me through almost gritted, but, it has to be said, *perfect* teeth.

I liked her immensely. Men like Charlie deserved women like Lupe. In macho South America, it was refreshing to see a woman so determined to get what she wanted, and on her terms. It was great entertainment watching her work Charlie. Poor Lupe was under the illusion that he still had assets, unaware that he had pissed and snorted them away long before.

We left them in the restaurant and headed back to the church. Unwilling to risk the thieves, Rosy had left her bag with a friend in the courtyard and crossed herself as she entered the gate to get it.

"Si-vil!" She came running out. "Where is jour ticket? Jour number is up on the board."

She snatched the little blue paper and ran back to the courtyard. I supposed I'd won a plastic crucifix, or a picture of the blue-eyed Christ.

Whilst I fumed and grimaced in gangrenous reverie, Rosy reappeared, triumphantly carrying my crimson prize. She thrust it into my hand, smiling.

A large bottle of ketchup.

28 DUPLICITY

Laura grabbed a large bottle of ketchup and squished it onto Todd's steak. She arranged the peas and fries and poured beer into a small glass.

"Here it is, hon. Come 'n geddit! Chow down!"

Todd approached the table, remembering that the sight of a dead cow swimming in gravy used to really turn him on. These days, it was just a texture experience. It had taken him a long time to get used to chewing something that pressed no buzzers or bells in his taste buds.

"That's my gal," he said, inwardly crying at the loss as he sat.

"So, what's it like?" Laura was curious about Todd's take on his new security job.

"S'nimportant position. Doors gotta be checked; alarms tested; keys signed fer. The boss speaks English, so that's OK, and them that don't, I don' need t'talk to anyways."

He shovelled peas; burped his baby Budweiser.

"So why they gotta send you to Cusco, hon?"

"It's only for twenny-four hours. Gotta pick up some chemicals for the lab. They need a security man they can trust. Them Peruvians'll rip 'em off, that's fer sure."

He hated lying to her, but the time to tell her the truth wasn't now. What he had to do would be over in a short while and when it was he had every intention of getting out of Peru, with her, back to civilization. Until then, he'd tolerate the rows, keep his head down, earn the money and do this thing that had been asked of him. It was the only option left. He couldn't get her out any other way. He was scared, very scared, but his mind was set.

As Laura opened her mouth to speak, the mobile phone in her handbag began to vibrate. Todd winced and took a huge slug of beer. Laura rummaged for the phone and stood up from the table, walking towards the far window. She had reassured Todd many times that her fling with the scientist was over, but their regular calls irked him beyond measure.

He daren't put pressure on her. She was short-tempered enough these days, and it was the last big row over money, back in Colorado together, that had given her the impetus to uproot and come to live in Peru. He couldn't risk losing her again. His love and loyalty were as solid as cement. He'd kill for her.

Believing she was telling the truth about the affair being over, Todd held his tongue. He knew the connection was cocaine. Besides, he couldn't condemn her. She'd put up with his drinking for all these years. There was no way he'd abandon her, no matter what she did now. She was going to be proud of him again when she found out how brave he had to be to get this next job done.

Yeah, she'd be proud alright, like when she first saw him driving those big rigs. Like it was before the accident.

Laura was talking into the phone to Stan Fischer in bad Spanish. Stan had been the first person in Arequipa she'd spoken to when stopping to ask for directions and a friendship had developed. From his connections, she'd landed herself an immediate job at the local mining company, teaching American business English to their management team. It was this excuse she now threw at the cowboy.

"It's work," she said, with her face temporarily turned away from the mobile and towards him, "they want me to do extra shifts tomorrow."

Now, through the earpiece, Fischer was giving her orders. She nodded and kept murmuring, "*Sí, no hay problema*!"

"These last figures are great, Lolly. It's just one week more. Keep the records as exact as you have been. Don't miss once. D'you have enough to finish? D'you need me to meet you?"

"*Sí.*"

"OK. Call my new private number 0549777777 tomorrow; can you remember that? It's easy, yeah? We can meet at the usual place, usual time. Any problems from Todd?"

She glanced across at Todd, now disappearing into the bathroom and slamming the door. Still she spoke in Spanish, knowing if Todd were listening, he had no clue as to what her words meant.

"He's going to Cusco, so it's no problem to meet."

"Lolly, honey, you're a brave girl. What you're doing is really going to make a difference. Say nothing to Todd. OK?"

"I don't feel so good. My breath's real bad and I can't control my temper. I just keep flarin' up."

"Honey, trust me. It's all gonna be fine. I'll soon have the money for you. And you and your cowboy can make a fresh start, I promise you."

"I hope so, 'cos if we stay here things'll never work out for him. He's never gonna learn the language. We're always rowing over money. He's a proud man. He needs to feel good about himself."

"You must never tell anyone, honey. You know what we discussed."

"*Sí. Sí. No hay problema.*" She closed the phone as Todd returned to the table, grimacing.

"You ain't eatin' nothin' agin', Laura?"

"I'm fine. I had somethin' earlier."

Todd snorted with contempt and finished the rest of his beer. He knew exactly what had done for her appetite.

"Todd, you wanna come see Anthony Sands play next Sunday?"

"That Briddish son-of-a-bitch? No ways!"

"Why not, Todd? He's a real talent. The people here love him."

"I ain't payin' good money t'see no Briddish guy with a geetar, an' that's that."

Laura got up from the table and flounced to the window, shouting:

"You never wanna go *anywhere*. You just drink yerself stoopid every goddamn night! Yer borin' me, Todd. You never do nothin' excitin'!"

Todd went to the fridge and cracked another beer, pacing backwards and forwards with frustration.

"I don' want you hangin' out with those Briddish people. They're weirdos. Him an' his sister. Artist! Huh! Looks like she don' know what a day's work is t' me."

"She's real successful, Todd. She don't need to hide her money. Ain't no reason to be jealous."

"She's got a slimy way o' talkin'. Kinda in riddles. Makes ya wonder what she wants."

"Well, it ain't you, that's fer sure, cowboy. She's queer."

"*What?*"

"Queer. Y'know – she likes the girlies."

"Jeez, I knew there was somethin' creepy about her."

"She ain't creepy. But she seems kind o' sad. I love the way she does her hair with them pretty colours. I don' even understand what she's sayin' half the time."

"Paintin' yerself up like a fifty-dollar whore ain't pretty, Laura. I like nat'ral. I don' want you goin' near Miss Fancy Ass Artist, you understand me, girl?"

"Don'cha tell me who I can speak to. You shut yer mouth."

Todd went across to her and held her: "Now *listen,* baby. I jis don' want no goddamn queers botherin' my girl."

Laura exploded, mouth twisted. She began screaming:

"Take yer hands off me, you bastard! Don'cha tell me what I can do! You stop givin' me orders about mah life! I'm sick o' you! Why d'ya think I left ya? Never asked ya t'come find me."

The ketchup flew past him and cracked against the wall.

“She ain’t ever bothered me. Fact is, one o’ these days I might like t’get t’know her better. An’ her brother. They’re real interestin’. Not like you, Todd. You narra-minded *asshole*.”

Oh, that sinking feeling in Todd’s stomach! She was overreacting again. Getting all bent out of shape over nothing. Every disagreement was turned into a major roaring row these days. He knew what he had to do to put a stop to all this and, by God, he was damn well going to do it… no matter what the risk.

29 AFTER THE FIRE

Clutching my ketchup, I walked Rosy to the bus and strolled back up to Yanahuara, past Todd and Laura's apartment. Even from the street I could hear their furious rowing.

As I neared my rose I was feeling mixed emotions. If Stan could be co-opted, the rose would soon have sisters, and our future together would be assured. But underneath my optimism lay a darker stirring. It was something Rosy had said when we were eating. She'd asked me if Ant might be interested in playing guitar for her if she secured a recording contract. A bean of jealousy was sprouting yellow tendrils around my heart. They might relate to each other in ways that excluded me. They were already curious about each other. I'd told him I'd begun an affair and he was genuinely pleased.

"That's great, sis. Is she Peruvian?"

"Yeah, she works at Gentrex."

"*No! Really*? Is that why you slept with her?"

"Hey! I'm not that cynical. I really like her. I met her by chance, singing in a bar."

"Man, what a weird coincidence! Gentrex! Does she know about the black rose?"

"Don't be stupid, Ant. Only *we* do. Oh, and Maica, wherever he is. She knows that I want Stan to clone a plant for me, but not that it's the rose. I'll let Stan know that it's a rose, of course, but not that it's black."

I told Ant everything. We never had secrets. My brother knew I liked girls before I revealed it. We were close and respectful of each other's privacy. He wasn't gay but he loved teasing my gay friends in London. He did it because he loved being outrageous and pushing boundaries. And, because of me, I supposed, he hated the hypocrisy surrounding homosexuality.

Gay boys adored him, especially the more effeminate ones. He was manly, but gentle: physically macho, but with a silliness that was unthreatening. The first week of my visit, he played at *El Paradiso*, Arequipa's main gay bar. To see the clientele fawn and fight over him was hysterical and intimidating. He tolerated them like naughty puppies: firm but kindly. Making it obvious he'd no intention of being overwhelmed, standing his ground, yet enjoying the energy and attention. I loved that part of him, because it was genuine, and showed how secure he felt in his own sexual skin.

As I neared our apartment, I could hear jumping-jack fireworks exploding. The Peruvian custom is to set them off for luck and blessings next to a crucifix of flowers on the roof of any new building, before the first inhabitants move in. It woke me sharply from my thoughts. The smoke seemed a little thick as I turned the corner to enter my little street. Firemen and police were staring up at my kitchen window, now belching smoke and steam as they hosed into the gap.

Apparently, Ant had returned, soused as a herring. Once he found out that the electricity had been cut off, he lit candles and started to make a good old British fry-up. Whether it was a candle that started the blaze, or a chip-pan fire, was unclear. No matter now. Left unattended as he showered, the flames took hold. Neighbours called the brigade.

Fuelled on cocaine and alcohol, Ant said sorry a thousand times. He clumsily mopped water into buckets from the sopping floor. The firemen departed quickly at the sound of my screaming; not so the sour-faced landlady, demanding a $2,000 redress. Ant began a row over the electricity bill, and dismissed her with assurances of future payment and $300 in new notes, pulled from my wallet in the lounge drawer.

So apoplectic was I when I saw the charred ashes of my rose, now truly blacker than deep space, that I threatened Ant physically, his strength no match for my incandescent rage. I grabbed a kitchen knife and waved it at him, screaming. He backed off, apologising, as my fury dissolved to tears of frustration and defeat. He put his arm around me, but I shrugged him away.

"I'm sorry, but we couldn't save her," said a distant voice.

I cried until I was stupefied with sorrow. A remote observer in the film of my own life. My love had been snatched out from under me and I was desperate; railing against the abyss; trapped like a rat and trying to run – anywhere, everywhere, away from the flames of death's combustion.

But now, cold truth acted as midwife. My bereavement was born at that moment and delivered up to me, wrapped inside a great, dull aching. Like a weighty, malformed child, it leant like a stone against my heart and gullet. And I begged time to return to the point before I possessed it. I screwed up my eyes and sobbed and begged. But time was deaf to my keening, and instead, slowed down from its bustle… so I could better savour my new, suffocating burden.

He'd burned my reason. I didn't have a reason till I found her. Now she was gone, what was the point of anything? After all, I could afford the air fare. Full belly, great clothes, all I needed was *meaning*. I'm just like all the other bloody *gringo* tourists here. That's what enraged me, the stark, unresolved truth of it revealed in the flames.

It wasn't really his fault, it was *mine*: to have invested my future in a fucking *flower*. It took all my willpower not to jack-knife into a foetal cringe.

"I'll go back to the valley, sis, don't worry. I'll get another one. There can't be only one. Don't worry, I'll talk to Maica. We'll sort something, really we will. Let's go and phone him, now!"

"He doesn't know I've got it, stupid! And besides, his number is unobtainable."

"Syb, he *owes* you. He left you to *die*! This time, he's got to pull out all the stops to get it and we're not paying him a penny!"

We're not paying him? This was typical of Ant, absorbing my cash by conversational osmosis. He would often talk about how 'we' should buy a new stereo or 'we' should visit Argentina. He meant with *my* money, always with me picking up the tab and him picking up my pecuniary property. He did it so naturally that it seemed almost churlish to question his forward planning. In this mood, he swept you along with his powdered enthusiasm and bright hopes. Everything is possible morale is high. It was only when it flagged and he turned back into a spiteful toad that the full implication of his philandering with my chequebook impacted.

The rage this would induce in me, against myself mostly, for indulging him, sent me running for the Valium, only ten *centimos* each, available over the counter. I strongly suspected that what held Peruvian society together were millions of enthusiastic, coca-fuelled men supported by their cheaply tranquillised women. But he was right about the valley. Without a single living cell of my rose left to clone, I only had one option. I desperately wanted the rose back by my side. This time, though, regardless of the poisoned valley, he could share the risk.

"I only wore the blindfold for the last few miles. I can find the valley without Maica. I *know* I can. I remember the sound of water; the bumps in the road. While I was blindfolded, I was fantasising that terrorists had captured me and that I'd have to recall the journey for the police, like in that old kidnap film with Cary Grant. I distinctly remember the sounds and the smells. They changed radically just before we stopped. Cow shit, water, jacaranda blossoms, more cow shit, strong eucalyptus, then two minutes later, we parked."

I knew we needed to avoid the Dioxin, but there must be other, unsprayed valleys nearby.

"Mmm. We'll need to hire a four-by-four. Bad roads up there, sis."

"Charlie's in Lima for the week, he flies at six. We could borrow his," I said, now angry enough at everything to feel a tremendous sense of invincibility. I knew, *really* knew, that we would not be caught.

"*Steal it*, you mean?" he grinned. "Well, it won't be that hard. He disabled the alarm. The local kids kept rocking the car and setting off for fun. Even if he’s fixed it I can go on the dark net, put in his number plate and order a new key fob. Takes about three days.”

I’d always known my brother had no social conscience, but I, of all people, had no place in lecturing him on that one.

“OK. When d’you wanna steal it, sis?”

“*Now,* Anthony. Right now!”

30 COW SHIT AND JACARANDA

Knowing Charlie's precarious finances, I doubted he would have a full tank, so I had the foresight to go to an all-night garage and buy two cans of petrol before we did the dirty deed. I packed a change of clothes for both of us, and a *campesino* bag containing fruit, crisps and hastily-made sandwiches. I wore Mavis' black wig and some tinted glasses, disguising myself through theatrics, not fear.

We found the car four blocks from Charlie's house, on the walk up there. Ant took the long route because he knew the car was unlikely to be on the driveway. Apparently, Charlie parks it away from the house so that no one knows if he's in when the debt collectors come knocking for the money he owes all over town. Anthony knew the blocks where Charlie usually parked it as he was often dropped off there after a night's partying.

Ant broke into the car with a coat hanger and a magnet, a trick he'd learned from one of the Peruvian drummers he'd worked with. Sure enough, the alarm did not go off. He knew exactly how to hot-wire the car to start it, sedately driving through the town before tearing up the mountain road. How surprised we were to find the gas tank already full and the car newly waxed. I knew we'd committed a crime, but I also knew if Charlie found out, it was unlikely he would prosecute. He'd just want money.

Alone with my brother for the entire journey, we had a chance to talk together, the way we had before he came to Peru. About Mum and Dad. About our upbringing. About how hard it was to find our tribe, hating wilful ignorance from the bottom and condescension from above. About our different views of Peru. About his addiction. About the rose and what it meant to me. About art. About music.

"People love music here, sis. They respect art. *Really* respect it. Not like the British. They respect the people who want to make it. Love the fact that you even want to try."

"Well, it's certainly a music-mad culture. All those bloody blasting radios biased to Latin sounds."

"No, you're wrong. They love British music. They all sing pop songs and they love the modern stuff. Good art transcends time, place and race. You *know* that. The first day I came, two young Peruvian boys stopped me in the street and asked me where I was from. When I said 'England', they pulled out an acoustic and gave me a perfect rendition of the Beatles' *And I love her*, complete with all the harmonies and the difficult chords. It was beautiful. It brought a tear to my eye. We all stood in the street embracing each other."

"They wanted cash, bro'. It's all they had to get it from you."

"No. It was purely for the love of the music. You didn't see the commitment they gave it. Pull a guitar out in company in England and you're accused of showing off, or you want pennies in your hat, or people are just bloody embarrassed by unsolicited performance and artistic commitment," he said. "Spill creative emotion for free and the Brits close ranks to freeze you out. It's an anti-art culture."

Yes, I'd seen that with my own eyes when he was younger. Deep down though, the great British public long for a vicarious thrill, but only when they're ready. Once they've *paid* for a concert ticket or gallery entrance, they positively demand to see you bleed with artistic commitment. But, though I knew his sentiment was genuine, I told him he was using it as an excuse to stay close to the source of cheap cocaine. He shrugged.

"Coke really works for me, sis. I get a lot done."

He did indeed, but his projects disintegrated like smoke the minute the drug wore off.

We continued to take turns to sleep during the fourteen-hour trip, but were unable to drive within a kilometre of the valley. The narrow road was cordoned off. Soldiers; police; roadblocks. Not that I wanted to return to the exact spot and risk Dioxin poisoning, but I hoped to be within the same climate and soil type to maximise my chances of finding another rose. I didn't want to believe Maica's tale: that she was the only one. I was sure he'd said that to elicit his high price.

Ant flashed Diego's fake press card. The dealer had it fabricated in Lima's backstreets to better facilitate his drug dealing to the rich and famous. But, while it opened mouths to us, it couldn't open the road. There was a big flag-burning rally by the coca growers, very anti-American. The wind had blown herbicide from the DEA's planes onto some of their legal crop in the next valley. Someone had shat in their cabbage patch and they were madder than a nest of hornets. They knew Dioxin was liquid death… that their livelihoods were gone.

Hundreds of legal, card-carrying coca growers from the *Empresa Nacional de la Coca* were there with hand-written placards, alongside many an illegal *cocalero*. Women were banging spoons against saucepans, while the men set fire to rubber tyres in the middle of the road. Ant informed me that *Sendero Luminoso* guerrillas were also involved, and had been secretly stirring up the growers with a big coke spoon. No longer true Maoists, the terrorists also had their finger in coca pie and had seen their assets summarily stripped by the deadly mist. The previous day, they'd cut off a policeman's head and stuck it on a pole.

Most of these shocking details were relayed to us by an old crone who had her hand out for money. Though I greased her palm for information, we still couldn't get access to the road. There were plumes of dark smoke where the Peruvian army were burning the fields. If there were any more black roses, they'd met with the same fate as mine. Black as hell now. Cremated. I was desolate.

We walked back down the dirt road in the direction we'd parked, having paid one of the locals fifty soles to guard the car. The man ignored me and pumped Ant's hand like he'd known him all his life, probably because Ant had proffered the money. I wonder how surprised he would have been to know that not only did the money belong to the woman, but that the same woman had also instigated the car theft.

We drove up the road towards Imata, pulling over so that Ant could urinate. I stretched my legs as he took a generous pinch of Atahualpa's dandruff, Bolivian style. Suddenly enlivened, he suggested:

"Let's walk through these clearings, maybe there are roses."

"That's the start of the bloody jungle!"

"It's just a few bits of green, and on the other side it thins out. Trust me, sis, I cycled up here when I first arrived."

"Ant, they kidnap people up here. White faces mean big ransoms."

"Not when we've got *this*." He pulled out a gun from his jacket.

"Where the hell did you get *that*?"

"From the glove compartment, when you were sleeping."

"Does it have bullets?" He flipped the chamber. Five left.

"There's a silencer still in the car side pocket."

"*A silencer? Charlie?* Christ, he's a dark horse."

"Yeah, he bought it from a police chief, one of Diego's clients. It's legal. He's got a licence. It's in his name."

"Look, you're not in a bloody film. Get a grip on reality for God's sake. You could kill someone. You've never used a bloody gun. You don't know how."

"Stop panicking, it's just a bit of insurance. D'ya want to find a black rose or not?"

I looked at him directly. My eyes held the answer. I couldn't come all the way here in a stolen car and return with nothing.

"Well, shut the fuck up and follow me!" he said. "We'll cut back any thorns of fear with the sword of purpose, sis!" And with optimistic gusto, he strode off into the bush, slashing right and left into the vegetation with the broken stem of a parñata plant.

"Guess what else I found?" he shouted back to me. "The spare valet key. It was in the back page of the car manual, so we don't have to keep stalling it to stop and we can lock it properly."

We walked for more than thirty minutes in a downward direction, peering round for anything that might resemble a rose. I had submitted to a little cocaine about two hours from Cusco. The thermos of coca tea I'd brought was all gone. I never want to have *soroche* again and coke is the natural cure. My nose was numb, but sensitive enough to register an acrid smell that was getting ever stronger as we descended.

"I think we're near water, Ant. Can you smell that weird smell?"

"No, can't smell a thing," Ant said.

Of course not. His nose had ceased to function as an olfactory organ; nightly nosebleeds, endless sneezing and blowing. Lately, he'd taken to snorting olive oil to ease the soreness and burning after a night's session.

As we turned towards the sun, we heard the sound of a river. The smell was overwhelming. The water and mud were a brackish brown with patches of rust red. Most of the plants were dead or dying and the strong odour seemed to point to one thing: pollution.

"Jesus! What have they been doing up here?"

"Refining coca," I said. "There was a programme about it on the news. Loads of deformed animals and fish. It's very contaminated in the southern jungle, and up here near the Huallaga Valley." Ant looked wary and genuinely shocked.

"Sounds like DEA propaganda to me, *contradrogas* trying to make the peasants stop growing it. *I've* never seen any deformed fish. It can't be the coca, it's natural. It grows wild everywhere."

"No, stupid! It's the refining chemicals for softening the raw leaves. Kerosene; borax; sulphuric acid; quicklime; carbide; acetone; toluene. That's the shit you've been putting up your nose every night."

"No, the chemicals are in *pasta*, the cocaine base. Maica's gear is highly refined. Ernesto, the bass player, he smokes pasta, the first refining, from when the leaves are mashed, before it's turned into crystal. He's a *pastrulo.*"

"That's why his teeth are rotted down to stumps and his hands shake," I reminded him.

"Yeah. Pasta Man Vibration!"

Ant started singing the Bob Marley version.

"Let's get out of here. It stinks! The water has a greasy rainbow film on it, look!"

"Well, it could be some other shit," he said. "Pesticides or herbicides. Maybe it's the Dioxin. The States dump it on coca. They can't sell it or use it themselves 'cause it's banned in the US. Maica told me. His brother's a farmer."

"No, it's definitely coca chemicals. It smells like your skin, times ten. Anyway, it's always polluted downstream from a refining shed. The programme said twenty-five rivers were dead in Peru, the worst poisoning in South America. Tons of chemical waste every week."

"OK, OK. I've got the point. Always look on the bright side, eh, sis? Let's go! You're not gonna make me feel guilty. If we're near a refining centre there will be people guarding it and I'm not in the mood for a confrontation."

"Well, that makes a change! Anyway, I thought we had the protection of your big gun."

"It's not *my* gun. Charlie's been carrying it around to wave at the wife's boyfriend. That's why he got the silencer – macho Latin bravado."

What a stupid, histrionic wanker Charlie is, I thought. Guns indeed! Silly bugger! Ant then enlightened me:

"He's been dressing up in a wig and dark glasses with Diego and following wifey round town to get evidence for the divorce."

I didn't mention that I'd seen the two middle-aged idiots with what looked like dead rats on their heads. Now I knew why. My own wig I'd removed and left it on the car seat curled up like a cat. I was sweating profusely and very tired. Back to priorities.

"What about the rose?"

"Stop moaning!" he said. "You're not gonna get one now so forget it. It's a stupid idea. It looked like shit anyway. I did it a favour by giving it a funeral. I'm bored. It's almost dark. Let's get to Cusco, pronto."

How Golden Boy had tarnished! Desperate for his drug, he was more than edgy, the fruit of his delicious poisonings now rotting on the vine. As he soured, unfeeling barbarity surfaced like a ravenous shark, tearing at the flesh of wounded kin: me. In this mood, his compulsion left him utterly dissipated and with less pity than a concentration camp warden. His personality had always been a switchback ride between saint and sadist. The perfect Christian metaphor: Good versus Evil.

Minutes after we began our trek back to the road we were horribly surprised by a black, daggle-tailed dog that ran out yapping, baring its teeth and attacking our shoes. Startled, I shrank back into post-trauma shock, expecting a bang. It came all right. Ant lifted the gun and aimed. A whistling sound rushed forwards. The dog rolled upwards in a flame. I heard a thick, foggy *crunch* as its head hit the earth.

My brother looked triumphant. "Gotcha, you little shit," he said. "I've waited *years* for that!"

"You bastard, Anthony! We'd better run."

I knew that the owner wouldn't take kindly to such a vicious despatch of his little mutt. He'd have no sympathy whatsoever for the killer; no care that a dog had savaged my brother when he was five years old and dragged him, screaming, from his bike.

Revenge is a tumour. The deadly shot excised it for sure.

31 A CUCKOO CALLS

We ran back to the car, breathless and aching in the high altitude. My coke had also worn off, and though the headache hadn't yet gripped me, it was in the post and would be delivered shortly if I didn't refuel. The sun was going down and we were both hungry. We had to return to Arequipa within forty-eight hours as Ant had two concerts, but first he was hell-bent on changing his brain chemistry.

We drove up the road through Cusipata into Cusco, where he wandered off to score. I booked us into a hotel, showered, changed my shirt, and went downstairs for a drink in the bar with a view of the car. I was thinking of both my roses with longing. Rosy was at Gentrex every day and evening this week. Suarez had loaded her down with work.

As I was about to drift off into sexual fantasy, my eyes settled on a man and woman across the far side of the square. They were animated and appeared to be arguing as they walked towards the hotel. My vision slowly focused as I realised who the man was. The malodorous Todd. Well, who was the woman? Maybe Todd had a bit of Latin pussy on the side, the old fox. But Todd couldn't drive. He was injured beyond that type of co-ordination, surely? How did he get here? Did she drive him up from Arequipa? He never took the buses. He was always saying:

"Goddam drivers! Ain't puttin' mah life in thar hands, no ways!"

So, did he fly to see her? That would be love then, surely? Or hard core lust. Maybe he'd come up with Stan's girlfriend, Neri, who often visited Cusco to see her family. Hmm... should I make myself known?

I left the bar and watched them enter our hotel. Curiosity overwhelmed me. I followed them upstairs, slipping up to my room, keeping the door slightly ajar. The hotel was a small, Spanish-style building with an inner courtyard and nine rooms on three sides of a veranda. They were to my left, and down two rooms, but Todd's loud drawl was unmistakable through the flimsy door. Incognito eavesdropping was necessary.

I put my dark glasses on and donned a straw hat over the now dishevelled wig. Sidling over to Todd's room, I stood outside with my back to their door, leaning over the balcony and looking down into the courtyard. I could hear him clearly.

"Where? How should I know? On the compu'da, I guess."

I couldn't hear the woman well, but she spoke in accented English. She said something like, "Brother will bring… he will show you." Then, "Everythin' with *Cuca* written on it."

Cuca? That was Spanish for cuckoo. It was also the name of a cheap mezze restaurant I used in my starving artist days when first in London.

"But thar's an inner office," boomed Todd, "an' I ain't got them special keys."

His tone was similar to the one he used with me. I just didn't feel that there was a big love affair between them. Then I heard her say:

"All the information on that, and on Della Fosby."

Who the hell was Della Fosby? Did this female voice belong to a jealous Latina, trying to bribe him with money or sex to find out about her husband's philandering? A husband or lover who worked at Gentrex? Yeah, that sounded plausible. Maybe the cuckoo in the nest was the other woman. Was Della Fosby the mistress? Their voices were almost inaudible but I heard the woman say something like, "…fuses …be careful." Todd said:

"But 'ahm gittin' out straight after. Ain't no use bein' here anyhows. She's more in love with that shit than she'll ever be with me."

Did he mean Stan and Laura? As the door handle turned and they started to come out, I distinctly heard her say "poisonin'."

Christ! Were they planning to kill someone? I scuttled back to my room as they walked down the stairs and into the square.

A few moments later I nipped downstairs to follow, but they caught a taxi and whizzed off. Curious, and now very hungry, I re-entered the bar and ordered an *empanada* and a beer. Whilst Ant was doing a deal with the local reprobates for his antidote to angst, I was reading a poster for the Festival of Paucartambo, near the edge of the jungle. It has the reputation of being one of the best costumed fiestas in South America and, on the poster, the colour of the earth where the locals were dancing looked the same dark orange as the valley. There could be roses!

One *falso* had turned Pigface into a prince, so I easily persuaded him to come to Paucartambo to look for the rose, but only with the promise that I would pay for yet more drugs when he ran out.

"I'm sorry I snapped, sis," he said, kissing my hand. We embraced. His body held all the dynamism of a young dog on a leash, straining for the next adventure. I told him about Todd. He was as bewildered as I was.

"Della Fosby?" he said. "Never heard of her."

We checked out of the hotel, bought more food, and filled up with petrol, then drove out of Cusco, crossing to the dirt road for Paucartambo. I was still talking about finding the rose and checking every hedgerow, eyes like radar. Anthony was optimistic, but his malady was only temporarily placated: like a sticking plaster on an alligator's egg – the hatching of a monster most imminent.

After five horrendous hours careering round a dangerous mountain road, we swung into Paucartambo. Ant had binged the cocaine in just a few hours. My mind was full of brooding fury sitting next to the murderer of my rose. A verbal storm was brewing as we drove the car over a beautiful stone bridge into the main square.

"I need a drink," he snarled, white flecks of spume at the side of his mouth, "got any cash?" I proffered twenty soles.

"What's this supposed to buy?"

"It's plenty for a few beers."

"Fuck beer, I want a bottle of rum."

"Sorry, Ant, but I can't change dollars till the morning."

"So that's it, is it? That's the night's entertainment? *Twenty fucking soles*?" He snatched the note.

Why argue with a rabid reptile? Yet, here is the same man who, less than three weeks earlier, after reading me poetry and writing me songs, had laid his head in my lap, sobbing at the shoeless children and the poverty in Peru, telling me how impotent he felt to affect any change. The rollercoaster was making me sick.

We tried to book in to a tiny hotel, having woken the owner with loud knocking. There was no room at the inn or any of the other two in town. We'll be sleeping in the car then. He headed for a cheap, fluorescently-lit café full of cock-eyed drinkers and mangy dogs, and ordered beer. All the natives looked at him and smiled. There was something about him, even in this evil distemper. He wasn't perfect looking, and scruffy enough not to resemble a rich tourist, but people just loved him. Charisma they call it, and Golden Boy had it in spades. The room just seemed to light up around him as the locals basked in his magnetic aura.

We were very tired and, after a few bottles, really flagging. The drinkers had gathered round us in a mixture of curiosity and opportunism. He was trying to tap more money from me to buy his new friends a bottle of rum and cement his position as all-round good guy.

So recently biting the hand that fed him, he was now in full entertainment mode, soothed by alcohol and an appreciative audience, showing off his knowledge of street slang and loving his status as clown and troubadour among these simple men.

He pointed at me and introduced me to them as 'the woman of his life', the famous sister with a talent like Picasso he said, with a grand sweep of his arm. The natives looked apathetic. Picasso? Christ! It was grandiose of him and inappropriate, a sort of 'look at us *gringos*, aren't we clever?' moment. These people had their own culture; had fought and died against being subsumed by Spain.

I managed to persuade him to an early night, and handed out some Valium. He snatched the packet from my hand and doubled the offered dose, washing the blue pills down with beer.

We drew a veil over the day as the temperature cooled to freezing. In the car, under alpaca wool blankets, we were soon embracing tightly for warmth and comfort.

32 PAUCARTAMBO

By contrast, the morning was warm, bright and very noisy. Ant required an alcoholic breakfast to rouse him so we found a bar in the main plaza.

The *'Virgen Del Carmen'* is a bite-sized carnival with a partly religious theme. From our table we could see huge bamboo frames laced with fireworks and ribbons being erected, fourteen-foot high and more. As they were hoisted into place, bands and musicians assembled in the square, which was swollen with stray dogs and laughing children. Food vendors were setting up kerosene lamps under greasy hotplates. I wondered if Mr. Todd would turn up.

Within half an hour, the festival came to life. *Capac Qolla* dancers began re-enacting the visual theatre of past terrors dressed as conquistadors and riding wooden hobbyhorses. They wore white, knitted balaclavas overlain with embroidered eyes and moustaches to represent the cruel *wiraqocha* – the white men who took their gold, raped their women and changed their culture and genetics forever.

Sporting whips, and with stuffed baby llamas on their backs, they were as frightening as they were beautiful, and reminded me of the painting '*Masken*' by the German modernist Heinrich Hoerle, or the exquisite club looks of the late costume artist, Leigh Bowery.

I changed $500 to Peruvian money and handed some to soles to Ant. He was raging and awful, and desperate for cocaine. His eyes scanned the bar for a likely source.

"Where will you get it from?"

"Syb, *this is Peru!*"

Frankly, the country was irrelevant. Ant could walk into any town in the world and score drugs within half an hour. He peered round again, draining his beer.

"Right, I'm off! What time is it?" he said, putting on his shades.

"Where's your watch?" I'd bought him a gold Piaget as a present, just before he came to Peru.

"Dunno," he shrugged, "it's somewhere." He turned to go.

"How'll you find me again? It's going to get pretty lively soon."

"I'll find you."

And he would. I was in no doubt. He's an animal, a great, instinctive, male animal. He would sniff me out.

"Don't worry," he said. His favourite phrase, flung at me, his teachers, doctors and friends as we all tore our hair out over his antics.

"Oh, thanks, bro'. Just abandon me in charge of a stolen car."

"No one gives a fuck, Syb. All they want to do is get blasted. You don't know Peru. No one likes to talk about it, but they're *all* at it." He slowly leaned forward and looked me right in the face saying:

"Didn't you know? No one takes coke in Peru. That is to say, I've never met more effusive, bug-eyed, truth economists in my life. It's the unfolding of the way. The unreal thing. *The beautiful lie*."

"Yes," I said, "and it comes holding hands with duplicity, meanness and spite. Not to mention all those gurning jabber-jockeys and their synthetic optimism."

He turned and left. The smell of *anticuchos*, alpaca meat, wafted up from the stoves nearby. Gamey. Strong. I bought two masks at a stall. Displayed alongside nylon baseball hats were glittering pictures of the Virgin, icons, crucifixes, and kitsch plaster statues in pink and orange. Plastic Peruvian Jesus. There's a title for a painting, if only I could be bothered to pick up a brush. Morose and in mourning, I reflected on the late black rose. My pep talks to her had been fruitless. What the hell was happening to me? Where was the motivation for my art? Where was the spark? Have I burned out? Is that it? The end of my art?

Supposing inspiration and creativity walked through the door right now, sat down either side of me, bought me a drink, and just when we leave to go, in holy trinity, back to the land of the living – BANG! *Senderista* bombs have another agenda and I burn to death. Or I drop dead unexpectedly. From a virus, let's say. Here one minute, cut down the next. Just like the rose. Why is it that external influences *always* dictate the plot, despite all hopes and plans?

Bang! Bang! Bang! Whoosh! They were letting fireworks off already; some eager beaver wanting to stir up the vibe. A ripple of adrenaline surged around the square as a helicopter flew over us. I put my mask on top of my head and strolled across to a small hotel to use the toilet and get more dollars from their ATM. The receptionist was busy with a couple of huge Germans, booking them in. They smiled at me. He had a stylish camera hanging round his neck. I wondered if he bought it for an u-n-b-e-l-i-e-v-a-b-l-y low price from the internet.

I was too hot to wear the fake hair, now stuck to the bottom of my bag, so I changed into a fresh top and tied a bandana scarf round my head, mindful that the car might be spotted and picked up. Anonymity, always loved her. Cloak of darkness. Wigs. Disguises. Always want the option of not being me. I was so chimerical with my looks that on two occasions, even Ant hadn't recognised me. "Shifting Sands" he'd nicknamed me.

The Germans were ushered upstairs. They had booked in advance and wanted hot water immediately. I tripped back out to the street, intending to return to the little bar, but was swept along by a band of cacophonous brass instrumentalists with costumed locals: lions, dragons, yellow-faced birds, hook-nosed harridans.

I couldn't contra-flow in this mosh-pit of bodies. To get back to the bar, I would have to swing with the rhythm until I had half-circled the Plaza. At the current pace, it would take twenty minutes. The helicopter swung back over the square. Every eye looked upward as it thumped the air. I was giddy with paranoia, but I swirled and clapped, determined to try and forget the valley, the rose. I tried hard to marvel at the creativity and to feel delight that others could so easily express it.

Extricating myself and re-entering the bar, I saw that Anthony had returned. He was telling his life story to an amused barman, mission a success, I gathered. He turned to greet me, a completely different person than had left.

"I've got a surprise, Syb. Come over here."

I followed him to a window seat. He pulled out a packet of grey powder and poured it into an orange drink he'd been holding.

"Check this out!" He offered me the glass. "It's mescaline. Got it from the dude setting up the fireworks. He's out of his box already. He's from Cusco. He sells grass too, so we can cruise down later. Quick, I want you to come up the same time as me." He grinned widely.

"You'll be painting after this, sis. It will blast away your block, baby. I absolutely guarantee it!"

Aha! As much as I dislike cocaine, I never could resist psychedelics. Whatever chaotic reelings may now proceed, I'd consider them a refuge: a chance to be diverted from my melancholy; from the carbon image of the rose I nearly died to possess; from the disintegration of my brother; from the sorrow of my past; from the emptiness of my future.

I'd tripped with Ant before and he was the best of company, and frankly, what was there left to stay straight for? Besides, if it was good enough for Juanita the Ice Maiden, it was good enough for me. Who knows? I might even die an honourable death: *Capacocha* – chosen for the Gods.

I raised the glass for a toast to nihilism – and drank the lot.

33 PROPELLER POLITICS

Gerry Kovaks wheeled the 'copter to the left, looking down at the revellers filling the tiny village square. He scooped low over the surrounding *chakras* then swung downwards toward the jungle. There, he hovered, relaying the news to his commander:

"Whirlwind to Orange Devil. Come in Orange Devil – copy?"

"Come in, Whirlwind, we hear ya' – copy?"

"Jeez, it's real windy up here, sir; getting a little bumpy. You were right. Mission Orange Squash sure stirred 'em up. They're massin' by the Bolivian border. Looks like a big time posse of *cocaleros*. Placards; donkeys; horses. Must be about two thousand of 'em. There's some kind of festival up here too, over the hill. But those folks just seem to be dancin'. May turn ugly, though, if they join up with the head-bangers, three miles down a-ways. Copy."

"Copy that, Whirlwind. Stay on it. Sheridan needs all the information, as up to date as you can get it. If there's trouble, we have to be the first to know; can't wait for the Peruvians to keep on top of it. Circle till you need more gas then go up a second time. Sheridan has to talk to the White House today, so make sure you keep me informed of any changes. Copy?"

"Copy that, Orange Devil."

"We might need you in Arequipa later. There's a gang of *cocaleros* down here makin' a big noise at the central *Municipalidad*. Might turn even uglier. Call every hour and report. Orange Devil over and out."

The 'copter scooped downwards and to the right. Within moments, the information from Kovaks' little bird was sent by encrypted text through the datasphere to the bigger eagle.

Wayne Sheridan was urinating when the call from Washington came through to the American Embassy in Lima. Now back in the capital, he rushed into the room with his fly agape as the secretary handed him the phone.

"Good afternoon, Mr. President," he wheezed.

"Howdy, Wayne. Schwab tells me you're doin' a great job down there on Project Phoenix with those cawfee plants."

Sheridan cleared his throat.

"Well, yes sir, there's real progress. They've got two great little varieties goin' here with increased yields. They'll make the people a lot of money, sir. Once they get the markets for this, the coca farmers will change their crop. There's a little unrest up in the coca fields because of Mission Orange Squash, sir, but nothing the authorities can't handle."

"What's the timeline? How soon will they plant them all up?"

"Next month, sir; they've hundreds of thousands of plants in the lab ready to go. Millions maybe."

"Can I have your assurance on this, Wayne? Nothin's gonna get in the way of those cawfee plants bein' ready? I know those Latinos. Everything is so *mañana* down there."

"It's looking good, Mr. President. I'm just waiting for the final figures from the lab. I'll send it all through. The pests and diseases are going…" He was cut short.

"We don't want any comeback from the green lobby on this, Wayne. These flies 'n stuff they're lettin' go, we may not be goin' with that one just yet. You understand me? Causes too many problems right now. Congress isn't good with science. Schwab's right, nobody likes bugs. All they need to know about is the cawfee."

"Sir, the bugs are a big part of it. If we leave them out, we might be looking at years before the farmers choose the new crop voluntarily. The bugs will wipe out the coca crop and leave them with no alternative but our cawfee."

"Go with the cawfee; stall the bugs, Wayne."

"We'll have to revise the projections then, sir."

"This is a guaranteed success, isn't it? Are your boys gonna come good on everything we're planning?"

The Drug Tsar gulped. This was the question that put his balls on the line and justified his massive salary. Used to changing goal posts from his time in the CIA, Sheridan still couldn't stop frustration strangling his voice just a little.

"Yes, sir, yes, well, on that you can be assured, Mr. President. Project Phoenix will deliver. We'll beat this cocaine trade, sir. This will be a real victory for the administration."

"We're countin' on ya!"

The phone went dead. The few moments of the president's time allotted to him had expired. The secretary came back on the line.

"Your report arrived this morning, Mr. Sheridan, but if there is any new data we would like to hear it immediately. The president has an important speech tomorrow on government drugs policy, as you know, so anything we need to hear, send it through the usual channels."

Call ended, Sheridan zipped up his fly and pulled out a pinging mobile phone from his inner breast pocket. He unlocked it and checked his texts. The first one of the morning had borne the message: '*Mission Orange Squash 100% success,*' sent from Kovaks, reporting the progress in Dioxin valley. The second was the update on the rally; an assessment of numbers, arms and men.

The latest text simply said: 'Call the sevens'.

34 THE WHITENESS

Forty minutes after we took the mescal, our eyes were misting and our throats began to dry. As I sunk down once again on the Andean turf, high above the normal line of consciousness, my mind flipped a thousand images, threading cold terror through sensuous beauty. Synapses stormed and crackled their impulses inside my skull. I'd been here before and knew the routine. Nausea; ringing in my ears; blurred vision. Why were some images sexual? And why, wreathed into the scramble, was there a progressive smell of burning? Where was I? In what place? And with what sense of knowing?

Oh. I'm starting to glow. My flesh is a dress, it drips like a waxen doll. The flame is my hair.

"Are we nearly there?" I ask Anthony.

"Yes, we are."

Streamers; streaming nose. The heat; the sponginess of my skin. Cow shit and jacaranda; toxic snowdrops; burning alpaca kebabs. Conical mass; smashed skull; monkeys in suits. Why's thar still apes around? Melted ketchup where the earth met the sky. Burning breath; foggy *crunch. Thunder. Heartbeat. Thunder.*

Colour. Colour. My relationship to it. My manipulation of it. Whoa! Here it comes, here it comes… cascading colour, disorientating and deranging me. Yellow light, yellow eye, yellow root, bag of lemons, golden boy, stolen gold, silver hair, green soldier, blue eyes, black dog. Scarlet edge, crimson flag, bruised maroon, nut brown skin. Cream sheets, white man, white powder, white knuckle ride, white balaclavas. Orange soil. Grey powder. Orange drink. Grey future. Orange dream…

M e s c a l i n e.

Peru replayed prismatic. An aura of colours fluttered around me… symphonic; flirtatious; provocative. These gorgeous, resonating frequencies teased me all the way to the altar: to marry my love of light's divisions back to my ability to use them. But, like a perfumed jilt, the dancing rainbow denied consummation, stifling my will to pick up a brush by the intimidating weight of its beauty.

I was glossy-eyed, gluey-nosed and giggling at the crowd. Time to play verbal tennis with Mr. Anthony.

"There's a lot of jiggery-pokery here today, Colonel."

"I should say so, Madam. A painted trollop such as yourself should keep off the streets."

"Might I take your arm, sir, whilst we venture forth?"

"Take both! And my bloody legs! They were never any good to me after Cullodden."

We start convulsing. What would normally engender a small chortle is now precipitating a physical tic, impossible to stop creasing up as both our stomach and spine jerk in comic spasms. We entered the throng in very merry spirits.

"Hey, *caballero*! Where can I get the Clapham omnibus?" Ant threw his hands out to a conquista-clone in a stitched, white mask.

"Geronimo!" I shrieked at him: "The devil damn thee black thou cream-face loon!"

The startled *cholo* gave my Shakespeare a wide berth. I thought it best to put the masks on now and handed one to Ant, pulling mine firmly over my face.

"Yellow-hair-wait-many-moons-for-firewater," I intoned, in Hollywood-style Native American-speak, pointing at Ant's blond halo.

We were treading a thin line between non-politically-correct humour and racism. I started braying with laughter like a demented donkey while trying to drag the trip in another direction, but I didn't quite succeed.

"Brunhilde," I yelled, eyeing the Germans on the periphery.

"*Who?*" Ant grinned, his antennae following the direction of my thumb as I jerked it to the right.

"Brunhilde," I said. "From *The Love Club*." He spotted the bosomy German and her boyfriend towering over the locals and cottoned on in a flash, instinctively understanding my humour.

"With Herrrrman, no less!" he said, peering over the mask, squinting through an invisible monocle, "Enjoying ze day out." He started goose-stepping, with his hand in a Nazi salute. We were becoming unmanageable and boisterous, but two masked women interrupted our puerile humour.

Like glittering birds, they wheeled and twirled in sequinned skirts and danced with us, while a band member blasted a huge white euphonium in my ear. The masks worn by this troupe were almost faceless; just the barest features of their conquerors. It was as if the natives had tried to de-humanise the Spanish, the way they themselves had once been reduced to mere chattels.

The bell was ringing in the white church tower and the frequencies had melted into the pipe, drum and folk music. It sounded like the instruments were revolving in a washing machine, flapping and flanging like a wonky wheel, the aural equivalent of a doubly-exposed photograph. My breasts felt tingly and my nipples were erect. Gentle fingers I invest – set fire to her velvet dress and burn her black to nothingness.

The dancing folded in and out, fan-like and frenetic. Faces in the crowd popped out at us, hideous cartoons, like illustrations by Maxon Crumb. I was hot. My mouth was very dry. Ant had his arms round both women and was kicking his legs out, singing, as he drifted farther from me. A dancer flitted close, wearing an intricately woven shawl. Each stitch was separated by a space in time, which had slowed down again so I could absorb the detail.

The angle of my head must have been childlike under the mask, because the dancer reached out and laid her hand on my bandana scarf. It was a mother's touch. She was the Madonna, the spirit of eternal motherhood, mother earth, *Pachamama*, unabashed to give that side of herself, which came so naturally. It moved me beyond measure, her lack of reserve, her intuition that a child such as I am would respond. Something in this mescal cactus affected the part of me that could elicit such a caring response. Certainly, I could never get it from my own mother, though no love was greater than hers for Ant.

I began to feel humility and oneness with these people, protected like a foetus. All sensation and no rationale. I started clip-clopping, the way little girls do when they pretend to ride an imaginary horse. Strangely, this rhythm attuned me to the crowd and I was swept forward and around the square, meeting up again with Ant, who had grabbed a bottle and was taking a huge gulp. Putting my hand out for some, I could see him sweating profusely. I held his arm. He sounded breathless.

"I'm bloody thirsty, sis."

We looked round for a drink stall and spied the Germans sporting a bottle of beer each.

"Follow the Krauts!" instructed Ant, and we pushed our way through the Peruvians to an open-fronted shop at the side of the square. The woman wanted a ridiculous price for her beer because we were *wiroqocha.*

"*No seas pendeja*!" Ant exclaimed, insulting the shopkeeper in hilarious street-speak. Everybody burst out laughing… except the Germans, who looked on, bewildered. We were slotting in far better than they. Loose. Slack. Slobbering. Ant successfully bought the beer cheaper, toasting the woman's health with more ribald slang. Her friends all screamed and giggled, opening like little flowers around him.

The Germans were younger than they appeared from a distance. Straight-laced, but not without a twinkle in the eye. Herman sidled over and lifted his camera. A large hand came down on my shoulder and a deep voice boomed: "You are English, yes?"

"No," a voice interrupted, "Norveejan."

It was Ant, who looks like a Viking with his high cheekbones and flaxen hair.

"*Sprechen Sie Deutsch*?" piped up Brunhilde.

"Yah, yah," Ant said, not speaking a bloody word.

In fluent German, Herman introduces himself as Dieter and his girlfriend as a most un-German-sounding 'Sue'. She is holding a festival brochure. I fall over laughing, choking on beer, but straighten to say:

"How doooo yooo doooo, Soooooo. Are yooo perooosing Peroooo?"

Dieter sussed. "Ah! You *are* English, yes?"

I nod, ending the game. Ant lifts his mask off. His eyes look like crested balls of lava.

"Are you liking ze show?" Deiter asks us, determined not to be put off.

"Yes," we both reply, rather meekly. The mescaline trip is about to peak and it's getting very, very hectic now. Heart rate up; sounds and colours intense; a weird rushing sound as if we are near water. Deiter is at least six-foot five and my head can't look up at that angle any more. I hold hands with my brother as strange chemistry struggles to right itself, deep in our brains. We are moving in blurred motion. Fogged.

The dancing party has enveloped us again and we're off, this time in a stoitering reel with a flushed Dieter and Sue. When we come to rest, Dieter hands Ant his camera. Ant examines it and turns it over in his hands, trying to draw some sensible conclusions.

"Vy didn't choo bring a camera?" Sue asks me.

"She doesn't believe in them," retorts my brother. "Thinks they make the eye and memory lazy, don't you, sis? Anyway, she's tetrochromatic. Cameras can't capture the colour she sees."

"Iz very goot, very cheap. I bought it from ze internet," Deiter gasps between the squashed *cholos* no taller than his belt.

That's it, I can take no more. All the loose ends of my life are joining up. Both Ant and I are now speechless, staggering to the pavement as the mayhem whirls around us. We fall, shambling and chaotic, into a paper-hattish logic.

Here comes, here comes – Wooah! – Pedro pokes a pipe of piggy pepper in a bull screen smoke shit. And where there's brass there's a monkey found dead in the boot of a Ford Fiesta. Chocolate melted in volcanic sulphur, available now at an off-licence in the Kilburn High Road. Of course, he's never been the same since he smoked that shag-pile carpet uncle Stan brought back from Egypt after the war. Where's Bob Marley when you need him? All on his Todd. He ain't got the keys to the inner orifice. It's a banger, throwing bangers. Gangbanger. Head-banger. Freshly spiked and poisonin' the whole world. Gun in the glove compartment. Chiropractor from Muswell Hell. Smokes like a vampire. Smiles like a cuckoo. White gloves in the light of the sea. Are you on one, matey? Big up your chest! *Habla bario*! Tottenham massive. Unpicking the petal, all the way from infrared to ultraviolet. Tuesday. Gravel. Evie! Evie! Where are you?

I lurch to my feet, Inca pottery patterns and geometric shapes now wreath around my vision. I am standing next to three llamas with ear decorations made from wool. Here's my chance to pet them. I move in on the animals finding the closest to be a white, fluffy alpaca who is noisily defecating. Déjà doo-doo. They're the same creatures I saw in the valley, I was certain. I recognised the ear tags. Lollipop gaudy. Their owner was dressed in white, coloured ribbons streaming from her hat. I asked the names of the animals.

"P a m e l aaaaa. Jeremeeee. Wilburrrrrr." Names that inferred the nineteenth century English overlords who built the infrastructure here. I am two seconds from collapsing with laughter, wondering if these names were a subversive act of mockery or a tribute, when my eyes take in new information.

Aaaaagh! I've just seen the way they've attached the tags. *Sown* into the animal's flesh at the tip of the ear. Dog's ear scarlet edge flung down screaming. Mauvism. Fauvism. Do you have a cunt? Bent and burning brush strokes; tiny tremors for white birds that ripped his face off on the lake.

Ant drags me back from near psychosis to hilarity, holding his beer bottle upside down as if it were a microphone. He is speaking with a slow, soft voice, whisper-talking as if on a BBC nature programme:

"As night ripened, the chaotic paradings continued. The drunken bands of parping brass, which had earlier spilled out of open-backed trucks from surrounding *pueblos*, were firmly entrenched in the four corners of the plaza as the *serious* drinking began." I pull the 'microphone' toward me, affecting a ridiculous voice:

"Yes, David, we are card-playing war cripples celebrating chaos. It's an eclectic mélange of euphoric paranoias. A lavish range of flavours phased in by Della Fosby, herself an exquisite corpse. Oh… it goes very slow. Your head is an egg you can hatch if you need to know…"

Ant retrieved the 'mic' and said to a nonplussed local:

"Well, you heard it here first, I and the Saviour murder together in cahoots. Mormons. Mona Lisa. Starberry Pields Pereber."

We stood together, swaying, close to a rusting oil drum full of rubbish. Ant aimed his empty beer bottle. The smashing sound made us look down sharply. At the base of the bin was a spilling plastic bag full of cotton wool and a pair of false teeth. As we leant over, the teeth seemed to move further away. My eyes became panopticons. We started screaming with laughter at the pink, gnashing dentures, then we noticed a drunk leaning against one of the bin bags, head bowed, shattered glass all around him.

"Maybe he barfed up his teeth," Ant wheezed, convulsed. "Too much tootin' an' a-tipplin'. The teeth responded by bailing out."

"Without a parachute," I spluttered.

"Hey, you – you with the rubbish bags," Ant screeched at the poor slumper, "*Recycle*!"

We looked up to see we were outside a ramshackle dental surgery. Banging on the glass, our own reflected masks looked like alien species. A man approached from within with a distinct underbite. It seems to be genetic here. So many faces with the bottom teeth pushed forward in front of the top ones. Even the llamas and most of the dogs have it.

"Physician, heal thyself!" Ant shouted. We dissolved into giggles and backed off into the vortex of bodies, the sound of helium-fuelled cackling flittering around our heads.

The Germans, who had long since given up trying to understand our addled frivolity, were now about fifty yards away, separated from the maelstrom, taking photos of the female dancers who were standing waist-high to Brunhilde and expecting tips. The smell of cash, even in this mayhem, sparked a feeding frenzy, and shoals of white balaclavas streamed towards big daddy Dieter.

We weren't the only *gringos*. There were several intrepid backpacker types, self-consciously trying to mingle in the name of good international relations, but the masked hordes seemed to always pick on us. We were easily absorbed again and toasted from circle to circle of *calientito*-swigging dancers. The warm, aniseed drink, cheap and potent, was sold from handcarts on every corner. It smoothed the edges of the mescaline, now subsiding into a comfortable flow.

The white clock tower showed how a seeming twenty minutes had been three and a half hours. Ant had scored coke from the barman, so my energy was reinforced by the pinches of white snuff
I had submitted to in an attempt to straighten out and keep *soroche* from spoiling the fun. Then we heard Dieter yelp. Someone had yanked the camera out of his hand, offering to take a photo of him and his *frau*. It was a man in a mask like Mr. Punch, with a huge penis for a nose.

“Maybe he’d like a glass of orange?” Ant cocked his head in their general direction.

“No! Ant, *please*. This isn’t a black and white war film. They’re not the enemy.”

“Spike the Krauts! Spike the Krauts!” he chanted.

However loathsome the Nazis, the sins of fathers and grandfathers should not be visited upon their progeny, and innocent German tourists should *not* have Mickey Finn mescaline slipped into their drinks.

– Or *should* they?

35 TRES CRUCES

As midnight passed, Ant persuaded a local policeman to take us to the Tres Cruces, about three hours away, to watch the dawn rise. Here, the sun and moon's coronas are polarised in strange mists as double and triple halos. Having read about the colours in the tour guide, back in the Cusco hotel, I was determined to see it, even if we were still having weird optical distortions of our own. Besides, without the rose or more mescal, I was desperate for a diversion.

Upward, to the edge of the Amazon jungle, we clanked and jerked in a battered truck towards the Valley of Smoke. Ant immediately bonded with the policeman by offering him, along with my $50, cocaine-laced cigarettes: *diabolitos*, whilst swigging from yet another bottle of rum. We were riveted by señor Bernardo's stories of the terrorists and *cocaleros*. He rolled his bloodshot eyes and reminded us that coca was cursed for the white man, whilst toking on *diabolito* number three with Ant. They started singing English pop songs.

It was the worst ride of my life. Again, one false move by the driver and we would be tipped hundreds of metres down the cliff. What the officer hadn't told us was that the road is open on alternate days to one-way traffic so, in the pitch black, we were going to Tres Cruces at the time allotted for everyone to go out. Emboldened by the fifty though, he felt it was worth the risk, even though it was past the midnight deadline. The danger only became evident when we encountered an irate driver going the opposite way, forcing us to reverse to let him pass on the edge of the abyss.

The truck headlights illuminated the spiny leaves of huge plants that covered the ridges in the mountainside, a type of prehistoric-looking bromeliad. Their flower spikes thrust a ten-metre lance into the air, the thickness of a small telegraph pole, laden with racemes of twenty thousand tiny yellow flowers. The fragrance was subtle, but distinct. As smokers, I doubted my brother or Bernardo were aware of such sensuous beckoning, drifting to us on the night breeze. I drew the scent to their attention and decided to use this as an excuse to talk about plants. About *roses*.

Señor Bernardo knew a great deal about the local plants, particularly the cosmic flora: ones that had curative properties and were used by the *bruhas,* local witches, and the *curanderos,* the herbal healers. Fascinating though this information was, I persisted. Were there any roses? Any very dark roses? Oh, to hell with it! Any *black* roses?

"Or any more cocaine?" my brother interjected, nudging Bernardo and laughing. The policeman looked angry and immediately began speaking in his native Qqechua. I recognised the words, since it was almost the only Qqechua I knew, and had memorised it from my travel book: Atahualpa's curse. I joined in, stumbling, all the way through. He was stunned to silence as I continued, flailing my arms for dramatic effect.

Eyeing me with considerably more respect than before, Bernardo did not even ask how I came to learn the curse. He'd obviously never been on a thirteen-hour flight with an earnest Swede with only a book as a distraction and then had to sit for eight hours at Lima airport waiting for the Arequipa plane. Fortunately, a bemused Peruvian student with whom I'd been waiting in the departure lounge had taught me some of the Qqechua pronunciation. Bernado cleared his throat, and turning to me without meeting my eyes, said in very clear Spanish:

"Yes, there are many beautiful flowers in Peru. Many roses. All varieties and colours."

"But are there any *black* roses?" I asked again, slowly and deliberately, "*rosas negras*?"

There was a silence for almost half a minute, punctuated with a phrase that sounded awfully like "*sikita muchay*". Qqechua for "kiss my arse", the only other bit of the language I recognised, having learned it from Ant via Ernesto. I repeated the question for the third time, saying I'd read that there was a black Peruvian rose.

"I have never seen one."

"Yes, but do you know anyone who has?"

"If God means you to see her, you will see her," he said. Then he flatly refused to say another word, except to make it clear he could get me a rose of any other colour I wished, at a very reasonable price. I wanted to strangle him. Ant hissed:

"Don't hussle. If he could make a buck out of it, sis, he'd take you to it right now."

The drive, though bone-shaking in the extreme, was well worth it. Such a strange refraction of light occurs at Tres Cruces. It was amazing. But as we were still jittering on the edge of psychedelia, we couldn't be certain if what we saw was drug-induced. The dawn light was lilac and yellow, fading out to grey, but ringed with orange and encircled by a weird lavender mist.

It appeared as if there were two suns rising, one triangulated and a boiling molten red. There was a sinking moon on the far horizon, also reflected in the cloud forest below us. I felt as if I were a character on the book jacket of a lurid sci-fi novel, clutching the arm of my muscular brother, staring up under the title:

'THEY CAME TO NEW WORLDS'.

We were the only *gringos* who had arrived in an open-top truck rather than on a tour bus, so the natives who knew Bernardo came out to stare. Once they realised that the return trip had been paid for, they all hitched a free ride back. The truck was full to bursting with toothless locals too preoccupied with Ant to look much at me. When they did speak, all they wanted to know was, did I have any children?

I was asked this question at least once a day, every day, since I'd been in Peru. They could not believe that a woman would reject motherhood, having few role models of women choosing other options, and their reaction to my negative varied from bewilderment to aggression. I could have made light of it, but I was sick of platitudes. Combative, confrontational me. I pointed out with great glee that since women had chosen to use the pill in Italy, they'd had the second lowest birth rate in Europe. Lots of hard core Catholic women *not* wanting babies.

Ant accused me of pissing on the vibe. I accused him of not using the opportunity to enlighten these *machistas* with his humour, drink and drugs. Once it was clear to all that I had no children, they had nothing to say to me. I asked every one of them if they knew of a black rose, but only drew blank stares, so I continued scanning the hedgerows, determined not to fall for my standard emotional trap, the one I learned at mother's knee – trying to make people that I don't like, like me.

Bernardo furnished Ant with a three-stringed acoustic guitar from one of the men. My brother twanged the strange half chords with amazing harmonic talent, as Bernardo tried to sing Beatles' songs, "*Hey Chood*", "*Starberry Pields Pereber*" and "*All Joo Nid is Luf*". The strays we had picked up swayed and clapped, delighted to be in the company of a *gringo* such as this. Liquid music flowed between them all like an emotional emollient, lubricating friendship, openness and warmth. But when I sang with them, they would not connect with me. They wouldn't even make further eye contact, save for a handsome lad of about eighteen who thought he'd try his luck. I was almost flattered until I remembered that, at that age, young boys will mount anything that has a pulse.

The truck was dirty, so I pulled some crumpled paper over to sit on and was staggered to find it was a two-week old copy of the British newspaper, The Observer, Review section. What the hell was it doing here? I tried to ask Señor Bernardo, but he was leading a rendition of the Rolling Stones' *Paint it Black*, of all things, so I kept quiet, irony rusting my ears.

In the dawn light, I strained to see the muddy print through the torn paper, making out a painting by Roddy Marks. It jolted me back to the life I had left in London. The journalist had mentioned me collectively with six other British artists, calling us "The Millennium School", saying that Roddy Marks was the leading light of "New Purism", whatever that meant! I was instantly furious, hating to be grouped with others. The very last sentence said that: "*Sybil Sands' output had slowed,*" as I was said to be having a "*personality crisis*", and had been missing from the London art scene for some time. "*It seems a shame that such talent should be so short-lived,*" some little shit had written.

Exhausted from the sensory overload, I slept. And time ran its ring, around everything. I woke with a jolt.

"Are we nearly there?" I asked Ant.

"Yes, we are. We're back at Paucartambo."

Bernardo was clutching at Ant, and trying to get him to visit his family home. A tug-of-war ensued, with me as the opposing force. I won. Ant was very drunk and became really aggressive, staggering back to the car with me, complaining that I liked to spoil all his fun.

He was in no state to drive to the Cusco road, so, as I filled up from our cans of petrol, he hung out of the passenger window shouting endearments in bad Spanish to the equally drunken policeman, tearfully waving us goodbye. Had it been genuine affection and the possibility of lasting friendship, I would have encouraged it, but, like so many of my brother's bondings, the memory would fade as the drugs wore off, until mention of it only brought the response, "*Who?*"

Countless times he'd brought back business cards from his cocaine socialising, enthusiastically telling me how important a contact he'd made. The following day, said card would be torn up to make filter roaches when smoking a joint, and when I asked him if he'd recorded the number, he'd croak:

"What number?" as he inhaled through it.

36 A COWBOY CONFESSES

The weather had turned windy and rainy. I couldn't face my brother's erratic driving, so he slept while I took the wheel for six hours till I was too tired to continue. I woke him and suggested we abandon the car in Cusco and take the plane home. He could only be persuaded by our usual carrot and stick relationship. I reminded him that we had to be back in time for his concerts. He realised his wages could be spent on cocaine, so he relented.

We took the car to a side road and parked it, grabbing a taxi to the airport. Ant complained bitterly. Had I waited to involve Maica to fence the stolen vehicle, he said, we could have made big money. It reminded me to telephone the duplicitous little *cholo,* but the bloody number was still showing as unobtainable.

As we arrived at the check-in, a crowd of disgruntled passengers was harassing the ground staff. All planes cancelled due to storms over the Andes. Next flight six in the morning, weather permitting. No option then, back out to the cab rank and back to the car. We revolved through the airport door, immediately recognising the bandy man in a checked shirt approaching us carrying a hold-all.

"Todd Whale!" Ant waved. Todd cringed, embarrassed to be spotted by two wasted-looking Brits.

"Hey! Todd! You stuck here?"

"Yeah. Goddam pussies 'r' frightened t' fly a plane in a few clouds 'n' rain," he snarled, anxious we should be reminded of his fearlessness with all things mechanical. Todd had work in Arequipa the following day, he told us. Ant commiserated, mentioning his concerts.

"We'll give you a lift in our car if you like," he offered, forgetting that it meant at least one more witness to our theft. Todd was compromised and jittery. So was I.

"Why d'ya' wanna' tek the plane fer, if you've got wheels?" he asked, removing his sunglasses and peering at Ant.

"I paid for Ant to return by plane to be in time for the concerts," I lied, "while I was going to drive back."

"You drive?" he said, uneasy that a woman might be in control.

"She's a better driver than I am, Todd," Ant said.

"Bet that don' mean much," replied the cowboy.

"You can run behind if you like, Todd." I smiled.

"Or, we could strap you to the roof," added Ant.

Todd relented, asking first why I hadn't brought the car to the airport.

"Some idiot blocked me in, so we grabbed a quick cab. Ant didn't want to miss the plane." Oh, the little lies we tell others, saving the big ones for ourselves.

"Where d'ya get the four-wheeler? Is it a rental?" he asked, as we drew up and I paid the taxi.

"Yes," we both said, a little too quickly.

"I need the bathroom," Todd declared, limping up the street to the *Servicios Higénicos Públicos*, probably shitting himself at the thought of my driving.

Ant was perky, and murderously hungry, loading up with beers, *empanadas* and chocolate. He had taken the money I gave him and scored more coke. When we were alone, I reminded him it would be wise not to toot in front of Todd. I started to repeat the details of what had happened in the hotel, knowing my brother would have already forgotten them.

It refreshed his curiosity, and he resolved to get as many beers as possible into Todd to lubricate the truth. I thought a tactic best serving this purpose was to pretend to sleep for the first couple of hours, 'waking' only if Ant were unsuccessful in gleaning the information. Ant, who has the persuasive power to make even the Pope smoke dope, was cracking open the first can of verbal laxative as we set off at speed toward Arequipa. Fresh cocaine and a few hours' sleep had revived his energies and driving skills.

There was a faint moon shining through a cloudy night sky as we left the lush valley and headed up Lake Titicaca road. I sank down in the back seat and strained my ears to hear their conversation.

"So, Todd, what d'you think of Peru?" was Ant's opening gambit.

"Hate the goddamn place," spat the reply. "Wouldn'a come here if it weren't fer Laura; wouldn'a be leavin' if it weren't fer her, neither."

"Things not working out?"

"Well, everythin's fine with me, but she kin't leave that stuff alone," he said, presuming Ant knew he meant coke. "Liquor, ah'd have no problem. Hell, everyone teks a drink." He took a pull on his can. "Jeez, y'know, she's inta' snortin', an' ah jis' hate what it does to her. Don' tek care o' herself n'more. Ain't looking after her teeth; her breath's all bad, just like her goddamn temper. Makes her goddamn crazy."

"What, violent?"

"Hell, yeah! When she kin't get it, she gits ornery; mouth all twitches down weird an' she trashes the place, screamin', beatin' up on me. Threw a jug at me yesterday, jist 'cuz she didn't like taste of the the fresh lemonade I made."

Hello! Where have I seen tantrums like that before? From pretend sleep, I deeply empathised with the cowboy.

"Was she like that in the States?"

"Nope. She never even drank much. Hates t'bacca. Hates weed. It's only since she come down here messin' about with the wrong comp'ny." At the mention of weed, Ant pulled a packet of grass from his pocket.

"Were you together in the States for a long time?"

"Yup, she's mah heart. T'gether six years. Never loved a gal like I love Laura, but she gits this notion in her head she don' wanna be in America n'more payin' taxes to a bunch of government jerks. Sure agree with her on that."

"Speaking of weed, can you skin one up for me, Todd?"

"Ah don' use it n'mores. Needs a clear head these days."

"Sure, but can you roll me one? Or you can drive while I roll."

Knowing that Todd's impaired eyesight made him a dangerous liability, I stiffen, waiting for the response. But Ant's guess is right. Keen to demonstrate his few remaining skills, Todd chose the role of roller.

"Hey, that's OK, fella," he said. "Jis keep yer eyes on the road."

They twittered on about Country and Western music. I knew Ant had no interest in it, but Todd was an aficionado. Then 'dad rock': The Eagles, Little Feat, Kenny Rogers. The names thudded into my consciousness like dull bullets. I nearly expired from boredom. It forced me to 'wake' and ask if Charlie had any Latin CDs in the car. Schlock salsa was better than this. Ant said he'd found only one but it the player couldn't play it, suggesting it was probably five-sole porno. Charlie was always boasting about his collection.

At no time did Todd show any curiosity about either of us, or ask us a single question. Conversationally in neutral territory, he was giving nothing more away. Nor would he smoke the joint he was offered. He was strictly a beer monster. The horrendous hogo from his shoes blended with the sickly stench of dope. Survival dictated I open the window, but just a fraction, as it was very cold and we were at the highest altitude of the entire journey.

Ant kept stopping, on the pretext he needed a pee, but in reality, because it gave him the privacy to take another toot of *caspa Atahualpa,* the Inca's dandruff. Then we hit the real bastard part of the road, bumping and rolling. I hoped the bloody tyres would hold.

They'd been yapping for more than two hours and still Ant hadn't asked him one direct question. This was typical. He'd been given a brief and then got too stoned to remember what it was. But one thing was for sure, he'd certainly managed to get quite a few lotions down Mr. Todd. So much so that the cowboy was professing tiredness, and slumped down as if to sleep, yawning loudly. Time to make my move.

"What were you doing in Cusco?" I asked him. I'd clearly instructed Ant not to ask this before I did.

"Er, er, sightseeing," Todd stammered.

"On your own? Or was Stan Fischer showing you around? His girlfriend's from Cusco. He bought her a house there."

I tried to sound wide-eyed... innocent; but when it comes to getting information I'm terrier/rabbit tenacious.

"That son of a bitch? *No*."

"Don't you like Stan?" I asked, knowing that Stan loathed him.

"He's the worst type of livin' slime that ever crawled on this planet, missy, an' that's the truth."

I was tempted to say: "What? Even worse than us Briddish?" but somehow I held myself back.

"Does he give you a hard time at work?" Maybe I could cajole more information with pretend concern.

"Don' ever speak to 'im."

OK, I wasn't going to get anywhere with that.

"Ah'm gonna get me some sleep now," he said, shrinking down into himself, as if to put a full stop to our conversation.

But as Todd Whale tried to slip the line and plummet to the depths, he was about to be properly harpooned.

"I can get you the key to the inner office," I said. He visibly rippled.

"*'Scuse me?*"

With no rose and no reason, I had nothing to lose by being agent provocateur. I repeated myself, leaning over towards his left ear. In the mirror, my brother quietly watched me do what I do so well: confront; discuss; commiserate; *plan*.

By the time we reached the outskirts of the White City, the racist cowboy had accepted he was going to need us 'Briddish', after all.

37 THE CEMETERY

My nerves were in knots by the time we reached Arequipa. Not because of the frightening new information from Todd, or the effects of our bingeing. Here we were at ten-thirty in the morning, in full view of Arequipa's citizens, driving a stolen vehicle. I'd hoped we could return the car before daylight. There was still the sound of helicopters overhead, and paranoia, previously tapping me on the shoulder, was now digging me sharply in the ribs.

Ant dropped us at the corner of the main road and zoomed off to return the car. Todd hailed a cab and departed. I'd made my brother solemnly promise not to breathe a word about the theft to anyone, especially Diego. But Charlie would know his car had been used because when I saw Ant drive away, I was astonished at the amount of mud on the vehicle.

My paranoia, now mixed with hunger, equalled nausea. A ceviche breakfast settled me somewhat, but when I came to pay for it, I realised just how much money I'd spent on Ant's habit. My wallet was all but empty. As I walked up to our apartment, Ant's drummer, was sitting on our step, waving at me. He was expecting to go to a rehearsal with Ant.

"*Donde está Anthony?*" Victor asked, eyeballs swimming. He was obviously drunk.

"He's coming in ten minutes," I said, but he was more than two hours. Diego had no cocaine, of course; Maica was still absent, so my brother was obliged to look elsewhere for fresh supplies.

Inviting Victor in to the apartment, I was immediately struck by the smell of burning. I couldn't even make a cup of tea. The electricity was still off, the fridge defrosting and dripping onto the floor. The drummer thought the cremated kitchen hilarious, laughing and reeling from side to side. Piqued by his lack of manners, it took all my understanding to absolve him, reminding myself he could have no sense that I was still half-crazed by grief; that to me, the kitchen was a crematorium. We had to find another apartment *fast*. I handed Victor the matted wig from my bag and left him giggling in the morning sun wearing it. I put the charred rose in a bin liner and started to pack.

Victor was a *pituco*, very pale skin, Spanish looks. A Mummy's boy, like Diego. Like Ant. He was funny and wild, which endeared him to my brother. But, like many sons who have been the apple of their mother's eye, he had an indefatigable belief in his own importance.

A fervent right-wing Catholic, Victor thought that Pope John Paul had single-handedly vanquished Communism in Russia and Eastern Europe. He had a T-shirt with the old Pope on it, which I tried to buy from him for my arty, ironic wardrobe, but he wouldn't part with it.

"We have a concert at two o'clock," he said lurching from left to right and throwing the wig down, "and at seven tonight, and one tomorrow. Good money!" Many of Ant's concerts were for the opening of new clubs and bars; most, if not all, funded by the product that inspired him to play.

Ant duly arrived, animated, unshaven, and ready for anything, but after so little sleep and a gutful of mescaline, dope, drink and cocaine, he looked like hell. As did I: crumpled, pink and puffy. He had a quick wash in cold water and changed his clothes.

He told me, out of Victor's earshot, that he'd parked the muddy four-by-four outside Charlie's house by mistake, forgetting that we'd found it several streets away, then added, laughing:

"That will confuse the bastard!"

"Oh God, Ant. He'll suspect something."

"What can he prove?" Ant shrugged. "And by the way, I kept the key… just in case we fancy another trip." He smiled. "Where's the gig again? Remind me." He grabbed his guitar.

"Victor said it's an inauguration of a new bar in town, but you may not have enough time to sound check, bro'."

We caught a taxi to the venue, but Victor informed the driver to take a detour via the city cemetery, fifteen minutes from the centre. He was insistent that we spent 'ten minutes' at the grave of his grandfather, before going on to the gig. We couldn't dissuade him, and since Ant needed him for the concert he decided to indulge him. But the visit would last almost two hours, thanks to elastic *'tiempo Peruano'*.

We stood in front of the cemetery gates as Victor paid the taxi.

"How come our culture can talk about sex and bodily functions, but not about death?" I asked Ant. "We don't even see the body. It's so quickly dispatched from hospital to morgue to crematorium or cemetery."

"Who wants to look at a fucking corpse? No one wants to contemplate death, before or after the event," he snapped.

But Anthony, in his numbed condition, is forgetting that only twenty-six months ago we both stood together at another cemetery. He forgets what is motivating my question. He shows not one sign of empathy or care. He does not squeeze my arm; neither does he hold my hand; nor does he seem to remember that the body of Eve, my lover of five years, had been burned in a grey, Hampshire crematorium on a sunny day just like this. And we had both crunched on the gravel, snivelling, back to the car; back to my empty, aching future. I was refused her ashes, or any part of them, subsequently scattered by her family on her granny's grave.

"I'm sorry, but we couldn't save her," a distant voice had said.

I'd cried until I was stupefied with sorrow, a remote observer in the film of my own life. My love had been snatched out from under me and I was desperate; railing against the abyss; trapped like a rat and trying to run – anywhere, everywhere, away from the flames of death's combustion.

But cold truth had acted as midwife. My bereavement was born at that moment and delivered up to me, wrapped inside a great, dull aching. Like a weighty, malformed child, it leant like a stone against my heart and gullet. And I'd begged time to return to the point before I possessed it. I screwed up my eyes and sobbed and begged. But time was deaf to my keening and, instead, slowed down from its bustle… so I could better savour my new, suffocating burden.

And the local paper had a quote from her teacher at the conservatoire:

'That such a talent could have been taken so suddenly by viral meningitis is a great loss. Cut down like a rose in full bloom'.

While The Times' obituary banner simply read: '*Eve Jardine, concert pianist',* and showed a picture of her beautiful face, smiling out at me. It happened so quickly. She was ill – then she was dead. Twenty-four hours. A cracking, tight head, easily silenced. Like Juanita's on the mountain; both images now entwined in all my dreams, joining the rose, the boot, the dog. She was thirty-two.

Anthony had wept with me at the funeral and never once let go of my hand. The relatives had waited to commiserate; except, of course, for Eve's father, who could never reconcile himself to his daughter's Sapphic love, and made no eye contact with me throughout, quietly heaving his shoulders with his son and wife.

Sure enough, Victor's relatives were waiting at the entrance to the burial park. A cemetery in South America bears little resemblance to those in northern Europe. The bodies are kept in family vaults or mausoleums, big marble monoliths, if you have money, that is. If not, they're piled seven high in a honeycomb matrix, one on top of another, over-ground, and sealed in white plaster.

There is a frame for photographs, names and tributes, covered by a pane of lockable glass, and metal rings for jam jars or vases to hold the flowers. Everywhere are pictures of Hollywood Jesus, handsome as any film star, with blue, blue eyes. I'd found a similar kitsch picture of Jesus among the litter when scooping sweet wrappers from Charlie's car floor. Odd. Was Charlie fervently religious on top of all his other peculiarities?

We strolled, or rather, helped Victor to stagger, down the main avenue on the way to the plot, which he had both metaphorically and literally lost. Various relatives were introduced. First, the women and girls: quiet, compliant, embarrassed to be kissing the cheek of a painted *gringa* who obviously had no business being at their remembrance day. Then the men, each of them as drunk as Victor. The egotistical, leering father; the louche of an uncle; the coke-addled brother-in-law.

I looked again at the women: their support network and facilitators, who had borne their children, made their food, constructed their lives. The men were indulgent and weak, hilariously funny, overtly sentimental and had probably loved these women with the exact same fervour they'd cheated on them.

A 'copter buzzed above us and we all looked up. The men leading the group up the avenue were all too drunk to remember exactly where poor Granddad was, even though they came here every year. Guided by a younger nephew, we finally reached the correct corridor of piled bodies. Footless and staggering, the men slowed to rest on a corner.

Out came the beers, cigarettes and two acoustic guitars. There, waiting with his wife, was Uncle Eduardo, squat and ugly, cracking his hairy knuckles. I recognised the second ape I'd seen outside Gentrex. A jut-arsed swagger-monkey in an ill-fitting suit, he was gibbering quietly to himself. It would seem Arequipa's short strings all join up into a web.

We stood in a ring, in front of the dead man, whose glass name-case they opened, while refreshing the flowers, both real and plastic. They offered up a toast with their beer. It was the anniversary, not of his death, but of his birthday, and they had come to honour him. Everyone, apart from his wife and son-in-law, had his blood running in their veins.

In the heat of the sun, and covered in little flies, amidst the smell of new and rotting flowers, of cigarettes, booze and sweat, my cynicism crumbled. One by one they sang a song for Grandpa, except for the monkey, now gibbering into his cell phone.

Ant, who fits naturally and with no self-consciousness into these scenarios, gave a rendition of '*Yesterday*' on the acoustic, and kissed the *abuela*: Victor's grandmother, wife of the deceased, who lastly sang a ballad to her fallen hero. Thank God for dark glasses. Victor kissed his fingers, and touched them against the faceplate of the grave. I looked around and away, squinting mascara and quietly sniffing.

"Eez beautiful, no?" he slurred.

The many faces of a white-skinned, blue-eyed Jesus, each as camp as the picture I'd found in Charlie's car, looked down upon me from the grave plates and cards, and suddenly, I understood. I knew that my own mourning had come to an end, that I had closure. That here, now, in this vastly different country, where magnetic fields revolve the opposite way to my birth land and the potatoes are purple – now I could let her go. Here in the cemetery, in this place of full stops, I must accept the truth. Evie – and *la Rosa Negra* – are gone for good.

Comforted though I felt, I was not having a conversion. I could not, did not, and will not believe in God. But I believed then in the desire and hope for a better future. I want to let these people know that I am not outside their experience. So I go across to Granddad, and say to his picture;

"I wish I could have known you, señor. You have a fine family."

I toast him with my beer, swaying with the drunks, because I don't know what else to say. My inability to care if I live or die won't be changed by this moment, but I can at least salute the effort made here by all of us. Though we are flawed, vain, drugged, lustful people, Victor is right. It *is* a beautiful thing to do.

I can see the reflection of Eduardo in Granddad's faceplate, still on the mobile phone, watching me. So I keep my back to them, and read the other graves, looking at photos of the dear departed, biting my lip.

Umberto Bernejo Dianderas: 24 enero 1996. Fresh carnations. Faded colour photo.

Maria Isabel Sandoz-Lazorte: Plastic flowers, doilies. "*Uniera sus vida a Dios*." Joined her life to God.

Jorge Angel Oquela Quispe: no inscription; fetid water; black flies.

Victor's cell phone rings. The gig promoter is beside himself at the lateness of the hour. We kiss everyone and leave. I try, in my white, Western way, to hug Grandma with Latin passion and sincerity, to let my body tell her that I, too, have lost my love and that I stand in solidarity with her in the face of sorrow.

Then, as we walked back down the neat rows to the main avenue, I saw it. Up and to my left, in an alcove beside the photograph of Terésa Valeria Lloque Yupanqui… in the shade.

It was no hallucination.

A black rose.

PART THREE

38 CARTER 612

It was windy outside and the swishing trees filled the dark laboratory with a soft, shushing sound. In the far corner of the room, Carter shivered and slowly looked around him.

His lips were numb and he was restless, scratching at his neck and ignoring the delicious meal in front of him. His penis was hard, had been so for an hour. Months of daily cocaine had damaged his heart and liver, but still, his sex drive was intact. Carter longed for female company, and for more cocaine.

Great interest was being shown in Carter. Money had been pledged, deals done. A small part of his brain, the *nucleus accumbens*, was a revolution – a frontier. Soon, it would be required for permanent perusal: sliced, sectioned, and pickled in a jar; the key to understanding addiction and all its complex tentacles. Carter's brain would open the door to millions, possibly billions, of dollars. But Carter knew nothing of the scheme. He wasn't to partake of the enormous wealth his test results would generate. He would not be given sanctuary or sobriety.

Deprived of females and family, Carter was doped each day and experimented on with ingenuity and invention. Some would call his treatment immoral; cold rationalists referred to it as 'necessary'. The man who plied Carter with cocaine believed the search for this knowledge was noble, regardless of the cost of gaining it. His own brain hard-wired for critical analysis, this son of science became a despot to those he imprisoned and drugged. But, in his single-mindedness, he *achieved.* He gained the information. He moved the game forward. Josef Mengele would have applauded.

Carter was most certainly advancing knowledge; in this he was a necessary participant, and though he could feel no sense of pride in his contribution, at least there was the cocaine to look forward to. Locked in, with no chance of escape, he flinched and shivered on his bed. His eyes, like small beacons in the dimness of the room, caught the dying rays of the six o'clock sun.

On the other side of the Gentrex building, Stannard Fischer handed over a paper with the words 'Project Cuca' printed at the top in large letters. Ramon Suarez studied the page.

"Are these the latest figures?"

"Yep. But we haven't been able to inhibit corticotrophin-releasing factor, or affect the melanocortin-4 receptor yet."

"But in all other ways it works, yes?"

"Yep. It's proven in all the other parameters."

Suarez continued reading. "Implanted microelectrodes in the brain of subject 612 measured all dopamine, serotonin and norepinephrine levels, including gamma-amino butyric acid and opioid peptides."

Fischer pointed to the paper.

"Subject 612 levelled off self-administration at five times the norm. The final transgenic procedure has stabilised the aggression and the breath problem."

"Give me all the data. I will write my report tonight," Suarez ordered. Fischer looked up. A facial tic thrummed at the side of his mouth.

"We have proof that *Cuca* is viable now," he said. "We can dispose of Carter with the others in the usual way. The experiments are complete."

"*Carter?* Who is Carter?"

"Er, Carter is my nickname for 612, the breakthrough subject. Y'know, the cart peptides in the brain? His levels are way beyond...."

Fischer stopped himself. He couldn't give more than the basics of science to Suarez, so he concentrated on pragmatics.

"There's several big bags of lab kill going up to the burner tomorrow morning. I'll dispose of the last experiment subjects by injection and send their bodies along with them, after I've removed the brains. We don't want any trace at the lab. We should guard against any of this falling into the hands of our competitors."

"Shouldn't we freeze the 611-612 series?" Suarez said. "We may need to refer to certain body organs after autopsy. Liver; heart; kidneys."

"For what reason?" Fischer's eyes bulged in annoyance.

"Long-term side-effects. Markets could be affected."

"The project directive is fulfilled. The human subjects show that *Cuca* works; the figures confirm it.

"Yes. Yes." Suarez had already collated the human test results from his own covert experiments, albeit without Fischer's scientific rigour. He was one step ahead, and had made his plans accordingly. Fischer was disposable now. He liked that feeling. He liked it a lot.

"Well, make sure I have the exact data, the amounts given, over what period of time and with what results. We need to anticipate future problems. I'll mention it in my report to señor Abelman."

Suarez clicked his case shut and put on his jacket – the dominant power play – to show *he* was the one to decide when the meeting was over. He deliberately spoke to Fischer as if he were in need of guidance.

"Any other questions?"

Fischer knew this game. He smiled, ignoring the bait. The air crackled as the two males faced each other. Suarez glanced at the insolent, bearded face. He had loathed Fischer from the moment he'd met him. His arrogance; his brilliance; his *luck* to have had the golden ride through Berkley and Harvard, while Suarez's talent and family money could only secure an education in Miami. But he felt himself to be the superior beast, secretly capable of far greater cunning.

"To continue at this level will require more funding. The original budget is spent," Fischer said.

Suarez seethed. The Americans and their money. *Always* their money. Controlling, bending people to their will. His jaw clenched as he tried to maintain superiority over the brilliant scientist by his diffident tone.

"The money is available to continue; you don't need to concern yourself with finance. Don't forget, this is a matter of the highest security. As long as we have the records we can repeat all the experiments. Dispose of the 612 series."

"As soon as I've removed the brains," said Fischer.

Suarez nodded agreement, picked up his case and closed the door behind him, sealing Carter's fate.

Fischer gathered his notes and replaced them in the folder. He walked swiftly down the stairs to the experiments block, and unlocked lab three.

"Hi, Carter, it's me," he said, and slid on a pair of white surgical gloves. He readied a scalpel. Walking over to subject 612, he lifted the quivering ginger guinea-pig out of his cage and cradled him in his arms, stroking him gently.

"Thank you, Carter, little buddy. I'm sorry it took so long. No one will forget what happened in your little brain, Carter, my friend, I promise. You're gonna make history."

Carter's penis went flaccid the moment he was touched. He hated being handled by humans unless it meant cocaine. Overdue his dose, he bit down on the surgical glove and leapt from the bench: skittering feet heading fast for the open door.

39 CUCKOO IN THE COCKPIT

"Head for the open door," Stan Fischer called to us as he came out of the building to our left. He pointed, waving to us through a dirty plate-glass window. Rosy spoke to a uniformed man and we were shown through a door near the baggage cart exit, out to the small plane ports at the side of the main runway. Stan approached us, smiling. The official melted away. Now that I had clues from Todd as to his Machiavellian nature, I started to search Stan's expression. The look in his eyes unseated my confidence; our nervous pilot had a definite tic at the side of his mouth.

It had been a hectic morning moving to a new apartment and we were late collecting Rosy from the Plaza Yanahuara. We'd taken a taxi out to the airport and the journey was a chance to get Ant and Rosy acquainted. Ant began by speaking in a local slang that had her laughing immediately. My brother rarely asks questions of new acquaintances. He mostly talks of himself. His opinions; his music; his adventures. It is executed with such hilarity and engagement that people without opinions or adventures of their own rarely notice.

Stan's red and white Cessna was immaculate, though now we suspected how he'd paid for it, we felt less impressed. Disregarding all social niceties, Stan launched into a tedious list of engine features: compression ratios, fuel consumption. Boys' toys stuff. We strapped in and took off. It was cramped. Stan ensconced in the cockpit and the three of us in the seats behind. Room for about eight people at a squash.

The Nazca lines, huge geoglyphs carved into the soil many hundreds of years before, would be upon us within the hour. We had to shout to be heard over the sound of the engine, but it was quieter once we were through the thin cloud at cruising altitude.

"Rocky, there's a couple of blankets at the back if you get cold," Stan said, leaning over his shoulder. *Rocky*? His pet name for her irked me.

"*Gracias*, Stan," Rocio answered, reaching for the blanket without offering to share it. Maybe she didn't trust my wandering hands, but nothing was further from my mind. I was thinking about the rose and the secret Gentrex project Todd had revealed to us, wondering how the brilliant Stan Fischer justified his corruption. It hadn't stopped me pushing *my* agenda, though. I had rushed to give him the flowerless stem of the rose as soon as I'd left the cemetery. Regardless of his villainy, I needed him.

"How's my plant doing?" I asked him. "Good?"

He inclined his head in sly acquiescence. I didn't push. I decided to wait. Before I could help Todd to steal the information he wanted via Rosy's 'borrowed' keys, I had to get the rose cells back from dear Uncle Stan, healthy and growing.

"Look at Misti! Is that steam? Ant asked. "Or is it smoking?"

Stan was handing back a bag of barley sugars as he spoke. We craned our heads to the left. The volcano's summit pushed through the cloud, which had ringed her below like a doughnut. Small white puffs coiled out of the crater. Ant asked if he, too, could smoke.

"Rather ya' didn't, old buddy," said Stan, sucking and slurping. "You need Bacban."

"What's Bacban?" I was curious. Stan didn't mention it for nothing.

"A revolution in modern medicine, developed by Stannard J Fischer, Ron Leiber and Arnold Merriman for Lifex laboratories, currently outselling all other 'Stop Smoking!' products on the market," Stan announced with comic pomposity. "They're genetically-modified tobacco cigarettes. Help you quit."

Ant offered a swig of his Cartavio rum to the twitchy pilot, who declined.

"How does it work?"

"Know how a permanent wave works in yer hair? The change of shape?" he asked.

I did. I'd had a Saturday job at a hair salon as a schoolgirl.

"Yeah, the lotion breaks the salt bonds inside the hair cuticle then the hair is bent round the rollers. Once they rinse off the first solution, they put on a second, which neutralises the ammonia and resets the bonds in the new shape."

"Clever girl! That's exactly what Bacban does, more or less. It alters the synaptic pathways inside the brain, the paths that take the nicotine into your brain's dopamine receptors. Bacban resets the nicotine in a pathway that can't take it up. I smoked for fifteen years; stopped five years ago. Used to be a forty-a-day man back then."

"Now he smokes sixty a day," quipped Ant.

We all laughed. Deflecting serious debate with humour is Anthony's stock-in-trade. It can be a useful delight in conversation but, for Ant, it's more than attention-seeking, it's fear of boredom; fear of reality; fear of committing his intellect and being held to account.

I pulled out my water bottle, to which I'd added the juice of half a lemon, it improves the taste of plastic. I had a drink and offered it to Rosy, then to Stan. He took a slug but spat the lot out in a horizontal jet.

"Jesus Christ! I thought you said it was water." He sounded furious, wiping his mouth and spitting into a tissue.

"Too bitter! Too bitter! Euk!"

I apologised for the adulteration, remembering his dislike of lemon in the restaurant whisky.

"I hear the coffee project is a success. It was on TV. Is Gentrex finished in Peru now?" I asked.

"Hell, no!"

"What are you working on then?"

"Professionally? Or personally?"

"Personally," I said, guessing that whatever he said was the new Gentrex agenda would be lies or politics.

"Paradise engineering," he answered.

"Brain chemistry? Designer drugs?"

"Yeah. And good ones. Dopamine substitutes; serotonin mimics; empathogens."

"Is it the new Soma?" my brother asked, delighted with the prospect of pharmacological playtime.

"Not exactly."

"Syb did a piece called 'Somanet' back in the 90s, didn't you, sis? Painted it under the influence of ecstasy. Sold for fucking thousands."

"Neural network stuff," I explained. "It was a collage made from MDMA pills, silicon chips and rubberised string. I made it just after ecstasy hit mainstream culture. We sat in many a bar and café back then, debating the merits and demerits of a drugged proletariat."

"I lay on many a bar and café floor; I am the drugged proletariat," laughed Ant.

"*Pills in a painting*? Weren't they illegal?"

"Not at the time. I got two hundred from a psychiatrist in Thailand and I painted over them. Sealed the work in a glass case."

I then explained Huxley's *Brave New World* to Rosy, who'd asked, bewildered: "What eez Soma?"

"It's a drug mentioned in a famous book. In the story, it was the drug that the State gave to the people to keep them calm and happy. Bit like Prozac. It raised the feel-good factor in your brain, just like ecstasy."

"Prozac makes me sweat and twitch!" Ant said.

"You sweat and twitch whatever drug you're on."

"I sweat and twitch more without them."

I faced the pilot, ignoring my brother's flippancy.

"What are you advocating, Stan? A daily cocktail of designer drugs for the masses?"

"Well, Sybil, you take pills to ease the pain of menstruation, don'cha? So, when people take pills to stop anxiety and depression, what's the difference? They're as much biological as psychological problems." He spoke louder. "I want a future of neuro-pharmacology on demand but preferably, gene therapy in-utero. No one ever needs to feel bad again. It'll be easier now the human genome is unravelled, and we can be trans-human." His mouth twitched.

"*Trans-human?*"

"Yeah. Genetically engineered by introducing cells from other organisms to correct and regulate brain disorders. No more anorexia; autism; obsessive compulsive behaviour; schizophrenia."

"Goodbye Mother Nature, and her random shuffle of our genetic pack! Soon, we'll get to choose what type of psychosis we prefer!" my brother quipped.

Fischer stayed silent. I wasn't going down this one. I wanted to stick to my mission. I'd already knew about suburban bio-hackers in their garage labs, busy tweaking Pachamama's teats and sending bits of warped genetic material through the post.

We were coming close to the Nazca lines. I hadn't known any details but I'd bought a souvenir mug with the Nazca monkey design on it, a perfect gift for Ant, whose monkey was now swinging mostly on alcohol, since Diego had run out of Maica's schnarfing powder.

"The Nasceñan peoples made the lines a thousan' jears ago." Rosy explained.

"Could've been earlier," Stan answered. "Can't carbon-date the lines. They've been repaired and redefined over the centuries."

"There are some whacky ideas why the lines were drawn. Celestial calendars, devotional walkways for the Inca shaman."

"Yeah. Ley-line markers. UFO runways." Ant continued my theme, waving his hands.

"*Mira!*" Rosy pointed and we leaned over to see huge figures and long, white, intersecting lines etched across the spreading hectares of desert plain.

"Hang on, everyone!" Stan instructed, and headed downwards to zoom in close.

"Look at that one! It's a huge hand with only four fingers."

"Yeah. Probably got them caught in the cookie jar," said the pilot.

Hmm… don't laugh too soon, Stan, old fruit, I was thinking. Ant read aloud from a guide book:

"*Figures are mainly situated on the slopes. Best known is 'The Astronaut', discovered 1982. It measures thirty-two metres. Others of the important figures are 'The Man with a Hat' and 'The Executioner'.*"

Stan zoomed up at a terrifying angle. We all strained backwards.

"I'm dying for a cigarette now!" Ant faked a shaking hand.

"Well, you're the odd one out here, Anthony, a real cuckoo in the nest. The *Cuca* in the nest, eh, Stan?" I dropped the C bomb: the Spanish name of the Gentrex conspiracy that Todd had told us about… and waited. I needed to know if Stan was all that Todd and his friends suspected. If the high priest of my rose's resurrection was himself black or white. Devil or saint. The answer seemed immediate. Stan inhaled the boiled sweet, choking. The plane slewed left. Rosy let out a scream.

"Take the controls!" Stan wheezed, coughing and spluttering. I unstrapped myself and lurched forward, across him. Rosy was pale beneath her darkness.

"Hold it straight," he croaked, as Ant handed him the Cartavio to wash down the barley sugar lodged in his throat.

It didn't take long for the pilot to be back in control and all was steady, except for Rosy's nerves. My slurring brother chirruped:

"Cuckoo! Cuckoo! I forgot you're a bird watcher, sis."

His sexual innuendo was funny, succinct and intelligent. He understands that provocation comes naturally to me. He's seen my art. My provoking of Stan amused him greatly. Nevertheless, I was certain the same tactics that had opened Todd's mouth would not work here. I hadn't expected them to. I was playing. What could Stan do? Throw us out for bad behaviour? I wanted to see him squirm. To unseat his omnipresent confidence. Our death lurch was unintentional, but nicely emphasised my point. And besides, I no longer had a functioning nervous system.

Stan searched our expressions. Ant – sloshed and smiling; me – impassive, unreadable. Mona Lisa mute. He cleared his throat and said very slowly:

"Y'know, Sybil, the cuckoo is my favourite bird. Subversive. Clever."

He was probably thinking, "*They couldn't possibly know.*"

Ant kicked my foot. Rosy saw him.

We see-sawed across the plains, taking in the spirals, trapezoids and strange, insect-like figures of the Nazca landscape. The scale of the work was breathtaking. The Nazca lines, though primitive, had great aesthetic power. I could see that several of the designs had been worked out by the same mind. I thought it was incredible for an artist's hand to have left something so beautiful for future generations. In a world full of destruction, how important a thing it is to be a creative force.

A terrible lump came to my throat.

40 TELEVISUAL TRAUMAS

Some might say that any sex is better than no sex. For me, climax is a hollow sensation when your brain does not connect to it, reduced to a sexual sneeze. Maybe it was because of the mescaline, a delayed after-effect. I'd not mentioned the Cusco trip to Rosy, nor had I betrayed Todd. Rosy knew nothing, though I'd been firing questions at her all week. Had she seen my plant at the lab? Had Stan shown it to her? Did he have a bench for private work? To my annoyance, she'd laughed, saying she'd been far too busy to ask, and besides, with thousands upon thousands of Petri dishes on the benches and trays, one group of cells looked very much like another, the only difference the numbers on their labels.

We were waiting for Ant to join us for a late lunch. He was due back from his beach concert on the three o'clock bus. Rosy switched on the local news. An item flashed up about the strike by the ENACO legal coca growers in the jungle. It was clear that their complaint was being taken seriously because of the amount of army personnel on screen. The *contradrogas* said that they needed reinforcements because, increasingly, terrorists were trying to take over the crops and poor peasant farmers were being shot at from both sides.

"Not to mention the pollution," I said aloud, which, of course, they didn't mention.

The news cut to an item about a body floating in the river. Nineteen-year-old man, believed to be homosexual. A photo flashed up. Pretty boy. He'd been shot in the back of the head after being tortured; two fingers cut off. Poor little devil.

"Who could 'av done eet? So many *maricones* are found like this 'ere." Rosy was staring at the screen.

"*Maricones*? You mean the gay boys? They regularly *murder* gay boys here? What about gay women? Have you told anyone in your family you are having a relationship with me?"

"No, of course, I would not to say it. My family would no understan'."

"How do you expect them to if you don't explain it?"

"Is no easy in Peru, Si-vil."

"It wasn't so easy in Britain years ago, but because people refused to hide and feel ashamed, there was a change of attitude. You have to wake people up and make them think. You have the right to make love to any consenting adult, no?"

Rosy looked downward, tilting her head. I could feel my anger and the desire to shake her getting the better of my compassion. I'm a warrior. Everyone who avoids the fight for justice is marked yellow in my book. It stirred the feeling that I could never fully bond with her. I felt alone and unhappy and it reminded me again that when minds don't meet, sex is never all it could be.

"Jou don' understan'. They could take my baby."

That piece of information slapped right across my self-righteous indignation and brought me to heel. Cruel truth inverted my judgment. I hadn't thought of such a spiteful injustice. It just hadn't occurred to me. Rosy was a warrior too. Only for motherhood, a state I could never even contemplate. The door burst open.

"*Holá*!" Anthony greeted us loudly, kissing Rosy's cheek. He put his guitar case down, excusing himself to the bathroom to strap on his powdered party mood.

"How was jour concert, Anthony?" she asked, as he reappeared, frothing and friendly.

"*Great!* Almost five thousand people; outdoor gig by the sea. Some idiot was riding a horse through the audience, then three guys jumped on stage completely naked and the mayor pulled the plug on the power and refused to pay us."

Delighted by his flamboyant company, she laughed. I couldn't. He'd scored coke from someone other than Diego, and since he hadn't been paid, he must have bought it on credit. He'd soon be tapping me for cash to pay the bill.

"Let's put some music on," he suggested. "Where's the CD box, Syb? D'you remember picking it up?"

"Forget your old tech, bro'; just put my iPod through the speakers." I handed it across, he ignored me. Since we'd moved apartments, everything but the basics was still in boxes. I remembered that I had thrown all the junk under the previous TV table into a big plastic bag. I began looking, ignoring Rosy, who'd disappeared into the kitchen.

"Blue plastic bag," I said, with conviction.

"Got it!" He found the assorted CDs and DVDs and rummaged through them. "Hmm, I'm bored with these. Ah, look! Uncle Charlie's contribution!" It was the one he'd found in the car.

"Charlie's? The one that wouldn't play?"

"Wasn't music, that's why! Probably porno, knowing Charlie. Found a flash drive as well. It's in my jacket."

"Anthony, you nosy, thieving bastard! How low can you get?"

"*Me*? I could limbo-dance under a dachshund dog, but *you*..." He rounded on me with reason: "... *you* helped steal his car, so don't be a bloody hypocrite!"

"Christ, bro'!" I hissed, shushing him so that Rosy couldn't hear. "Did you put the gun back and wipe it first?"

"'Course, sis! *Tranquila,* baby! Calm down! Oh! I've just remembered, the CD player is at Diego's."

Rosy reappeared with three sugary coffees. Peruvians have a love affair with salt and sugar, both of which I have screened out of my life, along with white bread, acrylic paints and Facebook. Cable TV was still blaring. Ant was staring at the other screen that dominates life, booting up the CD in the laptop, ignoring the iPod suggestion. It occurred to me he'd probably sold all his old tech for cocaine, but he still had the laptop I bought him. He loved computers. Apart from his musical talent, he was a hacker of sorts and had a box full of illegal software. He was so bright, a high-flying intellect of creativity and curiosity, but with a hideous, drug-addicted goblin in his mental cockpit.

I flip TV channels to find Winifred Harop, chat-show diva, asking:

"Can you explain for our audience, professor, exactly what you mean by addiction, and why some people can cure theirs and others can't?"

I turn up the sound. The professor is using her hands expressively.

"Addiction involves both biology and psychology. Users need their drug to avoid withdrawal symptoms but have to take an ever-increasing dose to get a high." Ant is cursing in the background:

"What? What the hell *is* this?"

The prof continues:

"There is a reward, or pleasure centre, called the *nucleus accumbens* in our brains, and a chemical called dopamine plays a vital role in sending messages to this centre. Drugs and alcohol, tobacco and even coffee affect dopamine levels in the brain, which will vary according to the individual."

"What about the so-called addictive gene?" Winnie asks on behalf of her audience, who crane forward, desperate for confirmation that their pill-popping habits and booze benders are entirely excusable and beyond their control. I crane forward, desperate for any information that might help get the monkey off my brother's back.

"Well, your genes don't dictate compulsive-addictive behaviour, but they can make you more susceptible." The professor is explaining three basic types of addict.

"One: the damaged soul medicating psychological pain."

Camera cuts to the audience, to an overweight, vulnerable-looking woman in her twenties.

"Under this heading come the sexually, physically and mentally abused, the socially awkward and the chronically shy."

Camera moves in, up close and personal.

"They can be helped by therapy and a gradual weaning off the drug, but are usually in a state of repression, fear, anger or confusion. Some recover, but those who remain well are usually those who can cut off all drug-using friends and have stable families to turn to for support."

The camera pans the audience away from the woman, now dabbing her eyes, then cuts back to the learned doc.

"Where eez ze music?" says Rosy.

"It's not music," snaps Ant, ejecting the disc from the laptop and pushes it in again. "Knew it wasn't. Won't open. Bet it *is* porno!" I did not look round but stayed with the programme.

"Group two is the hedonists." The prof pronounces it 'heednists'.

"Tolerance builds quickly as they become addicted to the good time. Rock bottom happens when their behaviour leads to crime, violence, hospital or financial ruin. Only then do they get the wake-up call. The richer they are, the longer it takes." Camera settles on bottle-blonde with a deep tan in row two. She looks like a washed-out negative of her own photograph. I still don't look round when Ant says, "*Jesus Christ!*" twice.

I drain my cup, supposing he is now looking at Charlie's favourite open beaver shots.

"Three: the group that has abnormal brain chemistry leading to low serotonin and dopamine levels. Feeling relaxed, happy, like you or I might do, is not possible without higher levels in the brain. Lethargic and depressed without their drug of choice, this group often commits suicide. Some suffer from what is known as bipolar disorder or borderline schizophrenia. Some have what is known as the 'warrior' gene, which predisposes them to low dopamine. There is no permanent cure. They will need medication for life… er… till death, which is usually premature." Prima toor. The camera in the back of my head pans to my brother. We keep our backs to one another, each fixated on a different screen. Rosy has been abandoned and quietly picks up her bag, opening the door to leave. She blows a kiss, making the sign for "call me". I nod, so does Winnie, looking sagacious, spectacles on nose, reading from a piece of paper:

"Statistics are frightening. In America today, more people than ever have addiction problems, but few recover, and lower income groups are most at risk." She looks over her lenses. "Is science making any progress in helping these people?"

"Yes, neuroscience is revealing clues to the process of addiction. We believe that some of the hard-wiring in the brain is genetic and some created by the type of early care, or lack of care, given to the child. Pharmacological therapies can make a difference."

"Doesn't that mean just substituting one drug for another?"

"Initially, yes, but some new compounds are permanently altering the connections in the brain."

"Jesus!" Ant says again.

Mindful of their star-driven entertainment business, the show flashes-up a parade of celebrities who'd boomeranged through the doors of clean-up clinics under the banner: "REHAB REGULARS".

They cut to the ones who hadn't made it.

"I can only guess at their particular problem," says the professor, "but addiction eventually killed these people."

Her voiceover sounds like a graduation roll-call.

"Judy Garland, early death from prescription drugs and drink. Marilyn Monroe, addicted to sleeping pills, believed suicide. Jackson Pollock, died addicted to alcohol. Janis Joplin, died addicted, choked on her own vomit."

"Better than choking on someone else's," I say.

Ant, who has obviously been listening to the show he wasn't looking at, hears my gallows humour and joins in as the prof continues:

"Jim Morrison, died through addiction, believed heart attack."

"...Too fucking fat to get out the bath."

"John Belushi, died addicted to cocaine."

"...But smiling."

"Jimmy Hendrix, choked to death on a cocktail of drink and drugs."

"...I'll have two Martinis and a Dead Man's Rattle, please."

"Billie Holiday, died from heroin addiction."

"...Permanently on vacation."

"River Phoenix, drug related death."

"...Gone down the Swance."

"Kurt Cobain, history of heroin abuse. Suicide by firearm."

We fall silent. Joke over.

"What a waste of talents," declares Winnie, followed by a cheery, "We'll be right back after these messages."

Ant shrieks at his screen, "*Clever! Very clever!* Syb, come and look! It's a dot. Right in the eye of Jesus!"

"Maybe he wants us for a sunbeam," I say, looking over his shoulder at the picture of the Saviour on screen, arms outstretched.

"Funny. I found an image like that on the floor of Charlie's car. Has he had a religious conversion?"

"Don't think so," Ant said, "but anything's possible with Charlie. He tried to buy coke from Joseph, that Mormon guy you like, last week."

Hilarious! Charlie had believed my confabulation! Poor Joseph. But the smile died on my lips as Ant's de-encryption disc began disintegrating the zeros and ones that made up the microdot in the now much-magnified Saviour's eye. Pixels slowly shredded outwards to the document beneath.

There, everything Todd had explained to us about the corruption at Gentrex was elucidated in bold type.

What we didn't know, was this revealed truth of Jesus, now made manifest, was simultaneously being read and absorbed with religious zeal on the other side of town...

41 DOUBLE AGENDA

Abelman flipped open the folder, but before he read the text of page one, he reflected on the man who'd prepared the document. He was glad he'd hired him.

Educated for twelve years in Miami, Ramon Suarez Montez was an ex-soldier and business man, reliable, disciplined, a brilliant administrator of resources. His report was concise. Abelman inhaled softly and read the print with the aid of a stylish, Philippe Starck reading lamp.

PROJECT CUCA

The 'Cuca' crop, genetically modified coca plants, are designed to be:

1. Resistant to all herbicides and fungi

2. Producing five times the normal cocaine alkaloid yield

3. Producing more addictive alkaloids

Half a million of these plants are already growing in the Yanahuara facility with 500,000 more ready in two weeks. Within six months they may be grown from their own cells and cuttings as they are totipotent. We do not know if the natural seed is hybrid, or a faithful replicate of the GM stock, as the first of these plants are not yet mature.

The two highest-yielding coca plant varieties are now fully modified for the Cuca project. They have been engineered to be resistant to all known fungi, ergots, herbicides and dioxin-based defoliants. Addiction studies done on mice, rats and cuys are conclusive, as are the human studies. Since the latest breakthrough with the 612 series, figures show that the addictive potential is both immediate and absolute.

It is my view that revenues will multiply five-fold and more within two years following distribution of this new product. Profit and investment projections are included as addenda. Costs will depend on the country of origin and staffing levels. Since Cuca and its 'super coke' yield will soon be the basis of all new business, we should concentrate investment in new indoor growing facilities, greenhouses and hydroponic systems, to propagate this new transcript.

I would suggest I now leave Peru for the Turkmenistan facility to work with the scientists on the product refinements for the best possible results in their climate.

Abelman smiled and opened a silver cigar box. Taking out a fresh Cohiba Sublime, he revolved the expensive Cuban stick in his tanned fingers, savouring the firm resistance of the silken leaves as he read the next page.

PROJECT PHOENIX

For project Phoenix, we are in a position to positively show:

1. Two GM coffee varieties viable at high altitudes, with good yields

2. Bio-engineered fungi effective on five varieties of low-yield coca
3. Continuing modifications on the moth and coca fly, both of which can devastate crops

By showing samples of infected coca leaves under laboratory conditions we can demonstrate to both the Peruvian and American Governments that real progress is being made. The Cuca crop is engineered to be immune to this infection, so for this demonstration we have selected a coca variety used by the indigenous population for tea and for chewing, but occasionally refined by locals in small family complexes. Its total destruction will not affect business as it has the lowest cocaine yield of all the varieties in South America.

When we demonstrate how this species may be affected, we are in a position to ask for further funds, so we may target the damage to the main crop varieties, which of course, we will fail to do until the Cuca crop is established in all territories in approximately two to three years. The GM fungi will not be released to the DEA until the new Cuca crop is successfully growing in large quantities.

The original $20 million investment will appear to be well spent with Gentrex. Figures are prepared, separate to this document, for presentation to the DEA for next week's meeting. I propose that we ask for a further $50 million based on our successes to date. This will finance Project Cuca Phase Two for propagating the GM cocaine crop. As our rival's crops wither and die, the market value of our crop will rise.

Abelman clipped his cigar and bit down, lighting and sucking the compact, moistened end, inhaling the fragrant core of vanilla-scented smoke. He ignited the first two paper sheets and dropped them into a metal waste basket by the open window behind him, swinging round on the chair to pick up page three.

EFFECTS OF GM CUCA COCAINE

Continuous cocaine use triggers an increased and persistent protein called Delta-FosB in the brain, as well as the release of glutamates. Normally, Delta-FosB is not produced until cocaine users have ingested several large doses over a period of months, but once Delta-FosB builds up in the brain, so does the compulsive need for cocaine.

Data from the GM Cuca experiments using guinea-pigs, rats and humans all show a rapid rise in this protein level, sooner than is normal. Increased craving begins at four doses and has peaked at ten, resulting in a five-fold increase in self-administration, therefore indicating that GM Cuca cocaine may be considered at least five times more addictive than normal cocaine.

The Cocaine and Amphetamine Regulated Transcript (CART peptide) is also a brain neurotransmitter. Low levels of this CART peptide also increase addiction. Cuca cocaine, after a seventy microgram doses, destroys the brain's ability to produce this neurotransmitter in large quantities, and therefore increases cravings. Subject 612 ingesting the latest refined Cuca cocaine has the lowest CART levels recorded. GM Cuca cocaine also permanently alters the dopamine receptors in the brains of both humans and animals.

In rats, mice, cuys and humans, levels of CART protein and MRNA affect feelings of hunger and satiety as well as addiction. Unfortunately, in our first trials, the animals suffered from fetid breath, obesity and gum disease as side effects, but new transgenic modifications have solved these problems. The extra expense and time to correct these problems was felt to be essential. It is imperative that users do not seek medical advice for this trilogy of symptoms, as digital records can be quickly compared for clusters of new diseases and may trigger a medical alert. We do not want any attention drawn to the Cuca effects until our markets are assured.

Suarez's clear exposition of the work allowed Abelman to easily grasp the complexities of Fischer's achievements. "Well worth his fee," he thought, "we should retain him at all costs." He burned the notes and turned from hard science to pragmatism on page four.

REQUIREMENTS FOR CUCA PHASE TWO

We will need at least 3,800sqm of a secure, temperature-controlled environment with electricity and water supplies. Facilities must include 600sqm of room-temperature storage, vehicle access and shelter for 25 vehicles, including HGV grade. Materials required include:

1,800 gallons buffer salts

300 gallons phenol

300 gallons ethanol

100 gallons chloroform

400 cylinders oxygen

6,900 gallons distilled water

300 containers dry gel matrix

300 gallons primer base

100 gallons cytokinin

100-gallon drum Ravocin herbicide

2,500 ultraviolet beta-type lamps

A list of technical specifications of the laboratory equipment will include centrifuges, chromatographs, microscopes and office and computer requirements. Costs of these are estimated on page six.

"What a great day," Abelman said to himself. The *Cuca* project had been his and Bill Lerner's idea. They would reap their reward in billions. He was sitting in his study in the seven-bedroom house in Challapampa. On the desktop sat a solid silver frame holding a black and white photograph of his mother in her glowing youth. She beamed out at her boy.

With two unread pages awaiting perusal, he leant forward to the mahogany desk. Reaching into a drawer, he moved aside the latest

Sotheby's New York catalogue. There, next to his P20 semi-automatic pistol was his private mobile phone with only four contact numbers.

As the evening sun lit the room rose and gold, he dialled Bill Lerner, still smiling.

42 *WAYNE'S COCAINE WORLD REVISITED*

Charlie's CD spilled out its ugly truth about *Cuca* cocaine. Ant checked the USB and confirmed the same information, similarly encrypted. He saved the report in a hidden file on his laptop and made a copy for Todd on clean flash drive, as well as printing a copy. I was incensed that Charlie had been part of it all. Fat, greedy, evil bastard! Ant was incensed for an entirely different reason. Not once had dear Uncle Charlie invited him for a toot of the super-coke.

"He's been keeping that one to himself, the sly shit," he said.

When we were first told us of the corruption at Gentrex by Todd, I was more shocked by his recruitment to the green cause than by the crime; but now that the double agenda was hard fact, I found it sickening. Todd told us that the Greenies saw bio-tech pollution as more threatening to life on earth than anything before it. They were already anti cocaine because of the polluted rivers. Put the two together and they were beside themselves with angst.

Green Soldier had received their tip-off about the GM coke from their Amsterdam branch. They knew Fischer to be the brains behind a massive drug ring in Amsterdam in the 80s, genetically modifying super-skunk marijuana, but the Dutch police never had sufficient evidence to build a case.

Todd said that the Greenies had a photograph of Stan in a Dutch restaurant with an Alec Abelman. They were both tracked to Gentrex. Green Soldier was desperate for proof of the plot, proof we now had in the document before us, courtesy of Sweet Jesus. Exposure of this scientific scandal would advance their cause worldwide and perhaps cause a moratorium on GM experiments, they hoped.

"Human guinea-pigs?" I spat, reading from the print-out we'd made, "Jesus! What Nazi swine! Anything for money!"

"They should have asked me. I'd have volunteered." Ant said.

Suddenly, we both felt like grown-ups. It was the most uncomfortable of feelings. It meant we had responsibility for something other than ourselves. We were desperate to pass the buck.

"Ant, let's ring Todd as soon as he gets off his shift. You know, when he told us about Gentrex, I still thought we were in some kind of good-guy bad-guy game. But it isn't a game, is it, bro'?"

Ant started flipping channels and pacing. He didn't answer. By chance, he settles on *America Today*, and a repeat of the recent discussion on America's drug enforcement policy.

"Right now, on planet earth, the most lucrative and popular recreational drug is cocaine," say a familiar set of white porcelain teeth.

The last time I saw this programme I was concussed. I didn't recall the gravitas of it all. The presenter I remember. He is slick. Yeah. He's the guy who likes sensational statements and constantly seeks to provoke them. A Texan drawl drifts out of the goggle box. Wayne Sheridan, looking like a genuine good guy. He is still neat, clean, oozing sincere concern and still fighting on the side of the Almighty, now sitting in the CNN studio in the company of a journalist, a lawyer, an addiction doctor and a social economist, whose names flash up on information bars every time they speak.

Ant goes to the fridge and pulls out a cold beer, hissing it open and gulping without having offered me one. I go and fetch my own, listening once again to the commentary.

"Isn't it true they also use pesticides on the crops?"

"It's used against the coca fly. Traces of it are in the finished product."

My brother has, apparently, been snorting pesticide, along with all the other muck. He is pacing the room, side to side.

"Coca is sacred," I hear one of the protagonists say.

"Cocaine is bigger than sacred," Anthony shouts. "It's the fuel of the digital age. The whole fucking system has been designed by a bunch of nerds spending twenty hours a day staring at a screen eating pizza and snorting coke."

I know he's right. Coke isn't just for hedonists and head-bangers. Like chemical messengers in computer chips, now cocaine is the chemical messenger in humans. The business world is rife with it. The art world is no different. Nevertheless, I stood my ground.

"Speak for yourself, bro', not everyone needs it!"

"Fuck off! Millions and millions of people use coke."

He is immediately combative. I have no stomach for a fight. I have to turn him, and quickly, or his panic at the prospect of having to take responsibility for what we now know will turn into rage.

"Yeah. OK, I'll admit it, cocaine *is* the twenty-first century. Without factoring it in, no future historian could understand the zeitgeist of our age. It's perfect for people unlucky enough to have a low feel-good factor. That is, not the shiny, happy people. The sad people. The chronically despondent. Like you. Like me. Except, I don't like it. It doesn't comfort me. But I know why people use. Remind me bro', did shiny, happy people ever create great art?"

He brightens. "*Happy Talk Keep Talkin' Happy Talk. Yes! We Have No Bananas*. Then there was the guy who sang '*Don't Worry, Be Happy*'…he shot himself!" Ant screamed with laughter, inventing outrage to emphasise his point.

Phew! I did it. Wherever his anger now goes, at least it won't dump on me for a while. I laugh at the snide examples, but inside I am wondering how many un-shiny people, collapsing into mental folds blacker than the rose, have dosed with drink and drugs and made great art. Quite a few. Quite a few: Joyce, Lennon, Coleridge, Kahlo and Cobain for sure. And Anthony Sands, my talented brother.

"The American Government appreciates the role of coca for the indigenous mountain people, but we have a duty to our citizens to stop the production of refined cocaine."

Ant interjects, "Bollocks. It's window dressing. He doesn't even know his own government is screwing him. It's just PR for the punters. He's bought into the 'good guy' role. Bet *he* sleeps well at night."

Sheridan waffles on, optimistically:

"Coffee varieties developed in co-operation with our two governments and Gentrex will bring a good livin' for Peruvian farmers."

"There's no way people are going to want *coffee* instead of coke," snorts Ant. "Why don't you tell them about the black rose, sis? That could be a great crop substitute for 'em. Make the country millions."

Ant, even if the rose were as fecund as coca, it couldn't compete."

"Why? You said yourself that the whole world would want one."

"Because once you, and your granddad, and Joe Bloggs from number sixty-three had a black rose, they wouldn't want another. One is enough. But *cocaine?* You can never have enough once you like the drug. Never! And super cocaine, genetically engineered to be more addictive? You must be fucking joking! It will give that feel-good factor times *five*. Pharmacology can't rival it as a commercial product. No commodity on the planet has a greater profit margin; sometimes it's more than two thousand per cent."

"One thing will kill off the trade," Sheridan says, focusing our attention. "*Disease.* That's why we've brought a modern company like Gentrex on board."

This is the second time I am hearing this information, only now, it matters. The group stiffens, as do we. Sheridan expounds, confirming half the information we received via Charlie and Jesus: Project Phoenix. Sadly, Wayne Sheridan does not know he has a cuckoo in the nest. He sounds like a zealot, the pitch of his voice now rising as he warms to his theme.

"Somethin' genetically engineered to terminate fertility within the plant, or to give it a lethal disease. A mould perhaps. Somethin' to kill coca forever; and cocaine addiction along with it."

“Fuck about with their coca and they’ll cut your head off!” Ant blurts. He’s right. They will. And if the peasants don’t, the ruling class will. Their economy depends on it. Sheridan pauses, then says to camera: “Biotechnology is the answer.”

Here comes the genie in fields of corn.
A scarecrow warns.

“Hooray for the Americans!” I say, in a British Bulldog voice.

“Dead-coca-crop-mean-many-votes-in-land-of-free,” he adds.

“And what do votes mean, children?” I ask.

“Power!” he booms. “And power means *M.O.N.E.Y.* Enough money to buy all the ‘super’ coke you could ever want!”

He laughs again. It hangs, uneasy.

I glance over to the computer screen. Ant flips back the Gentrex report to the picture of Jesus. I stare at the open arms and golden halo and in that precise moment I realise that I can never accept the concept of ‘sin’, only of utter sorrow, fear, psychopathy and delusion – the failure to control these, and the consequences thereto.

And I hope that if Jesus, or any of his pals and followers, had any wisp of power to grant or understand anything, that they can take from Ant the burden of his addiction, and free him from it forever. But I am a non-believer, and so this cannot be.

“Ant, what are we going to do?” I ask him.

“I know what I’m going to do. Have a nice few juicy lines of Captain Coke.”

Ant snorts three lines then turns slowly to me, smiling.

“You know, Syb, I absolutely *LOVE* cocaine. You don’t know how happy it makes me.” And, like a page turning over, I realise that the burden of his addiction is not *his* burden. It’s mine. Love ensured that. I had allowed it to nail me to my cross of martyrdom: I will suffer on your behalf, my brother, just like Jesus.

But Ant at least had his answer, had found his means. Junkies can be so joyful and positive when they've had their candy. They can achieve astonishing things. And I reflected on the weird intelligence of it as an antidote to having to deal with shit… where all of life's little problems are as nothing compared to the greater problem of servicing one big need, which, once serviced, renders all the remaining problems insignificant, and, for a time at least, allows a peace.

Who else but a using addict or a meditating swami can enjoy that state of mind daily? And what else but blind faith, or love – in any form it comes – can give you that serenity?

Ah..! Now I remember……making art.

43 WIREHEAD IN THE WATER

My brother and I had decided to sleep on the previous night's revelations before calling Todd. That way, we too could be children for a little longer, resting responsibility on the back burner. Besides, I had to get the rose cells back from Stan Fischer before we did anything serious against Gentrex.

Ant had gone to Diego's by the time I woke and didn't call me until very late in the afternoon. I was looking out of the window at the volcano when my mobile bleeped. The news he delivered was shocking and unbelievable.

"Stan's dead. The Cessna went down near Ica, on the coast."

"What? What are you saying, Ant? It can't be true!"

Like a bird diving to the sea.

"He must be dead. The plane exploded. It's just been on the news. There were loads of eyewitnesses totally freaking out."

"But my rose! My rose! How the hell am I going to get my rose? Stan's the only person who knows where it is. Rosy doesn't know," I howled. "She says there are thousands of Petri dishes full of cells. *Thousands.* She can't bring them all home, don't you understand? Only Stan knows. He can't be dead, Anthony. He *can't* be."

"Only Stan *knew*," he corrected my tense. "Don't worry, sis."

"*Don't worry*? Listen bro', it's in there somewhere. I'm going to get my rose. I'm going to break into the lab and get it myself. I'll pay Todd. He'll let me in. I'm going to get her. What the fuck have I got to lose?"

"Your liberty, possibly your life, and certainly your sanity by the sound of it." My brother was completely rational, chiding me, "Stop overreacting. Just bloody *ask*. Get Rosy to say Stan was cloning a special cactus and where did he keep the private work? You're not James Bond for fuck's sake!"

This was exactly the tone I normally adopted with him. God, he made it seem easy. Yes, that *was* a good idea, at least one worth trying before I decided to burgle Gentrex. He was right, I was too hysterical.

"It's the shock. You're right. I'll speak to Rosy. I'll ring her."

To have had the rose snatched from me a second time was unthinkable. But Stan's death was suspicious. I was overwhelmed with fear that he had found out about the rose and kidnapped her, then faked his own death. As my imagination boiled, I was frantically dialling Rosy's mobile and almost steaming by the time she answered.

"Rosy! Have you heard? The news about Stan? *Sabes algo?*"

No, she didn't know, and was shocked and upset, crying into the phone. In all the rigorous questioning I had put her through since Todd had told us of the Gentrex agenda, never once did she appear to be anything but an ingénue: innocent, ignorant; convinced she was working on a coffee project. She didn't use cocaine. She hardly drank. She was simply a Catholic, unmarried mother seeking her fortune as best she could, and I was utterly contemptuous of her ineptitude and lack of ability in helping me find the rose. I almost shouted at her.

"Rosy, *listen!* You must have seen it. You were there the afternoon I gave it to him in the café, the day I came back from the cemetery. You went back to work together. Think! *Think!*" I remembered the black petals falling off at my feet as I snatched the rose from its jam jar on the grave, immediately hiding it under my jacket. Stan had recognised the bloomless stem as a rose that afternoon. He'd asked me what colour it was.

"It's red," I'd lied. "Blood red."

Rosy sobbed her incomprehension. I was getting nowhere.

"Tell them Stan was cloning a cactus for you and you want to know where his private work was kept," I instructed. My tone was demanding, controlling. The rose might be alone somewhere about to die because no one but Stan and I knew of her existence.

Rocio didn't capitulate to my will, but asked why I wasn't upset at Stan's accident. I couldn't tell her the truth. She wouldn't believe me, or she'd panic. Even if I made her learn the cactus question, insisting she wrote down the answer, nothing would happen. Rosy swam in the sea of life with no compass, no sense of her own captaincy. She was 'done to' rather than doing. Passive to my aggressive. I couldn't trust her like I could trust my cynical brother. He knew the ways of the world and the type of psychos that could perpetuate the scam at Gentrex, and I loved him because he didn't fear it, he revelled in the knowledge, as long as no one expected him to take responsibility for it.

The quality of mother love Anthony received always made him feel like a prince. He bowed to no one. No one but me. Though I was unpredictable, and now, equally nihilistic, I was the only person who stuck by him and loved him unconditionally, so I mattered. Sure, he'd had girlfriends. Some of them even lasted a few months, but they all gave up on him when, for the fiftieth time, he'd come home drunk or drugged, snapping and snarling when withdrawing from his poison.

I hung up. I'd been wrong to involve myself with Rocio. My brother and I were not ready to have adult relationships. At this point in our lives, we were party to the greatest freedom of all: to not even care about our own existence. Strangely though, we weren't depressed by that. It was a release – from the material, from the need to belong. We both felt we'd learned enough. How arrogant is *that*? He was medicating. I was obsessing. Yeah, we were free all right.

It was early, but I needed a drink, so I nipped to the store to re-stock while I planned my next move. Though it would have been a healthier option, I bypassed the local juice man with his clanking bells and little white cart. It was mango season and the size and sweetness of the fruits gave him a roaring trade, surrounded by children clamouring for a cup of the syrupy, orange pulp, now half the price of papaya or pineapple.

But I chose the queue for serious liquor, and, while I waited, three separate strangers petitioned me for cash. My heart darkened. Declining open palms, I logged some bitter observations. They don't bleed you big in South America but they bleed you often, and there are *swarms* of them, like mosquitoes, with the power to suck dry a mighty moose.

Hard luck stories abound. Mothers dying of cancer; abortions; schools that won't admit little Alfonso without new books; grannies with sceptic boils. All are told with the expectance that you will say:

"Here, maybe this will help," and proffer some change.

Munchausen's syndrome, itself and by proxy, is a Peruvian epidemic. Though the poverty was mostly genuine, Mavis had warned me never to lend a Peruvian anything.

"They won' return it, *never*. An' when you ask them, they will lie an' say that it's been 'stepped on/stolen/shrunk/eaten by the dog'. But that's not true, man. You know they have sold it, swapped it, or are keepin' it for a time when they might need to sell it. They are greedy and selfish. Especially the *cholos*!"

She should have warned Golden Boy, who lent everyone everything. Half of Arequipa was wearing his clothes. He was recklessly generous, believing somehow that this would all come good when he needed it to. I loved him for his total lack of materialism, but even Ant became jaded eventually by the endless taking. Ernesto, the *pastrulo,* was the worst. He'd borrowed Ant's guitar tuners and effects pedals, kept them for weeks and then sold them for a packet of pasta base to smoke. I began to see just how much poverty erodes morals and loyalties; how liberal values are mostly a luxury.

Even Ant's 'friends', to whom he thought he was really close, were ready to sell him out for the right price. When I realised how addicted my brother had become, I asked his friend César if I could pay him to collude with his uncle at the Immigration Department to deport my brother for his own good. The perfidious Peruvian replied, 'No problem!' and swiftly quoted his price, whilst drinking and laughing with Ant the very next day.

But, having been the instigator of this plot to save Ant, I found myself without the stomach to act upon it. I recalled shouting at my brother:

"Bloody Latinos think *we* are the ones with cold blue eyes and cold hearts. They think that *they* are loving, warm and demonstrative, but they're full of petty deceptions. Cold blue eyes do insolence better than brown ones, but cold brown eyes belong to assassins."

I mused on how easy it would be to have someone killed for a few hundred bucks, and stood in the queue planning how it might be done. Oh God! The shock of Stan's death was wearing off, and here was I – ranting *again*!

44 THE KEY TO THE INNER OFFICE

I returned to the apartment and poured myself a drink, pacing the terrace and chewing my lips. The bulk of Misti seemed ever closer. The sky was clouding, and the top of Chachani, the highest of the three volcanoes, had disappeared in the mists. My phone rang. It was Todd, and I was ready with my bombshell.

"I need the inner office key for Wednesday," he said, reminding me of my promise. "It's the day with the least security. Lupez is off sick, Pachao starts his holiday, and De Silva's wife is havin' a baby."

"Things have changed, Todd. I'm going in, not you. I have to get something that's very important."

"What? What are you talkin' about?"

"Stan's dead. His plane went down. He had something of mine in the lab and you won't be able to find it. I'm going in, not you. I'll get all your stuff as well, don't worry. You'll get all the information you need."

"*No fuckin' way!* Listen, missy, I can't get you in. If anyone sees you, we're both finished."

"Don't worry, I'll be in disguise."

"I don't care if you're whistlin' Dixie; you ain't goin' in! If you don' wanna give me the key, jus' let me know."

"Come over to the house, can you?"

"Yeah, in a couple of hours, *and I want the key*." He hung up.

Todd had not reacted to the death of the hated Stan. No remorse. No delight. Nothing. But I was in no place to judge emotional shortcomings. I felt no guilt about my intended deception. We had garnered the secret information through a chance back door by discovering Charlie's CD and memory stick, and it meant that we could now give Todd the rope with which to hang Gentrex. But not yet. My brother and I were determined to delay it for different reasons. Our priorities were black and white.

When your back's against the wall, the way forward is clear. Calm descends on your fevered meanderings. A path is obvious. Unhindered by option, that's how I felt. I wanted nothing else, so I had no fear. The outcome, I was sure, would be to reclaim the black rose. All sense of wanting her for commercial gain had long gone. I wanted her because she was beautiful, alone, unique, inspiring, in need of my help and with no other friends – and she was *mine*!

I put down the phone and went immediately to the bedroom to get Mavis' wig. I carefully trimmed a fringe to match Rosy's style. The life mask, now fully painted, I slipped on, adding sunglasses. I wore flat shoes, my black trousers and her jacket, which she'd left at the house. I was her double, albeit two inches taller. When the bell rang, I answered the door, keeping the hall lights very low.

"Er, er, 'scuse me, Rocio," Todd stuttered, completely taken aback. "Is… is Sybil here?"

"You see!" I removed the mask.

"Jeez!" He was flabbergasted.

"Come in. I'll tell you the plan."

I was not going to be obstructed and I oozed determination and confidence. I told Todd that the plant Stan was cloning for me was a very rare and costly cactus worth thousands of dollars and that I would recognise it immediately. He thought I was insane risking so much for a plant. He wanted to know why I didn't simply explain to the Gentrex hierarchy what had happened.

"Stan was risking his job; any outside work was strictly prohibited due to cross-contamination," I told him, thinking on my feet. "They'll destroy or confiscate the plant for sure."

He demanded again that he should be the one to get the information from the Gentrex files and computers, information that was in fact, only three feet from him taped under my desk drawer on a flash drive. Given their intelligence in dreaming up a scheme like *Cuca* cocaine, I doubted the Gentrex conspirators would be so stupid as to leave information on an office computer. But Todd and his cohorts didn't seem to have thought that through.

Apparently, Todd had already stolen two Petri dishes of modified coca from Gentrex as evidence. Reassuring him, I explained that I fully understood computers, and was better placed to get what he required. I began to rattle off all the terminology I'd heard my brother use concerning the encryption of secret files and prime number algorithms. It baffled the cowboy, still mesmerised by the effect of my appearance, and he began to be won over by my embroidered lies.

"I can't teach you it all in time, Todd. It's incredibly complex nowadays, the way things are covered up. They partition the disc and hide stuff in the set-up programmes and 'help' files. One document can be broken up and placed in different folders. It's so hard to know what you're looking for. The information could even be in code, or cloaked in graphics. Without my de-encryption software, you'd be completely lost."

I gulped at my own lying bravado, overwhelming him with reams of jargon-precise bullshit, convincing him I was a digital diva. Deep down, I think he was relieved. He'd been intending to steal the big computer or laptops if he couldn't find the information he wanted. I assured him that type of tactic would give the game away and put his, and probably others' lives at risk.

Relenting, he knew that whatever his mechanical skills, computers had all but passed him by. His main complaint seemed to be that I was a woman, but he knew I wouldn't 'pussy out' and start screaming because he said:

"You people (he meant lesbians), you think you're as good as men, don'cha?" I smiled, unruffled. He sucked air through his teeth and realised that I was his best hope, so he took charge and started to give me instructions.

Todd told me that, dressed as Rosy, I wouldn't be questioned about late visits, because she was,

"... all cosied up to Chicau, the Head of Security."

"*How* cosied up?" I demanded to know.

"Well, they're an item, but he's married."

Bang! Balloon popped. My heart dropped back to earth like a stone. Not because she had another lover. Because she lied. I'd asked her specifically, many times, before I'd laid my hand on her, if there were anyone else. As I mentally abandoned one dark beauty, it made me cling all the harder to the chance of embracing the other.

"You could say you'd left your purse and have come over t' get it," Todd suggested.

"Yeah, and I'll have a hanky with me to act as if I'm crying, so I don't have to talk to anyone if I'm spotted. You can say my dog has just died." Actually, it was my love affair.

"Bedder make it yer mother. These fuckin' Latinos don' give a shit about their dawgs."

So far, so good. He would let me in at a specified time. I had no more than fifteen minutes before Chicau would return from his tour of the perimeter. Todd's shift was from six in the evening until six in the morning. We agreed to meet at 11.30pm prompt. Too early and I'd risk being in the building when others were working late.

I looked again at the squinting cowboy, amazed that he had put his energy into such a cause. But Todd had not been difficult to recruit because he hated cocaine and he knew Stan Fischer was supplying Laura. Jobless and drifting, and emasculated by his accident, Todd saw this as a heroic opportunity to right wrongs and settle scores, rescuing his lover from the jaws of addiction. Admirable and brave. And moral.

On the journey back from Cusco, he told us that he was persuaded to join Green Soldier by his friend, Steve Colby, who had been the pilot of Abelman's private plane in the mid-90s. Steve and his brother Jack were now hard core green activists. No longer flying for Abelman, Steve had immediately thought of his old friend, Todd, now living in Peru.

"Colby knew I'd gone to Arequipa to be with Laura," Todd had explained, "so I was the obvious 'in' for one of their men at Gentrex."

Steve Colby then rang Abelman, his old boss, persuading him that Todd was an ace security guard, an all-American, loyal foot soldier who served the hand that paid him, and, lo and behold, he got the job.

Not once though, in the entire unfolding of this imbroglio, did Todd name his female contact in Cusco, nor betray any more than was necessary for me know in order to help him. Though we now knew 'Della Fosby' was the Delta-FosB protein, we never got anything out of him about the woman who spoke it. Touching loyalty, I thought. Real integrity from a man most would consider just a redneck.

Whether he would have involved himself in the whole affair had Laura not been a victim is a moot point. The cowboy appeared to have no green philosophies or credentials prior to Peru. But no matter; he now committed himself with purpose and fury, intending to blow up the building with a device that would trigger a pool of gasoline, and put an end to what he described as the Devil's own work:

"It ain't right what those folk are doin', modifyin' them plants 'n' all, 'n' fuckin' around with God's nat'ral plan."

When I pointed out to him that wet-shaving his chin every day was, in some way, 'fuckin' around with God's nat'ral plan', he gave me a look as if to cut my throat with the proposed razor, so I kept quiet. According to him, genetic modification was:

"Ag'inst Mother Nature. An' the bast'ids that wanna make people addicted to cocaine should have their nuts sliced awf 'n' stuck down their goddam throats."

Yeah, somehow I agreed with him there. Until Stan's plane went down, I was quite content to leave the avenging angel gig to Todd, but now I felt delighted that someone was intent on exposing Gentrex, and glad that I could help. Their double agenda didn't surprise me, but I wanted them to fail. Hey! I like a good bang, and I was all for an explosion and fire as long as no one implicated my brother or me, and there were no casualties apart from Gentrex's stock price.

I didn't want to proselytise for the ending of biotech experiments, or for a drug-free life. I was, after all, a seasoned psychonaut and doubtless I would take psychedelics again. That I hated cocaine was immaterial. It didn't give me the moral high ground, for surely I would have used it had I liked it. Like my brother, I was weak and avoiding.

Perhaps I should have been working for Green Soldier or the Casa Verde project for orphaned children, or indeed, anything more worthy than wanking my ego onto canvas, but I wasn't. I was selfish and obsessive and I wanted the rose. Nothing now would stop me. I wanted her. I *wanted* her. And if Todd was the last gate through which I had to pass before getting her back, then I was prepared to do anything bar sexual intercourse to open that gate. I was even prepared to promise sex: to tease and to deceive, though not to deliver.

He left and closed the door, our pact sealed.

45 MASK

I removed all traces of my Rosy drag act, washed my face and sat staring out of the window. My brother had not come home as he'd promised, but had sent a text.

"You're my rainbow, sis. My rainbow. I know u always do the right thing. U r so wise and wonderful. So great to me when we were kids. I love you so much. U r my princess. I know u want to be wise and to know all there is to know, but I just want to stay stupid, deluded and free. Wisdom is a ball and chain. xxx"

I knew he couldn't handle any responsibility. I saw what had happened to that sweet little optimistic boy when we had sat together, first at Dad's bedside, then at Mum's, watching our family slip away. Powerless.

When Todd had first told us that Gentrex was modifying coca plants to make super cocaine, Ant's attention was titillated by the prospect of sampling it. Now, in the documents we had read on the screen, the implications of the double agenda had finally pierced his conscience. But he would postpone forever, if possible, the chance of acting upon the information. Ant desperately wanted it to be someone else's problem.

He rang me close to midnight, high and little drunk, saying again that he loved me, that I was all that mattered to him in the world.

"We should definitely give the information to the police, sis. They'll deal with it. It would be a big feather in their cap to catch such a bunch of villains and we may even get a reward."

"Bro', we're not in a Hollywood movie. These people are serious, hard core killers. The police would be bribed off and we would be silently slaughtered before we could leave this place. Use your head."

"No, you're wrong. Diego knows the police chief. I'm sure we could get him involved. He's a good guy. He comes to score once a week here."

"Anthony, *listen.* A drug-addicted policeman is going to be open to corruption. All they would have to do is threaten his family, or offer him a lifetime supply of coke, and he would bury the evidence. This country is built on cocaine, you idiot. You *know* that. Gentrex probably has every policeman and politician in its pocket. No one must know that we have this information. No one, Anthony. Except Todd, because we know he's on our side. OK? You must never, *ever* tell anyone, bro'. If I have ever asked anything of you, it was never as vital as this. It's our lives, Ant. My life and yours. You know I'm not afraid of dying, but I'm buggered if I'm going to die simply so that those evil bastards can get rich. Promise me you will keep this to yourself. *Promise me*."

"I promise, sis. I promise. I love you. I'll be home soon. I will."

He was such a child, but I was angry as well as touched, because I wanted to be a child, too. Sadly though, our family circumstances had robbed me of that. I *always* had to be the one to take the bloody reins.

Had I seen my brother face to face, I would have told him of my intentions to burgle Gentrex; I may even have invited him to join me, or at least to act as lookout. But if he were on a bender, he'd be in no fit state to help. Too reckless. A bloody liability. I gave nothing away, closing the phone.

Since vague sketching was as much as my artistic muscle could muster, I'd been idly doodling a likeness of Rosy before he called. My pad was covered in previous attempts, but now, tonight, I found it more difficult. The news about her affair with Chicau, well… my spleen must have leaked into my pencil. She'd begun to resemble the cruel queen in *Snow White*. Crumpling the paper, I decided to rest early to prepare for the coming storm.

That night, as every night since I had found her, the rose appeared to me in the dreams between the nightmares, her dark vulva folding me in, dissolving my fear. I knew that owning her would take me to the next part of my life; that she would somehow fill the void Evie left and maybe even deliver me into the arms of art. I was not going to give up on her.

Dawn brought the slow drip of adrenaline that woke me. I needed to talk to Ant, to be reassured that his night time truth fugue had not loosened his tongue. I called out. He answered, slurring, walking in to the bedroom, off his head, still dressed and not long back from his nightly revels. No, he assured me, he had not said a word, and I would be unharmed and safe and always his favourite girl.

He pulled my blankets up and kissed my cheek. "Sleep, sis," he said. And I remembered how we had slept together for comfort as children after our parents died, creeping to each other's rooms so we could wake up in each other's arms. When I told him, aged twelve, that he was too old for such things, he cried for a whole day and still tried to get in with me that evening. I'd had to remind him of the facts of life and the propriety expected of an older sister in such a circumstance. He had said then, with great indignation, that the world had a dirty mind.

I woke refreshed. The afternoon sun was strong and Rosy arrived two hours late for our lunch date. I was busy tanning myself, anxious that my skin should look darker to resemble hers, though I had some liquid makeup for my hands and face as back up. Ant had already eaten a quick breakfast and gone straight back to his dealer's before I got up.

On the bookshelf, still propped up, was Rosy's picture, and next to it the newly-painted mask. She was thrilled with the results.

"It eez beautiful, Si-vil. Can I take it now?" A couple more days, I told her, to fully dry the paint and then seal with matt varnish. She had no idea it was already finished; no idea where it would be worn in the meantime.

Having been worked to death the previous week, she now had four days' leave before a week of overtime. As she prepared food in the kitchen, she told me that her aunt was most upset because her children had sold the family pets, three cats and a dog, to the circus, to feed the lions. Apparently, in exchange for a ticket to the show, this was common practice, and the only way the circus could afford to feed their captive beasts. Often kids handed in their neighbours' pets. Rosy could find only humour in such a tale. I was appalled at the callous treatment of animals in Latin America.

She began asking questions about Ant. Did he have contacts in America in the music business? Could he help her make some more demos? Would he go on the radio with her and talk about her songs? My bean of jealousy had fully sprouted.

"Speak to Ant." I said.

I'd ceased to be angry with her for lying about Chicau. Everyone lies about sex in some way at least once in their lives. Everyone. We were well matched, I thought, using each other. Certainly, I was no better than she. I lured her to my house initially to get the rose to Gentrex; and now again, so I could steal her security card keys. Keys that I carefully picked out of her bag when she was in the *baño*.

She wanted me to make love to her, and came out of the bathroom in just her underwear. She swayed over to me and placed my hand against her mount of Venus, rubbing herself against me.

I thought what a beautiful animal she was, so lithe, graceful, and eager to mate. I could feel the damp through her panties. She placed her hands either side of my head. I anticipated her next move would be to push me downward, but I just couldn't. Not after what I knew. And not before what I was about to do.

Instead, I kissed her deeply and held her tight, pushing her head back and caressing her neck. I knew it was our last kiss. She sensed immediately that this was an emotion other than lust, so I feigned a stomach ache and she dressed again, knowing I was lying. She ordered a taxi and I prepaid it, promising to call her later. I waved her goodbye, knowing I may never see her again and drank cinnamon tea in silence. And then I prayed.

To whom or what I have no idea, but a more ardent plea for the fulfilment of personal ambition has yet to be voiced on planet Earth.

46 RUMBLED

At exactly 11.30pm, I was standing outside the Gentrex building alone wearing my wig, mask and dark glasses. The door opened a tiny crack and a sweating Todd ushered me in. I was surprised by the ordinariness of the place, the poky reception with its cheap furniture, the main lab and its ugly fluorescent lighting. Todd showed me to the locked inner door. I swiped Rosy's card through and it clicked open.

"I gotta go back to the main door. If anyone comes you'll hear me cough real loud. Hide 'til I can let ya' out. An' don' put the lights on."

I nodded, unable to speak well through the mask. I squeezed his arm and he shut the door quietly. I thought then that I really liked Todd. He had that rare quality so hard to find: the courage to stand up for his morals and fight the enemy, even though he was scared witless. Then it occurred to me that if this same moral conviction were applied to bombing abortion clinics, my sentiments would be entirely reversed.

I ran my torch over the Petri dishes and glass vials containing plant cells. There were so many. *So many*. Where to start? I began reading the labels: 611 RPR7; 611 RPR8; 611 RPR9; 611 RPR10. *Oh God!* Were they all in *code*? Wasn't there one that simply said, 'Sybil's rose'?

For ten or twelve minutes I searched frantically, running my torch over them and opening all the cupboards and drawers until I was startled by a scuffling sound. I could hear loud coughing and muffled voices. I slid under the largest bench.

Two men entered the lab. I could smell them. Expensive cologne; testosterone. When they switched on the light, I could see their reflection in the window glass. They wore white coats and medical masks, which they pulled down in order to speak. The taller one wore an elasticated lab cap. 'The Man with a Hat' and 'The Executioner'.

"None of his project notes or samples must remain. Get rid of everything you find, the quickest way you can, and search his house."

"Yes, sir. I will take care of it."

"Leave no trace, understand? No trace at all and nothing to link you."

"Yes, sir. What happens if they find a body in the plane?"

"Then we don't have anything to worry about, but we must prepare for other eventualities. How close are we to finishing here, Ramon?"

"Very close, Señor Abelman. As you know, 612 was the final breakthrough. Fischer solved the breath problem with a transgenic procedure using rose cells. All we need to do now is reinsert the rose gene into the *Cuca* plant cells."

It was Suarez speaking. His reflection showed a cruel, handsome face with thick, dark eyebrows and a small scar on his chin. Rosy had painted a deadly accurate description of him. Suddenly, I understood the implication of the union he'd described. *Cuca* cocaine was transgenic with a rose. Not my rose. *Please,* not her – my second dark princess – in bed with the enemy.

"How quickly can it be done? If he's with the opposition, we need to move fast."

"With all the staff working overtime, I think one week, maybe."

I hunched my knees close to my body. It was then that I saw something move near my foot. I looked down to see the cream whiskers of a small ginger guinea pig in the shadows. My breathing stopped. One small scuffle could reveal my hiding place.

"Who knows it all, apart from Fischer and us?"

"Fischer only knew about the human studies *he* did, not about the ten *cholos* in Goyaneche. He made the breakthrough with 612, so he knew it was five times more addictive. It's in the report. Cortez, Herrico and Gonzalez have all worked closely with Fischer in the inner office, so they know about the basic crop modifications."

"Do we need them for anything else? Are they expendable?"

The ex-army man paused before answering. His next sentence fell down on his staff like a guillotine.

"The whole workforce is expendable. Seven more days to tidy up the details, then we won't need any of them."

Thunder Heartbeat Thunder. I am a kneeling cliché.
So hard to breathe.

"Is everything here?"

"Yes. I will make copies of the final matrix and data and back it up; then I will remove all hard drives and laptops and destroy them myself."

"Do it anyway, but don't worry, the fire will take care of any remaining information."

FIRE? What fire? What are they planning? The guinea pig sneezed and scratched fiercely. I stared down and willed it: *Stop!* Stop little squeaker, *please* stop… or we're both dead.

"Make sure they are all here. All of them, understand? It must look like an accident. Fix the electronic locks so no one can get out. Can you plant some evidence to make it look as though terrorists or *cocaleros* have done it?"

"Er, yes. I have some souvenirs, things from my army days. I can leave them where they won't burn so they will be definitely be found."

"Good. Excellent. I shall be in New York tomorrow. Your money will be here Sunday at 1pm exactly: $200,000 and your number and pass keys for the deposit account for a further $2m. You will need to give the product samples directly to Muñoz and Barriga and they will hand your money over. Take the case, drive up to the house in Challapampa and leave your car. Umberto will take you to the airport for your plane at seven. Follow your instructions and wait to be contacted. Make sure the fire starts when you have a watertight alibi. Use automatic timers. All the lab personnel must be here and locked in. All of them, Suarez, understand? We don't want them offering their services to the opposition, do we? Like our friend Mr. Fischer may have done."

"Yes sir; all of them will be here workin' on a special project I have set with new deadlines. They are gettin' extra monies. They will be here."

"Shame they'll never pick up that pay check, eh?" joked Abelman.

"Yes, sir. Yes." Suarez laughed.

They opened the door to leave when a harsh, klaxon sound filled the air: '*Whah-whah*'. '*Whah-whah*'. Both men paused in the doorway. The guinea pig ceased scratching and looked up at me with glossy little eyes. *Jesus!* It was my phone! I'd put it in my pocket as a matter of habit, but hadn't switched it off. I had about five seconds of freedom left at most. An adrenaline rush so immediate filled my fight and flight pathways that I almost took off. I could hear all the dogs barking outside. Barking like lunatics. Howling. The cacophony almost drowned the second ring of the phone as I fought in my clothes to find it. Then, just as suddenly, they all stopped barking; a strange, empty pocket left hanging in the air, along with the hole where the ringtone had been.

Darkness closed in on me, as it had when the first rose had burned. I felt like a cornered rodent, the little one at my feet now disappearing into the shadows. In a transcendental state of fear, I was willing myself to find the best of lies. Sweat ran from inside my mask to my neck. Dripped down to my breasts. Should I go for their throats in an element of surprise as I made a bid for freedom? What would they do if I came out singing, cross-eyed and naked? A *tableau vivant* of self as surrealist. Or played the porn card? Throw my knickers on the floor. Pretend I've been having a quickie with Chicau. Might I have to submit to rape to get out of this?

My mind roiled, but my body was still. Here was the universal nightmare: leaden legs that cannot run… while the Devil approaches. My elastic friend time turned from treacle to brittle. Awareness came *within* the seconds, time's marker words, placed like goal nets either side of a tiny field of freedom, the remainder of my liberty the length of the pitch in between. Reflected clearly in the computer screen, they re-entered the lab. Sentinels of death. Psychopaths. Mummy's little boys.

Silhouettes, waiting to chew my lies.

"*What the…?*" I heard Abelman say. He'd drawn a gun from his jacket, his teeth glinting in a grimace.

And so – here it is, the greatest threat to my physical existence I have ever experienced. My nervous system has kindly switched back on, all bulbs blazing to burnout. I glance across at the rows of Petri dishes with their cells of life reduced and abstracted to simple numbers in endless serial codes.

One after another, Evie's relatives had been marked with serial numbers. With pink and red triangles; with yellow stars… perceived imperfections reduced to a deadly symbol. Filed onto trains. Into camps. Eve's grandmother had described to her the desperation and fear that could cause someone to sell out their nearest and dearest for the chance to take just one more breath. Now, in this flood of my own terror, I fully understand how such betrayals might come to be.

Do I still not care about dying? How authentic is my nihilism now? Not authentic at all. I want to *survive*. To continue. And more, I'd sell my closest friends to a brothel before I'd submit to ending it. This knowledge, that I could claw and clutch at survival above all else, above everyone else, gave a broad new understanding in the narrowest of moments.

I readied to spring from my crouched position, to kick and to punch and to run. My heart thumped out of me and into the floor. Was I fainting? Or was the room swaying? Abelman let out a yell as my body vibrated to an unknown rhythm. Suarez shouted, "*Terremoto*," as the floor rippled and shook. *Earthquake! An earthquake! Pachamama come to save me!*

"Must have been the sensor!" Abelman gasped. He thought my mobile ring tone had been the quake alarm warning.

Suarez shouted to stand in a masonry doorway arch, considered the best protection during earthquakes, and they ran to the outer lab and down a side corridor. I wasted no time nipping out from under the bench. *But where to run? What to do?* The floor was rolling and dust was coming down from the ceiling; panelling falling off walls; glass smashing; lights swinging and jerking.

Time shifted back from eternal to instant. In large black letters: '*NOW!*' wrote its name across my milky vision. Just as in the valley, '*NOW! NOW! NOW!*' The word flashed and thumped and impelled me to action.

I ran like the Devil himself was after me, out to the street, to the chaos and the crumbling masonry. At last, this self-important narcissist learns humility… that, and how to crawl through a broken metal door in three seconds flat without tripping over a fleeing guinea pig.

Yet still, I was hanging on to my wig, certain I would survive all dangers. I *willed* it to be so. Only in this mad, delusional state could I negotiate some basic path and keep my sanity.

47 UNDER THE WALL

I finally stopped running four blocks away from Gentrex. The tremors had ceased, but I knew at any moment there would be aftershocks.

I switched my phone back on. It was Ant who'd called. The streets were full of honking horns, and routes by car or taxi were jammed as everyone tried to get back home to loved ones. One of the power lines had fallen down on the Puente Grau and a taxi driver and his passengers had been electrocuted in the centre of the bridge.

Sparks were zinging and zapping as people cried out in horrified impotence, seeing the three charred bodies within. Hysterical matrons were on their knees counting the rosary as babies bawled and grown men crossed themselves and cried. Like frightened children they scattered screaming as the earth emitted its great big growling fart. And everyone and everything had tumbled down like little toys.

The quality of movement was all I'd expected, but the quality of sound? And of fear? That was terrifying and new, like a massive footfall in a forest of terrors. The bass frequency was more profound than my ears or body had ever experienced. I'd felt it in the most primitive part of my brain. This was the big one. A *juddering* seven point nine.

Threats from mere humans don't compare with it, since somewhere in your mental cache you carry the hope that with them you can at least talk your way out: cajole; persuade; manipulate a freedom. But not with this.

The resonance it made seemed to herald the most dangerous of beasts. But it was beyond the predator even, and far beyond our 'clever monkey' power to control or avoid it. Knowing there was *nowhere* safe to run, my ego was reduced to a small, guttural cry in the primordial jungle.

This quake, and the fear it induced, would remain permanently in my psyche, like the nuclear strike and tidal wave nightmares, filed forever in subconscious. Now, I too knew the power of *Pachamama,* and was bound together with the natives of Arequipa in mutual respect and apprehension, in humble acknowledgement of my frail insignificance. Only robo-sapiens and the trans-humans of the future will be immune to such terrors.

Exhausted and shaking, I caught my breath for a full five minutes before continuing to Diego's house, knowing my brother would be there, high as a condor and laughing. I dialled. He answered.

"Syb, you OK? Where are you?"

Apparently, the quake had had caused no problems at Diego's, apart from a small crack in the garden lawn.

"I called you," Ant slurred. "We knew there was going to be a quake because all the dogs started barking just before it happened. Diego says it's a sure sign when they go off like that, because they can hear the rumble before we do."

"Thanks for thinking of me," I said.

He was excited, like a child, his coca-fuelled brain waxing lyrical. He couldn't begin to imagine how the combination of his concern and my stupidity had nearly ended my life. I told him I had directly experienced the quake in full effect.

"Wow, Syb. Isn't it magnificent? The power of the planet! It's an invitation to the God Zone, where humans have to let go the controls and bow to *Pachamama.*"

Anthony loved extreme weather and rugged environments, referring always to Nature's force as the 'is-ness': that which *is* – despite us and beyond us. He frothed on:

"It's a leveller. Like ageing and death. Makes monkeys of all of us. The is-ness just lets you be a frightened animal and you don't need to apologise to anyone. It's a freedom, sis, where arrogance is futile. Where you can surrender your ego without shame."

Shame had always been beyond my emotional remit, I told him. It just seemed to bounce off me, like rain on an upturned bucket. I would see him within half an hour, I said, and hung up.

Turning the corner into a small alleyway, five blocks from Diego's street, I stuffed the wig into my pocket with the now broken mask. I must warn Rosy about the intended fire at Gentrex. I couldn't let innocent people die, but how to warn her without compromising Todd's agenda, or my own? Preoccupied, I almost tripped over a pair of navy and white Nike trainers sticking out from the remains of a collapsed *sillar* wall that I knew had stood at fourteen feet or more, now all but burying the groaning body underneath. I stopped dead in the dim street light as I realised who it was.

"*Maica*! *Maica*! *Christ! Maica*! Can you pull your legs free?"

I brushed grit from his bloodied mouth, yelling for help at the top of my voice. But no one was close. Those at the far end of the alley were running in the opposite direction. As I rolled the largest stone from his chest, Maica's dusty face gasped for air. His eyes opened. Small aftershocks still rippled beneath us as I dragged the smaller stones from his legs.

Judging by the fleck of blood at the side of his mouth, he had chest injuries, and his arm looked as if it were broken. He indicated his top pocket and his mobile phone. It was useless, completely smashed.

"Sybil! Sybil! *Gracias a Dios*! Call my house, *please*! Take the *cha*! Take the *cha*!" he repeated. "I am Yupanqui. No one must find me with it. Not the police. Not anyone."

He fumbled in his pocket for what must have been two hundred grams of cocaine wrapped in a plastic bag, and thrust it into my hand with his good arm. I stuffed it into my knickers, grateful for strong elastic and the power of Lycra tights.

"Don't tell my family you have it. Keep it safe. I will get it back from you. You will not cheat me. I know you have the rose. I have been in the north, in Trujillo. I was going to call you tomorrow."

I adjusted my clothes in the darkness, knowing what my brother's reaction would be if he knew his sister had such a prize. I felt no nerves. The police would be far too busy with the quake to stop and search a *gringa*, even though I was looking at twenty years if caught. Possession of a couple of *falsos* incurs a fine. If you cannot pay, you're sentenced to six weeks in jail. Rich man's justice. In Peru, the legal premise is guilty until proven innocent. Not only does the water go down the plug-hole the opposite way, but so does the law.

Maica gasped his home number and I recorded it into my phone. I called, but there was only a message service, so, in my clearest Spanish, I repeated that he was injured and I would be taking him to a hospital. I phoned Ant again, then Diego, both now engaged. I could not get through to the emergency services, all lines busy. I would have to commandeer a vehicle or pay to get someone to take him to hospital. I knelt closer.

"Will the cocaine ease the pain?"

"No, no, I can never use it. It would be wrong."

But not wrong to sell it to us white folk, presumably.

He gripped my arm. I could see a small triangle tattoo below the joint of his thumb and forefinger on his left hand. I had registered it on our previous meetings but now it seemed more familiar.

"You have the rose," he repeated. "She is beautiful, no?"

I'd ignored his first mention of the rose. Injured though he was, he could have been bluffing, but now it was obvious he knew, so why lie?

"Yes, she is beautiful. Are there other roses?"

I was desperate for another. I had to ask. He might die and take his secret with him.

"There is only one," he said. "It is the black rose of the Incas."

"*No* others? Are you *sure?*" I grabbed his shoulders. Was it a unique hybrid? Sterile? No viable seeds? I saw one at the cemetery. There *must* be more.

"The *chakra sagrada* has been in our family for so many years; we have kept the secret and have never seen another rose. Never. My grandmother used to dry the petals with coca leaf for the shrine to El Misti when she was a girl. You are the only one to see her outside of my family. I was cursed when I took you to her. I did it for money. Only for the money. The gods have taken revenge on me. The *contradrogas* have poisoned my land. My name is finished. My children do not want children. My coca is gone and I have deserved it all."

As if the puppeteer had sheared the strings of his creation, my spirits crumpled down with this news. He had animated me with his rose and I had come to life, breathlessly following his command, blindfolded and blown up in his *chakra sagrada*, his sacred field, to get what I wanted. He couldn't help me now; only Gentrex could deliver what I most desired.

Clenching my fists, I resolved to use every ounce of my diligence and wit to get it, clarity of purpose burning into my brain like a branding iron. I mentally drew a line through Maica's name, but I wasn't about to let him die. I rang the ambulance again, terrified that aftershocks would bring the remainder of the wall down on us both, but still I could not get through, not to Ant, not to Diego, it was maddening; so I sent a short text to my brother: 'Call me. Urgent. Need doctor.'

I pulled out Maica's handkerchief from the pocket where he'd had the cocaine, to wipe the trickle of blood coming from his mouth. Pieces of gold jewellery from inside the cotton square spilled out in the dust. Still frantically calling for help, I waved my arms at distant strangers.

"Birthday gifts," he wheezed, as I put the gold back into his pocket. "I am a shoe-mender. I have only worked the coca for them. The *niños* went to the *universidad*. They speak English."

He was talking about his children. Judging by the quality and workmanship of the gold, business must have been absolutely booming until it went 'boom'.

"Maica, why did you leave me to die?"

"I didn't leave you. I didn't leave you. I ran because I had broken the promise to my family. My son was less than half a kilometre behind us all the time. He found out I had taken you to the *chakra*. He warned me of the men on the hill when he phoned… the *contradrogas*. They shot down my *casita* with rockets. They killed Panchito, my cousin, and his little dog. After the explosion my son made sure you were followed to get *la negrita* back from you. You caught the bus at Puno, we knew you were safe. You are strong, *gringa*."

He grabbed my wrist.

"You will survive many things. They should have taken her away from you, but my son was afraid. He said the gods had willed it. He said you saved the rose from all the poison. He said you held her like the child you will never have."

Maica lay back, breathing hard, holding his chest. The remark was impertinent, poignant, and true. Amidst all my doubts, my greatest certainty is my lack of desire to reproduce. How perturbed I felt by a stranger's easy access to my private resolve. Such astute observation made me feel naked – vulnerable – *angry*. I did not want pity, or anything resembling it from these Catholic breeders. I rounded on him:

"I've been ringing and texting you for bloody days, but there was no answer. Why didn't you call?"

"Bad cell phone signal in Trujillo. I have been with my uncle trying to raise money for the *terroristas*. They wanted all the money I made from the coca or they threatened to kill my family."

He trailed off, convulsed in a coughing fit, more blood spitting from his mouth. I lifted his head; my fury was pointless.

"I thought if I paid them they would leave me alone. I could start a new *chakra* somewhere, but I could never give them mine because of the rose," he gasped.

"Is your son in Arequipa?" I hoped to call him, and enlist help.

"My son, he is wanted by the police. Years ago, he was a *terrorista*. *Sendero Luminoso*. I pray for him every day. When the *terroristas* started using coca for money, my son rejected them. He knows coca is C*apacocha,* like the rose. He would not use her or the coca for guns."

So, his son was a terrorist with a conscience. A selective conscience, of course, like all of us. I wiped Maica's bleeding face as he continued:

"When you said you wanted the rose, I knew I could use your money to pay the *Senderistas* to leave me alone, but I needed to ask my family. They all said no, but I was desperate. I had already sold all but one of the *combi* buses and given the *Senderistas* the money, and now they want more. Coca is the only way I have to make good money, but I betrayed the sacred rose. I am a Judas and the gods have punished me. You must put her back. She is *Capacocha*. Put her back in the soil of the Inca."

Tears squeezed out from the corners of his dark eyes, running down through my hands to his ears and neck. The Catholics had taught him how to writhe in guilt, but they didn't yet own his soul, for he called out the names of more than one god, of *Pachamama* and of *Misti*, the mountain deity. He was still a pagan at heart. He knew he was dying. He looked directly at me, sobbing. "*La Parca* is calling me. I can hear her voice."

Ant had told me that the mythical figure of death in this culture is not the Grim Reaper, it is *La Parca*, a woman, dressed in black robes. Seeking her dead son, she will take anyone to fill the void of her mourning. In Maica's mind, the veiled succubus was standing beside him and he had reconciled himself to her need. He told me in a whisper to tell his family that he loved them.

What can you say to a dying man? How could I make his last moments more bearable? I could not give him the only two things appropriate to ease his pain: morphine or love. With death at such proximity, I thought of Evie, of how she slipped from me. I held his hand and started to sob.

"You still have something good in this world Maica. Your children. Beautiful. Alive. You must recover for their sake."

This time I wanted a happy ending. For him. For me. For Anthony. I had not lost the greater part of my reason by indulging fantasy and sentiment. I was still aware that everything I hoped for could be thwarted and withered and would not bear fruit. But when the mathematics of infinite possibility is embraced, hope is not naïveté. Hope is motivation. Hope *is* reason.

"There were two flowers that week, one for my wife's grave. Always the rose starts to flower in the week my wife died. My beautiful Terésa."

"How did she die?"

"When my son was born. She only saw him for a few hours. She was bleeding so much. I took her to the hospital, but they couldn't save her. We put a rose in her coffin. Always I think of my Terésa when I see the rose. But the *chakra* is burned black now, the *contradrogas* have poisoned everything and the *terroristas* still want money."

I had not thought of our money contract until that point. To ask for the return of my fifty pieces of silver as recompense for being blown up was ridiculous now. He had not asked for the further $2,000 because I had the rose, only that I returned her to her rightful place. My stomach heaved from the weight of that request. How could I fulfil it? And, were it possible, did I want to? I could tell him the truth: that she had burned to death; that I had stolen his dead wife's rose from the cemetery; that the late Stan Fischer had taken the stem and grown some cells; that I had no idea where they were, or even if I could ever retrieve them since his plane crash. Maica started rolling his head from side to side repeating:

"*La Parca*! *What have I done*? *What have I done*?"

He drew in his breath sharply. "*La negrita* must live forever. Keep the secret or I no can make my peace with the mountain. El Misti will swallow us all. He will swallow us all."

So, here, amid these stones and dust, it occurs to me that though I have no morphine or love to give him, I can *lie*. I am a practised and convincing liar. I can promise him all he asks. I can lie to a dying man and offer him the illusion of salvation. As I open my mouth to speak, a little black dog runs out from behind me, yapping and snarling.

Its owner was swift in helping me remove the last of the stones from Maica's legs. He brought a flat sheet of plywood and we lifted Maica onto it and carried him twenty groaning yards to the back of a truck. The man's name was Salvador Condori. I gave him the phone number. He promised he would take Maica to hospital and ring his family. As we parted, Maica pulled me close to him and whispered:

"The cha. *Please* – burn it for the gods. Tell them you are sorry for taking the rose. Promise me, Sybil. Promise."

He stretched out his dark hand to me as I turned toward Diego's.

48 DIEGO'S HOUSE

Diego's house, like those around it, had sustained no quake damage at all. Walking down the path, I mused on Maica's imminent death and *La Parca*'s chaotic selections. Better she had taken Diego, keeper of my brother's soul.

"We are waiting for Maica," the dealer said, smiling widely with his big, stained teeth. The guests were sitting in the back yard, drinking wine. Fernando, Diego's Venezuelan friend, was there. I was greeted warmly, with questions about where I had been when the *terremoto* struck. My brother ran forward to embrace me.

"I've only just read your text, sis. Are you OK? Are you hurt?"

I shook my head, describing the taxi accident on the bridge, the chaos in the streets. I told them about Maica, that he was in hospital. They seemed to straighten up as if woken from a dream; their faces visibly paled. First, they asked if he were dead, then if I knew what had happened to the '*cha*'. Diego would now have to find another supplier, and fast, since he had several customers waiting.

The atmosphere turned strangely hostile. They hated that I had snapped them back to raw reality, away from their childlike excitement of the *terremoto* and anticipation of Maica's visit. Fernando looked at his watch and left, realising he could not score coke from Diego that night. It was Ant's Piaget watch. My gift to my brother. Now it was clear it had been swapped, or sold, for cocaine, or given away in the reckless, grandiose fugue that coke induces.

I explained that Maica's phone was smashed and that Diego should try to contact his family if he knew how. They all seemed vague, lost somehow. I wanted to slap them. Somewhere across the city, Maica was dying, perhaps within the hour, and I had an overwhelming urge to write a letter to him. He'd taken me to the black rose. He'd given me a *reason*, a focus. And though I was foundering, and the rose had been reduced to a few cells, I hoped I might truly thank him, or offer him some comfort before he died. Diego gave me paper and envelope as he readied two bicycles for a trip to the hospital with Ant. Not wishing to mention the rose directly, I wrote in large printed Spanish, as Maica's sight may be fading:

"*Maica, this is Sybil. I send you love. I send you my deepest respect. You took me to the heart of your culture and showed me perfect beauty. This meant so much to me as an artist. It will sustain me until love or art return to me, and for this I thank you. Please forgive your children. They will make you proud when you accept they have different dreams to you. They are young. They may yet have children to continue your name. You gave them the two greatest gifts: love and education. If they know how to love, they will not disappoint you. They will rise and fulfil their dreams and maybe some of yours, too; then they will know what a great papá you have been.*"

Aware of my dramatic tone without self-consciousness, I signed the letter and pressed it into my brother's hand. If imminent death is not the grand theatre where one can speak one's most heartfelt lines, then I have no place here.

Anthony promised me he would deliver it without showing Diego, who re-entered the room with a box of tissues and thanked me for taking care of Maica. He shook my hand with his dry, scaly fingers, kissing my cheeks with utter sincerity, then they left.

But the dealer's cheap aftershave lingered on my skin; his power over my brother lingered in my psyche. Diego was reptilian, waiting always with slitted eye to pick off his vulnerable prey. Whether he became a dealer in order to support his habit, or because it gave him the social caché that he was too lazy to achieve through hard work, no one knew.

A gifted poet, he was loose in principle and weak in conscience. Deep and shallow in equal measure. His personality had definitely been bent out of shape by his upbringing, but through laziness, neglect or fear, he had not unravelled the mess before he'd reached middle age and was disinclined to work on his psychological ghosts.

He was, nevertheless, one of the best-known dealers in Arequipa, with the finest quality merchandise, courtesy of Maica. The job provided him with an endless supply of 'friends' and a non-stop social life revolving around his product. Deigo was a narcissist, always well-groomed despite his self-imposed lack of funds due to his habit. Needless to say, a woman was regularly washing and pressing his clothes.

The woman's name was Christina, mother of Diego's children. She now appeared in the doorway and invited me in for *chicha*, the sweet, fermented drink made from black maize. I repeated the story about Maica. She understood that if Diego did not track his supply there would be no bread on the table and no rent paid.

Swaying under the influence of rum, she told me that his recent two-day bender had depleted all their resources, and she had no food for her children. Her hospitality was obviously aimed to elicit some cash from me. I was disinclined to fund my brother's favourite poisoner; he should look after his own brood. Changing the subject, I asked her about Maica. Had she known him long? Did she know his family?

"Yes. Diego met him in the jail. He mended the shoes. He has a beautiful Qqechua name, Maica Cauac: 'the eagle that guards'. He was in the jail for drugs. Maica lied to his family for so many years. His children thought he was an honest businessman with all the *combi* buses. They are ashamed their money has come from coca. They refuse to use their education to make money for themselves because it was paid for by coca. They think their life would be cursed. So she is an *empleada,* a cleaner, like her mother used to be, and he is a *terrorista.* They hate refined coca; they hate him for growing it because it is very bad luck when their family is Lloques and Yupanquis."

"Lloques? Yupanquis? What does that mean?"

"It is the names of the ruling families of the Inca. *Atunrunas,* the highest caste. They has the *triangulo* always... here." She indicated her left hand below the thumb and forefinger. "They were always the guardians of coca and sacrificed it to the mountain. It is very bad for them to use it for money. Dirty. The son is a crazy *Senderista*. His picture is on posters up near Puno. He strange. He think it his fault the mother she die. He look just like her. He don' have many friends but his cousin is the night cleaner at the Museo. He hides him there sometimes when he needs to come to town."

"The son *was* a *Senderista. Was*. He's no longer with them. Maica told me," I said, realising that this must be the same tattooed hand that had guided me to Juanita, the same terrorist Diego had described to Ant, for surely he can't know many and the connection was now obvious.

According to Diego, the rebel group had murdered an entire village, including two army officers, who were found with their hearts torn out. Hearts that the terrorists then roasted and ate as a gesture of power over their enemies, writing the news of their atrocity in blood on a wall.

Ant had told me that the terrorist was an ex bodybuilder and Satanist, of all things, apparently in reaction to his Catholic upbringing. He was now a social outcast living in the jungle. So, I had been standing alone in the museum with an ex Satanist who had eaten human heart. A man of charisma, culture and charm, who had shown me his history. A man who had also touched a black rose.

As I drank the *chicha,* I looked around me. The house was filthy, full of flies and dust. So much money passed through Diego's hands on a monthly basis and so little was spent on his family. I wondered how Christina tolerated it.

I saw three books on the table and noticed gold bracelets on Christina's wrists, all of them mine; then the borrowed CD player; the DVDs; Ant's iPod. Ant had been taking things from our apartment to pay for his habit, even though I was giving him a daily allowance.

Whether this was for extra cocaine or just to keep the dealer sweet was now irrelevant.

Already reeling from Rocio's infidelity and the knowledge that Maica's rose was irreplaceable, this third blow knocked me lower. I felt sick to my stomach. Addicts always become infatuated with their dealer. Ant would go misty-eyed at what he'd convinced himself was true friendship. Parts of it were, since there is a selfish mutuality in all relationships. We work hardest at those that advantage us.

How supportive would Ant be if Diego came out of rehab, clean and serene, with no intention of returning to his old life? My brother would drop him like a stone, just as he would if someone with better quality or cheaper *cha* were available. But right now, Diego loved to manipulate and control such a talented *gringo*. His only currency was cocaine and he used his power to the full. The bisexual dealer would transfix my brother as he measured the wraps, knowing that attention and affection would continue in a steady stream as he stroked his white goddess into paper *falso* envelopes.

To watch Ant dance for his Svengali made me angry, sad and sorry, reaffirming Diego's place as organ grinder to all the jumping monkeys. Anthony's relationship with this candy man had supplanted ours. I used to be the most important thing in his world, next to music. Our bond had been unbreakable until he tasted Peruvian cocaine. But I wasn't going to try and rival this coupling, even though my passion for my brother's gift was so strong and my sorrow at its dissipation so profound. I finished the *chicha* and stood to go.

Christina asked me if I had ever seen Laura with Diego. She was jealous; her husband had often remarked on Laura's generous curves.

"I haven't seen Laura lately, Christina. I've only been in her company three or four times," I said, walking to the door.

"She has not been to buy *cha* for eight weeks."

"Well, don't worry," I reassured her, "she lives with an American boyfriend, maybe he doesn't like her taking it."

"With the beard? I saw them togethers in a car on Tuesday."

"Yeah, that's him," I lied, empathising with the cuckold cowboy Todd, until I remembered that Stan had now left the stage quite clear for him.

I walked home. The streets were pregnant with anticipation, a million expectant ears straining to hear the next tiny rumble. Holding the broken mask in my pocket, I was thinking to glue it back together and possibly return to Gentrex for a second look, taking advantage of the chaos. My phone broke the silence.

"You OK, missy? I couldn't stop 'em. I thought you could hide OK. I came back for ya', but I figured you'd gotten out through the busted door at the side."

"I'm OK, Todd."

"Things need sortin' here an' I gotta look like I give a shit. It'll take hours cleanin' up this mess. I'll come to ya' at midday. D'ya get it all? Everythin' ya' came fer?"

"I got all you need, Todd." But sadly, not all I needed.

I hadn't even come close to that.

49 CHARLIE WIGS OUT AGAIN

Ant returned after dawn to find me in a yoga position on the floor, trying desperately to find some inner calm. He had sobered up and delivered my letter. Maica had read it before he died. Apparently, Diego was distraught that his partner in crime was gone.

"Latin men don't hold back tears," Ant remarked. "He really sobbed."

But I had seen my British brother Anthony cry many times, sometimes in rage and frustration when he couldn't get his candy, often because he was overwhelmed with sentiment when seeing abused children or beaten animals on the news, all too aware of his impotence in affecting change. Despite his enduring tantrums, he was very sensitive, it showed in his art. No one could listen to his music and think otherwise.

The missing *cha* had not been located. They hadn't dared ask Maica in front of his family. Ant was desperate. He would now have to spend my dollars on the harsh street coke, cut with all kinds of muck. He questioned me, in case I had seen the drugs under the fallen wall. Suspecting theft, Diego and he had gone back to the spot, pulling up each heavy brick in search of it, concluding that either Salvador Condori or Maica's relatives were the culprits. Little did Ant know it was hanging on a peg, only fifteen yards away, in the pocket of my suede coat. Ignoring Maica's request to burn it, I had kept it as a possible bargaining tool with whomsoever stood in my way of getting the black rose.

I mentioned my bracelets and the books, the old CD player, iPod and CDs. I told him I knew Fernando had his watch. The atmosphere soured.

"What's your problem? It was *my* fucking watch. Stop being such a control freak and mind your own business. I'll get the books and the CD player back. They're on loan. For someone so rich you're really tight-fisted, you know that? Is your precious little ego offended because no one could grovel a 'thank you' for your generosity?"

"No. And my ego is neither precious, nor little. I have a gold star, top-of-the-range, twenty-four-carat, *massive* ego. If you are going to insult me, bro, I insist on accuracy."

It transpired that the bracelets were given as a recent birthday gift to Christina, who had fed him and washed his clothes before I arrived. He appeared vaguely repentant, but really, in his heart, he was dismissing the incident as trivial because I could afford it. I thought he was like a wild dog, utterly self-serving, with only a patina of caring. Selfishness would motivate him to show a relative affection, wagging his tail for the hand that provided… but only while it fed, his eye always looking for opportunity elsewhere.

I told him about my breaking into the lab. He was furious, neatly manipulating faux concern into anger, to match mine against his theft of my property.

"You stupid *cow!* Why didn't you wait? I'd have helped. Stood guard with a baseball bat or something."

"You were on a bender, remember? Look at the state of you!"

He was hollow-cheeked, red-eyed and unshaven, his beauty shrouded by the white spectre. I made some breakfast whilst he showered. I knew that he was utterly changed by cocaine and that this was the final road into full addiction. He would never achieve his musical goals while he was a slave to such a drug. Only by relying on the goodwill of others could he move forward, yet he soon stopped the goodwill flowing by borrowing money and being unable to pay it back, shitting on yet another doorstep.

Just as we sat down to eat he received a call from Mavis. Her voice was so shrill I could hear it from four yards away.

"Anthony, you must come over right now! Charlie's flipped out. He's scarin' me."

"What happened?"

"They came for him *with guns!* He's freaked out, man. Come now, my house. Forty-two, Calle St Augustine."

"*Who* came for him?" Ant asked. I rushed to listen at my brother's side. Charlie had grabbed the phone and was gasping:

"Anthony, those *bastards!* They threatened me! I have to leave the country. They will kill me! You must go to my house and get some things. Now!"

"Sure, Charlie, calm down," Ant reassured him. "I'll come to you at Mavis's house."

"Yes, yes but *hurry*; they will find me. You don't know these bastards. You don't know what is happening to me. I must get out. Hurry Anthony, *please*."

"OK, I'll come right now."

Ant pocketed his phone, explaining the situation to me, walking into the kitchen to pick up a knife and hiding it in his jacket. From my life as a child with him, I had always known that it was a waste of breath to say "*Don't*!" So, I embraced him as he was about to leave. He was cursory in his affection, still embarrassed by his theft, or rather my discovery of it, so he pecked my cheek and left.

Though he was used to Peruvian histrionics, I could tell Ant was genuinely worried. Always there were dramas with Charlie, mostly constructed by Charlie himself, and usually of the more petty kind. But this incident was totally different. If Charlie were connected to the *Cuca* project and worked for the cartels, it may be very dangerous to associate with him.

What intrigued Ant was the chance of a toot of the super-coke, and it was this that was motivating his bravery. I knew it, and he knew I knew it. He was also curious to know if Charlie's buffoonery may have been a stunning piece of acting to cover up his cunning. Maybe his avuncular looks and whitening hair hid a mind like a steel trap: fluffy snow on a cold, barb-wired roof.

Ant took a taxi over to Mavis's house on the far side of Yanahuara, just one block from the Gentrex building. The debris from the quake was all over the road. Police had cordoned off the dangerous areas with white tape. Ant's cab had to stop short of the house, so he picked his way through the rubble on foot. He knocked five times before anyone answered. Mavis peeped from the upstairs window before descending and opening the door a tiny crack.

"Anthony! Come in man; he's really freakin' out. You talk to him!"

She quickly looked up and down the street, then slammed and triple-locked the door.

"Where is he?"

"In there. Back in the cupboard. He's locked himself in."

"The *cupboard*?"

"I know, I told you he was scared."

Charlie was coaxed from his hidey-hole with gentle reassurance. Unable to unlock it from within, due to shaking hands and the pitch black, he slid the key under the door. Ashen-faced, he was ushered to daylight.

"Anthony! Anthony! *Thank God*!" He flung his arms around his fellow addict. Ant was shocked by Charlie's appearance. His clothes were dishevelled and dirty and he was barefoot. Normally so well groomed, he was now unshaven, oyster-eyed and his lips covered in a white film. Ant said he had never seen anyone look that scared since the night before my first exhibition.

Apparently, Charlie had been visited by Suarez's henchmen. They'd met him at the airport from the early plane and frog-marched him to his car, demanding to know where '*it*' was. Charlie, nonplussed, was innocent of all charges, except adultery, corruption, greed, petty snobbery, drug addiction, alcoholism, and cocaine paranoia. Professing innocence only got him pistol-whipped. Ant could see a bruise at the side of his jaw.

"They keep saying I've stolen a flashing drive and a compact disc."

Ant turned white. He knew what CD and flash drive 'they' meant, but not how Charlie came to own it, or why the debauched Don seemed so genuinely bewildered if, in fact, he were in on the deal. My brother was about to be enlightened by the burbled facts:

Charlie had registered his car in a business name, a business that had subsequently gone bankrupt. His ex-partner in that business was entitled to some assets, since it was Charlie's drunken incompetence that had brought the restaurant they had both invested in to its knees. A lawyer's letter duly arrived demanding the car as a payable asset, but Charlie, having sought his own legal advice, refused to give it up.

But Ramon Suarez Montez, the ex-partner, enacted an illegal snatch-back, and Charlie woke one morning to find the car trailing out of the courtyard and out of his sight for the last time. This was why he was going to see the lawyer when I met him outside the Internet café. And why we had found the car so far from his house the night we stole it. It was no longer under Charlie's jurisdiction, Suarez was the new owner.

As Charlie tried to prove his ownership through the legal system, his wits ever duller from the spanking his monkey was giving him, Suarez had upped his own game and was in bed with the kind of crocodiles that could swallow Charlie whole.

But Charlie thrived on intrigue and hubris and could always find money to perpetuate it, especially when his social standing and reputation were at stake. He was determined to have his status symbol returned.

"Why does the greedy bastard need my car?" screamed Charlie. "He's got shares; he's got houses; garages; shops. He's already got three Mercedes! He's a fuckin' director of Gentrex! He's a *bastard!*"

What exquisite justice, I thought, when Ant finally told me the saga: others dirtied their hands achieving my goal, dealing out Charlie's karmic come-uppence. Something for nothing. Satisfying… *Rare.* Technically, we had stolen the snatched-back car and put Charlie's life at risk. By parking the car back on his driveway, Ant had made it appear as if Charlie had snatched back the ‘snatchback’, with all of Suarez’s private items on board.

I remembered that whilst on our expedition, my brother had prized open the glove compartment looking for a secret cocaine stash and found Charlie’s gun. He’d also checked every nook and cranny of the car for more coke, including the carpet flap he knew was used as a hiding place for *falsos*. Surprised to find the flash drive and unmarked CD, Ant had taken them out of nothing more than idle curiosity, leaving the other assorted bits: stupid serendipity now motive for murder.

The gunmen met Charlie at the airport and frog-marched him to the Mitsubishi, convinced of his guilt in taking the items. They drove into Arequipa, ignoring his denials, preparing to torture him, but were taken completely off guard when the Don bashed one of the interrogators in the face with his mobile phone, breaking his nose.

Charlie then scrambled out into Ecercito, the main street, where a shot would have attracted too much attention. He escaped his captors by ducking down back alleys, sweating henchmen and stray dogs in hot pursuit. One of the assailants had snatched Charlie’s gun from the glove compartment: the same gun that had done for the daggle-tailed dog. But when chasing Charlie, he let it slip from his gloved hand, and it skidded under a car. Since it couldn’t be retrieved without public attention, it was summarily abandoned; detected only when the battered blue Subaru exited its parking space and revealed it.

Mavis had been up all night, frightened by the *terremoto*, trying to calm Wishbone and tend to what appeared to be a vicious bite mark on his nose. Already disturbed and fretful, she opened the door to find a half-dead Charlie begging entrance, covered in blood from his captor’s broken nose and with one shoe on. All contrivances of the Peruvian pecking order had paled into insignificance as their mutual angst blended beautifully behind the blinds of number forty-two. Ant was dumbfounded.

"Help me!" gasped a breathless Charlie, grabbing Ant's hand. "You don't know… You don't know! I've seen *animals*! Horrible! Terrible! *Rats*."

Ant's guilt and junkie empathy kicked in, figuring the Don was having a major bout of *delirium tremens* and paranoia, but glad his friend was not party to the Gentrex agenda. He was very disappointed that it meant no super-coke, but wary that this mental collapse could be the price Charlie had paid for his 'super' high.

"Take my keys! Take them! I need you to go to my house. I must have my phone charger and my passports. Everything in my wall safe behind the picture of the Virgin. I will write the combination. I also need shoes, clothes. I'll write a list. Anthony, *please*... don't tell anyone my car was taken. Don't tell Diego, or anyone!"

Still preoccupied with his status, Charlie clutched a jingling key ring and a crumpled piece of paper, on which he quickly scribbled his needs.

"Wait here, Charlie. Just wait," Ant said, neither promising nor admitting anything.

"Help him, for God's sake!" Mavis hissed as Charlie shrank back into the gloom. "He's havin' a breakdown. I've offered him a *tuerto* of coke an' he don' wan' it; says he's never gonna use it no more an' no drinkin' either. Keeps seein' *cuys* an' rats. He says that one of them has his phone number written on its back."

Ant's hair stood on end. Even the snow-blind Diego had recently advised Charlie to come in from the blizzard of cocaine he'd been weathering. This was the result of excess, obviously: a warning not to push Madam Coca too far.

But the truth of it was that after the earthquake, Mavis's little dog Wishbone had been chasing Carter, the escaped guinea-pig, round the house all night. With 612 written in indelible ink on either flank, the little drug-addicted *cuy* had sought security at Mavis's through a broken air brick. Now, Carter was quietly ensconced in a sock under the bed quivering with cocaine withdrawal and fear.

Just like Charlie.

50 PURGATORY AND PYROTECHNICS

I slept, finally, but it was fitful, and the dreams persisted: falling walls; dark faces with elongated skulls; the smell of gasoline. I was woken by the high-pitched chiffering noise from a hummingbird on the balcony, hovering over hibiscus.

Alert for new quakes, I re-read the Gentrex report and finished the last page just as the doorbell rang. I leant out of the window, throwing down my keys to Todd. He wheezed as he came through the door, breathless and smelling of sweat.

"You got it? What happened?"

I handed him the CD, the flash drive and a print-out I'd made. He flipped through it, standing in the light from the window and squinting.

"Yup. Jis' like I thought. Fuckin' morons! Jail's too good fer 'em. Like t'git 'em on m'own fer a couple o' hours."

"OK, Todd, but you won't, will you? Leave that to the Greenies and get the hell out. Go into hiding. These people have long tentacles. Disappear for a while." I poured him a beer.

"What do you think happened to Stan? D'you think he's really dead?"

"Don' give a damn where that son of a bitch is, long as it's far away from me and mine. Be lyin' if I said I cared, but I don' wish him no harm. He's sure smart. *Sure is*."

He didn't even look up. I was unable to share my angst with him concerning the unknown whereabouts of the rose but I was determined that she should not be cremated again.

"Todd, don't burn down Gentrex," I said. "I overheard Abelman say they're going to burn the lab themselves in ten days and trap everyone connected to the project inside the building. They have to wait until the experiments are finished. Ant thinks we should tell the police maybe, let them deal with it. But I told him…"

"Those slimy bastards? They'd tek a bribe t' murder their own mothers. Don' you worry, missy. No one's gonna die. Todd Whale's cleaning up that rat's nest *real* pronto. They won' have time t' move nothin'."

He stood under the light again re-reading the document. I was about to ask him to elucidate when the television flashed a photo of Charlie. I immediately turned up the sound.

"This man is Carlos Silvestre Mendoza Gonsavo, wanted in connection with the murder of known homosexual Luis José Muñoz Pacheco, whose body was found two weeks ago in the Rio Chile. Mendoza Gonsavo is missing from his residence in Arequipa and may be armed and dangerous. The police are asking the homosexual community not to harbour him. Anyone knowing of his whereabouts should contact the Arequipa police."

After reading about the shenanigans at Gentrex, nothing about Charlie could now shock me. Not even an accusation of murder. I was sure he was in some way sexually confused or repressed. Transvestite perhaps. A difficult predilection in machoville. Maybe he was a psychopathic closet case who hated his gay side. But *murder*? No wonder he was so freaked out on the phone. I should warn Ant.

"Fuckin' faggots," spat Todd, looking at the screen.

"Not keen on the pink community, then?" I didn't know Todd could understand much Spanish, but he'd recognised the word 'homosexual'.

"If you mean faggots, no! It's goin' ag'inst nature what's got 'em all diseased." He drained his beer. Buttons pressed, I started to rant.

"Fuck off, Todd. This is the twenty-first century. No one should have to live in fear because of who they love. Repression in Peru is a horrible undercurrent. You have to be blind not to notice it. Hand-in-hand with all the Catholic hypocrisy comes guilt, social exclusion… even *murder*!"

"Ain't repressed enough if ya' ask me. Goddam TV's full of 'em."

He was right about that. As if by way of redress, the networks employed misogynistic gay TV presenters who devoted entire programmes to criticising the hair, make-up and clothes of women in public life. The anti-gay, Catholic population finds this hilarious.

"For Christ's sake, Todd. Imagine living in fear of being killed just because you're gay. The strain of duplicity must be terrible. Most gay men marry and have children as a cover. Being a homosexual in a macho is no easy gig. It's not that easy in any society, frankly. Some people are repulsed by you. Sometimes it's your own family."

"Sure be glad when I get out of this place, it's full o' fuckin' queers. I got us these." He produced four air tickets to Lima and thrust two firmly into my hand.

"You'll wanna leave too, right? Figured you'd tek yer brother."

"Is Laura leaving with you?" I doubted it. Coke is ten times the price in the Land of the Free. He surprised me with his answer:

"Yup, we're tekkin' the first flight at six in the mornin'. Yours are for four in the afternoon."

He looked straight at me and smiled.

"Laura 'n' me, we might even raise us a couple o' kids."

I put the tickets in my pocket, not wanting to poop the party. Babies born to cocaine-addicted mothers? Not a great idea.

"What do I owe you?"

"Nothin'. This'n's on me. I got me some expenses from Colby sent down here."

"Thanks, Todd. Good luck, man." I put my hand out to shake his, but he was already turning to go.

"Kin't say it's 'bin a pleasure, but it's 'bin real interestin'."

"Listen, Todd, you and Laura, stay in touch. I'll give you my email address."

I fumbled for a piece of paper to write on. From my *campesino* bag, I pulled out the picture of Jesus I'd plucked from the floor of Charlie's car when cleaning the evidence of our theft: the identical Jesus image that had revealed the double agenda. I asked Todd if he had a pen.

"Don' worry 'bout that. Laura's cuttin' all ties here. She's a real diff'rent gal. Ain't usin' coke n'mores and I ain't the kind 'o guy that sends them email things."

I threw Jesus down on the side table and turned to face him.

"OK, whatever. Good luck anyway, Todd. Hope all your dreams come true, man. You and Laura."

I asked him his schedule for the Gentrex explosion. He opened the door to descend to the street, adding casually,

"Don' be anywheres near the buildin' early mornin' t'morrow or the day after. Ain't decided which."

"No, Todd, *please*, not so soon. You can't blow it up till I've rescued my … er, *cactus*. *Please*."

"Too late, missy. Ya' had yer chance."

Then he left, closing the door. That was it. He'd gone. No 'Cheers, mate', no 'Thanks, pal', no '*Adios, amigo*'. I guess I was just too British or too gay to merit acknowledgement. But I shed no tears. No matter what I did or said, would Todd ever have liked me? Of course not.

Even my own mother found that one difficult.

51 ORIGIN OF SPECIES

Far from letting go of my hopes for the rose, I was acutely focused. I must try to get back into the lab, but my mask was not simply broken in one piece, it was badly chipped. There wasn't time to mend and repaint it, so what possible excuse would there be to go to Gentrex and ask for the rose cells? The *truth*? Almost, maybe. I could say Stan was cloning my cactus, like my brother had suggested. It was my best hope. I rang Ant to talk it through with him. No answer, so I texted him to call me, telling him of my decision.

With confidence and clarity, I strode down to Gentrex and banged on the main door. A bulky *mestizo* in a security uniform opened it. It was Chicau, monkey number one, the shaved ape who'd been servicing Rosy. I explained slowly in Spanish what I wanted. He was adamant that no unauthorised personnel could enter the building and he flatly refused me, shrugging his bulk and slamming the door.

Shit! Now I would have to try and contact Rosy and persuade her to join in the game, but, like my brother's phone, her mobile was only taking messages. She never used any apps or social media, despite me explaining how essential it would be for her career. I didn't know where she lived exactly, only the district, otherwise I would have gone over to her house there and then. I tapped the text furiously, banging the phone keys: *'Rosy, call me immediately you get this, S x.'*

By ten at night she'd not replied. I had only one option left, since Todd had made it clear that he would not help me a second time, so I returned to Gentrex, hoping that Chicau might tell me her address for a serious bribe. I could say I needed to refund her the money she gave me for the English lessons, as I planned to leave Peru. But no one answered the door, even though I banged for half an hour.

Exhausted and desperate, I phoned Todd and begged him once again to help. His answer was direct and clear. The gels in the inner office had all been boxed, ready to move that afternoon, and the lab was now cleared completely.

"A cactus is n'more important than a hill 'o beans, seems to me. Forget it. Don' be dumb," he said, and hung up.

I took two blue pills and fell asleep. The dreams were all in blue. Blue skies; Ant's eyes; the Prussian blue of uniforms. Indigo, woad and ultramarine. The seas of Greek islands. The canvases of Yves Klein.

When I woke, close to midday, a flood of yellow sunlight dispelled them. I made tea, and sat on the sofa facing Misti. On the table beside me was the picture of Jesus. The top edge looked like it had been torn from a ring binder. I stared at it for two seconds then picked it up. On the reverse, in blurred black biro was the number: 0549777777.

Folded sevens stained the paper.

I pulled out my phone and dialled. A voice quietly said, "*Holá*?" I recognised it immediately. I wasn't shocked, I was elated. I drew in my breath and asked for what I most wanted.

"Stan, where's my fucking rose?"

There was a terrible silence. My instinct to ring had been dead right. I could tell Fischer was incensed at his own stupidity in the midst of his brilliant plans. This must have been his one mistake. He'd forgotten to take the chip out of his phone and had answered by instinct. "Where did you get this number?" he hissed.

"I stole it, Stan. It's a long story. Don't hang up," I pleaded. "I won't say a word about anything to anyone. I absolutely, solemnly promise I won't say a bloody word, not even to Ant. I just want the rose. *Please*."

A short silence. Then the voice said:

"That was no ordinary rose, Sybil. Where d'ya get it? It was quite an inspiration."

"*Please,* Stan, I'll pay. What do you want? Tell me how to get her. Is she still alive? Are the cells growing?"

"They're doin' more than that. They got married."

"Where is she?"

"In the bridal suite."

I held my breath, now certain that I had been the provider of the means to strengthen the *Cuca* cocaine. My dark princess wasn't just in bed with the enemy, she was breeding with him.

"I've never seen a molecular configuration like that. It was awesome. A new insight. You're no artist, are ya? What biotech lab are you dealin' with? Lifex? Biodyne? Why d'ya involve me? Fall out with them over the money?"

"*What?* What are you talking about?"

"The rose. Who engineered it? Meyers? Ron Leiber? What colour was it? Blue, maybe? That would make the big bucks. Natural roses don't have blue genes. Is that what you added along with the human stuff?"

They coiled into my ear those words, then burst across the insides of my eyes like blackberry stains on a tablecloth, smudging like little bruises. Christ! Why didn't I think of that before? *Why did it never occur to me?* My head swam. My heart, mind and hope now traduced by this fresh oblivion – another death. But this time, the death of an ideal.

I'd presumed the black rose was a gift from *Pachamama,* but no, her apparent perfection had been vitiated by test tube. She was a transgressor, stomping on the standards my pretentious art had set for her. She was not a wild beauty, but a strumpet: a cynical moll, put into the world to lure riches. The secret petals in Juanita's purse disintegrated, the rose no longer a miracle of Nature, but a fantasy. Now, in an instant, I cast aside all notions of her worth, just as a man might do on the eve of his wedding, when his supposed virgin bride is revealed to be a whore.

Yet I knew that the disappointment and disgust I lay at her feet were of my own making. She was exempt from all guilt, unaware she'd been created to be pimped out by drooling, voracious whore-mongers who couldn't wait to prostrate her before the world.

But why should I feel revulsion? If the form were identical, the scent, the grace, the velvet petals, what did it matter? I'm a godless artist. Or rather, I *was* an artist. I used to think like one. So, why was there a need to venerate a biological force above that of the human mind, the greatest intellect in the known universe? Especially when such a life force required no intellect to exist beyond its own biological imperative.

A sudden memory of her unique fragrance jolted back my rationale. Maica's grandmother had picked the rose; used the petals in an offering to the mountain.

"...in my family for many, many years," Maica had said. I inhaled sharply. It *couldn't* be bio-tech. The rose existed long before anyone knew how to muck about with genes. A dying man did not lie to me, and I must respect his family's guardianship by not giving in to slanderous speculations about the origins of the black rose. She was worthy of loyalty, faithfulness and honour, and I suddenly found myself, with tears in my eyes, fighting for that honour.

"It's *not* bio-tech Stan. She's *real* and she's *mine*. Give me back the black rose. Tell me where it is."

Now it was his turn to inhale sharply.

"It was *black*? ...The *Inca* rose?"

I was silent. I'd said too much. Now, should he wish, he could deny satisfaction of a desire so strong in me it had strangled my caution.

"Well, well. I knew you were real bright but I didn't figure you were such a big player. The Inca rose! You found her. Wow! I thought it was a legend. Y'know, it's genetically different from any plant I've ever seen. It appears to have a large amount of human sequence DNA.

It's a whole new line of enquiry. I'd have taken it with me for sure, but I'm damned if I had the time."

He paused, "OK. It's too late for me to get it; things have gotten out of hand. I'll be out of the country in five hours. It's at my house in my private lab in Umocollo, in the back with the cacti. Three petri dishes on the left of the desk."

I thought that this was all the information I wanted from him, but I heard myself blurt out:

"Was Rocio sleeping with you?"

"All Peruvian girls with any brains are *brigeras*. The only chance they get to travel and have a better life is by using what they've got, for the short time they've got it. We're all prostitutes, remember? Doesn't mean she didn't like ya'."

And I realised that he had known about my affair with her all along, despite my discretion. Perhaps she had dribbled the details into his ear during one of their sex sessions. I clenched my jaw as Stan spoke right into the phone.

"But we've not had this conversation, *understand*? Even if you told people we had, you could never prove it. This phone won't exist on any network and I'll be far away before they drag the plane from the sea."

I'd already played my ace in this game. Now, I played the King.

"Abelman knows you might not be dead."

"*What? You know Abelman*?"

"I don't know any of them, but I broke into the lab looking for the rose. He came in with Suarez, so I hid under the desk. I overheard them planning to kill everyone connected with the Cuca project."

"*You broke in?* What did they say?"

I repeated it all, but said nothing about Todd or the greenies. I told him Abelman planned an 'accidental' fire at the lab to destroy all evidence.

"A fire? Shit! That figures."

"*Cuca*," I said. "They think you've taken it to a rival cartel." He was silent. "I know all about it Stan, all about project Phoenix having a double agenda."

As I spoke, I dismissed an image of me being quietly stabbed in an alley somewhere. I still haven't learned, after all these years, that playing dumb can be the most intelligent thing to do. I now thought of Stan as the competition, disregarding the fact that when ego beats caution, the game is usually lost.

"No you don't, Sybil," he said. "You know nothing about Project Phoenix. Anyway, what are you gonna do about it?"

He sounded rattled. I was confused. What did he mean? Were there more repugnant experiments on Gentrex's agenda? Fischer wasn't going to order my death, I knew that much. I'd looked him in the eye, he was no assassin. He'd obviously fallen out with the people capable of that.

"Nothing," I answered, truthfully. "*Absolutely* nothing!"

As Todd had reminded me, there would be no point telling the venal, corrupt, conniving police.

"What about the fire? It's unfortunate if innocent people die," he said.

"But not completely untenable, eh Stan? Can't make an omelette without breaking a few eggs." I spat his glib philosophy back at him. "I promise I'll make sure no one dies, and I'll keep my mouth shut, on one condition..."

"*What condition?*" He sounded angry, but I couldn't miss this chance to ask, although to expect anyone with *his* moral track record to keep a promise was a ludicrous proposition.

"You will never bio-engineer a black rose. Never! Let her be unique. Keep her secret. Never speak of her even. She is *Capac...*"

He interrupted: "So you can make serious bucks, right? Bet I'll be buyin' one in a couple o' years though, eh? From my local garden store? Or maybe not? She's worth more to science than commerce. You're sitting on a fortune, Sybil."

The remark sliced through all my idealistic protestations to the bone of my obsession. He had reminded me of my original motivation: mercenary, pure and simple, unsullied by the crazed emotional need I now had for the rose.

I was unable to speak, fuming at his presumption to judge me after all he'd done. And, of course, cut to the quick by his accuracy. But despite the fortunes he hinted at, I no longer wanted money from the rose. Hadn't wanted it from the first moment I'd held her. I just wanted *her*. I opened my mouth to begin my defence, but he spoke faster and with finality.

"OK, I've got bigger fish to fry. But this conversation did not happen, Sybil. It did not happen. I do not exist."

The line clicked shut to silence.

52 TORCHLIGHT

I rang Anthony again in a state of excitement. I had thought it better not to tell him about my call to Fischer until I had the rose in my possession. This time he answered.

"Where the hell are you, bro'? I've loads to tell you. I need to talk. Charlie's been accused of murder. It's been on channel four."

"*What? No! Really?* Er, don't worry. Charlie's cool. He's innocent. Trust me, sis. I won't be back for a few hours, though." He sounded high.

"Where are you, at Mavis's house, still with *him*?"

"No. I'm at a rehearsal."

"What? Without your guitar?" His Stratocaster and amp were in the hall. No point asking him if he'd slept.

"There's one here, sis, don't worry. I'll see you soon, princess."

"Are you playing tonight?"

He'd hung up, but it was the most likely scenario. He was always accepting gigs from complete strangers who wanted him to play at birthday parties and in their restaurants. Thinking he would be paid, he'd turn up only to find that payment was a jug of rum. Then he would get drunk because he couldn't refuse the alcohol and be unable to negotiate a better price. Man, the Peruvians had got him taped. They knew he was cheap. I was sick of him being treated like everyone's pet *gringo*, but he didn't seem to care as long as he was high. At least right now, he wasn't with Charlie.

OK, concentrate. Stan's house. I hadn't got the bloody address. How utterly *stupid* of me not to ask him exactly where his private lab was located. I rang the folded sevens again. Nothing. Not even an unobtainable tone. Stan was right, he no longer existed. But the rose did, and now it was within a ten-minute taxi ride of my possession. Rocio would know where Stan had lived. Umacollo is a large district and I didn't want to arbitrarily ask strangers about his address, so I had no choice but to call her.

Acoustic guitar was strumming quietly in the background and I realised that the ambience was identical to the call I had just placed to Anthony.

"Holá! Rocio. Do you know Stan's address? His house in Umacollo?"

"Holá, Si-vil. Poor Stan, eet eez so sad, so sad."

"Yes, but do you know his address?"

"No, er, no. Neri will know eet, but she is in Cusco wiz 'er family. She maybe does not know about ze accident even, poor Neri."

So, Rosy doesn't know where Stan lived. Where had they fucked then? In his car? In the cheap hotels that rent by the hour? Up against the wall in the dark of the night, like she did with me?

"Do you have Neri's phone number?" I said.

"No, I am sorry, Si-vil."

"What about Chicau, the security guard, will he have Stan's address?" My tone was clipped. She hesitated.

"I don' know, maybe."

"Well," I said, almost gritting my teeth, not caring to encounter her bulky paramour again, "do you have Chicau's number?"

"No, but I will see 'im at work next week." No she wouldn't. There would be no next week for Gentrex.

Suddenly, I felt sorry for her, not angry. She was as used as she had been using. I supposed that her life would play out dozens of such encounters before she aged beyond the sexual interest of others. The acoustic guitar continued strumming and I recognised the phrasing. No Peruvian shapes chords like my brother. His playing is distinctive. He was playing with *her*. Rehearsals, eh?

"Give my love to Ant," I said, and closed the phone, rapidly re-opening it to dial Todd. He might know Stan's address. No answer, leave a message. *Damn! Shit!* I sent a text. No immediate answer to that, either. I'd have to check Todd's house. I'd have to speak to Laura if he wasn't there, find out what she knew, somehow.

I waited at the side of my apartment to hail one of the numerous *tico* cabs. The narcotic fragrance of the datura flowers dangling low over my neighbour's wall began to bathe my nerves. There were so many psychotropic plants right here in the gardens: powerful hallucinogens like the San Pedro cactus, silver morning glory, leonotis, brugansia and passiflora. The northern jungle held even more: ayahuaska, yagé and piper mysthysticum, among others. Doubtless, Ant would get around to sampling them all if he stayed here long enough.

I finally caught a cab and directed the driver to Todd and Laura's apartment on the Calle Andina. The driver knew Ant and had seen me with him. Was I his girlfriend? Did we have children? No, I wasn't. No, we didn't. For the twentieth time since I had been in Arequipa, a taxi driver asked about my marital status and told me that it was my duty to have children and fulfil God's plan for me.

Depending on the level of my sobriety, I had, as in the truck at Tres Cruces, run the entire gamut of the argument over the last few weeks from the more acerbic comments on lack of imagination, to the overpopulation trip; the God question; the Christian church setting agendas for women's bodies. Blah blah, bloody blah. All the old chestnuts roasting on the fire. May as well have kept schtum. Man, I was sick to death of this one. I changed the subject to the earthquake.

"Where were you?" he asked.

"Hiding under the furniture," I told him.

"I was making love to my wife," he laughed. It broke the tension. I avoided making the earth-moving joke, it would have been lost in translation. Instead, I made small talk until he pulled up outside Todd and Laura's. As I fumbled with the change, his radio was blasting music at the usual ear-splitting volume. News of Stan's plane crash suddenly came on. We both stopped chatting to listen. The plane had been located in the sea by the coastguard, near Ica.

"*Que lástima*!" exclaimed the driver, seeming genuinely sorry.

"Did you know him?"

"*Sí, sí, un buen hombre.*"

Thank God for short strings.

"Do you know wherc his house is in Umocollo?"

"*Sí, Avenida San Miguel.*"

"Take me there! *Now!*" I said.

We zoomed off, the driver swerving sharply to miss a nut-brown, wizened women sitting in the diesel fumes on the curb. She was inches from the wheels of passing traffic, palms stretched open.

"What the hell?" I said. "Is she *mad*?"

"Their families make them beg to get the money for their food. There are no pensions here; no social security, *señora*."

Yes, this was an unforgiving jungle, and no wonder the animals in it were self-serving and ruthless. To be a woman beyond the age of fertility, poor and alone, is the lowest rung on the ladder in every culture on earth. Rosy must feed her child as best she could, singing for her supper, or fucking for it. I was in no position to stand in judgment. I just knew I could never make love to her again. I hoped she would manage to grab as much as she could for her life.

"*Ya estamos aqui*," said the *taxista*, announcing our arrival at San Miguel, as we turned into an avenue of yellow-blossomed trees.

My eyes were scanning the numbers: 173; 174; 175; 176; 177. When we got to 180 on the corner, the taxi stopped dead. Three policemen stood outside the remains of a luxury villa. The building was a black shell.

"*Puta madre*!" exclaimed the shocked driver, cussing strongly in Spanish. In contrast, I chose a succinct, but well-known Anglo-Saxon phrase. We stepped out of the taxi, open-mouthed, and just stared. Suarez. Suarez had done this.

Suddenly, I knew what I wanted. I wanted to go home. Because home is a place in your head, not a geographical point on the planet. Because home to me was to be lost in the concentration of making my art, and I was heartsick, art-sick and homesick for that place.

53 BANG!

I arrived back at the house, opened a half-bottle of rum and zoned out to the TV. Five shots later I was still watching the religious channel. A photograph of the Virgin, her passive head inclined to one side, filled the screen, as voices in lilting unison chanted a litany of her names: *Virgen de las Virgenes (virgin of virgins), Madre Intacto (mother with hymen), Madre Immaculata (perfect, unstained mother), Reina de las Virgenes (queen of virgins), Reina de la Paz (queen of peace),* ending with a crescendo *Rosa Mystica* (mystical rose). I threw my shoe at the screen and continued drinking.

The ritual bark-a-thon that accompanied every dawn woke me. Hundreds of sex-starved, solitary dogs guarding the roofs of the houses bark in impotent rage. For a moment, I thought they may be warning of another quake. I stiffened and waited for the room to shake as they howled their estranged pleas, to us and to one another. I'd collapsed next to the open refrigerator. My mouth tasted like a carpet slipper and I was lying in a sticky pool of guava jam. A text from Anthony showed on my phone. 'On my way home, sis. Be with you in an hour.'

I washed and made coffee, chewing four painkillers. The cocks were already crowing as the slit eye of the sun peeped from behind the volcano. The air was very cool. When I'd last stood in this quality of light and temperature, a violent explosion had changed my life trajectory. As I nursed my head and guzzled caffeine, sure enough, there came a loud 'BANG!' I felt a small vibration.

Terrified it was another quake and that the dogs had indeed foreseen it with their warning barks, I waited in the doorway, ears pricked. After three minutes, I ran up to the roof terrace and, in the sky to my left, saw an orange glow coming from half a mile away. It was Gentrex. Todd had kept his word. I watched for a few moments as the smoke and flames grew, then I took two pills. I needed to sleep, and to wait for my brother.

The sound of the toilet flush woke me. I could smell liquorice, cinnamon and blackberry. I called her name. "Rocio?" Anthony answered loudly from the bathroom.

"She's not here, sis. She's coming back later for dinner though; she's not working tonight."

"No one is," I said.

He opened the door, towelling his hands dry. I looked at my pale brother, straight in the eye.

"You were with her?" I knew the answer.

"Er, yeah. We were going through some of her material."

He was going through the material all right, straight to the flesh. I knew.

Dark petals opened as the gold guitar pushed home.

My profligate, prodigal brother can't hide his feelings. When he's at fault he looks guilty but defiant, or avoids eye contact. The yellow sprouting beanstalk was now fully grown, replete with ogre. My imagination became disturbingly pornographic. The positions of Giulio Romano. The Dream of the Fisherman's Wife.

The dog in haunches pumps behind – a gripping, slavering, one-track mind.

He began talking very fast about Charlie in the cupboard and the car. The whole story poured out. He'd been to Charlie's apartment, but it had been completely ransacked. A stooge had been posted outside, in case Charlie returned, but Anthony knew that from the alley behind the house he could climb into the bathroom window by standing on the dustbin. Charlie often climbed in that way to avoid creditors at his front door. Frankly, I was relieved that he was not a serious villain, and that my brother had not been at risk.

Ant was in ebullient form, laughing and animated as he told the story. He'd had managed to find the phone charger Charlie had asked for, and his spare keys, but not his two passports. Charlie was distraught that he couldn't flee the country, until Mavis formulated a brilliant plan to help him escape.

She'd dug out an old but valid Peruvian identity document belonging to her recently deceased aunt and decided to dress him up in full drag to resemble the creased photograph of Virginia Maria Del Prado stuck to the crumpled front page. Desperate to escape in one piece, he reluctantly agreed.

Shoes were the hardest to find, since Charlie was a size nine. Mavis had produced an old, battered pair with kitten heels, borrowed from a neighbour, but having seen the size of his tree-trunk calves, decided against a skirt. His hair she finger-waved over one eye and set with strong spray, then added a chiffon scarf, earrings and full face-makeup. A beige trouser suit was produced, a little short at the ankle, but wide enough in the beam, complemented by a pale blue, ruffled blouse. Ant said that, frankly, it was an improvement on the original Charlie, and not too bad a likeness of the old bird in the photo.

Whilst he told the tale, I turned my back to him. He'd obviously just had a line and was very high, hyper-ventilating and chewing his lips.

"Want a coffee?" he asked. "By the way, did I tell you that one of the guys I met at the last gig owns an abattoir? He gave me two bulls. I'm supposed to collect them tomorrow."

Ant was convinced that humour would soften me, but I caught, along with Rosy's fragrance, the unmistakable smell of cocaine in his sweat and on his breath as he walked past me.

"Scored twice then," I said. My face was stone.

"What?"

"You heard me."

There was a silence from the kitchen. I went immediately to the hall closet and checked the blue coat. The pockets were empty. He'd found the stash when he'd come back the previous day, probably whilst rummaging for money. I put the coat on, pulled out my suitcase and began to pack. The case was almost full when he appeared in the doorway with the coffee. I still did not turn round.

"Syb?"

I didn't answer. Emptying the drawers and walking past him to the lounge, I picked up my sketchpad, my Spanish tapes and shoes.

"Syb?" he said again, following me out.

I stopped and looked at him, my disordered, intemperate sibling. His eyes, usually bluer than the sky outside, were now beyond midnight blue, darker than deep space. He was flying high with the condors on the cursed cocaine, beyond me and beyond himself. His nostrils were caked in blood and his lips swollen. The eczema he had as a child had fulminated into purple psoriasis, all over his elbows and neck.

I knew this was no flirtation; it was as fixated a passion as he used to have for his work. As fixed as the one I had for the rose. Like me, he didn't want his obsessive love affair to end, no matter what it cost him. So, if it made him happy, I must not interfere. But I couldn't witness it a moment longer. I could not allow myself one moment of hesitation and passed him to continue packing. I had nothing to stay for now. No rose; no Rosy; no brother I could relate to anymore; no inspiration to paint. Nothing.

As if to mirror the curdled atmosphere, the scent of Rosy was fading, replaced by a sulphurous odour. Our Peruvian plumbing, maybe. Schnarfing powder doesn't just enter the lungs and bloodstream, it also goes down the back of the throat to the stomach. Cocaine-laced intestines make sour, ammonia-smelling scat. Ant turned, red-faced, towards me.

"She *wanted* me. I didn't seduce her. She practically swallowed me whole." He shrugged; white flecks of spume at the sides of his mouth.

"You're being used, bro'. She thinks a *gringo* in her bed and her band would help her get the record deal. She's a *brigera;* a *caprichosa*." I sounded like Mavis.

"*So what?* You didn't want her anyway. You *used* her to get the rose to Gentrex. She's a good-time girl, nothing else, so what's the problem? You said you could never love anyone after Evie."

He'd become so coarsened and numbed out. No tenderness or compassion anymore. No respect. Stealing, and using people, prostituting his time and affection. He was a better man before cocaine, but there was no telling him that. Cocaine had stolen him. He would justify this addiction any and every way possible, always making me seem judgmental and unforgiving. But I really understood. That was the injustice to me. I understood how he couldn't bear to be in his own head without some chemical adjustments. There was no blame; no shame. Just the observation that the price he had to pay for his high was a debasement of his finer feelings and the dissipation of his talent.

His compositions were still brilliant, but he wasn't playing at the same standard. I'd noticed that within the first twenty-four hours of being here. I'd already offered him a chance to get treatment at any clinic in the world at my expense. He'd turned me down. I had to switch off my love for him or his own delight in his addiction would have broken my back.

"The *cha* wasn't yours anyway!" he spat. "You had no right to keep it, Syb. People depend on that for their living here." He looked defiant, defending his theft as I packed my clothes and snapped the case shut.

"Did you sell the watch for coke? Or did you give it to Fernando?"

"Are we back on *that* again? Why ask?"

"That was a token of love, Ant. Engraved from me to you. Something special. A link between us."

"We don't need *stuff*, sis. They're only *things*. Things tie you down."

"But I wanted you to think of me every time you wore it. A talisman… to bind us together."

"We're already bound together. You're my blood. My princess."

"I thought you'd treasure it because I gave it to you. Because I mean something to you, Ant."

"So you bought it for *you* then, not for me."

"No, *for us*. But there is no us. Nothing matters to you anymore."

"I can't hold on to anything, sis, you *know* that. I'm not the kind of man who holds on to things. But I love you more than I've ever loved you. You're my family. My world."

I sat on the bed and we held hands. I told him about Maica's rose, his wife, and his coca field. About the conversation with Stan. About the last hope for my black rose, once again burned to dust. His palm was cold and clammy; his chemically-induced optimism insufferable.

"Don't give up! Maybe there's another one. We can go back and look. Anyway, what have you lost? You never even heard of a black rose till you came here, so what does it matter?"

It mattered so much, I didn't dare think of it, let alone express it. Regardless of my emotional investment, the fact remained that I had been responsible for tearing *la rosa negra* from her bed in the Inca soil, and he had accidentally burned her to death in our kitchen. The wizened stem from the second rose and the few cells Stan had taken were now also just cinders. I had no *reason. No reason. No fucking reason*!

I looked at Anthony once more, framed by the light from the window. It occurred to me that it may be many years before I saw him again; that I might, indeed, never see him again.

Cocaine can be a passing fancy for occasional users. But not for him. She was like a spider, eating his head, and he was oblivious to the web; in love with the sticky embrace. Now that I had read the *Cuca* report about the addiction process, I knew that even if he wanted to quit, his altered brain chemistry would fight his resolve. It was a greater act of love to let him live his addiction, free from all judgment.

Part of his journey as an artist was to wring the neck of mental excess and write out the experience. I knew for certain my dollars kept him sick. I knew too that if he were desperate and ill, I would, of course, be there.

I grasped the suitcase and stood up. As always, I could see the poetry in the tragedy. Art is often born in such moments, but, unable to produce it from the barren womb of my creativity, I simply turned my face away.

"*Fuck you*," he spat. "Go back to fucking London and your hipster prole art! Go back to that constipated, shagged-out old country! You stupid *cow*!" He kicked a chair, exploding it like matchwood. He sensed I would now abandon him. It tapped into the abandonment he'd felt when both Mum and Dad had died. He'd been so angry, his beautiful spirit crushed with sorrow. And I remembered his little fists clenching as he turned away from the nurses and stared out of the window.

The truth was I could never abandon him. My fate was to wake with his face on the screen behind my eyes every morning from this day forward. This I knew, because I knew the power of love and I wasn't afraid of it. But I felt so bitter that it hurt so hard. That everything I had loved so much, that had meant so much – him; Evie; my art; the rose. All now beyond my reach.

But Anthony could never suffer as I did because he had the magic dust that numbed his soul. He would be absolutely fine until it wore off and the rent wasn't paid and the guitar had to be sold for the next dose.

"Cocaine hardened you, Ant. Hardened you to stone."

He began to mock me in a dramatic tone.

"Well if you don't like it, *fuck off*! I don't need your money. I don't need anyone."

"Only cocaine, eh? I understand *numb,* Anthony. Remember *me*? I *know* why you want it."

He started kicking the wardrobe like a vexed child. I knew to never escalate the argument to his level. No one did tantrum at higher velocity than Ant. It was always a no-contest. That our mother tolerated it, nurtured it even, by constantly giving in to his demands, still surprises me. Rationale was always a stranger to him at such times.

"Put these back in Rosy's bag for me will you, without her knowing?"

I threw the two passkeys on the bed. Even though the doors they accessed were now charred splinters, I didn't want her to know I'd deceived her, or taken advantage. I wanted her to remember me with affection and respect. It was part of my narcissism to want to be liked. But, knowing my brother's fecklessness and memory lapses, I quickly added:

"If you don't, we might both be implicated in the explosion. Todd's just blown up the building. Oh, and give her this." I slung the two halves of the broken mask at him. He hardly acknowledged the information.

"Come with me, Ant. I have the tickets. They're dated for today." I placed his on the table between us. "It's dangerous to stay. The Gentrex people are serious villains, and the police might question you; you're a known friend of Charlie. Come with me. New York. Mexico. Berlin. Shanghai. We can go anywhere. Get away from this place, Ant. It'll kill you."

As I spoke, there was a dull rumble. We looked out of the window. A thin plume of smoke was rising from the far side of the volcano.

"Shit, it's Misti! Look, Ant!"

I was terrified. But Anthony? He picked up his acoustic guitar and began to sing me an extraordinary new composition, wrapping a beautiful chord sequence round poignantly truthful words:

"Everybody wants something from me – but I can't give them any-thing.
Everybody wants something from me – but I can't give it all."

His art transcends. A wonderful flame flickers in his moments as I watch. And I can only watch. Beyond my utter sorrow at his addiction, beyond the loss of the rose and my fear of the Gentrex agenda, an emotion far greater swamped into view. I was *jealous*. Jealous with a pus-green bile that burned my throat and rusted my tongue. He was still in command of his art, despite the monkey on his back – and maybe even because of it.

He sang in innocence, with the only form of expression that had any real meaning to him, and trumped my grand exit with the only card in his deck. The cold serenity of acceptance pressed down on my heart like an anvil crushing a flower: he was the better artist.

The one that, under any duress, could still create.

54 CHARLIE'S FINAL WIG-OUT

The earthquake had caused panic, but it was nothing compared with this. It had been more than four hundred years since Misti's last eruption and there were no procedures to follow, no evacuation plans. It was every man for himself and not a single taxi to be had. This simple plume of smoke had caused the streets to fulminate with people, all jostling in high Latin temperament; cars zooming through traffic lights. Predators would be taking full advantage of the disruption, and I felt race-conscious again, as if I had a sign on my head saying, 'Mug me. I'm white.'

With no cabs available, it would be better to walk to Mavis's house. I should say goodbye and elicit her help in getting to the airport. Mavis would know what to do. She was scatty but she was resourceful. Butch women like Mavis could be relied upon not to flap and scream. I needed to get off the streets until I could get to the plane in safety. So, clutching the little suitcase, and with my leather duffle bag on my shoulders, I dodged and weaved through the screeching traffic until I safely crossed over Ejecito, behind the big department store.

Charlie, meanwhile, had been shocked at his own transformation as Mavis revealed his female side with deft strokes of make-up brush and razor. She had even shaved his arms and painted his nails. Reinvigorated by sobriety, Charlie felt a burning need for retribution against the thug who had ordered his abuse and turned his home inside out.

When the volcano began to smoke, he'd rushed into the street in his sling-back shoes, clutching his handbag and spare car keys, hoping to snatch his Mitsubishi in the confusion. He knew his racial status would not help him now. He was just another refugee, without wheels of his own or the ability to pay the huge sums required to commandeer another set.

No longer fuelled by the white diet, Charlie was soon out of breath, teetering up the road towards Suarez's house. He borrowed a child's bike that was leaning against a garden wall. As wobbly on wheels as he had been on heels, Charlie weaved his way through the traffic for a further two blocks, cursing.

The Mitsubishi was parked directly outside a smart, painted villa. Charlie bent down and grabbed a brick, hiding it in his newly acquired handbag. As he approached, Suarez came out, clutching a small hold-all and a slim, black briefcase. Aware that he had not been recognised, the burly Don asked, in high-pitched Spanish, if Suarez would give him a lift to the airport, offering to pay. Suarez hesitated, compromised by the matron's request, then opened the driver's door and flung his luggage in the back, pulling himself up.

"I am not going to the airport, señora," he'd said, trying to extricate himself from any moral obligation. Charlie, knowing that central locking meant the passenger door was also now open, lost no time in climbing up into the passenger seat, using the brick to whack the shocked Suarez clean out of the open driver's door and onto the pavement. Charlie then jumped into the driving seat and roared off with the door gaping open, procuring briefcase and hold-all as the unexpected bonus.

Swinging round the backstreets to Calle St Augustine, just as I entered it, Charlie leant out of the car window, loudly calling my name. Despite his ridiculous clothes, I recognised the Don and called back. He did not see Wishbone run out in front of him until I screamed. There was a thick, foggy *crunch* as his little doggy head hit the curb. I rushed over to him and held his front paw, feeling the coarse texture of his little pad as I leant him against the gutter. He lay on his side, tongue protruding and his eyes glazed, but still breathing. I stroked his long, silky ears and talked quietly to him, then he let out a sigh and he passed.

The rumblings of *El Misti* were nothing compared to my rage.

Another death! Another death!

I rose off the pavement like a demented, possessed thing and cried out, my face distorted in a Munchian scream:

"I hate you, *Pachamama*! I *hate* you! I curse you and all your creation! Man's revenge on you is destruction! Destruction. Because you have no heart. No heart, and no feeling. So why the fuck should we?"

Because we can, Sybil. Because we have the choice.
Choosing it is a state of grace.

I knelt down and lifted Wishbone up into my arms, looking for a place to put his little body that was safe and sacred and clean. Men and women around us were crying, cradling frightened children. We howled in unison. Charlie put his arm around me having said how very sorry he was. He pulled out an expensive jacket from the hold-all and wrapped the dog inside it, carrying him like a dead child back into Mavis's house.

I couldn't go inside. To see her grief would have destroyed me. Charlie came out after three minutes, florid and sweating under the make-up, carrying a small canvas bag and a screwdriver.

"We have to go now, Sybil," he said.

"Mavis… is she OK?"

"She's staying with Wishbone."

I climbed up into the car. The smell of sulphur was stronger, the sky darkening by the minute. Misti, the erstwhile God, now smelled like the Devil. Though there was only the tiniest plume of smoke, thoughts of Pompeii and tons of pyroclastic flow raining down upon me stayed uppermost in my mind.

Charlie roared around the backstreets toward the airport, telling me how he had retrieved the car from Suarez via the house brick, and of his own new identity, Virginia Maria Del Prado, who suddenly turned to me and said:

"I admire you, Sybil. You are not like other women."

"Neither are you at the moment, Charlie!" I answered, bitterly trying to retain my sense of humour through trembling lips. He ignored the joke, straining his eyes through the windscreen wipers to see the road.

"Do you have a flight booked? It will be hell to get one."

"Yeah. A friend gave me a ticket."

"I am going to Cusco, then onward to Chile. Will you come with me, Sybil?"

"Thanks, but no." I patted his hand. He grabbed my fingers.

"What about your family, Charlie?"

"They can look after themselves. My wife's family has money. What will happen to Anthony?"

"He will be OK, short-term, as long as he doesn't run out of cocaine. Only music can stop him from destroying all he has, nothing else."

"Well, he has enough cocaine for many months. He must have taken what was in my safe because he didn't bring any back to me. But I did not want it anyway. I am finished with it."

"What about your murder charge, Charlie?"

"*What?*" Charlie was transfixed when I told him, hunching down as he drove, grateful for tinted windows. Mavis had no TV, so he was unaware of his new notoriety.

"Those bastards!" he spat. "They framed me! I am innocent! Oh God! All of Arequipa thinks I am queer! A murdering queer! I can never come back! *Never!*"

"You may not be able to if it's covered with lava."

He looked distraught. I almost felt sorry. He was more worried about being thought of as gay than a murderer. I could afford to laugh at that, aware that gay Peruvians could not.

We slewed round a corner as two women were trying to load a mattress onto the back of a truck. Charlie narrowly missed mowing them down. I used the incident to extricate myself from his grip.

"I am sure we're being followed," Charlie said, eyeing the mirror.

The streets presented a strange choreography as people manically nailed their houses shut with boards and planks to stop looters. The army was out in force. Shields, batons, facemasks; some had machine guns drawn. I was glad of Charlie's enterprising theft. I would never have made it to the airport without him. He swerved to avoid more people, then took a sharp right and stopped at some wooden gates. He jumped down, fumbling with the key to a padlock, explaining:

"This is a storage depot for one of my shops."

The gates swung open to a dusty yard and a brick building. He drove the car in and pulled hard on the handbrake, swinging himself out.

"Get your bags," he said, and opened the wooden door to reveal a red, three-wheeled tractor bike that he said belonged to his son. "We have to go the rest of the way on this, it is more versatile."

I jumped on the back, hugging my little suitcase, my duffle bag behind me. From the back of the shed I could hear Charlie's hysterical laughter. He flung open both the doors, shaking.

"*Es increíble! Increíble!*" he kept repeating, waving the screwdriver.

"Do you have enough money, Sybil? The ATMs will all be empty."

"Don't worry, I'm fine."

"Here, take this," he reached into the attaché case and pulled out a large handful of dollar bills. Almost forty thousand.

"Jesus, Charlie, where did you get *that*?"

"That bastard Suarez. I screwed the *pendejo* at last!" He started laughing again, waving his badly-painted nails at me as I backed off.

"It was in his case! Just take it, Sybil, take it. It is a present." After so much parsimony, I was shocked at this rash act. Charlie thrust the money at me. I shook my head.

"Please. You are not on the plane yet." He dumped a pile of cash in my hand and started stuffing the remaining notes into his bloomers and bra, laughing as he rammed even more cash into the arms of his frilly blouse. He pulled the bike out and re-locked the gates. Taking a small alleyway, barely wide enough for our shoulders, he zoomed between the buildings, earrings swinging, and we popped out like a champagne cork straight onto the airport road.

The army had flung a cordon around the terminal and had stopped all cars using the approach-way. Families with tickets were streaming up the road, luggage and children in tow, coldly abandoning their dogs and servants to their fate. Those without tickets had been made to queue. Charlie stopped to speak to a policeman, and I could see another, smaller bundle of notes change hands. We were immediately escorted by a police bike, up to the airport main door, ready to join the crush at the check-in.

To their great credit, and probably due to the number of guns present, the police were keeping good order, and frightened ground staff duly processed the queues. Having secured the car in his lock-up, Charlie seemed content to abandon the bike, knowing that the current contents of his bloomers could have bought a fleet of them. He had only a small canvas bag, but his trouser suit pockets were bulging, and he was still clutching the black attaché case.

Despite the volcano, the murder charge and his ridiculous drag, he seemed confident and in control until he was confronted with a poster of himself inside the terminal building. Shaking and sweating, he clutched my arm as he read the details of his supposed misdemeanour.

Then he rushed to a small corner of the concourse, close to the empty shoeshine stand, to hide behind two large pillars as he looked round for enemies waiting to intercept his bid for freedom. He had to be reminded that his mascara would melt if he didn't restrain himself.

"I was in Lima, I didn't do it. *I... I... Why would I have killed anyone?*" he hissed.

"Charlie, if the police catch up with you, you have an alibi, a perfect alibi; you won't be charged with murder. The Lima hotel will have records. Besides, you have enough money to pay for the best lawyers in town."

I could see the relief in his face. He knew, deep in his Latin soul, that justice only meant money, and the latter assured the former.

"This is goodbye then, Charlie. Please, take your dollars back."

I put my hand in my pocket. Charlie immediately crushed my hand with his.

"Shh! Not here. If they see that, you will never get on the plane."

"What? Why?"

"You don't know these fuckin' *cholos*; they will take your last penny and leave you with *nothin'*! They will tell you that you have to declare all monies leaving the country and make you pay them tax," he said, eyeballs swivelling left and right.

"Before you go to the bag search at the departure lounge, just fold two five hundred dollar bills in the back of your passport. Not the page with the picture, the one behind it. Show it to the tall *mestizo* with the moustache as you enter the departure lounge. He will treat you as a VIP and you will not have your bag searched. They know to look there and you will be waved through to the left side, past the X-ray machine. Keep the rest of the money in your brassière. No one will challenge you.

Get your ticket upgraded through to London first and you will not be searched in Lima with a through ticket on your luggage. Buy British

Airways or Iberia; only the Dutch airline searches you always. Trust me, we Peruvians know how it works here."

I took his advice, loaded up the passport and lined my bra, whilst Charlie did his best to cop a sly look at my tanned décolletage.

"Well, goodbye, Charlie. Thank you for everything."

I offered my handshake but he flung his arms around me, scooping me up in a bear hug. I hugged back, overwhelmed with gratitude and sorry I had thought him totally shallow.

"Sybil, you are the most fascinating creature I have ever known. Please, please answer me one question before I go to my plane."

"What, Charlie?"

"Do you have a cunt?"

55 AIRPORT ANTICS

The airport was full of frightened people, but the eruption seemed minimal. Light smoke was coiling in the opposite direction to the runway, with the wind keeping most of it from us. Local TV stations, with cameras trained on the mountain, showed continuous coverage and warned of a possible larger eruption. And everywhere, families who had been able to afford the last flights were struggling with their suitcased possessions.

I had changed my Peruvian money back to dollars, upgraded my ticket and checked in at the desk. Airport personnel, though jumpy, were all up to the usual antics, operating a maximum 'fleece-the-*gringos*' gig. The exchange rate had suddenly plummeted in their favour and the cost of carrying suitcases had tripled. This was their last chance to milk the cash cow for a while and they were making the most of it. Who could blame them?

Handing over my small case, I saw the check-in clerk look sideways as she stuck luggage tags on my ticket, also tying a label on my duffel bag. But, as I turned to go, she did not put my case on the conveyor belt. She kept it by her feet. Two female police officers approached, flanked by two plain-clothed customs officials. Every eye in the airport seemed to stare, including Charlie's ex paramour, Lupe, who was in the queue for the Tacna plane on the arm of a geriatric Don Juan.

The policewomen had truncheons, guns in leather holsters and shiny boots with trousers tucked in. They were glamorous and stern, ushering me into an office adjacent to the money change booth.

"Why did you come to Peru?" They looked me up and down slowly as they asked.

"I am an artist," I told them, in Spanish. "I came here to paint."

I said I was finding it difficult to work, that I'd come to their country for inspiration. For the passion. The flame. To connect to the rage I need to re-ignite my artistic self. To find the special energy that lets me know I was and always will be an artist. That throwing paint on canvas and sculpting is not futile and indulgent, but the only way I might be who I am.

The officials murmured to each other. One of them rolled her eyes. I'd have got more respect if I'd said I was looking for UFOs at Machu Picchu. The body language of those who find you pretentious is the same in every culture. Avoiding eye contact, they leant slightly away from me, their lips curled a tight zip as they scratched around in my hand luggage.

Whilst the women did the pat down and looked in every pocket, cuff and crease, the men were searching my suitcase in the outer office. They thought I was smuggling cocaine, obviously, and watched my demeanour for giveaway details of guilt. Couldn't they tell from my utter defeated silence that I wasn't up to such an adventure?

I was down to my T-shirt and underwear. Would they stop short of the vaginal intrusion? And what of the bra? I almost had a fit of giggles. There was gold in those hills, but an offer of money at this stage would seem to confer guilt, so I had resigned myself to them finding the cash. The superior officer barked in Spanish, with hands on his hips. Did I know that trafficking drugs carries an immediate prison sentence? Yeah, I knew. I knew they'd found nothing in my luggage. This was an attempt to intimidate me into a confession in case I was carrying the contraband stash in my stomach or vagina.

Expecting violation at any moment, I mirrored his stance and told them all in loud Spanish that I hated cocaine from the bottom of my heart. Hated its lie; hated its pretend sincerity; hated the smell, the taste, the bullshit; hated everyone who sold it and pitied everyone who took it; hated the way it numbed out the finest of caring emotions and burned them into a fierce and malevolent need. And I told them that

Atahualpa had been right to curse it – and that I added my curse. Then I stood back in a moment of grand hyperbole, as befits someone of my theatrical nature, reciting Atahualpa's words in Qqechua. My party piece. They backed off, handing me my clothes and returned my suitcase to the check-in.

Now dressed, I left for the departure lounge with a menacing dignity. I spoke quietly to the tall *mestizo* and walked straight through, past the conveyor belt, $1,000 lighter, just as Charlie had instructed. I was incredulous at the corruption, but of course, not averse to taking advantage of it. Sixty yards away, all the staff were eagle-eyed and watchful. Here, where it really mattered, they were blind.

To distract myself from rage and indignation, I bought a magazine. Since art was no longer inspiring me, I turned to science: *American Scientific Review*. I also bought a quarter bottle of rum and some crackers at inflated prices, conscious of still being watched. If it were by the officials, I understood why. My diatribe had been so fluent and lyrical, and delivered with such sincerity, that they could be forgiven for thinking it was animated by the very product it was damning. Besides, why would I pay a thousand dollar bribe if I wasn't hiding something? But I doubted the hand that slipped the cash so deftly into his cuff would be beckoning the authorities anytime soon.

I sat quietly, grimacing and slugging at the rum. No doubt Charlie too would still be musing on my genitalia as he belted himself in for the flight. I doubted Suarez would catch up with him, even with his influence and money. Charlie was a formidable force when sober; but addiction is pernicious, and Charlie had a self-indulgence that knew no bounds, so his chances were slim. And I thought of the brave cowboy, now safely back in the USA, soon to be impregnating Laura in their little house on the prairie.

So, *American Scientific Review*. I began to skim read. The waitress brought me the lemon tea I ordered and I poured a tot of rum in. The television in the café area was blaring news of the explosion at Gentrex.

"This is believed to be an act of sabotage by *cocaleros,* who were planning a march on the parliament building in Lima next week to demand that the DEA stop spraying their crops. It is known that militant elements were agitating to close down the Gentrex laboratories and stop their programme to develop fungi that will affect coca crops."

The magazine slipped shiny in my fingers. It offered a double-page spread, '*Addiction: New breakthrough in pharmacotherapy*', and listed Bacban, the anti-smoking drug Stan had boasted of developing. It talked of the "*revolutionary approach to rewiring the brain*" and the pioneering work done with Lifex Laboratories in Colorado. "*Bacban is the first real success in a line of enquiry that dates back to the mid-1980s*," it read.

How could Stan Fischer still get the Bacban royalties if he'd faked his own death? Maybe he'd just been on a straight salary. Maybe he didn't care about money. Christ, I'd misjudged him. Me, the once über-astute assessor of character had slipped. That I'd read him wrongly unseated my confidence and reduced my current sense of self-worth even further.

The article mentioned new drugs currently in trials for the rehabilitation of cocaine addicts, including ibogaine, psilocybin and DMT. Hmm. Maybe with the right drug therapy Ant could shrug off his monkey at last. I was almost optimistic until *Scientific Review* informed me that "*…the co-operation of the subject to undergo this therapy is a crucial key to unlocking addiction patterns*".

I slurped my boozy tea, biting into the lemon. How entirely opposite Peru was to England. Such a contrary culture. Not just the water/plughole reversion, but the dynamic of its psyche was so extraordinarily different. It was not a country that had expanded, conquered and prospered, but a country of conquered people. Conquered by greedy, racist, despotic Europeans. But, despite the natives' subjugation, there remained a stubborn separation in those who had not been integrated or allowed to benefit from the vast wealth of their conquerors.

After hundreds of years, this peasant class still had the means of production of a weapon now so great, so powerful, that they cannot be overwhelmed or beaten, unless some superpower decides to do the unthinkable and push the button.

Like the Afghans with their poppies, Peruvian *cocaleros* know their crop is worth more than gold and sophisticated weaponry. The native people must surely realise that Atahualpa's curse has come to pass. When the Spanish burned Atahualpa's body, legend says a condor flew out of his ashes and soared across the mountains. Such is myth. Sad, poetic... the beautiful lie. But Anthony had been just as cynical in trusting such a tale.

"Atahualpa was as much a despot as any of them in his day," he'd said. "He just wore better drag and had better drugs."

We'd scooped up sheets and flowers and paraded about as we had as children, dressing up and making believe we were King and conquistador, re-enacting it all, with me screaming theatrically as he 'cut' my throat. My playful brother. I knew he would not be on the plane.

The volcano was rumbling louder now. The thread of electromagnetic energy that runs between all people was speeding up and fluttering. Strangers' eyes met mine with humility, humanity and fear. Those who tried to retain pride or posture were made to seem ridiculous. The roar of Misti, the force of *Pachamama*, rendered us all insignificant, no more than fleas on the arse of a dog.

Page twelve of my magazine sported emphatic fonts and jolly, coloured diagrams illustrating '*Side effects of Bacban therapy*'. It listed irritability; temporary drooping of the side of the mouth: 'Bell's palsy'; aversion to citrus tastes; and bad breath. Apparently, the symptoms recede immediately the therapy ceases. I bit into the lemon and drained the tea. The lightbulb snapped on.

"Laura Snow," I said aloud. "*She never smoked!*"

In a situation of such high tension, as we all awaited exodus, it wasn't surprising people were talking to themselves. I wasn't the only one. A woman opposite looked over, and murmured something at me.

"Laura never smoked," I repeated. Yet, according to Todd, she had all four side effects of the Bacban cure: bad breath; irritability; the facial tic; the aversion to lemon. Indeed, Stan had the last two symptoms himself, even though he took the Bacban cure more than five years ago.

I looked up at the Departures list. My flight had opened. The intercom invited me to board. A small jerk of adrenaline tightened my throat. Slowly, my intellect focused and the lemon penny dropped. *Jesus!* Could Stan have been using himself and Laura as guinea pigs for something else? Right under Gentrex's nose, but with their money, their time – and with the cartel's distribution network? The cuckoo was "subversive, clever," he'd said. "You know nothing about Project Phoenix," he'd said directly, and deliberately, to me.

Now I realise what he'd been hiding, the clever bastard! He's been developing the genetically-engineered super-coke alright. Sure, it gives a rabid addiction, but he's engineered it like Bacban to completely re-wire the brain; a cauterising of the dopamine receptors that process cocaine. Cure by excess! And delivered by the uptake system of the addict's choice, just as the GM cigarettes had done. Binge yourself clean!

Brilliant! Breathtaking! What brains! What balls! That must be why he'd faked the plane crash and escaped. They won't know what they've got until they've processed and sold it. Then, after a seeming increase in demand, they'll be ending the very addiction they think they are fuelling.

Maybe he was working for the DEA all along. Or was he a maverick vigilante, fighting his own private war? Did Todd know this?

Did Laura tell him? I smiled from my boots upwards. A condor flew out of the ashes.

The secret science drips with handsome karma.

Why hadn't I *seen* it? My instinct had been right. I *knew* he was a good guy. Stan's designer cure had been laid like a cuckoo's egg inside the other cuckoo's egg in the Phoenix's nest. Gentrex think they fooled everyone, but Stan fooled them all. He was more than just a good guy. He was a saviour. If his product were taken up by the cartels, millions of snow-blind users across the world would have their habit terminated in less than four months. Maybe at last there *could* be a cure for Ant. If only he wanted one.

Euphoria lasted a full forty seconds before rationale swirled up to overshadow my epiphany. There would be more developments. Many more. If this cocaine were five times as addictive, why not heroin twenty times as addictive? It's a new war, that's all: this time in the test tube rather than on the battlefield. But just as expensive, and with just as many casualties. Whatever new designer drugs were made by this technology, they would continue ad infinitum as money dictated direction.

Stan had done a fine job, won an important battle, and probably would save thousands of lives.

But the world needed a thousand Stans to win the war.

56 STANNARD HAS LANDED

A large man in a larger suit was standing with his back to the sixth-floor window, almost blotting out the Washington sun. He was drenched in Blue Mountain Breeze: the cologne that Billie had bought him from Minsky's last Christmas. The harsh fragrance filled the office, which was neon-lit, airless and clean. No one with an artist's eye or creative sensibility had chosen any object within it. Function prevailed over form. Man and office were a match.

"It's a fine job, Stannard. A fine job! Yup! We gotta real chance to win this war," he said. "I'm proud of ya'. But we need a full de-briefin' before I call the President." He congratulated his colleague, walking over and putting his hand on the younger man's shoulder.

"Love the buzz-cut, by the way. Almost didn't recognise ya' without the beard. OK. Let's start with the product. Did you bring any back? I still have the demonstration four grams from our last meet, but we hav'ta account for all of it, Stannard. Sign it off. Y'know… *security*. Procedure."

"OK, Wayne, but before we talk about the details, what happened to Laura Snow and her cowboy? Did they get out OK?"

"Sure, they were followed from the airport in Denver."

"They didn't know you were there, did they? I told you I wanted them kept out of the loop."

"Nope, they had no idea. Went to her mother's house, I believe. Then they drove up to Telluride. We had two security guys following them. They could be offered a witness protection programme, if you want that."

"No. Not that. Can you drop her out of the report? Does she have to figure? She did a great thing, an' I want her left in peace."

"Well, they'll need to know the cowboy blew up the buildin'."

"Why? Only *we* know, Wayne. Can't we say it was Gentrex themselves? I'd like that, Wayne. It might be a condition of me being absolutely thorough in my debriefing."

"Well now, Stan... we can't just..."

"Why not? We know Suarez and Abelman were planning a fire. The artist told me. I reported their plan."

"Artist? What artist?" The fat man looked quizzical, then slowly enlightened by his own deduction. "A gun artist? You mean a hit man? You never mentioned him before. I thought you were working alone."

Sheridan's fat fingers drummed on the desktop. Fischer turned and gestured him to stop, flustered by his own faux pas in speaking about it. He was tired. Very, very tired. Missing his footing.

"Wayne, you don't need to worry about any breech. The artist will never speak of anything that happened."

"Is he dead?"

The scientist took one nanosecond to decide whether deception should prevail over truth.

"Yeah, dead," he said. "No more art."

"OK. We'll talk about it later. So, how much did you bring?"

"I have half of what they refined from the first little harvest in the Huallaga Valley field: sixty keys."

"Sixty kilos? Hell! Did you bring it in Bobby's plane?"

"Yeah. Frank's got it in the lab now. But you know they moved over half a million plants, and forty thousand Petri dishes with cell growths. There were three hundred thousand cuttings growing in Abelman's Challapampa house, as well. Then there are the nursery fields they set up in Eastern Europe. There was a half key that Laura Snow sold to Mendoza, and she reckoned at least half was still in his safe. He was the guy Laura used as her guinea pig; it'll all be in the report. He was the double-blind, because he had no idea he was snorting *cuca*, unlike us."

“We don’t have to worry about the Huallaga valley field. Mission Orange Squash got all that. The administration wants no publicity on that one till we’re finished debriefing. How long will it be before the cartel realise what you’ve done? We had a timeline of two to three months. Does that still hold?’’

“Well, that’s only for someone taking pure *cuca.* Street stuff can be cut up to eighty, maybe ninety per cent, so it’ll be a good few months and maybe even a year before the dealers to realise the clientele is dropping.’’

“We’ve made sure every major dealer known to the agency has been covertly supplied. The CIA had a team of a hundred and ninety guys working undercover for over two months now, pushing our own field crop from the California facility. We’re hopin’ that this country will be free of cocaine addiction within eighteen months to two years.”

Sheridan leant forward over the desk and spoke and with reverence.

“Stan, let me tell ya, the President will give you anything you name if that happens.”

Fischer sat down opposite the drug Tsar. He had much to tell and much to keep to himself. And when all the details were delivered and signed into a report he was going to take some time off.

“I’m due vacation once we’re through here, and I may be off everyone’s radar for a while,” he said, stretching.

“Well, that’s just fine by me, Stan. Wish I could join ya’. I gotta meet with Troy Pender and Dan Burstein from the CIA this afternoon. We gotta talk Turkmenistan and make us a plan. Where will you go?”

“I dunno,” said the scientist, cracking his knuckles. “I’d like to relax and kick back for a little while, and well, maybe, just, y’know – smell the roses.”

57 UNDER THE DOOR

Smells can generate powerful emotions. Rose perfume. Sulphur. Body odour. The airport was awash with smells, mostly of fear, which had loosened my bowels. Time to visit the lavatory. Fifty *centimos* was the usual price to gain entry. It also bought you three sheets of paper. Now, the cost had risen to five soles for only two flimsy sheets. I entered the orange cubicle, resting my bag on the floor, still incredulous at Stan Fischer's coup. I wondered if he'd been a bad-guy-gone-good from his Amsterdam years. Maybe he was trying the same thing with weed and it didn't work.

So, my last few moments on Peruvian soil are to be spent in a lavatory. Quite apt when I considered my life had just slid down one. I'd lost it all, even my grieving – my excuse for apathy. But, as I constructed that thought, I felt uneasy. I felt… *judged.* Because teachers, agents, gallery owners, parents, and my own darling brother, have all accused me of indulging high drama… of hysteria and hyper-sensitivity. 'Melodramatic,' they say. And, of course, I wear the title among them as my crown of thorns. I wear it in resignation of their ignorance.

When they used such a word, did they think I was *acting*? A deliberate *exaggeration* of feeling? That would be an injustice to me. If I were gifted with 20/20 vision, or perfect pitch, or an uncanny accuracy in sport, or a talent for maths, I would not only be accepted, but *congratulated.* But a capacity for high and low passions capable of sickening other folk within minutes has long been my private rollercoaster. Why then, does my ability to experience, define, and emote in greater range than is usual evoke the negative judgment of 'melodrama'? And why does it irritate?

My range doesn't mean I'm unstable, or that my experiences are more worthy, or less worthy. Only more *intense.* For certain, my antennae pick up nuances others miss, and in this bandwidth I am a chronicler, sending back postcards through my work. Only now… I couldn't work. Now there wasn't any point to me. No point at all.

I started to pee, but could only manage a trickle. A woman walked into the right-hand cubicle next to me. She sat on the pan but did not, by the sound of it, appear to be doing anything. I coughed and fidgeted. My ears strained to hear her excretions. I stared under the gap of the door at the tiny feet. The silence was palpable and embarrassing.

In states of extreme stress, I already know that time and space can appear to warp. I keep very still in the rising warmth and claustrophobia. I feel sick and light-headed. My eyes widen. Déjà-voodoo. Yeah. The cubicle. The tiny feet; the bus station. I remembered the weight of the rose in my arms. The concussion of my consciousness back in Puno. I need Valium. Where are my pills? Where are they? Panic begins as a tingle on my scalp. My heart is a drum.

In smoky outline, Juanita, the virginal child, appears before me. She is rising, stepping with tiny feet, swimming in her mescal dream. Higher. Higher. Where the earth meets the sky; petals hidden deep in her feather purse as the shaman drone and sing. From Peru's past I see a pagan religion that can never fade. A thousand more years of Catholicism and still it will only be stronger, dictated to its people from the thin air of the icy mountains; from the unknowable sky.

I bend down again to look at the little shoes in the neighbouring cubicle. I hear rustling. A brown, tattooed hand wearing a gold ring and bracelet slips a clinking bag to me under the partition. *What*? *What*? Is this discarded contraband, and she a drug mule desperate to divest herself of evidence?

"*Take it!*" a voice says. And time draws back, objective.

Inside the bag were three Petri dishes of tinted gel with a cluster of greenish cells in the centre, the lids elevated, with at least an inch of space above the growth; seals neat in paraffin wax where the lid met the dish. I could smell perfume.

"Rocio, is that you?"

"*No se preocupes, todo es seguro.*"

...The phrase from my phone text that night at Charlie's. The mystery elephant was now, most certainly, in the room.

"Who *are* you?"

"Ssh, don' worry. It eez for you. *Es la rosa negra.*"

I screwed up my eyes, staring into the bag, incredulous.

"Who *are* you?" I hissed again.

"Instructions for cultivation are inside. Follow them exactly, an' in three jears you will have the rose," the voice said. "Bring her back to us, Sybil. Use jour spirit. Make her live."

"How did you know I'd be here?"

There was no reply.

A crowd of noisy German women entered the *Servicios.* I squatted down on the floor to look underneath the neighbouring cubicle. No one. Pulling up my tights and zipping my skirt, I flung open the door, but she was gone. I carefully inserted the gels one by one inside my bag, along with the envelope, cushioned against my folded jumper, and ran out of the restroom, bumping into several people and snagging my jacket on a cleaning cart. The untimely obstruction sent me into a rage.

"Out of the way! Out of the way! *Quítate! Apúrate*!" I yelled at the back of the cleaner's head. What kind of stupidity makes someone keep cleaning an airport when there's a volcano is erupting down the road? '*Fear of dismissal; mouths to feed.*' P. O. V. E. R. T. Y. seared its indignant name across my vision.

In guilt, I pulled out most of the money from my bra and pressed it into the cleaner's hand, shoving her hard sideways and squeezing past the cart. At least I could make a real difference to one life here. Leaving the woman gaping, her gold front teeth glistening under the lights, I ran out, desperately searching for the little shoes, for the little Ampato maiden, but she was lost somewhere in the milieu.

I was elated, dizzy, frightened. Now with *this*, the escape route, the chance to make sense of it all. Who the hell *was* she? Someone had followed me here, despite the chaos, the inconvenience. Or maybe she'd waited at the airport, knowing I'd come through. She wore an elaborate gold ring with a black stone. I recognised it. I closed my eyes to conjure its origins.

Maica! Maica Cauac: the eagle that guarded the rose. The ring was part of the gold birthday gifts that spilled from his pocket. The dark hand wearing it must be his daughter. So, yes, it's logical this *cholita* would know about the rose. But how did she get the gels? Did she know about Gentrex? And why the secrecy?

Most of all, why would a penniless Peruvian be doing anything for a *gringo* that wasn't for self-advancement and money? If she knew how much I wanted it, why didn't she offer to sell it to me? Then I remembered. Her hand was tattooed. Maica's family was Yupanqui, selling the *Capacocha* rose for money was cursed for them.

As mystery faded, pragmatism clarified. I could now get to the plane with the gels undiscovered. I'd already circumvented the X-ray machine and there were no more searches. Like Charlie had said, once in Lima, only the Dutch airline search at the gate. Despite the vast amounts of cocaine grown here, my carrier and final destination had the reputation of being very lax and rarely called your bag out. When it came to airport security, Todd had been right, "the biggest goddam assholes were the Briddish".

The cleaner, for instance, if she gave me a packet of cocaine now, it would not be picked up at all until I reached London, and judging from the last three times I had re-entered my country, the customs weren't even manned. No one. It was like the grave, you could just… *Wait*!

Didn't Christina say that after an expensive education in a private school and top marks in English, Maica's daughter was working as a cleaner? An *empleada*, in Arequipa? At the airport, maybe? Oh, God! Was she the cleaner at *Gentrex*? Or at Stan's house? Or maybe both? Had she known about the double agenda? If she were working at Gentrex, then maybe, yes. They had all treated the lab cleaner like an ignorant *cholita*. She spoke mostly Qqechua and they thought she was just a peasant, but this clever girl had understood every word they'd said. But what was she hoping to gain? Why would feigned ignorance advantage her? I ran back to the toilet to find her, but the cleaning cart, brushes and blasting transistor had been abandoned, so I rushed back to the concourse and scanned the territory like a condor seeking prey. It *must* be his daughter. It *must* be. Who else? Perhaps the cart may have clues as to her name.

I returned to the mops and chemicals, shocking my fellow travellers as I rifled through the polishes, sprays and tiny rubber gloves. The dainty hand, descended from Juanita's tribe, had given me a black rose, the same genus as the one in Juanita's purse. Now she had gone, cushioned at least by the money I'd thrust in her hand, but gone to a different life. Not so the six German women waiting to urinate, and whom I queue-jumped to loud complaints.

Inside the cubicle, I rested the bag back on the floor, plonking myself on the pan. A smell of rotten eggs permeated. Was it bodily excrescences? Or the mountain's breath? With my face in my hands I pressed my eyes tight until there was only blackness. For the first time in Peru, I was grateful for distorted Latin music. The blasting transistor, still atop the abandoned cart, covered the noise as I racked and gagged and banged my fist on the orange walls, hysterical with overload.

The Germans became agitated, banging back on my cubicle door, their guttural voices distorted now to Qqechua cries, gurgling from the lips of the Inca chief, garrotted by Christian conquistadors. I gave way to emotional incontinence, drooling and snivelling and sobbing. Then I started laughing wildly, like the mirth of mescal. Cackling. Hooting.
My mind's eye zoomed from an aerial shot of the orange cubicle, down to the interior of my bag. I leant forward and lifted out the secret thing that could change all my fortunes, as I tried to think through what would now happen.

The crackling intercom called to board my flight again.

58 THROUGH THE GATE

I've been lost in this desert for forty days and forty nights, emotionally fasting; numbing out my grief; looking for a reason. Now, the parable of Christ's temptation comes to mind, unconsidered since my childhood days at Sunday school. Lucifer has come to sit beside me, perfumed with sulphur, smiling and pointing to the material riches of the world.

"You're hungry, Sybil. Eat your fill. Go to bed with commerce. Get rich. Suck corporate cock. Have whatever you want."

He shows me a beautiful London studio overlooking Hampstead Heath; a house in southern Italy with fabulous light for painting; endless materials of the highest quality; a landscaped garden and a trickling stream; the finest of healthcare; all the books money could buy; studio assistants preparing my canvasses; my own *staff!* All my aesthetic dreams realised alongside the fame and caché I would have as godmother to the black rose. A place in history, not necessarily now as a painter, but as a philanthropic Bohemian who had brought something beautiful to the world and enriched both the poor and the wealthy.

Sybil, you didn't create it. It isn't your original work. You can't claim it as intellectual property. It won't define you.

"Ah," counters the Dark Angel, "but it will make you rich. *Famous*. Your fame can promote your art. Make it easy on yourself. Bow down and worship me, and I will give you the world. Think of the freedom."

I am thinking of it.

Now, again, I sense the swarming of suburbia; the conceit of connoisseurs; the swill of commercialism and the froth of fame; a permanent end to privacy, to anonymity. And among it all, genuine wonder, enjoyment and delight in the rose's beauty; the prying into her dark vulva; the nuzzling of strangers.

Sybil, it's only a fucking flower.

I stood over the toilet bowl, attendant that I held the possibility of hope in my hand. I could see the dirty, shoeless children all in paid education. The Black Rose Foundation and Trust. Is that what the little Yupanqui maiden was depending on? Did she know all this? She couldn't hope to do any of that here in this macho society, where everything would be taken from her the minute anyone smelled money; where her government would restrict her visa to travel abroad, to develop her Inca rose. Why would she think this particular egomaniac had such magnanimity? What had she seen in me that could have given her cause?

When Evie died I was powerless, but I can, right now, deny *La Parka* her spoils. One cell is a potential plant; one seed a potential forest. I don't need to sell the rose. I could still keep her private in my London garden. No one need know. Maybe I could donate her to science. A miracle and a curio; a natural trans-genus for dissection and dismemberment, to be pored over with forensic curiosity. Not this time by awe-struck plebs, but by men and women of learning, legitimately wielding scalpels, and with all the correct credentials proving their right so to do.

The gels were out of the bag and two seals opened, poised over the bowl, my sweat dripping onto the seat. I scooped the contents, first of one, then two dishes into the pan and pulled the chain, wiping my fingers on my jacket to better grip the third. I tore half the seal. The intercom called the flight for the last time.

Responsibility, for anyone or anything else, is a burden I cannot bear. What had this black rose ever given me but an insight into my own miserable self? Why can't I, just for *once*, gain more than I lose?

I clutched hard to the last Petri dish in my hand. But to destroy her could not my erase guilt, not now I understood all the implications. All I wanted was to keep painting. Now, here I am, in an existential drama, in an orange airport lavatory, like in some cheap novel.

Satan, my sulphurous tempter, whispers his seduction in perfect biblical phrasing one last time:

"*All these things will I give thee*
– if thou wilt bow down and worship me."

Like Juanita, I have been taken up to the highest mountain and shown all the kingdoms of the world, and the glory of them, and expected to embrace the dark. To sacrifice myself to ignorance. To become immortal. But I will not. I refuse to be held to account. I'm stepping off.

And off I step...

Sinking to my knees I descend, a rushing sound in my ears, the same sound I'd heard when I held Eve's limp body in her hospital bed; when I'd held Wishbone; when I'd held my little brother and they buried Mum next to Dad. The voices outside are barking and gurgling in guttural German. The hand drier is whooshing and spinning as chains flush and doors bang.

The wall is *so* orange, and I know it's exactly the right colour, right here, right now. Like the soil on the mountain. Like Evie's hair and the mescal drink and the Plastic Peruvian Jesus. The colour warms me. But the colour warns me. And I really *know* that if I don't move my mindset forward at this moment it will be trapped and crystallised like an insect in this amber light, stuck and motionless and never flying again.

I breathe to the full capacity of my lungs and stand up. I am no longer alone. They are all here with me, rolling past each other, igniting my passion, vivid and clear and shining. Rosa Mystica; Mummy's little boys; The Devil's in therapy, God's gone bald; Virgin of Virgins. Yes! Here they are! Crystal Concubine, Cabbage of Culture, The Death of the Monarch in Grand Theatre ...all here. All waiting for their birth. My new work. My new paintings. I can see them! I can see them!

The envelope! There was an envelope in the bag! I rummage and find it, tearing it open. On one side of the sheet are typed instructions for the further growth of the plants. On the other, in spidery writing:

"Querida Sybil, my friend Todd told me you would be on the four o'clock plane so I am bringing you this present in memory of my father and to thank you for your bravery in getting our movement the information we needed. Papá showed me your letter. You said many wise things. I know you deserve the rose because I saw you in Puno. You carried her like a child, so I know la rosa negra will be safe with you. She is Capacocha. You must give her eternal life." Juliana.

Inside the envelope: a bracelet of tiny, brown, *pashaquilla* seeds. A talisman I know does not work. I slip it on my wrist, honk into toilet paper and dry my eyes; then seal the lid back on the final dish.

Personality crisis? What fucking personality crisis? They can kiss my shiny white arse. How dare they try and write me out of the script! *Me* . . . *I*. . . I can conjure from my imagination that unique thing which can have no life unless I will it. Art *is* my child – but there's no age limit to producing it – and no need for a partner. I am *Capacocha* for the truth of it. My gold star, top-of-the-range, twenty-four-carat, massive ego told me so. It told me that my creativity, my intellect, will be laid out bare-arsed – to be spanked always by critics without the smallest clue as to how to create for themselves. Those silly, pompous, self-aggrandising fuckers who think they know better than those who do the work. Ha! Hello, my dear friend rant! Shock wearing off.

I take the final swig of rum. Beauty *is* worth preserving. There is too much ugliness in the world. Whether I keep the rose a secret or not I don't need to decide right now, but I do know this...

I am rising I am rising I am rising

And right now, the black rose is rising with me

...right up the steps of this plane.

...*FROM THE AUTHOR*

At the beginning of the twenty-first century, I lived in Arequipa, Peru, for four years. The city is 8,000 feet above sea level, so the brain, heart and lungs of new citizens have to acclimatise to an altitude with low oxygen. As was predicted, I began to experience *soroche*, the altitude sickness, and each night I would have psychedelic dreams.

When I woke, I tried to remember the dreams in detail, but could only catch a few metaphors or tableaus, which I wrote down in my notebook. After several weeks, the dreams subsided as my body became used to the thin air.

Some months later, I re-read the notes. The phrases seemed to be linked… connected to each other in a fractured narrative.

From these notes, and the feelings they engendered when reading them, White City Black Rose was created. A small portion of the dream phrases are included in the text.

22944228R00194

Printed in Great Britain
by Amazon